The Mindruler

I0565121

Steve Pillinger

Book One of
The Mindrulers
series

Cover picture by Jennifer Pillinger.

ISBN: 978-0-6399077-1-0

Although some of the characters in this book were inspired by real people, they remain entirely fictitious, and any identification made with actual persons is the reader's interpretation, not the author's intention.

Note also that the theological speculations in this book represent the characters' attempts to understand the situation in which they find themselves, and do not necessarily reflect the beliefs of the author.

Readers may notice in this book that pronouns referring to God (he, him, his, etc.) are not spelled with capitals (He, Him, His). This does not imply any disrespect for God. It simply follows the example of most English versions of the Bible.

Table of Contents

To my family
who played the game,
inspired the story, read the drafts,
and kept me writing.
This is your book!

Acknowledgments

This book has taken shape over many years, with helpful input from many people. Those who have been there from the beginning are my family, and many of the characters and events took shape during the happy hours we spent playing the 'Family Game'. You know that this story is yours as much as mine.

Then there are my 'beta testers'—the intrepid band of friends who read my half-baked drafts and made constructive comments. Thank you for your perseverance!

Among these special mention must be made of the Beardlings, my fellow-writers in Thame, Oxfordshire. Andrew and Victor, you so often put your fingers on the exact issue that needed correcting; our sessions of coffee, laughter and helpful criticism have improved the story immeasurably.

To Fiona Veitch Smith, whose penetrating and insightful critique several years ago transformed a slightly rambling story into a book worth publishing—I can only say a deeply heartfelt thank you!

Last, in pride of place, is my wife. She read it all, not once but a dozen times. She ruthlessly slashed excess verbiage, transforming my writing style. The movie-like 'scenes' she pictured provided seminal ideas that enriched the plot time and again. It is no cliché to say that this book could not have been written without her.

... Nor, in our little day,
May His devices with the heavens be guessed,
His pilgrimage to thread the Milky Way
Or His bestowals there be manifest.

But in the eternities,
Doubtless we shall compare together, hear
A million alien Gospels, in what guise
He trod the Pleiades, the Lyre, the Bear.

O, be prepared, my soul!
To read the inconceivable, to scan
The million forms of God those stars unroll
When, in our turn, we show to them a Man.

from 'Christ in the Universe'
by Alice Meynell (1913)

Titles to follow in this series:

The Restorers
The Strongholder

Dramatis Personæ — Who's Who

Alanya	Dûrian name of **Lannie** (Elaine) Catterick, displaced website designer.
Armanet, Lord	Joint leader of the failed Rebellion against **Bishop Shambor**. (*See also* **Dôrion**.)
Berenel	Mother of **Jomel** and wife of **Taboru**; sister of Lady **Nelláy**.
Bishop Shambor	Bishop Suffragan, *de facto* ruler of Dûrion and of the Dûrian Hearth.
Chand	Acolyte at the Temple of Gadesh in Stillárre. (*See also* **Guriet**.)
Damion	Former village Elder and spiritual leader of the Manor community.
Danîsha	Dûrian name of **Denise** Thompson, displaced widow (semi-retired).
Denise Thompson	English name of **Danîsha**.
Denny	Older teenager in the Manor community, son of **Frem** and **Margay**.
Dhelgor	Mindbender and Captain of the Bishop's Guard in Stillárre.
Dôrion, Lord	Joint leader of the failed Rebellion against **Bishop Shambor**. (*See also* **Armanet**.)
Ennel	Young single woman, member of the Manor community.
Estaron	Secretary to **Bishop Shambor**.
Father Martin	Vicar of the Round Church of Leston in Oxfordshire, UK.
Fira, Lieutenant	Hawk-faced former officer in the defeated Rebel army, and leader of the Manor community.

Frem	Husband of **Margay** and joint 'Keeper' of the Manor community, responsible for health and childcare. Father of **Denny**.
Frengor, Brother	Member of the Lightist order of Travelling Priests.
Garset, Captain	Lightist officer in the Dûrian armed forces.
Ganneret, Lord	Land Elder (Baron), member of the Dûrian nobility; father of **Perrely** and husband of **Nelláy**.
Gelmion	Dûrian name of **Gilbert** (Gil) Denbigh, displaced university lecturer.
Gil Denbigh	English name of **Gelmion**.
Guriet	Acolyte at the Temple of Gadesh in Stillárre. (*See also* **Chand**.)
Gwargif	Emissary of the Dorbians, sent to find the 'Warriors of Light'.
Jomel	Temple prostitute in the Cult of Gadesh. Cousin of **Perrely** and daughter of **Taboru** and **Berenel**.
Lannie Catterick	English nickname of **Alanya** (Elaine).
Margay	Wife of **Frem** and joint 'Keeper' of the Manor community, responsible for health and childcare. Mother of **Denny**.
Martin	*See* **Father Martin**.
'Neesh	Nickname for **Danîsha** (Denise).
Nelláy, Lady	Wife of **Ganneret** and mother of **Perrely**.
Ongaret, Brother	Member of the Lightist order of Travelling Priests.
Perrely	Young Dûrian girl of noble family. Cousin of **Jomel**, daughter of **Ganneret** and **Nelláy**.
Sarmion	Priest of the Temple of Gadesh in Stillárre.
Shambor	*See* **Bishop Shambor**.
Shere and Khan	Alanya's nicknames for **Shîrin** and **Cârin**.

Shîrin and Cârin (Shîr and Câr)	Twins, wisecrackers, and former Rebel soldiers serving under Lieutenant **Fira**. (Full names: **Shîrinor** and **Cârinor**.)
Shiván	Dûrian name of **Steve** Harston, displaced university student.
Shivvie	Nickname for **Shiván** (Steve Harston).
Steve Harston	English name of **Shiván**.
Taboru	Stillárre merchant, originally from Selmion. Father of **Jomel** and husband of **Berenel**.
Teynel	Dûrian orphan girl in the Manor community, Danîsha's protégéé.
Veynel	Older lady responsible for domestic matters in the Manor community.

For notes on the pronunciation of many of these names, see the Appendix *How to Pronounce Dûrian Words & Names* (p. 430).

For help understanding the **Dûrian language** in the early chapters of the book, see the Appendix *Some Basic Dûrian Words and Phrases* (p. 438).

Maps of Dûrion and the Dûrai Region

Key to Map symbols and shadings

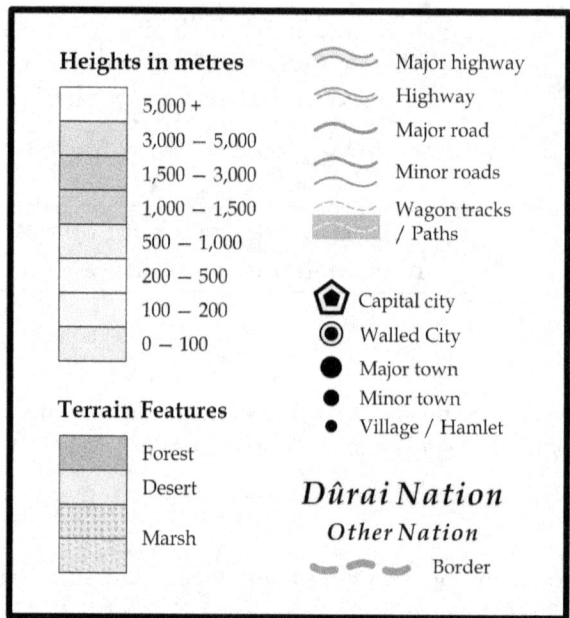

Heights in metres

	5,000 +
	3,000 — 5,000
	1,500 — 3,000
	1,000 — 1,500
	500 — 1,000
	200 — 500
	100 — 200
	0 — 100

Terrain Features

Forest

Desert

Marsh

Major highway

Highway

Major road

Minor roads

Wagon tracks / Paths

Capital city

Walled City

Major town

Minor town

Village / Hamlet

Dûrai Nation

Other Nation

Border

Note: The **Dûrai Nations** are Dûrion, Selmion, Thrinar, Marûvin, Pandiar and the city-state of Calardane.

The primary Dûrian unit of distance is the *aldor* (plural *aldoret*), which is equivalent to approximately one and a quarter kilometers or three quarters of a mile.

Map 1:
The Dûrai Region

Map 2:
Central Dûrion

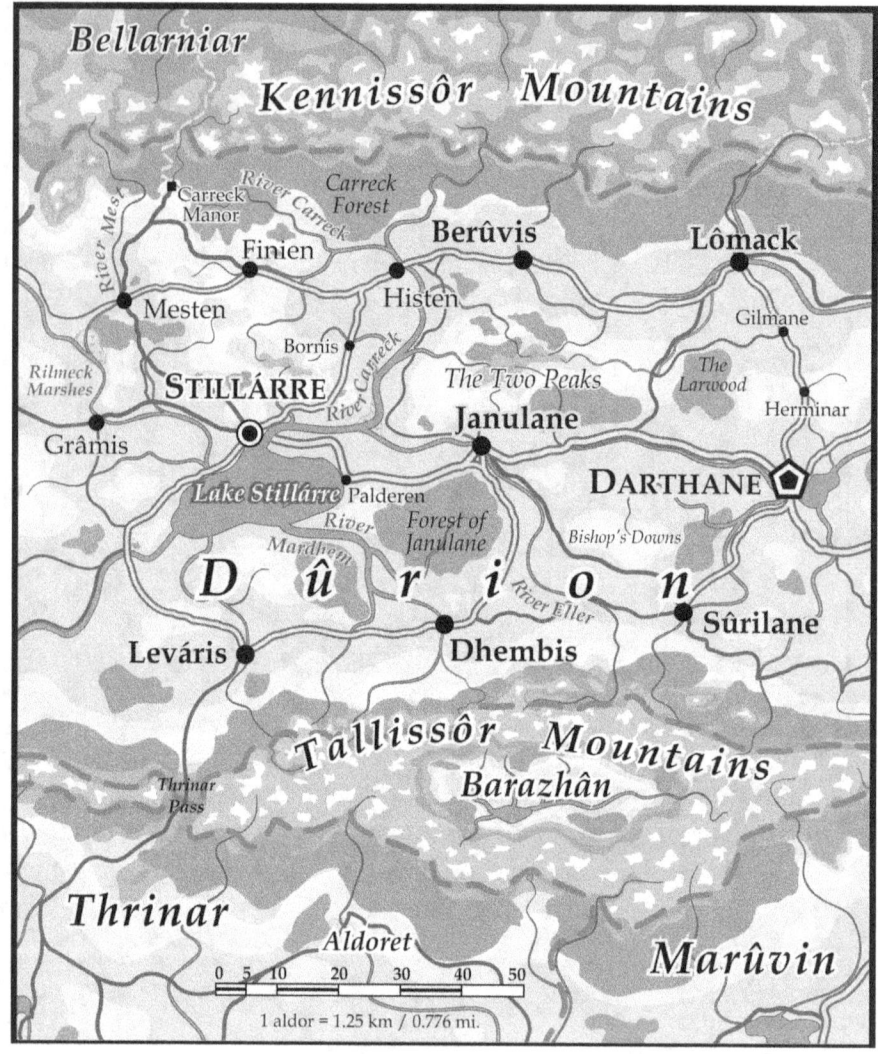

Chapter 1: *Unexpected battle*

ODDLY ENOUGH, it was the arrow Steve noticed first. It stood almost vertical, the iridescent feathers shimmering in a shaft of sunlight. He lay half-asleep, admiring it. Then the sounds began to filter through: the distant clash of wood and metal, faint cries, whizzing noises and dull thuds, all against a dim uproar of voices.

He sat up—and *difference* crashed into his brain. The trunk of a tall tree rose in front of him. All around were the feathery fronds of a plant that looked vaguely like bracken. Further off were other trees. His bedroom in the house he shared with three other students had turned into a forest. Instead of stacks of CDs and sci-fi novels there were tree trunks; instead of the debris of discarded McDonalds wrappers and unpaired socks there was a carpet of leaves.

The stray sunbeam faded, but the arrow... With a cry of shock he leapt to his feet, his heart pounding. A squat figure lay face-down beside him wearing a brown knee-length tunic, interwoven bands of metal covering his upper body. The arrow stuck up between two of the bands. A circular helmet and a small, oval shield lay in the bracken. His dark hair was matted with blood. He looked very dead.

Approaching shouts brought Steve's head snapping up. A crowd of similarly-dressed men was sprinting towards him through the trees. They carried swords and bows. For a terrible moment he stood frozen—then his legs burst into action, and he shot off out of their path.

After dodging round several tree trunks, he dived into a clump of bushes and hunkered down. Peering back cautiously, he saw that the brown-clad men had reached a small, rocky rise, and were turning to fight. A larger group wearing dark green were chasing them. Many of these had capes swirling from their shoulders—a green sea crashing against a small, brown island. Short swords rose glinting like surf amidst a confused roar of weapons and voices. Cries of "*Halaa! Gidas ar!*" "*Colas i bondat!*" "*Atenámbaret!*" rang out above the din.

Steve watched, unbelieving. It was a real battle. Bodies were falling, people being killed. The fighting surged to and fro. Then the defence began to crumble, and the brown-clad survivors took to their heels. There was one in a light-coloured top with longish auburn hair and no armour. A woman? The green sea swept over the rise, leaving broken bodies in its wake.

Steve stared after the disappearing soldiers, his mind in turmoil, his heart racing. *Is this a dream? If so, it's the most real dream I've ever had.* He pinched himself. It hurt. He wiped real sweat from his forehead. *Dear God, what's happened? I could have sworn I was starting my third year at the good old University of London. Yet right now I seem to be running for dear life from a mediaeval battle! Has my brain blown a fuse?* He paused, chewing his lip; then shook his head violently. *No way! I'm perfectly normal – it's my surroundings that aren't. But then... isn't that what every loony would say?*

More shouts and pounding of feet. The fugitives had taken a wide turn and were charging towards him. He leapt out of the bushes and sprinted off in a different direction. A large, grey animal broke from cover right in front of him. It had branching horns and a broad, rather stupid face. A bovine stag? He yelled, and barely managed to dodge it. Heart pounding, he ran on through the bracken, stumbling across small streams and gullies, tripping over hidden rocks, pausing briefly behind the huge tree trunks to see if anyone was following.

When the sound of pursuit had faded, he collapsed panting beside a small stream. For a while he lay on his back, the tall bracken arching over him. He felt one of the fronds idly, his overstretched mind in neutral. Strange—like everything in this mad forest. It looked like bracken, but it wasn't. It was a light yellowish green, and more feathery. He allowed the fine filaments to stroke his fingers. Through their delicate tracery he could see the immense trees. He'd never imagined trees could be so high. Their trunks reached up endlessly to the distant canopy of leaves.

He levered himself up on one elbow, and looked into the stream bubbling along beside him. The water was totally clear, the smooth pebbles on the bottom distorting one way and another with the flow of the current. He put his hand in. It was delightfully cool. He scooped some up and poured it sloppily into his mouth. It had a wild, invigorating taste. He drank again and again, wishing he could lap like a dog. Finally he flopped back, and his eyes closed.

Thudding feet abruptly ended his nap. He sat up to see the crowd of fleeing brown-coats rapidly approaching. *Why can't they leave me alone?* He leapt up and sprinted off through the bracken.

Suddenly he burst out of the forest into daylight. He skidded to a halt. His eyes widened. He was at the edge of a broad, grass-covered bowl of land almost surrounded by the forest. At the centre stood a ruined castle, the masonry blackened with fire. It was strangely elongated, like a sawn-off skyscraper, and the top half bulged outward. There were ramparts and several shattered towers. Tendrils of grey smoke curled up from the building into the overcast sky.

Two pairs of hands seized his arms. He yelped and tried to wrench himself free, looking from one side to the other. For a moment he thought his delusion had worsened: the smooth-skinned olive faces of his captors appeared identical. Then the one on the left said, "*Fenda limmeri af orrila, Shîrin?*" The one on the right grinned and replied, "*Dembar bissimaheynor.*" He produced a dagger and flourished it meaningfully. Steve flinched, but felt a spark of relief. At least he wasn't seeing double. He stopped struggling.

Behind them a harsh female voice barked, "*A temmas!*" and Steve found himself running willy-nilly between his twin captors towards the castle.

* * *

Lannie Catterick wandered among the tall trees in a daze. She couldn't believe this was happening to her. Where had it sprung from, this forest? She'd fallen asleep on the couch last night, after setting this Sunday aside to pull together the shattered pieces of her heart—those that Matt hadn't crushed under his number twelve heel. For two solid weeks he hadn't answered her calls or texts…

And now this! She couldn't *cope* with an unexplained forest right now. It had no right to be here. She wanted to scream at it to go away—but there were those other screams in the distance, real out-loud ones. Was this a sophisticated version of hell? Maybe she wasn't the only one who'd been dumped here against her will.

On the other hand, there was no way hell could be this beautiful. The trees were immensely tall and straight, with a smooth, grey bark; many were covered with luxuriant creepers to a height of twenty or thirty feet. What kind of tree *were* they? She'd never been strong on botany. But harmony of colour—that, as an artist, she could appreciate. The tree leaves were a rich, deep emerald; the creepers and the scattered clusters of thick shrubbery were a darker, bluey-green; and the feathery ground cover was a range of lighter shades that she couldn't quite define, but which blended in perfectly. Occasional outcrops of steel-grey rock or swirls of russet and ochre foliage added contrast.

And over it all lay a pale golden wash—as if she were wearing tinted glasses. The artist in her craved her sketch pad and acrylics. If she'd chosen to be here, it would be the perfect place to find heart balm.

If only Matt were with her now. *If only…!* If only she'd bitten her tongue Friday-before-last, instead of lashing out again. Well, the engagement was over; there was no point reliving the agony. When she got back from wherever *this* was, she'd throw herself into her work. She loved her job with Garfield Web Design, and was a rising star in the company. She'd rise higher, and to heck with emotional attachments.

Shouts and a confused uproar continued in the distance. She found herself walking towards it. Why not? Misery likes company. Might as well find out what other tortured souls had been dumped here.

A small creature burst out of the undergrowth ahead of her, and bounced off rapidly through the feathery ground cover. A rabbit? No, too sleek. A squirrel? In her brief glimpse it had been light brown with coffee-coloured spots. She'd never heard of a spotted squirrel. At least it knew where it was going in this forest, which was more than she did.

Shouts suddenly broke out closer by, with the clash of metal and cries of pain. A fight! God in heaven, what had she got *into?* There was a sudden thudding of feet, and a crowd of people in armour came running pell-mell over a nearby rise. Lannie froze. *Armour?*

Then there was a whooshing sound, colours flashed in the air, and the men began yelling and falling. Fear spread like icy fire through her veins. It dawned on her that it was a rain of arrows the instant before a sharp pain erupted in her arm, and a long, thin object with iridescent feathers dropped to the ground at her feet. Her scream mingled with the other cries. Blood began to ooze from a gash all the way down her right forearm. Then her immobility vanished. Clutching her arm, she ran for dear life with the armoured soldiers.

They crested a rise. Ahead there was a long line of bushes at the bottom of a narrow valley. They stampeded down the slope into the bushes, branches whipping at Lannie's face and limbs. She glimpsed a dim space with a rock wall opposite—then the solid ground gave way beneath her feet. With a scream she tumbled down a steep slope and landed on a couple of soldiers at the bottom, jarring her injured arm. She opened her mouth to cry out, but a smelly hand clamped over it. "*Hssst!*" a voice breathed in her ear. She tried to pull the hand off her face, but the soldier had her in an iron grip, his other arm round her waist.

Her eyes gradually adjusted to the gloom, and she swivelled them round to see as much as she could. They were crammed into a narrow ravine overshadowed by bushes on either side. The soldiers sat or lay just as they'd landed, completely silent but for laboured breathing and accidental whimpers from those who were wounded.

Shouts and running feet could be heard on the ridge above. Lannie's eyes, along with many others, followed the sounds round to the head of the valley. Then they faded away.

There were sighs of relief, and the hand was removed from Lannie's mouth. The soldier it belonged to uttered a crisp command in a penetrating undertone: "*Felleneynor!*"

With a shock Lannie realised it was a woman. She glimpsed a narrow, intense face and smouldering green eyes above a hawk-like nose; then the female warrior seized her good arm and began pulling her up the rocky slope of the ravine. The other soldiers swarmed after them. Lannie cried out as her injured arm was bumped, earning a searing glare and a "*Hsst!*" from Hawk-face.

The narrow-faced commander led them back the way they'd come. She moved at a brisk trot with Lannie in tow. They passed the bodies of comrades lying where they'd fallen, and there were soft groans from the survivors. Lannie noticed that none of the soldiers were taller than her. At five feet two she found it novel and rather pleasing.

They continued running between the widely-spaced trees. Lannie was able to keep up—but she saw no reason to stay with this army. She jerked her hand free of the Hawk's grip and dashed off between two bushes.

"*Thallas!*" At their leader's muted cry two soldiers leapt after Lannie and brought her crashing to the ground. She yelped as pain exploded in her wounded arm.

"Em is temmas."

Lannie was propelled firmly back to Hawk-face, one soldier gripping her uninjured arm, the other grasping the collar of her blouse and brandishing a knife.

"Fendi sharrila denôro?" The commander spat the words out in an intense undertone, hands on hips, eyes flashing. She pointed in the direction Lannie had tried to go. *"Limmeri af tonûr bondanet gedila bisti? Aa?"* Lannie stared at her coldly. Hawk-face held a hand up. Shuffles and muted comments ceased. *"Jillima!"*

In the silence Lannie heard a distant thudding of feet punctuated by faint commands.

"Jilli? Aa?"

Okay, she got the point. Lannie nodded slowly. With a scornful glance Hawk-face turned away. *"Em diminas. Felleneynor!"*

They set off again at a rapid trot, Lannie flanked by the two soldiers. After a while they heard cries behind, and the pace increased. Their pursuers had picked up the trail.

She was beginning to feel faint and wondered how much longer she could keep going, when the whole group skidded to a halt. Fear flashed through her. A soldier ran up and whispered something to the Hawk. The leader strode forward, followed by Lannie and her guards. There was brightness ahead where the trees ended. Lannie stifled a gasp at the sight of a tall young man — well, tall compared to her new companions — in jeans and a T-shirt, standing with his back to them, staring out of the forest.

Two of the leading soldiers leapt forward and pinioned his arms. *"A temmas!"* Hawk-face spat out, and before the man could make more than a token struggle he was running with them across open grass. Lannie caught a glimpse of wide blue eyes and tousled blond hair. Ahead was a burnt-out building. They charged through a shattered doorway. There was rubble everywhere. Lannie had a jumbled impression of smouldering heat, walls covered in soot, charred carpeting and fallen roof timbers. They emerged into an inner courtyard. On all sides were the collapsed remains of what looked like a mediaeval castle.

Lannie glanced at the young guy in the T-shirt. He raised his eyebrows and shrugged. She compressed her lips.

The Hawk plunged down a half-covered passage leading off the courtyard. She reached into a recess in the wall that might once have held a lamp. A moment later Lannie gasped as a section of the wall slid aside, revealing a narrow stone stairway. Then the whole group was hurrying down the stairs into the bowels of the earth.

Chapter 2: *The Forest Hilton*

AS THEY FELT THEIR WAY DOWN the narrow stone stairway into the darkness below, Steve found himself beside the auburn-haired girl he'd noticed earlier. He liked looking on the bright side, and she was the only bright side available—an oasis of normality, wearing a cream top and black trousers. She was short and slim, with a light scattering of freckles on an elfin face. Not really his type, though. There was a determined tilt to her chin that might be better viewed from a safe distance. She held herself very straight, and her steps were quick and determined: a focused, ambitious person.

"Hi!" he said. "Welcome to the Forest Hilton. I'm Steve Harston." He grinned and held out a hand.

She glanced at him briefly. "Hi." She ignored the hand.

Okay. Not such a bright side after all. He'd have to look for another. As in, *have* to. He couldn't let himself drift into that old, familiar downward spiral. The pit of despair was a place he never wanted to see again. He stifled a sigh as they continued their careful descent into the darkness. It was a little too symbolic for comfort.

They reached the foot of the stairs. The masonry door ground shut; it was pitch black. Everyone shuffled forward into what felt like a large open space. There they waited.

Look for the silver lining, Steve said to himself. *There always is one.* Well, in the present situation he was grateful to be alive. And even if his companion wasn't feeling sociable right now, at least she was *here*, and she spoke English. Maybe her 'arrival' had been as sudden as his own. Give it a day or so and they'd be chatting away merrily. He felt his spirits lift, and breathed a sigh of relief.

After an age the door opened again, shedding a dim light down the stairway. Someone at the top called out, "*Shildanet fellenathar!*" and there were exclamations of relief all round. "*Neymelet mallas!*" the boss-woman's sharp voice commanded.

One of Steve's twin captors thrust a small pot into his hands, and took from his bag what looked like a weathered piece of grey bamboo. It had ridged joints at regular intervals. The young soldier dipped a finger into the pot and brought out a glistening lump of soft, reddish clay. Steve watched, puzzled, as he smeared the clay around one of the joints on the stick. Then he grasped the stick with both hands, one on each side of the smeared joint. With a sharp motion he snapped it. There was a flash and a crackle, and both sides of the broken stick were burning. Steve and the red-haired girl jumped.

"Yikes! An outsize match!"

The soldier raised an eyebrow at their startled reaction. He lifted one piece of the 'match' to the wick of a small lamp held in a bracket on the wall. A bright flame arose. He retrieved the pot from Steve and moved on to another bracket. Steve saw that others were doing likewise. Then he glanced round and uttered a crisp "Wow!" at the amazing sight that was taking shape all around him.

They were in a vast underground space. As he took in the details he realised that it was an enormous kitchen. It stretched away in every direction, the roof supported by massive pillars. And it was fully set up. A substantial cooking range stretched along one wall, with pots, ladles, fire tongs and other implements ready for use. Chopped firewood was neatly piled in niches in the wall. One recess housed a closed barrel—presumably containing water, from the large dipper on top. Shelves on another wall were stacked with sets of crockery. Open sacks of grain and beans, other closed sacks, barrels, boxes and huge earthen jars lined the walls.

Four long tables stood in the middle of the room, with wide, backless benches on either side. There were seven or eight open storerooms, some containing more goods, others with empty racks of wide shelves. Passages ran off on three sides, with glimpses of yet more rooms.

Soldiers were hurrying down the passages, investigating. Cries came from one of them, then a heavy banging sound, as of a door being pounded. Steve wondered what they'd found.

* * *

Denise sat in the dark, thinking wistfully of her comfortable little cottage in England. The others were all huddled around her—whoever they were. Heavy breathing, sniffs, and an occasional whimper from one of the children punctuated the silence. A reek of sweat and fear filled her nostrils. The brightly-dressed foreigners had bundled her into this storeroom when shouts and the thud of running feet were heard upstairs. Denise shuddered. She just hoped it wasn't more of those soldiers in outlandish armour. She'd seen enough of them yesterday.

Where am I, and how did I get here? On Tuesday she'd been living her normal, quiet life since retirement: helping at the local library in the morning; visiting friends and phoning her daughter in the afternoon; babysitting in the evening for her neighbours. Finally home by eleven. She had settled into her armchair with a cup of tea… and must have fallen asleep in her clothes.

The next morning she'd woken in that incredible forest with a battle raging all around. Nothing had made sense. Mercifully the civilians had run across her before the soldiers did. They'd dragged her along with them to this hiding-place under the ruined castle. But now…

A rumbling and grinding noise made itself heard through the storeroom walls. There were gasps and low moans, and Denise felt the bodies all around her tensing. The hidden masonry door was opening — their hideaway had been discovered! A sound of feet on the stairway followed, accompanied by a distant murmur of voices.

The volume of sound slowly increased, punctuated by exclamations, though no individual words could be made out.

Minutes passed, and the rumble of voices continued.

What were the intruders waiting for? If they were looking for survivors of the battle, why didn't they *do* so? Or was it a trap, to lure the fugitives into revealing themselves? Denise found she was holding her breath, and let it out slowly. She felt as taut as an overstretched rubber band.

Other sounds mingled with the muffled voices, and a dim glow appeared under the door of their hideaway. The fugitives drew a collective breath. The intruders were lighting the lamps. It was going to be a thorough search. Her heart clenched. *Will I die in this foreign basement, not even knowing where I am?*

A thud of shoes on the stone floor of the corridor outside their refuge. A brief muttered command, and a low moan of fear among the fugitives. Denise felt bodies pressing back against her, away from the door.

The door handle rattled. One of the kids squealed in alarm. The man at the door called something out — it sounded like a question. Everyone froze. The question was repeated.

There was a long moment when no one breathed. Then boots crashed against the door. The women and children inside screamed, and the men cried out. Everyone huddled even further back into the room. Denise found herself gasping for breath, bodies pressed against her on all sides. The well-made door quivered, and quivered again under repeated blows.

Then, with a splintering crash, it flew open.

*   *   *

Lannie stared out over the large, unexpected kitchen and the brown-clad soldiers hurrying about on meaningless tasks. She was angry and confused, and her wounded arm was throbbing viciously. *Who are these people? What am I doing here?*

There was a crash and a sudden outburst of screams and shouts from one of the adjoining passages. She took an involuntary step back up the stairs. *Not more fighting!*

But then the shouts of alarm changed to cries of delight, and a few moments later what looked like a flock of brightly-coloured birds came pouring into the kitchen. People wearing ankle-length garments in vivid hues greeted the soldiers with obvious relief and joy. Some had heavier robes or thigh-length jackets; and some had dyed hair — purple, blue and even green. All wore home-made sandals with thick soles. Like the soldiers they had olive complexions and oval faces with huge eyes, like those on ancient Greek pottery. And she was pleased to see that, like the soldiers, they were short — few stood taller than her own five feet two.

There was one exception, though. Her eye was caught by a taller figure who seemed to have been swept aside by the maelstrom of embracing foreigners, ending up just nearby at the foot of the stairs. This one was dressed differently — Lannie's eyebrows shot up as she registered a grey pleated skirt and powder-blue cardigan her grandmother could have worn. She looked up at the woman's face and their eyes met. Lannie gasped. It couldn't be!

"Mrs. *Thompson!*"

"Lannie Catterick!"

"What on earth are *you* doing here?" It was one of the old biddies from the church she used to attend in Birmingham — a knitter and a flower-arranger! Somehow this was the most surprising thing that had happened today.

Denise Thompson's face lit up. "I might ask you the same, my dear!" She moved to embrace Lannie, but at the last moment grasped her hand instead. "I haven't seen you for what? A year, year and a half? Fancy meeting you here!"

Lannie nodded, searching for something neutral to say. But at that moment the older lady noticed her wounded arm.

"Oh, you're hurt!" she exclaimed. "What happened? An arrow? Let me have a look. I've had first aid training." She peered into Lannie's face. "You're pale and sweaty from shock. Come and sit down. I'll get some water." She led Lannie to one of the nearby tables, pointed to the bench and bustled off.

The young guy — Steve — was grinning. "Well, well. You can't even go to the back of beyond without bumping into someone you know."

Lannie nodded briefly as she sank down on the bench.

"Don't pay any attention to me," he said, his grin lingering.

She didn't.

Denise came back with a leather water flask. Lannie drank eagerly, then Denise trickled water on the wound and bathed it with her handkerchief. She neatly wrapped the grey scarf from her neck round Lannie's forearm. In the background the joyous reunion was continuing. Impromptu singing had broken out in parts of the room.

"There! That'll do for a while," Denise said, raising her voice a little.

"Thank you."

"So did you also —"

Denise was interrupted by a shout that rose above the singing. "*Hây! Atenámbaril collinathar* sen *hinnay!*"

In a moment the three of them were surrounded by the brightly-dressed people. They all stared at Lannie and Steve, pointing and jabbering together in awed excitement. The words *Atenámbaril, Atenámbaret* kept popping up. Lannie heaved an impatient sigh.

Denise frowned. "That's what they called me, too."

"Well, whatever it is, we seem to be celebrities," Steve said. "I should have brought my plastic smile. Hey, d'you think they'll put us on a chat show?"

To Lannie's relief, Hawk-face brought the press conference to a sudden end. "*Essin!*" she bellowed, striding through the crowd. She turned to the multicoloured civilians, her face thunderous.

"*Atenámbaret? Estembar lassar târ Atenámbaret! Dôrion i Armanet dissi-lathen sûlack?*" The commander harangued them for two minutes solid, eyes flashing, her harsh voice vibrant with indignation. Lannie watched as the brightly-dressed folk wilted. They stared at the ground, shuffling in embarrassment.

"I guess we can forget the chat show," Steve murmured.

* * *

The locals turned their attention back to the soldiers, and the three English-speakers heaved sighs of relief. Denise sat down beside Lannie, and Steve parked himself opposite them. Denise folded her hands on the table and eyed him with interest. A good lad. Blond, blue-eyed, a broad grin. Not tall, but muscular. He reminded her of Tim, her eldest, as he'd been ten years ago. Twenty-one or twenty-two, she would have said.

"Well, let me introduce myself. I'm Denise Thompson; I'm a retired teacher. I live near Birmingham, and I work... worked part-time in our local library. Lannie and I go to the same church."

"Ah. So that's why you greeted each other like long-lost buddies."

"Yes, Lannie and I know each other, and you two have met, of course, but—"

"We've bumped into each other. But we haven't really *met*, if you know what I mean."

"What?" Denise paused, taking in the young man's quizzical grin and Lannie's stony silence. "Oh." She blinked. "Then I'd better do the honours. This is Lannie Catterick. She does some kind of computer art—don't you, dear?"

This brought a frosty correction. "Website design."

"Of course, I remember now." Denise's eye lingered a moment on Lannie. There was quite a chip on *that* shoulder. She turned to the young man. "And you are...?"

"Steve Harston. Until today I was in my third year at the University of London, doing Linguistics and Study of Religions. Now... I'm here with you guys."

Denise glanced from Steve to Lannie. "Don't tell me. You both fell asleep in your clothes and woke up in the forest."

Steve pulled a face and nodded. "Spot on. What about you, Lannie?"

She gave a curt nod and adjusted her injured arm, which she was holding carefully.

Steve turned back to Denise. "But you were already here, Mrs. ah—"

Denise laughed. "Call me Denise."

Steve grinned. "Denise, then. When did you arrive?"

"Yesterday morning. The evening before I'd fallen asleep in my armchair, and I woke up sitting on a rock in this forest. Then these people found me—the ones with the bright clothes. They were running away from the fighting, and took me with them. I think they must have been staying in this castle before it got burnt down in the battle. Anyway, they knew how to get down here. We had a right panic when you lot arrived! But I'm very glad you did." She nodded emphatically, looking from the one to the other.

"Are there any other English people around?" Lannie asked.

"Not that I know of."

"So it's just us," Steve said. "Here we are; and we haven't the foggiest idea how, where or why. Well—at least we have a roof over our heads, and we haven't been slaughtered in the fighting."

"What's this, 'count your blessings' time?" Lannie asked caustically.

"Better than counting your curses," Steve shot back with a grin.

They were interrupted by Hawk-face, who started calling out instructions in her harsh voice. Her real name, rather appropriately, turned out to be 'Fire-ah', and she seemed to have taken charge. Everyone got up and headed in different directions.

A woman about Denise's age with blue-tinted hair, whom she'd heard people calling 'Margay', brought a large bowl of reddish-brown tubers which she tipped out on the table. She sat down beside them with a friendly smile, then took out a knife and started peeling. More women arrived, carrying bowls of outsize pea pods and other vegetables, all unfamiliar to the three foreigners. Denise found a knife and started peeling tubers. Lannie heaved a sigh and joined in, shelling peas.

Steve stood up. "I'm sure the men must be doing something useful too..." He looked around, and saw a group carrying boxes out of a storeroom in one of the passages.

Lannie sniffed. "Kitchen work too humble for you, is it?"

"It's okay—just doesn't use enough *muscle*." He ran to the next table, planted his hands on it, and vaulted over in a single smooth movement. There were gasps and cries of alarm from the locals. Steve performed an elaborate bow then trotted down the passage to join the work party.

"Silly idiot!" Lannie said amid the shocked foreign babble.

Singing broke out around the tables as they worked on the vegetables. Eventually they were peeled, washed, chopped and added to large pots simmering on the stoves. An exotic, mouth-watering aroma began to waft through the kitchen.

Steve returned with the work party and helped arrange the benches in two wide semicircles facing the cooking range. Denise, Steve and Lannie joined others washing hands and faces at a large trough on the wall beside the water barrel. Then all the adults seated themselves on the benches, while the younger ones served the food. Denise found herself looking into the sweet face of a young girl of about ten or eleven. Her light olive complexion was flawless. She smiled, bobbed her head, and said in a clear voice, "*Dîmeri neldin.*"

"I'm more than ready for it, my dear." Denise returned the girl's smile and took the wooden bowl and spoon. She dipped the spoon into the dark-reddish vegetable stew, and raised it to her lips. Her eyebrows shot up.

"Why, this is *delicious!* It's like… I don't know what it's like… but the *flavour* is just—"

"Supercalifragilisticexpialidocious?" Steve suggested.

"I'm glad it doesn't have meat," Lannie said.

"You're a vegetarian?"

"That would follow."

"Well, well. This place is full of surprises."

The stew was followed by a variety of fruit—golden berries, red citrus-like spheres, and some chewy purple sticks that burst in the mouth, giving off juice and filling the nostrils with a sweet, spicy aroma. 'Pop-sticks', Steve called them.

When everyone had finished, the young people collected the utensils and washed them at the trough. Laughter and the sound of splashing drifted across the kitchen. Denise wondered exactly what—or who—was being washed. When it was over a group of rather damp youngsters came trooping back to join the circle around the stoves.

One of the civilians, an old man with long white hair and kindly grey eyes, raised his hand. Silence fell. He turned to the three foreigners. *"Estûrar, mel anéy nalestas. Eréy len min lassen."*

"The official welcome," Steve murmured.

"Damion ganalestis." Pointing at his own chest the old man repeated clearly and slowly, *"Da*–mi–on*"*.

Exchanging glances, they obediently chorused *"Day*–mee–yon*"*. The locals laughed and drummed their hands on their knees.

Damion pointed to the narrow-faced commander. *"Fi*–ra*"*. She nodded curtly. Steve, Denise and Lannie intoned, *"Fie*–ra*"*. Again the drumming of hands.

Damion turned next to a large man in a mauve tunic sitting beside blue-haired Margay. *"Frem."* They repeated it, and Frem's kindly face lit up. He laid a hand on his wife's shoulder and said, *"Mar*–gay*"*. Again the chorus, and the transparent delight of their hosts.

The roll-call continued. When the old man reached the twin soldiers who had escorted Steve into the castle, he announced them together: *"Shîrinor i Cârinor."* The two young men grinned broadly like a pair of Cheshire cats. Denise, Lannie and Steve tried to repeat the names, but they came out rather mangled. The twin on the left frowned. *"Shee*–rin!*"* he declared. The one on the right followed immediately with *"Kaa*–rin!*"*

"Hah! Shere and Khan," Lannie said dryly. Denise and Steve both laughed. The twins had a sleek, feline look about them, just like Kipling's tiger—though without his evil cunning. "Shere and Khan" they chorused.

Khan responded with a comment that had all the locals chuckling.

Finally it was their turn. The old man pointed at Steve. Steve spoke out his name clearly, but there was a confused response with several different pronunciations—which brought a faint smile to Lannie's face. "Sounds like you have a choice between 'Steep' or 'Sheep'!"

Steve threw her a dark look. "Hold it, hold it," he said loudly, raising his hand. "Ste–*pha*–nus." The group began their imitations, and the name finally came out as 'Shi–*ván*'.

"There you go," said Steve triumphantly. "Shiván speaking. Not a sheep in sight."

"Idiot," said Lannie.

It was her turn next. But when she gave her name as *"Lan–ny"*, a sudden silence fell. One of the younger women started sobbing. "What on earth...?" said Lannie.

"Probably a close relative," Denise murmured. "Killed in battle."

"Oh. E-*laine*, then," Lannie emended. "I hate my proper name." She was relieved when the locals adapted it as 'Alanya', which had a pleasantly exotic ring to it.

Denise escaped with 'Daneesha'.

Finally Damion looked across at Steve. *"Dem anéy ostalendi, Toldor Shiván?"* Commander Fira scowled, but said nothing.

A complete silence fell. All eyes were fixed on Steve. "Oh boy," he muttered.

"Um, sorry, I don't understand." He made a helpless gesture with palms turned up.

There were encouraging smiles and nods from several around the circle. The old man imitated Steve's gesture, spreading his arms wider and looking upward for a moment, before returning his expectant gaze to Steve.

"Give thanks for the food!" hissed Lannie.

"You mean *pray?*"

"What else can he mean?"

Denise shook her head. "I wonder what god they pray to."

"Dunno, but... Let us pray," Steve said.

They bowed their heads and Steve uttered a short, conventional prayer of the kind you'd hear in any school dinner hall. All three looked up. The entire group was staring at them in astonishment. After an awkward moment, Damion spread his arms wide, palms raised, and looked upward, his gaze focused beyond the wood-beamed ceiling. Everyone followed suit.

Then he began to sing — a long string of liquid syllables on a single baritone note. His voice was strong and mellow. Others joined in, each on a different note, but all in harmony, tenors, basses, sopranos, altos, each blending in at their own level. The sound had such an ethereal purity that the hairs on the nape of Denise's neck rose.

Then Damion's note changed; and all changed with it. The music flowed from one chord to the next, seemingly spontaneous, yet always co-ordinated, always in perfect harmony. Denise found tears in her eyes at the sight of those yearning faces with their large eyes staring upward, pouring out their hauntingly beautiful song.

The final note faded softly away. The three foreigners sat spellbound. For those few moments the dim, ordinary kitchen had been transformed into a cathedral of light and music.

Denise noticed that their hosts had now returned their hands to their laps, and were staring into the small flames of the cooking stoves. Damion made a short statement; all responded in unison. He spoke again, and again came the response. Denise saw tears glinting in many eyes. Were they mourning those lost in battle? But that song had been a prayer. She had no shadow of doubt about that. Who were they praying to? A supreme Creator? A loving Father? Or a harsh, tribal deity who had exacted a blood tribute and needed to be appeased?

No. That song had radiated trust and longing.

Damion was speaking again—a resounding declaration. The group responded in kind, once more raising their eyes and hands heavenward.

After a final moment of silence, they turned to their guests, smiling and uttering words of friendship they could not understand.

———————————————

Chapter 3: *Perrely and Jomel*

PERRELY CLUTCHED HER MUD-SPATTERED CLOAK and hurried home along the main road to Berûvis. How could she have forgotten Uncle Taboru and Aunt Berenel's visit? Father would be furious, and Mums would be *so* upset. Mums had reminded her on Freyneril, the day before yesterday. But yesterday she'd been helping Kindler Dorlion distribute food to the homeless; and today... well, Brother Frengor of the Travelling Order had been preaching in the fields next to the Wayside Chapel, and she'd been looking forward to that for weeks.

But what could she say to Father and Mums? They shuddered at the travelling priests' exuberant outdoor worship, calling it cheap emotionalism. They would berate her for not attending Hearth in the sedate and decorous fashion appropriate to a lady of her status. Yuck. Not that she had anything against dear old Kindler Dorlion; his heart was in the right place, but his sedate and decorous rituals were not for her.

And what about Uncle Taboru, Aunt Berenel, Jomel and the rest of her cousins from Stillárre? They were cultists, so no explanation would make sense to them. They'd simply be offended that she hadn't been there to greet them.

Oh, well. They knew she never stuck to the conventions, and did peculiar things like going about on her own. After all, her family followed Prince Orrénne — the most famous loner in history!

As she slipped in through the back door of the manor house, she thought of Jomel. They'd been such friends once. Two cousins the same age, both attending the prestigious Hearth School in Janulane. 'The girls', as both families called them, had spent alternate holidays in each other's homes. It was a couple of years now since they'd seen each other. It would be nice to have a good old natter with Jomel again.

Reaching her bedroom, Perrely hastily shed her muddy outer garments and pulled on the new tunic and culottes in shades of pastel green that Mums thought looked so smart. With her jade scarf thrown just so across one shoulder, she'd project a decorous image the family could be proud of. She looked in the mirror, tidied her hair, and wiped some mud off one cheek. Then she went down to the reclining room.

It was pretty full, as expected. Her eyes briefly took in her own family, then Uncle Taboru and Aunt Berenel with all her cousins... Was *that* Jomel? No! That fashionable young lady in a smart, dove-grey jacket? Dear Prince, it was!

"Perrely, where have you *been?*" her mother cried.

"Do you know what time it is, young lady?" The usual from Father. "We've been waiting all day for you. Your cousins have been wondering where under the sky you'd got to—and so have we!"

"Ah, be gently with her, Ganneret." Dear, easy-going Uncle Taboru. A cloth merchant who had moved to Dûrion decades ago, he had never lost his sing-song Selmian accent. He was a short, thick-set man with a warty face and ears that stuck out from his head. "We know this niece Perrely. She does what she does, yes, girl?" His eyes twinkled at her.

"I'm sorry," she said. "I meant to be here, I really did, but, um, there was a meeting on today, and I forgot and, er, went." Not so good.

Her mother heaved a deep sigh and Father frowned at her. *They know exactly where I've been,* she thought, *but they won't mention it because Hearth and Travellers both follow the Way, and they won't want to air our differences before cultists.*

"There's mud on your socks," said her younger brother Barlet. "You've been to the Travellers' waymeet, haven't you?" Bless him, the observant little brat.

"Ah—yes."

"What, one of those Lightist meetings out in the fields with the *peasants?*" Aunt Berenel exclaimed. "Who did you go with?"

"No one. I went alone."

Her aunt's eyes and mouth became perfect circles. She turned to her sister. "Really, Nelláy, how can you let her do such things? Now that she's finished school, you're just leaving her to run wild?"

Perrely subsided into a recliner, her heart sinking. Oh, dear Prince, don't let this develop into a family row.

As if in answer Uncle Taboru intervened. "Come now, Berenel, let us not throw aspersions on our dear brother and sister." He turned to Perrely. "Girl, why do not you and Jomel go somewhere and catch up your news. You two must have much to talk, no?" He beamed at her.

She felt a rush of gratitude to her cultist uncle. The Way did not have a monopoly on ordinary kindness. "I'd love that." She turned to her cousin. "Jomel, is that *you?*"

"Yes, our daughter has changed, has she not?" said Uncle Taboru in a rather flat voice. "But go, you two, and get acquainted again."

* * *

Perrely's mind struggled to adjust to the assured, worldly young woman beside her as they walked between the cream-painted pillars of the colonnade that surrounded the central courtyard with its bushes, flowerbeds and fountain. The inward-sloping green roof tiles were dotted with darker patches—Father needed to have the moss seen to.

They sat on the stone bench facing the fountain in the welcome shadow of a dark-leaved *shey* tree. The gentle tinkling of the fountain soothed Perrely. She turned and looked her cousin up and down. "You know, I hardly recognised you when I came in. You've changed so much!"

"Have I?" Jomel's lips quirked in a lazy half-smile. "You, on the other hand, haven't changed a bit. I'd have recognised you anywhere." She let the silence hang between them.

Perrely searched Jomel's carefully made-up face for familiar landmarks. Close up, of course, she could see the likeness to the fun-loving girl she'd known two years ago. But that's all it was; a likeness. Even worse: a death mask. The eyes that stared back at her were empty—their sparkle gone. The girlish dimples had vanished along with the puppy fat. Her face had a classic beauty now that Perrely knew men would fight over—the perfect, pale oval surrounded by a halo of dark hair, and those stunning, blue-green eyes. But it was a closed face, with the lifeless beauty of a pressed flower.

"What happened, Jomie?" she said softly.

"What happened? I grew up," she said lightly. "And what about you? Up to all your old pranks, it seems. Wallowing in the mud with the peasants!" There was amused condescension in her voice.

"Well, there *was* a lot of mud, I grant you, but I cleaned most of it off. Trust Barlet to notice my socks!" She chuckled; but instead of the delighted giggle of former days, it drew only a quirk of the lips from Jomel.

"Really, though," Perrely said seriously, "it was a wonderful celebration. There was a man there who'd come on crutches — he couldn't walk without them — but the Light touched him, and he threw them away and danced! Isn't that marvellous?" She looked wide-eyed at her cousin, willing her to delight in what she'd seen.

"Oh, yes, we have plenty of that sort of thing in our religion, too," Jomel said in a bored tone. Perrely felt as if she'd walked into a closed door.

"You do? In the Cult of *Minórre?*" She knew that Uncle Taboru and his family were specially devoted to the god of the harvest; but she'd never heard of their priests healing the sick.

"Oh, no, I've joined the Cult of Gadesh now," Jomel remarked casually. Perrely's eyes widened. The Cult of Gadesh! The most vicious, most depraved of all the Lightless religions. The cult of the demonic Worldruler himself! The cult of the Mindbenders. She stared at her cousin in horror.

"No, Jomie, you haven't. Tell me you haven't," she whispered.

"Oh come, don't give me that shocked Lightist reaction, as though we're all monsters! There's a lot to be said for it; many... benefits, and so on. But let's not talk about religion, since we'll never agree. Tell me about yourself. Any men in your life?"

Perrely could hardly wrench her mind away from the appalling picture of her dear Jomel having the life squeezed out of her by the Cult of Gadesh. "No... none. I think I'm... just not ready for marriage."

"Okay, so Mr. Right hasn't turned up yet. You'll know when he does. Then I expect you'll fall desperately in 'love'." There was a hint of mockery in the last word.

A cold stone settled in Perrely's heart. "What about you, Jomie? Is there anyone you love?"

Jomel looked away. "No."

"No one? You're very beautiful, you know. Isn't there someone who loves *you*?"

"Not that I'm aware of." Her voice was hard.

"I'm sorry."

"Well, don't be. You're in the same situation — you just said so."

"No, Jomie, I didn't say that. I said I hadn't found a man to marry. But I have found love — a different kind of love. It's not the same as a man's love, but it's just as real. The One's love is a kind of warmth inside— Anyway, all that stuff they preached to us at school—it's true, Jomie."

Jomel stared at Perrely for a moment. There was the tiniest flicker of something in her eyes; then they emptied again.

"Yes, well, I'm glad you have all those nice feelings. But a real man is a hundred times better—as I'm sure you'll find out one day. Anyway, enough about love. Tell me what you've been up to all this time."

The conversation turned to the small doings of everyday life.

Before long they got up and strolled back through the fountain garden. Glass-panelled doors lined the outer sides of the colonnade, opening into the many rooms of the manor house. They headed for the large reclining room on the right where the rest of the family was gathered.

"Ah, so it is that the girls have finished talking at last!" Uncle Taboru exclaimed as they entered. Her parents and Jomel's were stretched out comfortably, propped on their elbows, on a semicircle of the burgundy-upholstered recliners that dotted the wide expanse of ochre floor-cover. On other recliners in the background the five younger siblings sat or squirmed or squabbled. Perrely's older brother Larion sat aloof, as usual, tapping his fingers and looking bored.

"I'm glad you girls are back," Mums said. "Do you think you could do something with the children? They're getting so restless…" She and Jomel's mother were sisters, and they looked it, with their dark hair, deep-set eyes and long, rather mournful faces. It had been a scandal when Aunt Berenel, a noble-born Dûrian, had married an immigrant Selmian merchant; but the two families had since become good friends.

Perrely took one look at Jomel's sculpted eyebrows raised in shock and rescued the situation. "Don't worry, I'll take them outside." She raised her voice. "Hey kids, anyone want a game of strike-ball?"

There was a chorus of excited affirmatives, and they all scrambled out of the reclining room with Perrely while Jomel arranged herself elegantly on a recliner.

Perrely was unable to chat again with Jomel before Uncle Taboru and Aunt Berenel left the next morning in their carriage. But she continued to hurt for her cousin. Somehow, someday, she had to dig behind that mask and find the friend she'd lost.

* * *

Perrely was smiling as she walked down the alley in Berûvis, the town nearest to their home. This was the poor area, but the double-storey tenements still had their characteristic green roof tiles, though discoloured and with many gaps. The usual flowerbeds beside the road were missing, though; instead she had to thread her way around piles of litter and the occasional unconscious drug addict. She wrinkled her nose in distaste. These pathetic pieces of human debris were not called 'stinkies' for nothing.

But she was so glad she'd visited the old man again. He'd been pathetically pleased to see her, and had thanked her a hundred times for the bread and beans she'd brought. Of course, she shouldn't really have raided their own larder; but her allowance had run out, and the old fellow was so poor, with a useless family who hardly bothered about him. That made it okay — didn't it?

Well, Cook wouldn't have thought so if she'd caught her; nor would Mums or Father. She sighed. Sometimes doing something wrong seemed the only way of doing something right! Even now she was in the wrong for coming into town alone. Her parents knew she often behaved like a loner. They allowed her a certain amount of freedom, though many condemned them for it. Never mind that she was only following the example of Prince Orrénne himself!

The narrow street between the tall tenements opened into a broader way. This would take her home, through the market square. She breathed a sigh of relief, glad to be back in the town proper. Here flowers lined the well-fitted yellow paving stones of the wide street, the walls of the houses were clean, and the windows gleamed with unbroken glass. In the distance she could see the high stone arches of the town's aqueduct, which brought fresh water from the hills not only to Berûvis itself, but also to nearby areas including their own manor house.

Her thoughts turned back to Jomel and the Cult of Gadesh. Something terrible had happened to her cousin; something that had killed her on the inside. Mums had told her yesterday that Uncle Taboru and Aunt Berenel were very worried about Jomel. She'd left their comfortable home outside Stillárre, and had a live-in job with a tin merchant in the city. They hardly saw her these days.

And when they did, she was a stranger. Perrely wondered whether they knew Jomel had joined the Cult of Gadesh.

It suddenly occurred to her that there were a lot of people hurrying down this street. Up ahead a rumble of voices indicated a large crowd in the square. She frowned. It wasn't the country market today. She hoped she'd be able to push her way through. She had to get home in time for the midmeal.

As she approached the square her heart sank. It was filled with a huge throng that overflowed into the side streets. She started forcing her way through, elbowing people in the ribs, tramping on toes, getting roundly cursed. Only the fact that she was well-known in the town saved her from rough treatment. She'd almost reached the main road out of Berûvis, when a single name stopped her. *Armanet*. It was on everyone's lips. *The* Armanet? The leader of the Lightist Rebellion?

Maybe there was good news! Everyone was talking gloomily nowadays about the Rebellion losing momentum. But it *had* to succeed. Bishop Shambor was promoting other religions besides the Way of the One — though he was supposed to be their spiritual leader! He had to be stopped, and their nation of Dûrion restored to its wholehearted devotion to the One and his Son, Prince Orrénne.

She had just been emerging from childhood when the Rebellion started — but how she had rejoiced when she heard that Lord Armanet and Lord Dôrion had proclaimed themselves Restorers of the Way! People had flocked to them from all over the north and west of Dûrion. For six years she had eagerly followed every scrap of news about the Rebellion's progress. What a great day it had been when they'd captured Stillárre, Dûrion's second city! They'd suffered reverses since then, but they *would* recover. It was said that even now they were gathering more troops in the north-west.

Of course, Father didn't support the Rebellion. Nor did the Travelling Order whose itinerant priests did so much to bring hope and practical assistance to the poor under Shambor's tyranny. She couldn't understand their rejection of the uprising. They said Armanet and Dôrion didn't have the signs of the One's Restorers that were prophesied in the Book. To her it sounded like splitting hairs.

She pushed toward the front line of the crowd, near the centre of the square. Infantrymen in green capes were stationed at intervals, preventing the people from pressing in any further. A way had been cleared through the square, and a throng of people lined either side.

She addressed a grizzled townsman standing beside her. "*Ney li omalend, isset.* — Good day, friend. What's happening?" He turned with a scowl that quickly faded when he recognised the pretty, fair-haired girl in crumpled upper-class clothing. "*Illi dîmend,* Lady Perrely." His long face settled into mournful lines. "Are you the only one who doesn't know?"

"Know what?" A terrible premonition squeezed her heart.

"That it's over, Lady," he said sadly. "The Rebellion. It's failed. The Bishop's army captured Carreck Manor several days ago. Armanet couldn't break out."

Every word struck Perrely like a nail driven into her flesh. It was over? The rebels, on whom all their hopes had been pinned, were defeated? Shambor, with his wicked perversion of all they believed in, had *won*? In a single instant the eager longings of six years were snuffed out. The blood drained from her face.

"And the rebel army?" she heard her voice croak. "Did they — were they all — ?"

The man swallowed, and his eyes moistened. "I'm afraid so, m'Lady. My son was with them. The Bishop's men burnt the manor to the ground. No word of any getting away."

"What about Armanet?"

"Captured. That's what this is all about. They've dragged him through all the western towns; now they're doing the same here."

"Oh, no!" She stared unseeing at the crowd on the other side of the cleared way. She'd known Lord Armanet since she'd been so high. A quiet, friendly man; a well-respected merchant in Berûvis. She remembered the passion with which he'd pleaded the rebel cause. As a result, the townsfolk of Berûvis had been fervent supporters of the Rebellion — she among them, though not the rest of her family. Now her family had been proved right. It had all fizzled out. She squeezed her eyes shut to block the tears. *Why,* dear Prince?

A hush fell on the crowd. Through it came the steady clip-clop of horses' hooves. Five riders of the Bishop's Guard trotted into the square, their silver helmets gleaming and grey cloaks rippling. A wail arose from those they passed. They came abreast of Perrely, and she saw what lay behind them. Then her voice, too, uttered a cry of anguish and her hands flew to her mouth.

Tied by long ropes to the central horse, was Lord Armanet. At first, perhaps, he had been running to keep up with the riders; but some time ago he must have fallen. Now he was being dragged along the rough stones, his clothing ripped to shreds, his skin being scraped from him. His hands were still bound by the ropes, keeping his head off the ground; but the rest of his body was filthy, raw and bleeding. He had hardly enough rags left to cover his nakedness.

At a command the riders reined in, and Armanet collapsed in a bloodied heap. The Guard Lieutenant dismounted and walked back to the fallen prisoner. He kicked him. Armanet groaned, and the crowd groaned with him.

"People of Berûvis!" the Lieutenant shouted, his arms akimbo. "Look at this miserable pile of human wreckage before you. This is the man who claimed to be your 'Restorer'! What has he restored? Nothing! What has he given you? Only death, heartache and despair."

Armanet struggled painfully into a sitting position. Tears streamed down Perrely's cheeks. He was one solid bleeding wound, his hair matted, his face haggard. Yet his eyes as he sat there were clear and calm. He surveyed the crowd with an inner dignity no one could touch.

The lieutenant laughed. He pointed a derisive finger at the rebel leader. "Look at him! This... *thing* is the man who would have replaced our radiant Bishop! Now he knows what happens to those who oppose the One's anointed ruler. You people of Berûvis believed in him—but now you can see how he has deceived you. Greet your noble leader! Go on, give him the homage he deserves!"

Maybe the officer imagined howls of abuse would be hurled at Armanet, Perrely thought later. Or more tangible insults, like eggs and turnips. If so, he'd sadly underestimated the loyalty of this town to the rebel cause. What actually happened was clearly the last thing he expected.

Utter silence fell on the market square, broken only by the faint rustle of clothing. The rustling increased, and Perrely saw a man on the opposite side of the cleared way go down on his knees. Another knelt beside him, and another. She turned, and saw the people behind her all sinking to their knees. Her heart swelled with pride. She and the townsman beside her did likewise. In a few moments the entire square was kneeling before Armanet in the ancient act of obeisance.

The lieutenant screamed at the crowd to get up, threatening dire reprisals; but the damage was done. Someone started singing the Song of Allegiance, and the officer's ravings were swept away as the whole throng joined in, pouring out the anguish of their hearts. Perrely heard her own voice singing with them. Tears streaked the blood and dirt on Armanet's face as he slowly raised one hand in benediction. His eyes shone with gratitude.

Before the Song ended the rebel leader was jerked to the ground and dragged out of the square as the Guards resumed their journey to Darthane. There he would face Bishop Shambor and the ultimate defeat: mindbending.

The last chord faded, and the people dispersed in silence. They would suffer for today's act of defiance.

Chapter 4: *Common denominator*

STEVE GROANED. His heart was hammering and his breathing was ragged. They were pointing at him. All of them. *I didn't mean to!* he wanted to scream. *It was an accident!* But nothing came out. The whole playground was advancing on him, friends and enemies, all pointing and chanting, "Monster, monster, it's a monster! Kill it, kill it, kill it now!"

He ran for his life back into the school building. There, in the counsellor's office, he faced a panel of six adults. "Sit down, Mr. Harston," said the headmaster—a black-haired man with hard eyes. The face of the English teacher next to him was kindly, but she was shaking her head sadly. The rugged features of the sports master in his football jersey registered disgust. Two faceless men sat stiff and unbending, their heads turned in his direction. At the end of the table his mother was quietly weeping, her head in her hands.

"Sit down, Mr. Harston."

"Y–yes, sir," Steve stammered. He looked around, but there was nowhere to sit. "I'll just… get a chair."

He stumbled out into the empty corridor. There was no chair. There were no chairs anywhere. He hunted high and low, in room after room, but there were no chairs. At last he found the caretaker in his small cubbyhole, who laughed scornfully at Steve's question. "We've no chairs for the likes of you."

Steve blundered out of the caretaker's room, straight into the forest. Small bodies in banded armour with brown and green cloaks lay in the bracken, many with iridescent-feathered arrows in their backs. He stumbled over them. There were shouts, and an arrow whizzed past his ear. He tried to run faster, but the dead soldiers seemed to grab his shoes, holding him back. He forced himself past a clump of bushes, then froze in front of a large tree with a brown-coated soldier pinned to the trunk by an arrow. Sightless eyes stared at him from a chalk-white face. The soldier's arm lifted and pointed at Steve. His lips formed the word *"Monster!"*

Steve gasped, tripped over the soldier's boots, and fell forward. Outstretched fingers seized his neck and began to squeeze.

"A–a–a–agh!" Steve yelled.

* * *

Denise was lying awake on her hard shelf-bed. The previous evening everyone had been allocated a sleeping shelf in one of the storerooms. Lannie was sharing with five others, including two children. She wasn't too pleased about it. Denise, however, was happy to be with a group of older ladies, including blue-haired Margay; and Steve was quartered with four soldiers and a strapping teenager called Denny, the son of Margay and Frem.

She heard a distant noise and wondered what it was, so late in the night. It had sounded like a shout. She lay listening for a while, then heard sounds of someone in the kitchen. She climbed carefully off the shelf—the middle one of three on one wall—so as not to disturb the sleeper below. The stone floor was cold; she fumbled for the sandals she'd been given and pulled them on, then wrapped a blanket around her. She walked out into the passage and on towards the kitchen. Maybe Lannie or Steve was up, and they could chat.

But no, the midnight cook turned out to be the teenager Denny, Margay and Frem's son. He had filled a pot with water and put it on the wood-burning stove which was never allowed to go out.

Denny saw her and poured out a flood of words that passed her by meaninglessly. Denise shook her head and shrugged. More words followed, with gestures towards one of the other passages: presumably where his sleeping quarters were. Denise shook her head again. "Sorry, I wish I could understand you."

By now the pot had boiled. Denny went to a nearby shelf and took down a glass jar containing a dark, grainy substance. He sprinkled a couple of spoonfuls into the simmering pot, and a sharp but pleasant aroma wafted through the kitchen. Denise recognised it as *chass*: the local equivalent of tea or coffee. It had a strong flavour, slightly bitter, and seemed to be a mild stimulant. She felt she could come to like it.

After a few minutes while the *chass* brewed and the teenager continued to talk (maybe thinking that repetition would get the message home), he took a couple of two-handled mugs down from a shelf and turned to her with an enquiring look. "Yes, please!" He grinned and turned back for more mugs. Understanding at last!

Denny filled seven mugs, using a primitive strainer with fine cloth to filter out the grains. Chass was always served black and without any sweetener, which was fine by Denise. He handed one mug to her and put the others on a tray. With a smile and a final burst of gibberish he headed off down the other passage. Denise shook her head. A whole room-full of men unable to sleep? That was unusual. Maybe it had something to do with that noise she'd heard earlier.

She sat on one of the benches in the kitchen with her hands cupped around the warm mug, sipping the strong brew from time to time. It was comforting to have something warm inside her as she tried to grapple with this new situation.

It was the suddenness and complete inexplicability of the change that defied all logical thought. One moment she'd been in her familiar surroundings in England; the next, in a ruined castle in a foreign country among people speaking a foreign language. It was too much to take in all at once. She was so grateful that Lannie and Steve were here as well: without them she would have doubted her sanity.

At the same time, however, she was aware of an undercurrent of excitement running through her thoughts. Wherever she was now, it was certainly far enough from England to qualify as 'overseas'. And all her life she had longed to go overseas! Tied by circumstances to a mundane teaching job in Birmingham, she'd had the soul of an adventurer. How often she'd felt caged, had longed to spread her wings and fly away to a place where people really needed what she could give; where there weren't so many do-gooders competing with one another; where she could bring love to the truly loveless and hope to the truly hopeless...

This might well be such a place! She hadn't forgotten the home and family that she'd so suddenly been snatched away from; she would want to return to them before too long. But in the meantime, this country was clearly torn by war and suffering; could she learn the language and start helping to bring healing in her own small way? For however long it took before she, Steve and Lannie found their way home. Then maybe, sometime in the future, she could come back?

She hoped so. She so very much hoped that here at last she could spread her wings and learn to fly.

* * *

"You're very quiet, Steve," Denise said.

It was breakfast time in the ruined castle and Steve, Lannie and Denise were sitting at one of the long tables in the kitchen eating fruit and savoury biscuits with the brightly-dressed locals. Commander Fira and her troops had left earlier: Steve guessed they were out in the forest checking on the enemy green-coats who had chased them yesterday.

Steve glanced up at Denise. He shrugged. "Bad dream. Just need to shake it off."

"Oh, I'm sorry. I suppose we'll all have those for a while." A thought seemed to strike her. "Did you make a noise and wake the rest of your room?"

Steve blinked. "Yes, as a matter of fact I did. How did you know?"

"I heard someone in the kitchen and found Denny here making chass: seven mugs, including one for me. He took the other six back to his room. I wondered what had woken them all up."

She gave her infectious, bubbling chuckle, and Steve managed a smile in response. Lannie continued eating a biscuit, staring into the distance with unfocused eyes. Well, Denise might be the only sociable one among them this morning; but he was endlessly grateful that she and Lannie were here. Without them it would have been a hundred times harder to struggle back from that old, familiar despair, as he needed to do now.

Breakfast ended with a round of communal singing—which these people seemed to do at every opportunity—followed by a buzz of conversation and the clatter of dishes as the locals deposited them in the large washing trough. Steve, Denise and Lannie followed suit. After helping with the washing up, the three of them spent the rest of the morning carrying water down from the pump in the castle courtyard, washing clothes, and preparing vegetables for the midday meal.

Steve went through the motions mechanically until it came to him that he had to do something different to break out of the pall cast by the nightmare. Numbly performing unfamiliar tasks in an alien environment was like an extension of the dream—and was only bringing him closer to that downward slide into despair.

He put down the squash, or whatever it was he'd been peeling, and trotted into the open area beyond the kitchen tables. He took a short run, and began cartwheeling past the end of the table where Denise and Lannie were sitting.

"Watch it! Be *careful!*" Lannie snapped, jerking aside as Steve's legs whirled close to her head.

"Gotta keep fit!" he gasped as he shot past the other tables. There were cries of alarm and some laughter. When he was upright again he caught the end of a sharp exchange between Denise and Lannie.

"...needs to do his own thing."

"Fine, but not at the expense of my head!"

"Don't you worry about your head. He knows what he's doing."

"You think so? He nearly decapitated me!"

"Nonsense." Denise smiled indulgently.

Lannie stared at her, bereft of words. For the first time that day Steve grinned.

He grabbed an empty bucket and charged up the basement stairs four at a time. At least fetching water provided a few moments in the open air. The soldier guarding the masonry door to their hideout waved him through, and he trotted down the ruined passage to the archway where it gave on to the inner courtyard. As he entered the open space he sucked in a welcome breath of fresh air.

The courtyard was tiled, and in the centre was a large stone trough. A metal pump stood over it, twisted by the heat, but still working. On all sides were the collapsed remains of the castle, with blackened upper storey rooms open to the elements where the inside walls had collapsed. There were still wisps of smoke rising from the debris of the fire that had destroyed the castle. Only one of the corner towers remained almost intact.

Steve looked up at the sky between the surrounding ruins. It was overcast, but bright. That was it: he needed to get a proper look at the countryside around the castle—especially that incredible forest he'd been too busy to appreciate yesterday.

Leaving the bucket beside the pump, he entered a different passage off the courtyard and found his way through a maze of rubble to the broken front door. A little invigorating pantomime made the door guard laugh, and he allowed Steve out a short way on to the green grass beyond.

Steve stood staring as he took in the grandeur of his surround-ings. What a *place*. Ahead, separated by about four hundred yards of grass, was the forest. His eyes rose, and rose, till they found the canopy far above. He turned slowly to his right, and gasped as the bright sky above the forest was replaced by towering, snow-clad mountains. He kept turning, taking in new vistas. On all sides but one the tranquil forest surrounded the castle ruins with its majestic mountain backdrop. The remaining area was open, where the land fell away in a jumble of small hills towards distant, blue lowlands.

Stillness settled over him, his anxieties fading in the face of such serene beauty.

Where *was* this?

At the guard's urgent beckoning Steve reluctantly went back in-side, wondering how these people—whoever they were—could kill one another in such breathtaking scenery.

* * *

Fira and about half her force returned around midday, carrying two more wounded soldiers whom they made comfortable on bed-shelves in another of the storerooms. Then everyone sat down for the midday meal of crunchy nuts and beans on a savoury doughy vegetable, eaten with the fingers.

Fira addressed the group, all five feet one of her standing ram-rod straight at the end of one of the long tables. From the civilians' reactions it seemed the news was good. Denise wished she could understand.

"I hope those green-caped soldiers have given up and gone home," she murmured.

"That's not likely, is it, after the way they chased us yesterday," Lannie retorted.

"How is your arm?" Denise shot back. It was freshly bandaged.

There was a moment's silence. "It's better. Margay put some ointment on it. I'll have a scar, though."

Steve nodded solemnly. "An honourable trophy of war. You can show it to your grandchildren: 'The day I fought for freedom in Neverland'."

Lannie gave him a look. Denise chuckled. She was glad the young man had recovered his sense of humour. Then she sighed. "I wonder when I'll see my grandchildren again."

Steve's eyebrows shot up. "You have grandchildren?"

Her cheeks dimpled. "I have three, actually."

"Three? But you're so young and fit. You can't be a day past thirty-nine."

Denise laughed. "Flatterer. I'm fifty-six, and I don't care who knows it. I married young. My eldest, Tim, has two children — Ben, who's just turned eight, and Ellie, who's four. My daughter Rosemary has just had her first. Anthony, they're calling him..." She stared unseeing at a wooden serving platter in the centre of the table; then sighed. "With George gone these two years, it does get lonely sometimes."

One of Denise's new roommates arrived with a tray — an older woman with a rather severe expression called Veynel, who was in charge of the kitchen. *"Chass len temmis."* Steve and Denise each took a steaming two-handled mug. The hot, black liquid had a pleasant aromatic fragrance. But Lannie wouldn't try it: she said she didn't like hot drinks without milk and sugar.

Lunch was over and, as usual, someone started singing. Others joined in, harmonising, and soon the basement resounded with a cheerful melody. It had an alien feel to it. Rhythm? Harmony? Denise couldn't pin it down. Yet it spoke to something deep within her. Other songs followed, some more upbeat, some more downbeat; all heart-warming.

When the last chord faded away, she heaved a deep sigh. "Oh my, these people can sing! That was wonderful. If only I had my guitar."

"You play the guitar?" Steve said.

"Very well, as I remember," Lannie murmured.

Denise shot her a glance. There was a glimmer of a smile on the red-head's face. "Thank you, my dear." To Steve she explained, "I play in our church music group. I'd just love to learn these songs."

"Bondanet, felleneynor!" Fira rapped out, and she and her soldiers headed up the stairs once more. The three foreigners helped clearing away the dishes. After that there was nothing else to do, so they settled themselves again at one of the tables. Several of the locals in their technicolor shifts were sitting nearby chatting.

"Those bright clothes," Denise murmured. "They have a sheen to them — but the fabric isn't nylon or polyester. It's hand-woven."

"Yes, I noticed that," Lannie said. "They'd be a big hit if they were discovered."

"Another thing," Denise went on. "What about the colours of their hair? Margay's is a dark blue shade. But it isn't dyed. The colour goes right down to the roots."

Steve nodded. "Then we have the strange animals—that deer I saw which looked like a cow; and you mentioned a spotted squirrel, Lannie…"

"—and all the plants!" Denise added. "I haven't recognised a single one. The tall trees might be California redwoods, but they're not red. The bushes, the creepers, the bracken—even the fruit and veg we've been eating. They're *all* different."

"And the *light*!" Lannie said. "Everything has a golden tinge. As if we were wearing tinted glasses—even down here. I keep wanting to take mine off."

"You're right!" Denise exclaimed. "The leaves of the vegetables were all a yellow-green."

There was a moment's silence.

"So where are we?" Steve said quietly. "And how did we get here?"

The questions hung heavily in the air. Finally Lannie spoke.

"There's only one answer that covers everything, and I'm not ready to deal with it yet."

"Come on. Say it. Make you feel better."

"No it won't."

"Alright, *I* will. We're on a different world."

"Nonsense!" Denise protested, hearing the alarm in her own voice. "I'm sure all these things can be explained. We just don't know enough yet."

Steve shot her a sympathetic glance. He opened his mouth to speak, then changed his mind. "You could be right. But wherever we are, how did we get here?"

"Maybe we were drugged and kidnapped…" Denise began.

"What on earth for?" Lannie cut in. "It's not as if we're millionaires, or diplomats, or spies. And where have our kidnappers gone?"

"Obviously we don't know!" Denise responded tartly. "None of this makes sense, so one suggestion is as good as another."

Lannie snorted. "Okay. Try another."

"I will! Could we all have been on a plane which crashed, and we survived, but we're suffering from amnesia…?" Her voice tailed off. "No, we wouldn't all have lost our memories."

"You've hit it!" Steve exclaimed. "Whatever happened, happened to *all* of us. We arrived here at more or less the same time. Can we think of any... meeting or event before then that we might all separately have gone to?"

They began brainstorming, but soon ground to a halt. Meetings, outings, entertainments—all drew a blank. They tried mutual acquaintances, with similar results.

"Okay." Lannie ran a hand through her hair. "Denise and I live in the same city. Let's try the two of us. Did you go to that concert by the Birmingham Philharmonic last week?"

Denise shook her head.

"Or the Hobbycrafts and Art Materials event at the National Exhibition Centre?"

"I'm afraid not." She chuckled. "And I don't think you came on our Ramblers' Club outing."

Lannie snorted. "This isn't getting us anywhere."

They were silent for a moment.

With a sigh Denise murmured, "We had a special speaker at church last Sunday, but of course you wouldn't have been there."

"As a matter of fact I was, but I didn't see you."

"Really?" Well, well. "It was a good service, wasn't it?"

"It was a good sermon."

"Yes, that vicar from Oxfordshire gave us plenty to think about. Father Martin, they called him. Strange title for an Anglican—"

"Father Martin!" Steve exclaimed.

Denise stared at the young man, whose eyes were wide. "You know him?"

"He gave a guest lecture in our department at university."

"About linguistics?" Lannie looked sceptical.

"Yes, he has a doctorate. He's both a scholar and a clergyman, and he's well respected in the academic world. I went to see him later at that church of his in a village called Leston—about something different—"

"So did I," Denise said.

"Um—me too," Lannie added.

They stared at one another.

"This—could—be—it," Steve said softly.

"Okay, so we all went separately to see Father Martin." Lannie was frowning. "I don't see how that got us here."

"Oh, my dear, but it fits in." Denise's heart was beating faster. "Father Martin asked me whether I'd be willing to live in primitive conditions if God sent me to a different country. I said I would, never believing it would actually happen. But here I am!"

A pleased smile gathered on Steve's face as she spoke. "Same with me! I've been elected chairman of the Christian Union, and… well, leadership positions have never worked for me. But Father Martin said I'd learn about leadership 'somewhere quite different'."

Lannie shifted impatiently on the bench. "Oh, come on. Just because a preacher threw in the words 'somewhere different' with each of us, you're saying the Almighty magically transported us here? That's a load of crap."

"He said that to you, too?" Steve asked.

"Yes, but that's not the point. We—"

"*What* did he say?"

"I— He— We spoke about my broken engagement, okay?"

Steve raised his hands defensively. "Okay! But he said you'd find the solution 'somewhere else'?"

"Yes. But we're trying to work out how we got here, and three conversations with a vicar don't answer that!"

"Break out of the mould, sister! We wanted to find a link between the three of us—and we have. We all went to see Father Martin. He spoke to each of us about a 'different place'. And here we are, in the most 'different place' you could imagine! We don't know how, but those conversations must have had something to do with it."

Lannie was silent for a moment. "Well… Maybe."

Denise shook her head. Could it be true? Until this moment she hadn't connected her present situation with what Father Martin had said to her. Yet it did 'fit', as she'd said to Lannie. Perfectly. It was just that she hadn't expected quite such a sudden arrival here!

Dare she hope that this *was* the 'different place' Father Martin had been talking about? And for Lannie and Steve too?

Chapter 5: *Lannie escapes*

BISHOP SHAMBOR DOM BELDET sat in his ornate reception room in the great Cathedral that towered over the city of Darthane. The ruler of the nation of Dûrion was an imposing figure in his deep blue robe of office trimmed with silver. A silver stole hung over his shoulders. Shiny black hair framed a broad, powerful face with dark grey eyes. Strong hands were clasped together on the desk in front of him.

Behind him a circular stained glass window filled most of the room's outer wall. Its multicoloured light streamed on to the polished blackwood desk, where it created a darkened replica of itself around the broad shadow cast by the bishop. Chaise longues and occasional tables filled the rest of the room, arranged in clusters on the wide expanse of thick blue floor-cover. The walls were lined alternately with bookcases and blue-and-silver hangings. A water clock trickled quietly in one corner. In another the bishop's secretary, Estaron, stood writing at a sloping table.

Facing Shambor across the desk was a gaunt figure draped in bloodstained rags. He stood propped up between two Guardsmen, a light of defiance burning in his eyes.

"Greetings, old friend." The Bishop's voice was deep and mellow.

"If I'm your friend, Shambor, you must have some vicious enemies," the prisoner rasped.

The Bishop nodded slowly. Here was a man who really believed in the rightness of his cause. Such strength was rare.

"I know you no longer consider me your friend, Armanet; but you will. You will."

"Never."

"Your rebellion has failed. Your last stronghold has been destroyed. Your followers are scattered. Yet still you defy me?"

"You may have me in your power now, Shambor, but I serve One whose power is greater than yours. I may have failed, but *he* will overthrow you!" Armanet was trembling with the effort the words cost him.

"Put him on a recliner, then leave," Shambor told the Guardsmen. "You can go, too, Estaron." The secretary's pale blue eyes regarded him for a moment, framed by black hair and an unlined, self-contained face; then he carefully sanded the wet ink and walked with unhurried steps to the door.

Once the rebel leader was comfortably arranged on one of the chaise longues and the Guards had left, Shambor went to a glass-fronted cabinet on the other side of the room. He took out two tall silver goblets and a decanter of *shandil*, the alcoholic liquor brewed from *farn* grain. He placed them next to a beaker of water on a nearby table. With his back to Armanet, he took a vial from the pocket of his robe and shook a little dark grey powder into each goblet. Then he half-filled them with the amber-coloured shandil and topped up with water. He mixed both drinks vigorously with a blackwood stirrer.

He came back to Armanet, a goblet in each hand. "A drink for old times' sake." He took a deep draught from the left-hand glass and held the other out to Armanet. "Don't worry, it won't fuddle your wits. It's half water."

"D'you think—I'd drink—anything *you* offered?" the invalid ground out.

"It'll help the pain."

"I can endure a little pain."

"Oh come, Armanet. You're in my power. Why be petty when I extend a courtesy?" He held up the left-hand goblet. "See, I'm drinking it myself."

Armanet gave a hoarse croak of a laugh. "Very well. I'll drink—the rest of *that* glass. You can have the other."

Shambor shook his head sadly. "As you wish." He held out the used goblet, and watched suspicion warring with need in the man's mind. He was in constant pain. A tiny mental prod in the right direction did the trick.

Armanet slowly reached for the glass. "Sip for sip, then."

Shambor drank slowly, reminiscing between swallows about the good times before the rebellion. Armanet matched his sips. Gradually his face relaxed.

"Ahh, that's good. It does help the pain. Thank you." His words were slightly slurred. The goblet was nearly empty when his eyes closed and his hand slipped. Shambor deftly caught the glass before it hit the floor.

"Sleep well, my enemy," he murmured. "When you wake, you'll be my friend."

He shook his head to clear the fuzziness. Ah, *teméyn*! The wonder-drug that opened the doors to the Realm of the Mind — or, as his detractors would have it, that made mindbending possible. He, of course, took it every day, and was only slightly affected by a medium dose. Decent people like Armanet had no resistance at all.

Now to perform the operation. He snapped his fingers above Armanet's face. No reaction. Pulling up a stool, he sat beside the unconscious man and focused his drug-enhanced mental powers on Armanet's right eyelid. It slowly opened and closed again. Good. Concentrating hard, he made a tiny pinprick on Armanet's right cheek. The cheek twitched, and a droplet of blood appeared. Shambor clasped his hands tightly in his lap, index fingers extended, and focused his mind to stir up the particles in the blood, creating miniature currents and generating heat. More intense particle activity sealed the blood vessel, cauterising the wound. A small brown mark replaced the blood.

He was in good form. So much for the practice run. Now into the mind itself...

The access point was easily located. Inside, he searched for the node that transmitted commands from the conscious mind to the rest of the body. Each new mind was a fascinating puzzle. As he made his way through the maze of unexpected branches and dead ends, he picked up the memories and thought patterns of the subject. There was great determination and strength of purpose in Armanet, sadly wasted on a futile cause.

After half an hour of painstaking searching, he found the crucial node. He secured it and poised his mind for the delicate action to follow. The slightest inaccuracy, and Armanet's body would be beyond his own *or* Shambor's control. Exactly the right incision had to be made and the *teméyn*-charged node redirected to accept Shambor's telepathic control. Sweat beaded Shambor's forehead. This was no slave, who could be discarded if anything went wrong. This was the rebel leader, and having him mindbent was essential to Shambor's plans.

With infinite caution he sliced down through the node: so far, and no further. The strands recoiled and he patiently trapped them and bound the upper group into the intricate pattern known as the mindlock. There. Now Armanet's mental commands could only be transmitted to his body with Shambor's approval—as long as he continued to receive teméyn. Shambor carefully splayed the lower group into receptive positions and bound them in place. Now they would respond to Shambor's telepathic commands—dependent, again, on teméyn.

With a sigh of released tension he straightened himself on the stool and stretched. The job had been perfectly done, though he said so himself.

He went to the wall cabinet and poured himself more shandil—without the teméyn. He returned to the stool and sat sipping. After a while a shudder ran through Armanet's body.

"Now, Armanet, nod if you hear me."

There was a pause, then Armanet's head moved slightly forward and dropped back again.

"Listen carefully: You will take half a finger-width of teméyn every morning with water or chass. You will now forget that you were commanded to do this, but you will *not* forget to do it." He paused for the victim's mind to process the instructions.

"Very well. Armanet, wake up!" He snapped his fingers.

The eyes opened, and the rebel leader looked up at Shambor, puzzled. Confusion turned to shock, followed by a moment of dazed comprehension, then horror. Shambor felt that powerful personality struggling desperately within the newly-created prison of his mind, trying to force his tongue and limbs to defy his new master. At last the shattering realisation dawned: he was mind-bent.

"You were mistaken in opposing me, weren't you, Armanet?"

There was a pause. The eyes had a trapped look. He would work on that.

"Yes—I was," the man's voice croaked. Shambor smiled. Of course it was not Armanet who had said that, but himself. When he had perfected his control this man would sound like Armanet, have all Armanet's quirks of speech—even Armanet's choice of words—but at Shambor's direction.

"Do the people still believe in you, Armanet?"

"Some do." There was no pause this time.

"Would you lead them against me if you had another chance?"

"No."

A puppet. Yet potentially far more. He could have risen to great heights in the Realm of the Mind—even become a Mindbender himself. What a great Mindbender Armanet would have made! Shambor sighed again at the waste.

"Why would you refuse to lead the people against me?" he prompted.

"Because you are the rightful Bishop of Dûrion. Treason against you is sacrilege. I misled people. I would apologise for all the death and misery I have caused."

For a moment Shambor exulted in the totality of his victory. His mind had overcome the final stronghold—Armanet himself—and the rebel cause was now truly dead.

"And are you my friend now, Armanet?"

"Yes. But I betrayed our friendship. I committed treason."

"Treason is punishable by death, my friend. But first you will make a public recantation to persuade all your followers of the error of their ways."

"Yes, my Lord Bishop."

Shambor bestowed a mocking smile on his latest slave.

* * *

For three days Lannie had been *sick*. And she was ready to scream at being cooped up in this dismal basement.

Blue-haired Margay had come each morning to check up on her. On the first day Margay had felt her forehead and clicked her tongue. "*Heyss! Estûril dôrim thonda.*" She'd done a rather effective mime of stomach cramps, and Lannie had nodded. Margay had left, and Lannie gathered from the enthusiastic mimes of her roommates that the other two foreigners were also sick. *Great. Eat foreign food and this was your reward.* Margay had returned with a foul-smelling concoction in a wooden mug and made Lannie swallow the stuff. The treatment was repeated twice daily. It wasn't fair. Steve and Denise had recovered after just one day, while she'd carried on feeling like crap.

Privacy was definitely going to be a problem here. She didn't know how much longer she could survive in a single room with three other women and two kids. She was not a particularly sociable person. She enjoyed the occasional outing with friends, and attended the local gym. Otherwise work occupied all her time—most of it solitary. Matt, her ex-fiancé, had been the one exception... She was fond of her family, and turned up for obligatory events like Christmas, birthdays, and her brother Dale's wedding. But her parents' circle of country society and old money set her teeth on edge.

Even with such a limited range of social contacts, she needed to get away by herself to recharge her inner batteries. She often went for solitary walks. That was going to be a problem in this blighted place. She still needed to sort herself out about Matt. She had to get away into the forest, where she could be truly alone in the deep silence. Her whole being craved that.

Yesterday there had been a general exodus after breakfast. At noon they'd all come back, full of loud talk, many carrying white bags full of fruit, nuts and tubers they had collected in the forest. Steve had dropped by, looking bushed.

"What have you been doing?"

"Digging. Planting. Picking fruit."

"Oh! We're starting a farm now?"

"Seems like it."

They'd all trooped out again a couple of hours later.

Today Lannie was feeling better—and she had an escape plan all worked out. When Margay came in and mimed washing and dressing, she groaned and turned over. Margay tried again, and Lannie showed such a woebegone face that the older woman's expression softened. *"Aay, Alanya. Deril am hinnay, bas."* She shook her head doubtfully, gave a brief smile, and left. Lannie heaved a sigh of relief.

She waited until the last foot tramped up the basement stairs. Then she washed quickly and pulled on her cream top and black trousers. That made her feel more herself. Less conspicuous, too. She left the room and went to the kitchen—empty until Veynel and her crew returned to prepare late-morning chass. She started looking through the supplies. Eventually she found what she wanted: a couple of white food collection bags. Her passport to freedom.

It went better than she'd expected. One of Fira's guards stopped her at the ruined front entrance of the castle; but when she flourished the bags and pointed to the forest, he smiled and waved her through.

She crossed the wide ring of grass to the forest, and walked nonchalantly under the trees. Then she began moving quickly from one clump of undergrowth to the next, pausing frequently to listen for the sound of voices. Finally she relaxed. She sat on a rock and inhaled deeply. A clean freshness filled her nostrils. All around her stood the tall trees, and under them was the profound stillness of an immense cathedral. Her soul revived like a wilted flower. She admired again all the blending shades and textures of green, and noticed with surprise that she was no longer aware of a golden tint. Her eyes must have adjusted.

For a long time she sat there, soaking in the peace of her surroundings. Then she began to think.

Okay, Matt first. Get that out of the way, and she could turn to other things — like the chilling possibility that this was a different world.

Her first thought, to her surprise, was whether she still loved Matt. She had trouble visualising his face. Somehow, in this very different place, he seemed unreal. She remembered some of the good times they'd shared together; his sudden bark of laughter — the way he'd raise one eyebrow at her when she posed a cheeky question — and his sharp answers. He could give as good as he got. That was one of the things that had attracted her to him. But did she really love him? She stared absently at a tall clump of bushes. They were covered in clusters of golden berries — the same ones they'd enjoyed as dessert in the castle basement.

She'd been devastated when Matt had broken the engagement. After a week she'd swallowed her pride and phoned him. No reply. She'd emailed and texted. Nothing. That weekend she'd felt utterly down and desperate. Almost as desperate as she'd been three years ago when a creeping paralysis had gradually reduced her to immobility. In that dark time a friend had taken her to church, wheelchair and all, and she'd 'found Christ' — along with a wonderful sense of peace.

The feeling had faded in the months following, especially after her recovery and meeting Matt; and she'd gradually stopped attending church. But in her agony following the recent break-up she'd gone there again, hoping to recapture a little of that peace. Instead she'd been unexpectedly stirred by the sermon.

A few days later she'd gone to see that preacher — Father Martin, the man Denise and Steve had also visited — to discuss her broken engagement. He'd challenged her to *listen*. Her mind went back to that day, only a couple of weeks ago…

It had taken Lannie an hour of slow driving in her black sports car through narrow country lanes to find the little village of Leston in rural Oxfordshire. The church on the village green was unmistakable from Father Martin's description: the walls were a creamy white, and there was an unusual circular tower at the centre. The sign at the door read simply, The Round Church of Leston.

She parked and went in — then stopped in surprise. The internal layout was quite different from other churches. The floor was covered with a durable dark blue carpet, in pleasing contrast to the white walls. Windows with rich yellow glass let in a warm light. In the nave, chairs were arranged in circles around small tables. There was a counter at the end with a coffee machine, mugs, and kitchen equipment. What would have been the crossing — the intersection of the two arms of a cross-shaped church — was a circular area forming the base of the round tower. It contained several rows of chairs set in a three-quarter-circle facing the communion rail and altar in the chancel beyond.

Standing at the coffee counter was a young man in everyday clothes with a thick mane of blond hair. A smile lit his face when he saw Lannie. "You must be Ms. Catterick." He had widely-spaced eyes of a startling light turquoise colour, smooth bronzed skin and a strong chin.

"Yes, I'm Lannie."

"A cup of coffee?"

After helping her to a latte — which was surprisingly good — Father Martin led her to the front row of chairs in the circular sanctuary. Her eyes were drawn to the Irish cross on the wall above the altar. She noted absently that it was unlike other such crosses she'd seen. The vertical bar was unusually long; and there were other subtle differences she had no time to analyse.

She and the priest started chatting, and she was impressed with how easy he was to talk to. She told him about Matt, how in a moment of frustration she'd snapped at him, and now their engagement was in ruins. Father Martin listened, and asked a few penetrating questions.

"You said you appreciated my talk the other Sunday." There was a twinkle in his eye. "Could that be because you don't find it easy to listen to others?"

"People are so boring."

Father Martin laughed. "It's refreshing to talk to someone honest. But seriously… do you feel that maybe your inability to really listen to Matt has been part of the problem?"

She'd known it would come to this. "Definitely. I wanted to discuss that with you. You mentioned several ways –"

He held up his hand. "No. No tried and trusted methods. This goes deeper. Lannie, I believe you already have the gift of summing people up quite accurately. You can quickly tell what kind of person someone is – and whether they're likely to be useful to you. Am I right?"

She frowned. "I don't like that way of putting it, but – yes, I can."

"Then let me ask you: Are you willing to use that gift in a different way? Not just to label people as this or that type, but to find out what they're really like. Are you willing to listen to people? And to discover the truth about them?"

The questions brought her to a halt. Everything she'd been going to say died on her lips. The truth about people. That had never concerned her. People fell into obvious types who behaved in predictable ways. As far as she was concerned, why they did so had never mattered. Once she had someone labelled she knew how to handle them – or ignore them – while she carried on doing her own thing.

But here was a challenge she hadn't faced before. To go beyond just labelling people. To listen until she really understood what was making the other person tick. Could she...? But Father Martin was right. She knew in her heart that this was the fatal flaw in her relationship with Matt – and with many others. He was the one who understood her, and made all the adjustments. She had never consciously tried to discover the truth about him. For anything to change she had to start learning how to do that.

The priest had been sitting quietly, watching her as she wrestled with it. Finally she drew a deep breath. "Yes, I am."

Her eyes flicked up to the cross above the altar. Was that a flash of light? Nonsense, stress was making her see things.

Father Martin nodded soberly. "I know you came because of the situation with your fiancé, but I don't think you'll learn the art of listening in that situation. You'll learn it in a different place. It'll be hard, and you'll suffer in the process. But it'll be worth it."

She had accepted Father Martin's challenge, and spent the rest of the week trying to contact Matt again, without any response. She'd cried herself to sleep fully-dressed on the Saturday night. The next day... she'd woken up here.

There'd been no opportunity to start developing that skill of listening.

At first she'd dismissed Father Martin's comment that she would learn this skill 'in a different place' as irrelevant. But it didn't seem so irrelevant now. Did that mean she should concentrate on learning to listen here, so that if she and Matt did somehow meet again, they might have a chance of mending their relationship?

A distant sound broke in on her reverie. She froze. Was that a voice? There it was again, nearer—a muted call, "*Alanya!*" Her name—the one the locals used! Now she heard other faint echoes—"*Alanya!*"—all drawing closer.

She wasn't going to be found and dragged home! She looked around desperately. The golden-berry bushes! It was a big clump, with loosely-packed foliage. She dashed to it and dived in, scrabbling frantically through the outer branches.

She was thinking she'd burrowed far enough, when her hand fell on a human foot. She yelped and jerked back—to the accompaniment of a masculine English swearword. She just had time to notice a very ordinary British shoe, before it whipped away and she found herself staring into the face that belonged to it.

Chapter 6: *Boy meets girl*

IT WAS A LONG, SERIOUS FACE interrupted by a small moustache. Above was a once-combed mat of black hair, greying at the temples. Underneath were a corduroy jacket and a neat blue tie. Two grey eyes, wide with shock. "Who the hell are you?" he gasped.

"I might ask you the same," Lannie shot back, trying to keep the tremble out of her voice. Another unwitting arrival in the forest! How many more would there be?

The eyes subsided as he took in her normal appearance. "Thank God. I'd given up hope of finding any civilised human beings in this place."

Not far off a voice called, *"Alanya!"*

She put a finger to her lips.

He nodded.

Lannie reviewed her options. Her quiet day was shot. She couldn't try and slip off again—she now had this unwelcome intruder on her hands. She'd have to take him back to the castle. But they weren't going to be caught and marched home by Fira's henchmen.

The cries gradually grew more distant. Her companion turned to her, twigs and leaves riffling through his dark hair.

"Name's Denbigh," he said. "Dr. Gil Denbigh."

"I'm Lannie Catterick." A courteous instinct prompted her to extend her hand; but she quickly withdrew it when she saw how filthy it was. A charming half-smile crossed her new acquaintance's face. His eyes now held a lot more appreciation. Lannie winced inwardly. *Hero meets pretty girl in the undergrowth.* "Are you a medical doctor?" she countered quickly.

He blinked. "Ah—no. Doctor of Philosophy. I lecture in Linguistics."

"Oh. Pity. There are quite a few wounded where I'm staying." She started to manoeuvre herself out of the golden-berry bushes. Dr. Denbigh did likewise. They stood for a moment brushing the dirt from their clothing. Her companion was disgustingly tall, Lannie noted. She hated being reminded of her short stature.

"You're staying here?" he asked, fixing her with an intent look.

49

"No choice. I arrived unexpectedly, just like you. At a guess I'd say you fell asleep in your clothes last night and woke up here?"

He blinked again. "That's exactly what happened. Are there others here besides you?"

"Two others."

"And you all arrived the same way?"

"Yes. Here, take this." She handed him one of the food collection bags she'd brought. "Fill it with berries." He might as well make himself useful. She began plucking the golden-berries and dropping them into the other bag.

* * *

Since early that morning Gil Denbigh had been struggling to cope with an unfamiliar state of mind — utter ignorance. He didn't know where he was. Or how he'd got here. It was an unnerving experience.

Fighting off panic, he'd tried to reason it out. Was he dreaming? Had he lost his grip on reality?

True, he'd been under a lot of stress lately. His lifelong ambition — to be Professor and head of Linguistics at the University of London — had been within his grasp. There was only one other contender, with less experience but more publications to his credit. In an effort to establish a secure lead, Gil had submitted a flood of articles to linguistic journals. Including a paper 'borrowed' from a junior lecturer. This had come to light. Accused of plagiarism, Gil had been given one week by senior colleagues to 'consider his position'. One week to choose between impossible alternatives, both of which meant public humiliation. And with it the cast-iron certainty that he would never now be offered the Chair of Linguistics.

Had this driven him over the edge? He'd begun to think so when he'd seen those small men in armour searching through the forest. Horrified, he'd made a dash for the bushes. But then he'd found this young woman. She was real. And normal. The relief had been stupendous.

He eyed her appreciatively. She really looked rather appealing in a diminutive way. He'd always had a soft spot for redheads; add to that her blue-green eyes, the scattering of freckles, and her small but lithe form... It was a shame that right now she seemed more confused than *he* was. Handing him a bag to collect berries! He put it in his pocket and smiled at her indulgently.

"My dear, I think we need to get away from here. Those were soldiers who passed by just now. I'm sure there'll be other berry bushes. We should leave this forest, with your friends, and find the nearest town, where we can—"

The girl—Lannie—had stopped her berry-picking and was glaring up at him, hands on hips. Her fiery eyes complemented her auburn hair.

"Oh, so you're taking charge, are you? You know what to do, do you? Tell me, when did you arrive here?"

"A couple of hours ago."

"Well, Doctor Know-all, I've been here a week already. Those soldiers are my friends. I have reasons for not wanting them to find me. In fact, I don't particularly need *you* right now. So you can either fill that bag and follow me to a safe place, or try and find your town. I wish you luck."

She turned back to the bushes and started plucking berries with quick, violent movements.

Gil took the bag out of his pocket, an amused half-smile on his face. Lannie was straining to reach a cluster of berries higher on the bush. He plucked them with ease and put them in his bag. His smile widened at the furious glance she gave him. "You leave me no choice," he said. "I'll come with you, of course."

"And what's that supposed to mean?"

"Just that I prefer the company of an attractive woman with a whole week's experience—"

"*Doctor*—"

"Denbigh."

"Whatever. Let's get one thing straight. I'm willing to take you to a safe place because I'm a decent person and this forest is dangerous. But one more comment like that—just one—and I'll leave you here to rot. Do I make myself clear?"

Gil stared down at her intense face and the cold glitter in her eyes. "Sorry," he said. "That was inappropriate."

They picked berries in silence until both bags were full. Then Lannie jerked her head and said curtly, "This way."

He followed her through the trees. Things were looking up. Lannie would get over her huffiness. Girls always did. With her around — and a safe place to stay — this could turn out to be just the break he needed.

* * *

Denise groaned as she eased herself on to the bench at the kitchen table. She was over the stomach cramps, but her muscles weren't used to hard labour like this. Steve sat down beside her. "I'm famished!" he declared, and began rapidly digging into the roasted vegetable wraps on his platter. People were streaming into the kitchen, eagerly collecting their food from Veynel and her perspiring helpers at the stoves.

The young girl who had served Denise her first meal in the kitchen — Teynel, her name was — came hurrying over with her bowl. She sat on the other side of Denise, who smiled warmly at the pretty child with her large, turquoise eyes. The girl grinned shyly. "*Ney li omalend, Mâra,*" she murmured, before digging eagerly into her soup.

Denise had noticed that the children and younger women all called her *Mâra*. She assumed it was a title of respect. But there was more than that with Teynel. The girl seemed to have attached herself to her, often sitting with her at meals and in the evenings. Denise longed to find out why. She wished she could speak to Margay, who looked after Teynel, though she was too old to be her mother. Meanwhile Denise was growing increasingly fond of the child.

When they'd collected the second course of golden-berries with deer's milk Steve said, "Strange about Lannie, isn't it?"

Denise's head shot up. "What do you mean?"

"You didn't hear? It seems she left the castle this morning, and no one knows where she is."

"*What?*" Denise stared at Steve aghast. "And you're only now telling me? I thought she wasn't well yet. She's gone out? What if she runs into an enemy patrol?"

But she hadn't.

Denise looked round as silence slowly spread across the kitchen.

Lannie was coming down the stairs accompanied by a tall, very English-looking stranger.

Fira leapt to her feet and strode to the foot of the stairs. Her face was livid.

"*Alanya! Denôro sharrini? Bondanet li min bissitar!*"

"Well, I've come back," Lannie said. She showed the lieutenant two bulging collection bags and dumped them on a table. "This is Dr. Gil Denbigh. He'll be staying with us for a while. Excuse me." She pushed past Fira with the tall man in tow. He was staring around with raised eyebrows.

Denise closed her mouth, which had been open. *Another* unwilling arrival!

"Lord love a Doc!" Steve exclaimed beside her, his eyes wide.

"What?"

"I know that man. He's my linguistics tutor at university."

"Good heavens!"

"Just 'heavens' will do. Not much love lost between us."

A murmur was spreading across the tables. Denise saw again the wide-eyed stares as the local folk registered the new arrival. The words *"Atenámbaril cârim!"* rose above the buzz. Fira, who'd been staring after Lannie with a thunderous expression, rapped out *"Essin!"* and the locals fell silent.

Lannie and Gil came to their table. The doctor's eyes widened when he saw Steve.

"Mr. Harston. Fancy meeting you here." His voice was a little flat.

"And the same to you, doc. Um, sorry, I know that last paper of mine was a bit late—'fraid I haven't brought it with me, but I could do a re-write here, if you think that would...?" He let his voice tail off, eyebrows raised.

Dr. Denbigh sighed. "Always the humorous quip. Well, it seems we're in this together, so we'll have to make the best of it."

"Well said, Doc! Let's look on the bright side. We'll learn to appreciate one another here in the Forest Hilton. Looks like you and Lannie have already started. Great! Make yourselves comfortable, and I'll get you both some food."

He leapt up, did a quick handstand, and headed for the stoves. Gil shook his head.

Denise held out her hand. "I'm Denise Thompson. Is he like that at the university, too?"

"He never lets up... Gil Denbigh." They shook hands.

The newcomer turned to Lannie. "This is very snug. What happened to the castle? The fire looks recent."

"Oh, yes, it's recent. When we arrived there was a war going on."

"I'd guessed as much from all the arrows lying about."

"Then you should also have guessed that it's not such a clever idea to go looking for a town."

"I assumed the war was over."

"Well, you assumed wrong. Fira—that's the hawk-lady who yelled at me just now, she's in charge of the soldiers—she has guards on duty all the time."

Dr. Denbigh's eyebrows had risen again. "Then it was rather foolish of you to be out by yourself, wasn't it?"

"I needed to be alone, all right?" Lannie snapped. "Instead of which I get soldiers hunting me and you turning up."

At that moment Steve arrived back with two bowls of soup. Gil started eating, his face thoughtful.

He and Lannie were still busy when Fira gave the signal to return to work. Everyone began streaming up the stairs.

"What's happening now?" Gil asked.

"Back to work. You'll like it," Lannie told him sweetly. "Plenty of hard physical labour to keep you fit."

"What?"

"Yes, they're making a farm in the forest. Digging, planting seeds, picking berries and stuff."

Gil looked thunderstruck. "Working on a farm? You said nothing about that!"

"You didn't ask."

"I'm not a farm labourer. I can't do that kind of work."

"My dear man, there's no such thing as a free lunch. You've just had yours, so now you must pay for it." With a scornful glance she pushed her bowl aside and headed for the stairs.

"It's not so bad, Doc," Steve said soothingly. "I'll give you a hand—show you where to dig, and so on."

"Thanks," he muttered.

Soon Dr. Gilbert Denbigh, Senior Lecturer in Linguistics at the University of London, was walking up the stairs carrying a spade.

Chapter 7: *Vision*

PERRELY REFUSED TO ACCEPT that Armanet's capture meant the end of the Rebellion. Look at how they'd honoured him in Berûvis: kneeling before him, even singing the Song of Allegiance! The people still believed in Armanet, trusted that he would overthrow the Bishop and restore godly rule. Shambor might have won a temporary victory—but the One would have the last word. The Book was full of stories about courageous people who opposed heresy against tremendous odds; they had their setbacks, but they always won in the end.

On Anderil she'd made a vow to the One to pray three hours a day—for the rebel cause, and for its leader. She'd done so on Marneril; on Dûrneril, yesterday; and today. Her requests had become increasingly bold.

"Supreme One," she implored as she knelt beside her bed. "Illumine your Name by an act of sovereign power! Release Armanet from Bishop Shambor, even though it seems totally impossible! If he's been mindbent, break his mental bonds! If he's imprisoned, let him escape! Restore your people's confidence by a miracle. Demonstrate to everyone in Dûrion that there is only *One* true God!"

She reminded the One about examples from his Book where exactly that kind of miracle had occurred. She pleaded that Armanet's followers, his scattered army, and all who opposed Shambor's despotic rule, would be so electrified by his miraculous escape that they would rise up like a mighty wave with Armanet at its crest, and sweep Shambor and all his evil works from the land.

She sighed and wiped her eyes; then stood and stretched. She was happy that the One had given her this boldness before him, and had no doubt he would grant her request. Now she only had to wait, restraining her impatience, for news of Armanet's escape and all that would follow.

* * *

Armanet limped slowly to the temporary wooden dais at the inner corner of Cathedral Square, flanked by two soldiers of the Bishop's Guard. Hundreds of people filled the wide plaza in the shadow of the magnificent building that crowned Darthane's Cathedral Hill. Hundreds more crowded on balconies and leant out of windows to watch the final end of the Rebellion.

Ten days of rest, medical care and good food had done wonders for the rebel leader's physical condition. They had all but destroyed his mental condition. He had known that Bishop Shambor was secretly a Mindbender. He had feared being mindbent ever since his capture. But the reality was far worse than anything he'd imagined.

To be a prisoner in his own body! Unable so much as to scratch an ear if his jailer disapproved. To feel that mocking presence in his mind, sometimes moving him like a puppet, exulting in his helpless fury. It was almost more than his proud spirit could bear. Only blind trust in the One carried him through.

Worst of all was the knowledge that in a few moments he would be betraying all the thousands who had pinned their hopes on him. Those in Berûvis, who had done obeisance and sung the Song of Allegiance even in defeat. Those whose sons, daughters, brothers, parents, had died following him. Those of his loyal troops who still lurked in hiding… What would they think when they heard that he had recanted at the end, sworn allegiance to their hated enemy? He wept with dry eyes for their pain. This would kill the Rebellion more surely than any military defeat.

He reached the dais and walked up the short flight of steps. To his right was an oddly-shaped wooden block. Beyond it stood a burly man in a dark, knee-length tunic, his hands gripping the haft of an axe. But immediately in front of Armanet was Shambor in his episcopal chair, resplendent in the blue and silver of his office. Behind him stood a row of Mindbenders in blue robes. The Bishop's secretary and ever-present sidekick Estaron stood gravely to one side in his best white tunic, arms clasped behind his back.

Armanet found himself going down stiffly on one knee and bowing his head. A low groan of shock rose from the crowd. Shambor touched Armanet's head in the traditional blessing, then stood. Armanet stood with him.

As from a great distance Armanet heard Shambor speaking of his, Armanet's, misguided actions in stirring up the people against their anointed Bishop: of his inevitable defeat, his capture, his repentance; his desire now to make a public recantation.

Shambor returned to his chair, and Armanet stepped forward. There was a deathly hush. Then he heard himself speaking, and shame overwhelmed him. His own voice, with his own mannerisms, declaring that it had all been a terrible mistake: speaking out those lying words loud and clear. Blaspheming against the faith he had sought to restore. Breaking oaths he had sworn. Betraying those who had trusted him.

At last his voice fell silent. He saw the bitter lines on many faces. Then he turned and knelt once more before Shambor. Now his humiliation became total as the unthinkable happened: Armanet, leader of the Rebellion, swore the oath of allegiance to his enemy Shambor, usurper of the Dûrian episcopacy.

It was with a sense of relief that he found himself walking towards the executioner. At last it was over. He heard Shambor declaring sorrowfully that Armanet's repentance, though genuine, was too late. Treason had been committed, and the law must take its course.

He knelt at the block and bowed his head. His last thought was a prayer that the One would send others to finish what he had started.

* * *

Perrely knelt again at her bedside, her upper body sprawled across the covers. She wept uncontrollably, her head resting on her arms. This was the darkest moment of her life.

Today Father had come back early from work, grim-faced. He'd sent his employees home. News had come from Darthane. Armanet had been executed. Not only that, but before they beheaded him he had publicly renounced the Rebellion, recanted his heresy, and sworn allegiance to Bishop Shambor. This had happened before a thousand witnesses.

Perrely had fled to her bedroom and wept. She had tried to pray, but had broken down and wept again. They had brought her the daymeal, but she couldn't eat.

She'd been so sure. How could she have been so wrong? How could the One have allowed her to make such bold requests, when he knew the exact opposite was going to happen? How could he have let it happen? Didn't he care about the evil Bishop Shambor was doing? About the thousands who'd died trying to stop him?

Had they died for nothing? Was he going to let Shambor get away with it?

No. He did care. Enough to have sent his own son into this evil world. Orrénne had died at the hands of men just like Shambor. She wept again.

She knew Armanet must have been mindbent when he renounced the Rebellion and swore allegiance to Shambor. She remembered the calm assurance in his eyes as he'd sat, covered in blood and rags, in the square in Berûvis. She knew he would never have betrayed those who sang the Song of Allegiance to him. Some of those in the square would understand that; but many would be unable to see beyond the fact that the one to whom they had pledged themselves had betrayed them. They would be confused, disillusioned, bitter.

The Rebellion was over now. Armanet would be remembered, not as a martyr, but as a traitor.

Perrely found she had no more tears to weep or prayers to pray. She looked up at the wooden *ambon* on her wall—a circle for the world, crossed by a vertical rod for the One who had died for it.

If anything was going to be done about Shambor, *he* would have to do it.

* * *

The weeks had passed and it was Anderil again. But today was different. Perrely stared in wonder at the huge trees. It was the first time she'd been in one of Dûrion's mountain forests, and she was awed by its grandeur. She wandered slowly from one great trunk to the next, drinking in the fresh woodland scents, the deep silence, and the fascinating interplay of light and shadow.

She glanced up, and to her surprise saw a grey-haired lady walking across her path some way ahead. She had a cheerful face, but was dressed in the strangest clothes Perrely had ever seen. Drab, thick and clumsy they looked. She was carrying a stringed musical instrument made of redwood—a *bellaril*. She didn't see Perrely, and passed out of sight.

Perrely followed the direction the grey-haired lady had taken, but there was no sign of her. She sat down beside a forest stream and trailed her hand in the water. She was looking at a small hill on the other side when an extremely tall man with a moustache appeared over the crest of it. She gasped. He must be taller than Bishop Shambor! He, too, was dressed in outlandish garments — a dark blue corded jacket, a narrow blue cloth knotted around his neck, a white blouse, no robe, and ankle-length breeches. He stopped and pulled a glass out of his pocket — a *blaise* with two handles. He lifted it towards her and looked through it. Then he turned and disappeared beyond the hill.

Perrely debated whether to follow the man, but decided she'd rather just enjoy the beauty of the forest. She hadn't been doing so for long, when she saw a red-haired gentlewoman crossing the stream further down — at least, she assumed she was a gentlewoman, since she was wearing straight black culottes. She was only a little taller than Perrely, and she was marching through the forest with a quick, determined stride, holding a large shell to her ear. It looked like a *bess* from the Thrinari beaches.

Perrely climbed languidly to her feet. *I'd love to stay here all afternoon*, she thought, *but I suppose I ought to go home*. She strolled along the stream for a while, until she had to take a detour round a clump of undergrowth. Then she stopped.

A young man was standing beside a creeper-clad tree trunk. He was thickset, well-muscled, slightly above normal height, and again oddly dressed — no cloak or tunic, just a white, short-sleeved blouse above a pair of faded blue ankle-length breeches. He was looking at her. He had a friendly, open face and warm blue eyes; and clasped to his chest he held a thick book with an orange-and-black cover. He smiled, then turned and walked away.

As Perrely stared at the young man, it suddenly struck her like a hammer blow. These people she'd seen: they had been very strange — and very alone. Words from the Book echoed in her mind: *I will send strangers and loners to rebuild the broken path and restore the Way and cleanse my rescued people.* The Restorers of the Way. Could *these* be…? She hurried after the young man.

All four strangers were gathered together in an open glade. They turned and saw her, and their faces lit up. The gentlewoman was holding aloft a great gold-and-silver ambon that sparkled in the sunbeams lancing down through the trees. Her heart skipped a beat. Another prophecy: *They will hold high the Rod of Truth.* The blond-haired young man beckoned her to come and join them; and she did.

A deep peace and a sense of 'rightness' settled over Perrely. She heard her Prince's voice saying softly, "This is your place, my daughter, to be with the ones I have sent."

The picture slowly dissolved into a wooden ambon mounted on a wall. It took Perrely a moment to get her bearings. This was her bedroom. She was kneeling beside her bed, where she'd been asking the Prince to show her the way forward.

Well, he'd shown her more than she'd bargained for! Her heart was aglow with the peace of that final scene, yet her mind was full of questions. Was this really the Prince's way for her? Or had she dreamed what she wanted that way to be? She'd been so bitterly disappointed that the Rebellion had failed, and Armanet and Dôrion had proved not to be the Restorers of the Way. Was her imagination now trying to invent a substitute, a new set of Restorers?

Yet those scenes had been so real, so vivid! She could recall every detail of the strangers' appearance. How could her mind have invented such an outlandish group of people? But if this— vision (she couldn't call it a dream) was truly from the Prince of Peace, was she meant to leave home and find them? Surely not...

"Dear Prince Orrénne," she murmured, "I was wrong last time, and I'm so afraid of being wrong again. I don't want to do anything until I'm really sure. If these people I've seen are real, and they're the true Restorers of your Way—and if you want me to be with them—then please... will you bring them to me?"

It seemed to Perrely that the Prince smiled.

Chapter 8: *Dream renewed*

DR. MARTIN FELLOWES sat at the front of the Round Church of Leston, looking up at the Irish cross on the wall. Above him rose the circular tower that gave the church its name. It was full of mellow afternoon light from the yellow-tinted windows that ran around the top, under the dome. The cross, also, was illuminated by a shaft of golden light from the western window of the apse.

He loved this church; and he enjoyed his work here in Leston. His parishioners were a mix of rich and not-so-rich, and they gave him plenty of challenges and rewards as he sought to shepherd them. When time allowed he also pursued his other love, linguistics: writing articles, attending conferences, speaking at universities. He'd always had a gift for languages, and could have opted for an academic career; but the One Creator God had a different plan.

It was a lonely life, though; and sitting here, in the semicircular auditorium under the tower, he was always reminded of another place of worship, far away, where his heart was and all he held dear. It was in the service of that place and those people that he endured his periods of exile here. He knew the One would bring him home when his present task was done; but this had been a long stretch, and he hoped that time would come soon.

Meanwhile he sat waiting for another visitor who might, or might not, bring that homecoming closer.

He bowed his head in prayer for her. An older lady: but Light had touched his heart as he spoke to her. He hoped she would come. He hoped another light would validate the Light's touch this afternoon.

His thoughts went with brief longing to his wife, Shindorel; and to the old bishop whose prayers had brought Lannie Catterick, Denise Thompson and the others across his path. Was Lannie already in Dûrion? Probably. He wondered where she was and how she was doing. Would Denise also be an *Atenámbar*, despite her more advanced years?

He would soon find out.

* * *

As Denise carefully guided her trusty old Volkswagen through the twists and turns of Oxfordshire's country lanes, she thought about the young vicar, Father Martin, who'd preached at her church last Sunday. He'd spoken about the way so many people in this modern world were crying out to be listened to, but only encountered deaf ears and self-absorbed minds.

His message had struck deep, because that was exactly what she herself had been struggling with recently. Her church had decided to send a team to help out at a rural church in Kenya for four weeks. It was the church started by Margaret Weston and Joyce Davis, to whom she'd been sending small monthly gifts for three decades now. She'd eagerly put her name forward, confident that her many years of contact with the church would guarantee her a place—only to be rejected in favour of a younger person who wasn't even sure she could spare the time.

When she'd tentatively raised the matter with her vicar, he'd repeated all the reasons for the decision—the trip was intended for younger people, the person chosen needed this challenge to put her faith into action, and so on, and so forth—without really listening to Denise's pain.

As Father Martin concluded his sermon Denise decided she had to speak to him personally. The injustice of her church's decision still rankled, though it had happened months ago. At least this young vicar with his deep-set, compassionate eyes would listen, and she'd feel understood at last. Ever since her teenage years she had longed to serve God overseas; and now even this short, four-week opportunity had been denied her.

As an eager young Christian on the threshold of life, how she'd burned with eagerness to do things for God! To go out into the wilds where he was unknown; to trumpet the message of his love from the hilltops. To care, and suffer, and struggle to reach out to people living in darkness and misery, so that they, too, could discover the unbelievable joy of God's presence...

But then, she'd had to earn a living. She'd trained as a teacher—a temporary measure, to keep body and soul together until she could follow God's calling to serve him overseas. She'd started teaching, just for two years—which somehow expanded to five. Then George had asked her to marry him; and she'd been plunged into inner conflict, keeping the man waiting for months. But everyone advised her to settle down and give up her impractical ideas of working overseas. So, in the end, she had; and ended up teaching for thirty-three years.

She'd loved George, and hadn't regretted marrying him. Yet she'd never shaken off the underlying sadness of a dream lost, a vision abandoned. She'd thrown herself into her teaching, and knew she'd been loved by her pupils, and had a positive input in their lives. But it had never felt like her ultimate goal, her life's work. She'd taken an avid interest in Christian work overseas, gathering information, attending meetings, subscribing to newsletters, and giving what she could to a number of organisations and individuals — including Margaret Weston and Joyce Davis in Kenya.

Then had come early retirement, and George's sudden passing a year later. As she learnt to live with that, her thoughts had turned again to her old dream of serving God overseas. Did she dare to believe that God still wanted that for her? That she wasn't too old? That God could still use her overseas after all her years at home as an ordinary housewife and teacher?

How wonderful it had seemed when she'd heard her church was organising a month-long trip to Kenya! This was God's answer — yes, he *could* still use her! The Kenyan trip would be the first step: she would find out what she was capable of, and how she could follow it up with other shorter and longer-term avenues of overseas service...

Then the rejection. She was too old. Overseas service was for young people.

She pulled the car over into a lay-by until her vision cleared.

* * *

Denise entered the Round Church of Leston rather uncertainly, looking about her in surprise at the modern decor. The church seemed empty, apart from the semicircular rows of chairs in the central sanctuary: there, with his back to Denise, sat a young man with a thick mane of blond hair. His head was bowed in prayer.

She felt terribly awkward about taking up Father Martin's time, and paused among the coffee tables at the entrance. But he must have heard her come in, because he rose and advanced towards her with a smile. He was dressed casually in tan trousers and a blue polo-neck sweater. There was no sign of a clerical collar.

"Mrs. Thompson! It's good to see you. Do make yourself at home. Would you like a coffee?"

"That's very kind, but… no, I'm fine, thank you."

"Okay. Then let's find a seat at the front, and we can talk."

Denise was struck again by the intense, single-minded gaze of his brown eyes. It was as if one hundred percent of his attention was focused on her, and he was hearing both what she said and what she didn't say.

Father Martin escorted her to the first semicircle of blue upholstered chairs that faced the altar and the unusual Irish cross on the wall behind it. He quickly put her at ease, and sat quietly listening as she poured out to him how all her life she'd longed to work for God overseas, but now, at the first real opportunity, had been turned down. To her embarrassment she broke down and wept, clasping and unclasping her hands in her lap.

Father Martin leant forward and took her hands in his. Reluctantly she met his gaze, knowing she must look a fright, eyes red, cheeks blotchy. But his face only showed compassion. "Denise," he said gently, "God is well aware of your desire. He knows just how much you have to give to others. He shares your passion to spread his love in distant countries, to people as yet untouched by it."

She nodded, and heaved a shuddering sigh. "I know. I shouldn't be making such a fuss. My contribution is to pray and to give, both of which I can do from home. I must just accept that."

"No!"

She blinked, startled.

"Denise, what if the time has come to play your part much further afield? Not just for four weeks, but a good deal longer. Would you be willing to put up with primitive conditions? To stick around when the going gets tough, so you can share the truth of God with people who desperately need him?"

She gaped at the young man. This was the last response she'd expected. He was completely confirming her lifelong vision!

Her chin came up. "Yes, I would!" she declared firmly.

For a moment a brighter light lit the altar. If she hadn't known better, she'd have said it came from the metal cross on the wall.

Father Martin smiled. "I know it seems impossible now, but I believe God will give you exactly what you've been longing for."

She stared at him. There was joy in his eyes. He seemed genuinely happy for her. The tears started again, and she felt his arm go around her.

He might be wrong. She might never end up overseas. But there was at least one person who truly believed she wasn't past it. That God could still use her. That her dream was not nonsense.

Map 3:
Carreck Manor and the surrounding area

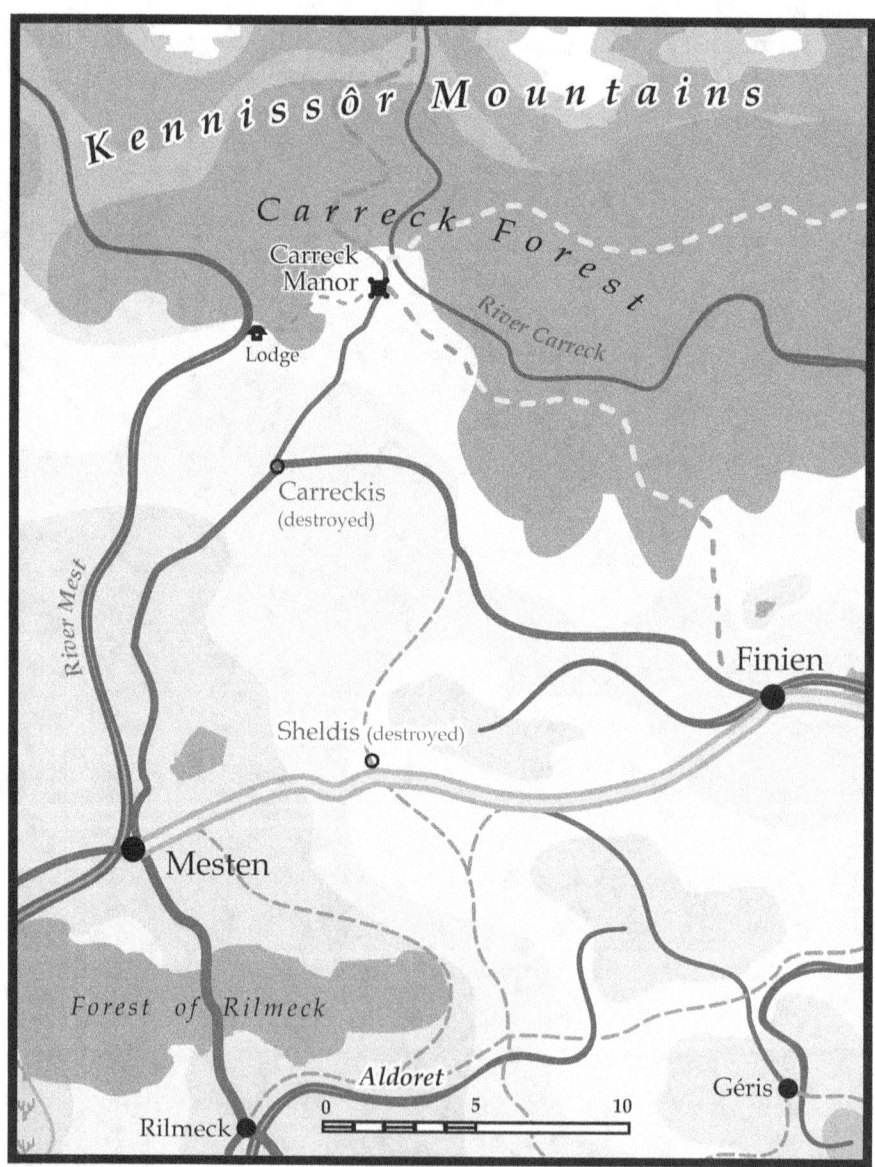

Chapter 9: *Fireclay and information*

DENISE SIGHED WITH CONTENTMENT as she stared out over the wide River Mest gliding past the meadow where the group were eating their midmeal. What an incredible vista it was, utterly deserted and unspoiled. Tall forests and snow-capped peaks lay behind them, and in front the river wound its way through tumbled foothills into the blue distance. Not a road or a car or a tourist in sight. Westerners would pay thousands to visit a place like this—and here she was, for free!

Ten days had passed in the ruined castle, and today was a welcome break in their daily routine. They'd come to this beautiful spot to collect fireclay: the red putty that caused the bamboo-like firesticks to burst into flame.

The party of ten locals and four foreigners had set out at dawn, with a two-hour walk through the forest to get here; followed by hard labour the rest of the morning, repairing the three rowing boats. They needed these to get to the reddish sandbars in the river, where they would scoop up the clay in wide-mouthed bowls. Back at the castle it would be strained through a fine cloth, dried out, mixed with oil, and patted down into little earthenware pots for use with the firesticks. They'd found the boats in a boathouse attached to a dilapidated building which their companions said was once a holiday lodge used by the 'Elder of the Manor'.

Denise was struggling to get used to all the new words they were learning. The name of the region they were in was 'Dûrion', and the people were 'Dûrians'. The castle where they were living Steve called 'Carreck Manor'. Steve was their resident expert on the language: he had made amazing progress since their arrival. She and Lannie were some way behind; but poor Gil, the linguist, had started late and was still at the baby stage. You had to give him credit, he kept plugging away. Even now during the meal he was repeating words after the twin soldiers, Shîrin and Cârin.

"Gelmion!" Steve called, and Denise smiled at the black look Gil gave him. Gil didn't like the Dûrian names they'd been given, but she and Shiván were using them regularly now. They matched the brightly-coloured Dûrian shifts and local sandals they all wore.

"Gelmion," Steve persisted, "we've been thinking back to the time we all arrived in Dûrion. Tell me, did you go and see anyone in particular back home before you found yourself here?"

Gil broke off his lesson to stare at Steve. "No," he said heavily, "As it happens, I didn't visit a travel agent to buy a one-way ticket to a ruined castle in a foreign country where I don't know the language."

"Tut, Doc, anyone would think you didn't like this place. What I mean is, did you… happen to visit someone you wouldn't normally visit? Before waking up in the forest?"

Gil seemed on the point of snapping off a scornful retort. Then he blinked, his eyebrows shooting up. "I … might have done. Why?" He came over to join them.

"Who, Doc — who?" All three were staring at him.

"It was that visiting lecturer — Dr. Martin Fellowes. You heard him, Steve."

"Father Martin!" Denise exclaimed.

"Did you go to that church of his — the 'Round Church' in Leston?" Lannie asked.

"Yes. *You* went there?"

Steve cut in. "We all did, Doc. Welcome to the club."

Lannie was looking at Gil intently. "Did Father Martin speak to you about learning something 'in a different place'?"

Gil swallowed. The question seemed to unnerve him. "Yes. As a matter of fact, he did."

"Well, well," Lannie said, looking at Steve. "It seems you were right."

"What are you implying?" Gil demanded. "That this priest *sent* us here? Ridiculous!"

Steve was unusually serious. "Maybe, but just consider the facts, Doc. The only thing all four of us have in common is that we recently visited Father Martin. He told *all* of us that we would learn something new in 'a different place'. And if this isn't a different place, then I'm a Martian."

"Well, that's open to debate. But how are we supposed to have got here, then?"

"Weren't you listening?" Lannie said impatiently. "We don't know. What you've just proved is that our visits to Father Martin must have had something to do with it."

Gil nodded, frowning thoughtfully. "Interesting. That opens up a lot of possibilities. But we don't know how we got here, or where we are. I have an idea about that, though."

"Tell us, Doc," Steve urged with a grin.

"Well, my guess is that we're somewhere in central Asia. Mountainous, remote—and people still fighting with swords and armour."

"Interesting. That opens up a lot of possibilities," Lannie mimicked. "But here's a different possibility for you: 'Shiván' believes we're on an alien world."

Gil let out a bark of laughter. "So that's why you didn't get your assignments in on time, Mr. Harston. Burying yourself in science fiction!"

The young man gave him a dark look. "Alright, laugh. But explain a few things. Why is the light here more golden? Why have we recognised none of the plants or animals? Why have we seen— count them!—zero western-type things? I've been to some far-out places in Africa, and even in the most primitive villages you'll find coke cans and battery-powered radios. The Manor basement has piles of stuff in crates, barrels and sacks—how come *not one* has a manufacturer's label?"

"Asia is different from Africa—less dependent on western aid. In any case, it's circumstantial evidence. There may be a perfectly good explanation for those things."

"I'm *so* glad to hear you say that," Denise murmured.

"Such as what?" Lannie demanded.

"Well... The people here seem a conservative lot." Gil shrugged. "Maybe they've deliberately turned their backs on western decadence. Like the Amish in America."

"Oh, now *that* would make sense," Denise exclaimed.

"No it wouldn't; it's totally far-fetched," Lannie retorted, her eyes on Gil. "They've just been fighting a war. Surely they'd want Western technology to help them win."

Denise bit off the sharp retort that sprang to mind. Soon Lannie and Gil would be going at it hammer-and-tongs again, and they wouldn't want *her* involved. She was beginning to think the two of them enjoyed these verbal duels.

"Wars have been fought before to preserve a traditional way of life," Gil said.

"Maybe, but here the enemy *also* fought with swords and armour. If they were the non-traditional ones, why didn't they use guns?" Lannie stared at him triumphantly.

Gil gave her his celebrated half-smile. "Inconclusive. This could be a remote area, fighting their own little tribal war. Governments often turn a blind eye to local conflicts."

Lannie glared at him. "Alright, what about their clothes?" She gestured at her own dark green shift. "This is a high-quality fabric, hand-woven, but with a sheen to it. Light and supple, almost waterproof—yet comfortable to wear. Western companies would pay millions for this! How come it hasn't been exploited? No government would turn a blind eye to a goldmine!"

Gil shrugged. "Again, inconclusive. Maybe it's genuinely undiscovered, and you can make your fortune. Maybe it's uneconomical to manufacture abroad. Maybe it doesn't travel well. There could be a dozen reasons other than saying *therefore* we're on a different planet."

While Lannie glared, Steve commented peaceably, "Only one way to know. Have a look at the stars one evening."

Lannie rounded on him. "Oh, and that's very easy, isn't it? Perhaps you haven't noticed that the Manor door is guarded at night? In any case, it's always overcast in the evenings." She jumped up and went to get seconds from the communal lunch basket.

After a moment's silence, Steve turned to the nearby Dûrians and started chatting with Margay and her husband Frem. Denise picked up that he was trying to find out what the war had been about. Lannie rejoined them, and all three listened in to Steve's conversation. It went slowly, with many repeats and queries; but Denise shook her head in admiration at the vocabulary 'Shivân' had already picked up. He broke off from time to time to translate for them.

"It seems like the war was between two different religious groups," Steve told them. "Our lot here, the losers, who believe in only one god; and the government lot, who believe in many gods."

Gil snorted. "Well, that's great, isn't it? We've landed in the midst of a sectarian conflict."

"I asked them how the civilians got involved in the war—and Frem said most of them are from a couple of nearby villages. The villages were destroyed, but they're all Light— Lightians? Lighters?

70

Oh, heck, 'Lightists' — it's the name of their one-God religion — so they took refuge with the rebel soldiers, who were making their last stand at Carreck Manor. When the enemy set the upstairs on fire the villagers escaped down the emergency tunnel into the forest."

"How did you understand all that? You're learning too fast!" Lannie complained.

Steve turned his head and pointed to his ear. "Haven't you seen? Built-in translation module."

"Idiot."

With another snort Gil went back to Shîrin and Cârin, who cheerfully plied him with more words and phrases.

"You two have been learning pretty fast as well!" Steve told Lannie and Denise, his eyes bright. "Haven't you noticed? Look at the good old Doc over there. A linguist of linguists, but he can hardly put two sentences together yet. That's the stage the three of us ought to be at, too, after only a couple of weeks. But haven't you felt sometimes as if you already know this language?"

"Yes, I have!" Denise exclaimed. "It's as if I knew Dûrian long ago as a child, and the more I hear, the more I remember."

Lannie nodded. "That goes for me too," she said. "When I learn a new word I think, 'Of course! I knew that!' "

"Exactly," Steve said. "Father Martin told each of us we'd be learning things 'in a different place' — and that's just what's happening."

"So somehow we're on a fast track with the language," Denise mused. "That must tie in with why we're here... Can you ask the Dûrians who they thought we were when we first joined them? Remember how Damion and the locals treated us like celebrities? They obviously thought we were special, and kept using that word *Atenámbaret* — which we still don't understand. But then — "

"Yeah! Then old spoil-sport Fira came along and pricked the bubble. Well, I'll give it a go..."

He turned to Frem and Margay again, but soon the whole group was involved. Two of the soldiers seemed vehemently opposed to whatever Frem and Margay were saying; and the twins — Shîr and Câr — kept firing off what sounded like humorous comments from the sidelines.

Finally 'Shiván' paused to translate. He mopped his brow. "Whew! That was like lighting a fire cracker and finding it's linked to the whole box. Okay. You heard them—the big question is whether or not we're *Atenámbaret*. The villagers, like Frem and Margay, say they think we *may* be, because of… something I couldn't follow. The soldiers—apart from Shere and Khan, who just kept cracking jokes—say we can't be, because the whole war was about this issue: the two rebel leaders also claimed to be *Atenámbaret*. But the villagers say, Well, they were defeated! So they couldn't have been. But for the soldiers that's like saying everything they fought for was rubbish… So-o-o, who we are is a pretty explosive issue."

Lannie nodded. "Which is why Fira blows her top every time anyone says that word."

"Do Frem and Margay think we're their new rebel leaders?" Denise asked, frowning. That was the last thing she wanted.

"Could be. I dunno." Steve scratched his head. "Wish I knew what *Atenámbaret* means."

"Didn't you ask them?" Lannie demanded.

"Of course I did, and they reeled off a whole lot of stuff I couldn't understand."

Just then Frem announced, "*Felleneynor! Kion lîsim lasa.*"

"'Let's go. It's the sixth hour'," Denise translated. "Oh dear, that weird time system again."

They stood and stretched, then clambered into the three rowing boats with their Dûrian companions. It would be a long afternoon scooping up the red clay from the river sandbars, but a welcome change from digging and harvesting.

Chapter 10: *Forest hearthtime*

AMID THUNDEROUS APPLAUSE from the packed auditorium Steve stepped forward to greet their distinguished guest.

"Welcome, your Grace!"

The Bishop in his mitre and resplendent vestments looked Steve up and down. "Hmph. You?" Steve was suddenly conscious of his scuffed shoes, shabby jeans and un-ironed T-shirt. The bishop turned to the rest of the reception committee. "He won't do! Can't you find someone decent to introduce me?"

Phil Richardson jumped forward, the picture of a Smart Young Christian, while Steve shambled off the stage, mortified.

He sought refuge in a room next to the auditorium, but was horrified to discover that the bishop was leading a discussion group there. Turning his eyes on Steve the prelate said, "...Whereas what we see before us now is obviously *not* the kind of image we want to project." There were titters of appreciative laughter. Steve turned to leave, but the door was gone. There were no doors in the room.

The bishop's voice dripped scorn. "He can't even find the door!" The laughter was louder and longer. The bishop bombarded Steve with questions he couldn't answer while he blindly stumbled round the room looking for the door. "Look at him! He calls himself the Chairman of the Christian Union, and he hasn't a clue what he's doing!"

The students surrounding the taekwondo floor laughed and jeered. Steve felt a dangerous rage welling up within him. The bishop faced him, sideways on, hands at the ready, immaculate in his purple *dobok* or taekwondo uniform. Steve glanced down at the tattered sackcloth he was wearing, and his fury went up a notch.

The bishop danced forward and patted him on the cheek—first the left, then the right, a mocking sneer on his face. Steve's control snapped. His right fist lashed out with hardened knuckles in a deadly punch to the bishop's throat.

There was a sickening *crunch*.

Steve woke up with a jerk and a half-smothered cry; then lay still, shivering. It was pitch dark. He was in a ruined castle in an unkown country. There were stirrings in the other beds of his shared storeroom-cum-bedroom, which soon settled down. The red rage of his dream faded into the familiar desolation of despair that always followed.

No! He would not allow depression to gain a foothold. He disciplined himself to go through the mental exercises that had helped him so often in the past.

Look at the facts: Since that one dark episode years ago—the 'accident', as he thought of it, which in fact had not been as terrible as his dreams—there had been no repeat of what had happened. He'd worked hard to develop a cheerful, outgoing personality that appealed to others. You could call it deception; but he knew he had become more positive as a result.

In fact he'd been too successful. Towards the end of his secondary schooling, and at university, he'd begun to have leadership roles thrust upon him. That was disastrous. He'd been agonising over his latest leadership predicament when he'd fallen asleep in his clothes one evening and ended up here...

Okay, enough about that. *Look for the silver lining:* This was a totally alien place where it was only natural that old fears would resurface. Yet despite his dreams he hadn't gone over the edge into depression. He'd maintained his cheerful persona and become a useful member (he hoped) of this new community. That, he had to admit, was partly thanks to the presence of Denise, Lannie and Gil.

Which brought him to the third exercise: *Remember, you're not alone.* Even if the other three had not been here, God would still have been with him. He silently repeated one of his favourite Bible verses: "For God has said, 'I will never leave you; I will never forsake you.'" He believed that. He had to. Without God he could never have climbed out of the deep pit of despair he'd fallen into after the 'accident'—nor the subsequent episodes of depression. Thankfully those had dwindled as he came to the end of high school, and he hadn't had one now for several years.

Lying in the darkness he silently thanked God he was not alone.

* * *

Today was Anderil, that blessed oasis of rest after six days of work. Denise was grateful the Dûrians had a seven-day week. It gave a familiar structure of normality to their new lives.

She could hardly believe three weeks had passed since their outing to fetch fireclay. Their daily lives now centred on the small community in the Manor basement. Hard labour had become an accepted work routine, with welcome breaks for relaxation. They were tougher, browner, more mentally alert. Gil and Lannie had passed through a phase of anxiety about their jobs; and all of them had blue moments when they longed for friends and family. They wondered what had happened after they disappeared. Police searches? Listed as missing? Even pronounced dead?

But these worries led nowhere. There was simply nothing they could do. Gradually the anxieties had receded and life back home became a distant dream. With their Dûrian friends Steve was 'Shiván' now, Denise 'Danîsha', Lannie 'Alanya' and Gil 'Gelmion'. As their fluency in Dûrian increased, understanding grew and friendships deepened. A new world was opening up, and in spite of the tight security and hard work, there was a simplicity and peacefulness to it that they'd come to appreciate.

Today the sun was only occasionally hidden by clouds, and 'hearthtime' — the Dûrians' gathering to worship their God — was being held in the forest. Danîsha loved that. Even when she couldn't follow all that was being said or sung, her heart was lifted by the sheer beauty of her surroundings. The cathedral of trees was donning new vestments with the changing of the season. Summer green was sprinkled with autumn gold; and the forest was filled with mellow light.

She sat with Margay in the inner ring of split logs that formed their meeting circle, soaking in the peacefulness of the scene. Many of the Dûrians had already arrived, and the fire in the centre had been lit for the *Limmeris Narac*, the Remembrance of Flame. Damion was waiting for stragglers before uttering the Call to Song. Meanwhile the Dûrians were filling in time in their normal way, by singing. It was a cheerful tune, and Danîsha's foot was tapping to the rhythm.

Young Teynel came running up to sit beside Danîsha. "*Ney'i tarrend, Mâra!*"

"*Illi steylend, Teynel.*" Danîsha smoothed the girl's soft, dark hair and adjusted the comb that held it in place. She'd learnt from Margay that the girl was an orphan from a village where almost all the adults had been killed in the war. Frem and Margay — the 'Keepers', responsible for health and welfare in the community—had been looking after Teynel. But they said Danîsha bore an uncanny resemblance to the girl's grandmother; which was why Teynel had attached herself to her. Danîsha had grown very fond of the gentle, affectionate girl. Teynel helped fill the gap left by her own grandchildren, so far away.

* * *

Gil leant against the shattered arch of the castle entrance, hands in pockets, watching the locals cross the green. They were on their way to their hearthtime in the forest, and he was waiting for a chance to slip back inside.

"I think you might try a little harder to fit in." It was Lannie coming out. She paused with raised eyebrows. Gil snorted with exasperation, and saw the smile she tried to hide.

"Is that so? What if there are things in this culture that I don't want to fit in with?"

"When in Rome..."

Gil snorted again, then allowed himself a half-smile. "Oh, so when we first met, you came alone to the forest in search of my company?"

"I needed to be alone then! But I haven't done it since, have I?"

"Very commendable. But what about our Sunday walks? If fitting in is so important, the four of us shouldn't be wandering off on our own every Anderil afternoon."

"That's the exception that proves the rule. It makes it even more important that we should fit in the rest of the time."

"Maybe so, but extracting that concession from Guv'nor Fira was like squeezing juice from a rock. She only gave way when Damion and Margay came in on our side."

"Right! So at least some of the Dûrians supported us. We weren't going totally against everyone."

"They supported us because they knew we couldn't fit in."

"Which doesn't stop us from trying!"

"Okay. But certain needs require exceptions. Well, I have one of those needs, which is to respect my own convictions by not pretending to worship a god I don't believe in."

"Wow. You have convictions?"

"Ouch."

"I don't think that's a conviction: you just want to be alone to do your own thing."

"Which is exactly what you wanted when we first met."

Lannie rolled her eyes. "Back to square one. Okay, I was wrong to go off on my own. To the Dûrians that was a terrible thing to do—just like missing their treasured hearthtime!"

He liked how her chin went up again, but he could trump her.

"Perhaps you're right. Perhaps being alone isn't such a good thing. How about we go together?"

He looked straight at her. She opened and closed her mouth, then flushed and looked down.

"Well?"

Her head came up with a gleam in her eye. "If that's what it takes."

Of course, she wouldn't admit defeat, or that she liked his company. He smiled to himself.

They strolled over together behind some fellow worshippers and sat down on one of the split logs. The double circle was full now, and the twins Shîrin and Cârin made space for them with elaborate courtesy. In the centre the fire was burning brightly, and old man Damion lifted both hands and began singing the Call to Song.

* * *

Steve's mind was buzzing with questions as the hearthtime proceeded. This was their sixth Sunday with the Dûrians, and every week the words became more familiar to him. Even the Dûrians' form of his name—Shiván—had become his new identity. When Damion read from the Dûrians' holy book, he found he could pick up the gist of the passage quite easily. It was all about 'walking in the light'—an amazingly Christian theme.

As Danîsha had said, learning Dûrian was like rediscovering the language of his childhood. *Melléy*, the Dûrian word for 'hearth', had slotted into place as their term for the community of Lightist believers—the church. And *Atenámbaret*...? It was simple, really. *Aten* was to restore, to rebuild something the way it was before. *Am* was 'one'—or *the* One, their name for the Creator God. *Bar* was a path, road, or way through. *Ambar* was the name of their religion: 'the Way of the One'. Therefore *Atenámbar*? A Restorer of the Way of the One. And *Atenámbaret* was the plural.

Shiván had long believed that God had a plan for those who trusted him; and he was now slowly coming to the conclusion this was what God had brought them here for: to be the Restorers of his Way in Dûrion. Easily said, but a huge thing to come to terms with. Especially when they knew so little about the Way of the One. For starters, they needed to know whether they would be restoring what had already been there – the Dûrians' own religion; or, if that differed from Christianity, restoring faith by sharing the more complete truths of the Christian Way.

Today he could make sense, dimly, of what was being said. These Dûrian Lightists worshipped 'the One Creator God', and him only; but was this the Judaeo-Christian God, or some other form of Creator-worship? On Earth, as he'd learned in his Study of Religions course, monotheism was rare: the big three – Judaism, Christianity and Islam – were the principal monotheistic religions. It was fascinating to find a monotheistic religion *here* on what he was convinced was a different planet.

More significant was the fact that individual Dûrians frequently addressed God as their *Bânor* – 'Father'. On Earth Christianity, as far as he knew, was the only religion where God was called 'Father' in the context of a personal, individual relationship.

But what was their constant reference to this *Keldon Orrénne* all about? Was he a prophet, like Moses, or Mohammed? He seemed mighty important, because the whole of the Remembrance of Flame was about him – that moving ceremony Elder Damion was leading right now, and which they celebrated every Anderil – every 'One's-Day' – as well as every night after the daymeal. He still hadn't sussed it out properly. It seemed very similar to the Christian sacrament of Holy Communion. In which case, was 'Prince Orrénne' another name for Jesus Christ?

That was a shocking thought, which he knew many sincere Christians would reject outright. But after seeing at first hand how similar the Lightists' understanding of God was, he couldn't dismiss it so easily.

Damion uttered the final declaration of the Remembrance of Flame, arms wide as he gazed up toward the distant canopy of the forest. Shiván couldn't follow every word, but he caught the ending: "... We will shine with the Light of the One Creator God, which Orrénne passed through flame to kindle in us." Then the ringing challenge: *"Will you shine for him?"* Followed by the full-throated response, *"We will shine!"* Finally everyone repeated the theme statement—*"Flame turns the Dark to Light."*

What was all that 'flame' stuff about? A way of describing suffering? Or was it something completely different?

Soon some of the women would be bringing mugs and kettles of chass from the kitchen, and everyone would gather for an al fresco 'tea-time'. He must nab Damion quickly.

Shiván walked over to where the old man was sitting alone on one of the logs. "*Vildor*—Elder," he said, "may I ask you something?"

"*Kim, estûr*. Ask, stranger." Shiván sat next to him. Damion looked at him with a kindly twinkle in his deep-set grey eyes.

"Why did Prince Orrénne pass through the flame?"

"We have repeated this every day in the *Limmeris Narac*, the Remembrance, and you do not know? He did it for you, and for me."

"So he... died?" Danîsha came over and joined them. Gil and Lannie followed.

"Yes. But death did not hold him. He turned the flame to Light."

"Uh, right. And when you say 'flame', do you mean, like, fire? Or do you mean the pain he suffered?"

"Flame is flame, stranger."

"So you mean—he was *burnt*?"

"What else? Or does flame not burn where you come from?"

"Er, yes. Flame does burn. Yes, it certainly does." He stared at Damion and rubbed his chin. He looked at the others. What was this? A human burnt offering?

He tried a different tack. "And, er, who was it who burnt him?"

"The *Garlizane* of Selmion. He condemned Prince Orrénne as a *tordhey* and gave him to be burnt on the *narlis* of Gadesh in Orselm."

Shiván blinked. Right. Okay. "And Prince Orrénne died? *Before* he turned flame to Light?"

"Yes."

Gil rose and stretched. "I can't follow a word," he said in English. "I'll leave you to it." He wandered off towards a trestle table laden with steaming kettles and mugs of chass.

"Did Orrénne die to save *us* from death?" Danîsha asked. "Good one, 'Neesh," Shiván murmured.

"He did. You know this. You have received his Light."

Shiván felt his pulse quicken. So it *was* an atoning sacrifice! Orrénne was sounding more and more like Jesus.

"Afterwards, did he… live again?"

Damion nodded tolerantly, like a pastor being quizzed by children. "*Acariméstina.* He lived again."

Resurrection! The parallels were coming thick and fast now.

"If people believe—about him—are they reborn as children of the One?"

Damion smiled. "Of course. *You* are children of the One Creator God. Gelmion is not."

The three stared at one another. The parallel was complete. But then… Who *was* this Prince Orrénne? He was clearly not the same historical person as Jesus Christ. Yet he seemed to have died the same kind of sacrificial death as Jesus had.

Lannie turned to Damion. She looked troubled. "How do you know… that Gelmion is not a, er, child of the One?"

"He sees, not by the Light, but by his own understanding."

Shiván translated Damion's response.

"And me? How do *I* see?"

Damion smiled. "You have seen the Light, daughter, and the Light has claimed you. But you have closed your eyes. Light is shining all around you. Open your eyes."

Lannie was silent.

Danîsha asked Damion, "Do you know… um, a man called Jesus?"

"I do not know this name."

They were silent for a moment. Finally Shiván sighed and squared his shoulders. It had to be asked. "Is Prince Orrénne the son of the Creator God?"

Damion nodded, his smile broader. "*Tarrathen.* — You've discovered it. *Andon lasa Orrénne*—Orrénne is the son of the One."

There it was. Clearly stated, totally unambiguous.

"Orrénne is the *Son of God?*" Lannie queried in English, her eyes wide.

'Neesh looked thunderstruck. "But… Jesus is the *only* Son of God! How can someone else be, as well?"

Suddenly everything fell into place for Shiván. He knew how Orrénne and Jesus could both be the one and only Son of God: they were the physical forms the eternal Son of God had taken on two different worlds. Lightism *was* Christianity. These people were their interstellar brothers and sisters in the faith. A shocking thought for Christians, as 'Neesh's reaction showed; but all the evidence was in. This wasn't the time to discuss it, though: people were milling about, laughing and talking and drinking chass. He would talk it through later with Lannie and Danîsha.

* * *

After chass-time the four foreigners set off into the forest on their own, watched with shaken heads and doubtful mutterings. The Dûrians found their need to be away from the crowd extremely strange, even socially deviant. But the word *Atenámbaret* had featured in the plea Damion and Margay had made for them with Fira, and the hawk-faced leader hadn't looked happy. They'd speculated whether this need of theirs for privacy somehow supported the villagers' view that they were the true Restorers of the Way.

After a while they came to a parting of the ways, where one faint track headed off to the northern plantings, the other to the south.

"I have a suggestion," Gil said. "Let's split up here. Two of us go north, the other two south."

"And how would we split?" Lannie asked. Was there a faint twinkle in her eye?

"Well, I thought you and I might head south...?"

"Fine by me."

"Right!" Shiván nodded solemnly. "I detect a well-laid plot. Let's you and me head north, eh, 'Neesh? Shall we meet back here again in — say — an hour's time?"

"Sounds good."

Danîsha opened her mouth to protest, then closed it. With a wave Gil and Lannie strolled down the southern track.

"I don't like this, Shiván," she muttered as they set off in the opposite direction. "I *don't* think the Dûrians would be happy about us splitting into mixed pairs — especially Lannie and Gil! You've seen how rigidly they separate the unmarried men and women in the basement."

"Yeah, I know what you mean. But what can we do? Gil and Lannie obviously planned this in advance. We'll meet up again, and return all together to the Manor."

81

"Well, I still don't like it. I'm worried about Lannie falling for Gil. He strikes me as the sort of man who could easily have a quick affair. I'd hate to see Lannie hurt. Is Gil married?"

"Ah — no. Divorced. I don't like to slander the good old Doc, but his reputation at uni is pretty much what you've just said."

"Oh dear."

* * *

For once Lannie and Gil didn't immediately fall into an argument. Gil told her amusing stories of some of the linguistic field trips he'd been on to remote areas in West Africa. She told him about her 'county' upbringing, and some of the gaffes she'd made in polite society. He asked if she ever painted for pleasure. She said she wished she had more time for it, and told him how she'd been itching for her watercolours and sketchpad ever since arriving in Dûrion. He said he'd buy her some the minute he found a town with a British consulate.

Lannie didn't reply. She felt a sudden pang at the thought of Gil leaving. They walked on in silence for a while.

They reached a glade dotted with pale yellow flowers lit up by sunbeams filtering through the high canopy. There was a low ridge at one side. They sat on a jutting rock looking out over the flowery lawn.

Lannie sighed. "This is beautiful."

"Far from the madding crowd."

Silence fell again. Gil chewed on a piece of grass. Lannie sat thinking about the tall academic beside her. Her opinion of him had changed since he first arrived. Then he'd seemed brash and overbearing, and a little too eager to get to know her. She'd looked forward to seeing him crumple under the heavy work regime of the Manor community. Only he hadn't. He'd shaped up well, doing his share and more at times.

Although at first she'd been irritated by his argumentativeness, recently the arguments had become a game between them, just for the fun of it. He was strong-minded, and stood up to her, unlike most people... In fact, she admitted to herself, she enjoyed being with him.

She hadn't intended this to happen. She still loved Matt — didn't she? She couldn't sort out her feelings. Gil was *here*, and Matt was far away—maybe beyond reach forever. But Gil was a lot older than her; and, more important, his philosophy of life was quite different. Right now, shaken by what Damion had said and mindblown by the idea that Christianity might span the stars, she didn't feel able to cope with Gil's scepticism.

Jesus Christ had seemed very real to her three years ago when she'd been paralysed with Guillain-Barré syndrome; then that reality had been killed off by church. She'd come to regard her 'religious phase' as an emotional reaction, quite understandable in the circumstances. Now she'd discovered people with identical beliefs on what could well be an alien planet... and for her the whole issue was wide open again. She wasn't ready for Gil to start poohpoohing it.

That being the case, did she dare allow her feelings for him to develop any further?

Gil glanced at his watch. "Twenty minutes to go. We'd better start—"

He didn't complete the sentence. They both froze. Not far away a muted command was rapped out. They heard the snuffle of animals, clink of metal, and rustle of cloaks. Lannie felt the blood drain from her face. Gil motioned her to get down. He crept along to a bush, and, hidden under the lower branches, peered cautiously over the ridge. A moment later he came hurrying back.

"Soldiers!" he murmured.

"With green capes?" Lannie heard the tremor in her voice.

"No, blue. They have horses—or camels—couldn't tell which..."

"Then they're the enemy. We must get out of here!"

They ran doubled over across the glade and on to the track. Lannie led the way. Her heart was in her mouth, expecting any moment to hear shouts and the whoosh of arrows.

Two figures suddenly reared up in front of her, and she stifled a scream. It was Shîrin and Cârin, on duty as lookouts. Gil nearly cannoned into her.

"*Alanya i Gelmion—dâr fillen?*" Shîr said. Câr added something *sotto voce*, and they both chuckled.

Lannie gasped out a single word: "*Bondanet!*"—'Soldiers!'

The smiles vanished. "*Fillas o heyn. Sheck, sheck!*" Cârin gestured urgently towards the manor. Shîr put a couple of fingers in his mouth and produced a warbling bird cry. It was answered from nearby, and echoes came from further afield. Lannie and Gil charged on down the path.

They reached the spot where they'd parted from Shiván and Danîsha. They weren't there. "You go on to the basement," Gil said. "I'll dash up the northern way and find them."

"No— Gil!" But he was already off, making good speed on his long legs.

Torn with indecision, Lannie hesitated. She almost sobbed with relief when she saw Shivvie and 'Neesh appear, strolling down the path. They caught sight of Gil, and hurried towards him. Only when he'd begun pointing urgently toward the Manor did she pick up her feet and dash for safety in the old ruin.

Chapter 11: *Jomel makes a plan*

IT WAS LATE AFTERNOON IN THE CITY OF STILLÁRRE, and Jomel was preparing to leave her rooms at Juleron the tin merchant's house. The ceremonies would begin at the Temple of Gadesh soon. She sat on the edge of the wide, canopied bed, pulling on her tooled leather boots slowly to delay the inevitable moment.

Her thoughts went back to that time with cousin Perrely at her home in Berûvis. Perrely's life seemed so simple and idyllic compared to hers. Sometimes she wished... but it was too late for that. This was her life now. Her parents thought she earned her wages as an apprentice to merchant Juleron; they would be horrified beyond belief if they learnt she was a temple prostitute.

The job had given her status, though—both fame and notoriety. When she set out shortly to walk to the temple, some of those she met on the way would greet her deferentially. Others would cross to the other side of the street. She tried not to care.

She finished working one boot on and sat holding the other, staring unseeing at the handsome brass fire irons opposite the bed. Her work was certainly profitable. She was steadily accumulating a substantial nest egg. She had her eye on an apartment closer to the temple—a very nice one, freshly redecorated, with gold and old-pink wall hangings. It would be wonderful to have a place of her own. *But what will I say to Mummy and Daddy? They'll want to know how I can afford it on an apprentice's salary. How can I explain where the money comes from? But then... it's only a matter of time before they find out anyway.* She shuddered at the thought.

She remembered Sarmion the priest's unctuous words this morning—that he'd heard some important new visitors would be attending the temple tonight, and he hoped she'd be on her best form. She was their rising star! Everyone loved her! (He omitted to mention the other devotees, who cordially detested her.)

So once again she had to exert all her charms to snare new patrons for the temple. She was so tired of it all. She had to escape this tawdry life as a temple whore. Since she'd never be allowed simply to leave the Cult of Gadesh, her only hope was to rise within it—to become an Initiate, maybe even a Mindbender. She'd made a few plans to hasten that day, and tonight she would set them in motion.

She finished dressing and left Juleron's house with a determined step.

* * *

There was a whistling sound and Jomel screamed as her back erupted in agony. *Gadesh!* The fellow was whipping her! It was business as usual at the Temple in Stillárre, but this session was not going according to plan. "*Kem'ma!*" she screamed in Selmian as the lash bit into her again.

"Stop? Sweetheart, I've only just begun!" the man declared in the same language, his voice gloating. The leather lash descended a third time, and Jomel's screams dissolved into sobs of anguish. He must have had the whip hidden in his clothing. *Fool!* she castigated herself. Why hadn't she mind-read this Selmian merchant? "A wealthy donor, do all you can to please him," that fat fool Sarmion had said. So she'd paid special attention to her clothes. She should have paid attention to what he was thinking! Even when he'd insisted on binding her wrists and ankles, she'd played along 'to please him'.

Her frenzied writhing was doing nothing to loosen the cords, so she tried to focus her mind on inhibiting the maniac. Then the lash landed on her shoulders, and she screamed again.

Mercifully at that moment the door burst open and Priest Sarmion charged into her cubicle with his two acolytes. They pulled the man off her. Sarmion told him the session was over, and he had the gall to say, "I want my cash back, priest!" Sarmion made soothing noises and led him out.

"What happened, Devotee? So charmed by the patron that you forgot your powers?" There was a smirk in Acolyte Chand's voice as he and Guriet started untying her hands and feet. They never let Jomel forget that the acolytes and other devotees hated her because she'd used her position to good advantage. She was the favourite of the priest and the junior Initiates. But Chand was right, though she hated to admit it: she *had* forgotten her new powers of mesmerism and mindreading. She had only received them from the god a couple of days ago, and was still perfecting them. She should have seen what was in the merchant's mind from the start, and used a little mesmerism to calm him down.

Chand and Guriet finished untying her and she sat up slowly, rubbing her wrists and ankles. Then she stood and wrapped a sheet around her waist. She could feel blood trickling down from the wounds on her back, which were stinging viciously.

"Are you two just going to stand there and watch me bleed?" she snapped. "Guriet, get some cloths from the cupboard. Chand, go and fetch Chery to bathe my wounds." Right now she could do with some female attention.

"Oh, *yes,* your exaltation, right away, your exaltation. We can't have the priest's pet suffering, now, can we?" It was Guriet's whining voice. He rummaged in the corner cupboard and began dabbing roughly at her back.

"Think what a wonderful story this'll make for the adherents, Guri," said Chand. Guriet sniggered. "A moral for us all, never to allow success to make us complace..." Chand's voice tailed off and he departed abruptly. Her mesmerism did work when she remembered it.

Priest Sarmion returned a few minutes later, exuding sweat and apologies. He looked nine months pregnant in his grey priestly robe. "Jomel, my dear, I am *devastated* by what has happened," he said, every jowl and double chin quivering. "If I'd had any idea that monster would *hurt* you...! You need time to heal, of course. No work for a week!" He beamed at her.

She felt like asking if he'd given the merchant a refund, but instead forced out a thank you. Sarmion left blethering about how important she was to the Temple of Gadesh.

Soon afterwards Chery arrived with warm water, towels and a small jar of salve. She was like a breath of fresh air—an eager young adherent, thrilled to be of service to none other than Jomel herself. She had only been in the Temple a couple of weeks. Adherents were the new recruits. Once they'd proved their commitment they would become devotees, like Jomel, or acolytes like Chand and Guriet. Then, eventually, if considered worthy, they would win the glittering prize of full membership as Initiates of Gadesh.

While Chery twittered over her, carefully bathing her back with warm water, dabbing it dry and gently applying salve, Jomel remembered herself at that stage. Six months ago. Was that all? It seemed like a lifetime.

It had started with that prick Chand. How could she ever have fallen for him? But he'd seemed so sophisticated at the City Elder's Reception. Full of the exciting experiences he'd had at the luxurious new Temple of Gadesh on Stillárre's market square. High, mystical worship! Animal sacrifices (and sometimes, he whispered, even human ones)! Personal powers offered to new adherents! Sex for the asking! Very different from the endless boring rituals of the Temple of Minórre that her family attended. Chand's words breathed the heady aroma of forbidden fruit. The Cult of Gadesh had a sinister aura of power and intrigue even among the other cults.

And so she'd started attending with Chand. The gleaming marble temple had overawed her with the vast space of the central sanctuary. The roof seemed higher than the towering *colárre* trees of the mountain forests, and indeed the massive supporting columns were sculpted to look like colárre trunks, complete with entwining creepers of painted stone. At night they had twinkling lights in the vault to resemble stars, giving the impression that the ceremony was taking place out of doors in a real forest.

And what ceremonies they were! Grey-robed priests swinging censers to the accompaniment of eerie Selmian melodies that made one's hair rise; menacing ranks of black-robed Initiates facing the high altar; a blue glow of unearthly light emanating from the marble walls, contrasting with the roaring fire on the altar.

White-robed acolytes would lead in the sacrificial animal — usually a bovine, but once an enormous *garzin*, a killer bear from the Tallissôr Mountains. As the animal was slaughtered beside the elevated altar and offered to Gadesh in the fire, chants and incantations would begin softly and build gradually to a thundering climax, accompanied by breathtaking demonstrations of power by the Initiates — howling gales sweeping through the temple while the fire remained untouched; earth tremors, voices from the spirit world, healings of the sick, appearances of the dead, manifestations of the gods — even of the Worldruler himself, when all fell prostrate before the towering black form above the flames.

After the sacrifice came the time of pleasure, when food and drink were provided, dancers, acrobats and musicians performed, and worshippers could visit the little cubicles leading off the sanctuary. There pleasures of a more intimate nature could be had for a modest fee.

After a month, both she and Chand had been inducted as adherents. They'd pledged themselves body and soul to Worldruler Gadesh, and were invited to petition for personal powers. Chand, the fool, had besought the god for the gift of command over animals and forces of nature. What a futile power! Flashy sensation was all he wanted; and that was all he got. For a while the poor twit had revelled in making dogs attack passers-by and summoning up breezes to blow people's hats off—which was all adherents could manage. She, however, had sought a more significant power: the ability to arouse love in another. Chand had soon fallen way back in the crowd of men clamouring for her attention.

Then a couple of months later the trap had been sprung. She had been commended by Sarmion the priest for her significant progress, and offered entry to the next level—becoming a devotee—in return for certain services. These turned out to be making her body available to worshippers—one of the most successful means of attracting new adherents. Far from being a recipient, she was to become a provider of the Temple's 'intimate pleasures'!

She shivered as she remembered her horror at hearing those words—and the far greater shock when she'd immediately been raped by the priest and acolytes. Her screams and struggles had been met with the taunting reminder that she'd pledged her body to the god—so what else did she expect? As if it were some comfort, she was told that Chand and the other young devotees were also now 'servicing' worshippers. It was quite a normal 'step on the ladder'.

Something died in her that day.

She hadn't dared confess to her parents how she—and they—had been dishonoured. One of her new 'patrons'—Juleron, the tin merchant—offered her a live-in position at his business house; which gave her parents the impression that she was establishing her own career. They left well alone, though they could see the change in her.

Of course her only work for Juleron was to serve as his mistress, and to be available to the senior Gadeshites whenever they desired her. Her main work was at night, as a temple prostitute. The humiliation of it struck home afresh. She was nothing more than a common whore, she told herself, at the mercy of perverts like the recent merchant. She'd given herself to Gadesh, and this was her reward.

Well, she had plans to change all that — and now was just the right time to put them into practice.

* * *

When the adherent Chery had carefully eased her clothes on to her, Jomel told her to fetch Priest Sarmion again. He arrived a few minutes later, and squeezed himself into the patron's chair.

"You wanted to see me, my dear?"

"Oh, Sarmion, thank you for coming. That's so kind of you. You know what makes all the devotees respect you so highly? You *care* about us. Any other priest would have made a devotee come to him. But you came to me. That's *so* special." You couldn't lay it on too thick for Sarmion; in any case, she needed a cover for the cautious use of her powers of mindreading and mesmerism. They weren't supposed to work on her superiors; but she might just swing it with Sarmion...

His broad smile gave way to a sentimental sigh. "It's *you* I care about, Jomel. You've become so popular! All our top patrons are asking for you. You hardly have time these days for a humble priest..." Jomel felt a surge of triumph. Sarmion was attracted to her anyway, and off his guard. Both love-arousal and mesmerism were working. A quick peek in his mind... Yes! A lonely, unattractive man's desire for a caring relationship with a pretty girl. Not just sex — he could have that any time. He wanted an on-going friend-ship. Right, he would have one — for as long as it suited her.

"*Do* you care about me, Sarmion? Really care?"

He was suddenly very serious, and there was a gleam of excite-ment in his eye. "Of course I care, Jomel. I always have. If there's anything I can do for you..."

"Oh, Sarmion." Her lips trembled, and a tear ran down her cheek. He heaved himself up on the bed beside her. A podgy arm descended on her wounded shoulder and she stifled a cry of pain. She nestled close to him. "I'd really like to spend more time with you, Sarmion. You've always been so good to me. I'd like us to be real *friends*. Would you like that, Sarmie?" She peered anxiously into his face. The poor slob was trembling with eagerness.

"I'd love that, Jomel, I really would," he said hoarsely. He bent to kiss her, but she continued quickly, "We could spend more time together during the day, maybe." Her hours off, but that was part of the plan. She looked into his mind, and a sudden exciting thought seemed to strike her. "I could come with you to the district shrines! That would be fun, wouldn't it, Sarmie?"

"Just what I was thinking, Jomel! We could take a packed lunch and make a picnic of it." His large, dog-like eyes were burning with devotion: dream-come-true time.

"Yes! That would be great... Oh." Her face fell.

"What is it?"

She heaved a sigh. "I was letting my imagination run away with me. It would be wonderful to do all those things, Sarmie, but I was forgetting my patrons. I really need the sleep during the day, or I can't keep going through the night." She looked up at him mournfully. Mesmerism now — a careful nudge.

Sarmion cleared his throat. "Well," he said, "we might be able to do something about that. What you need is a wealthy daytime patron. Then you could have the previous night off, and — "

" — we could spend time together after I've serviced the patron! Do you really think you could find me a daytime patron, Sarmie?" Mesmerism. *Mindbender Dhelgor. Say Mindbender Dhelgor.* The most powerful Gadeshite in Stillárre. If she could fascinate *him*, her future career in the Cult of Gadesh was assured. He would lift her out of the rut of temple prostitution. He might even sponsor her to become an Initiate...

The priest's face took on a portentous look. "Oh yes, I could, Jomel. I have an idea I could interest Mindbender Dhelgor in you."

"Dhelgor! Not the Captain of the Bishop's Guard?" Jomel whispered, her eyes round.

"Yes, the Captain himself," Sarmion declared.

"Oh, Sarmie, that would be *wonderful!*" she gushed, looking up with girlish delight into his besotted grin.

Chapter 12: *Instruments found*

THE KITCHEN WAS A SCENE OF FRANTIC ACTIVITY, fires being doused, food packed into storerooms, bedding and all other signs of occupation removed. Gil heard Fira calling his name. There she was, on the far side, with Lannie, Denny and the children. He pushed through the crowd with Steve and Denise. Fira spoke rapidly to Denny, pointing down a nearby passage. The young man set off, beckoning them all to follow. Lannie's face was pale. Gil took her hand. She didn't snatch it away.

They passed several doors. Denny pushed open the last on the right. In the dwindling lamplight from the kitchen they had a brief glimpse of a storeroom piled high with all kinds of goods. There was just enough room for everyone to squeeze in and find places on the floor. Then Denny closed the door, and the light vanished. Several of the little ones whimpered; two scrambled on to Gil's lap. There were grunts and the sound of something being dragged against the door: Denny preparing the defence.

They settled down to wait.

"Why does Fira shove us with the kids each time?" Gil muttered.

"Saving the women and children?" Steve suggested.

"Speak for yourself."

"*Hsst!*" Denny said. They did so.

It was pitch dark, and the kids kept fidgeting. One of those on Gil's lap started whimpering, and he gently stroked her hair. His other hand continued to clasp Lannie's. She was sitting close, leaning against him. He wished he could put an arm around her... but not yet.

He thought grimly of what would happen if the enemy burst in. There was lots of stuff in this room. Good ammunition to pelt intruders with. It would only be a stay of execution, but he'd make sure the bastards paid a price before they got their hands on Lannie. Or the kids.

Time went by. The air became thick with the smell of sweat, fear, and small children. The little ones on Gil's lap fell asleep. The older ones became restless. Two started whispering, and Denny nervously shushed them.

* * *

Shiván was sitting half under a table, little Grildon asleep on his lap. He moved a hand to support himself better, and his fingers fell on two small disks on the dusty floor. Without thinking he picked them up. They felt like coins. He thrust them into his shirt pocket.

Noises from the kitchen! Everyone tensed. Grildon woke up and cried out—Shiván hastily clamped a hand over his mouth then gently rocked him in his arms. The child slowly relaxed. Then there was a sound of approaching footsteps. The tension in the darkened room shot up again, and Shiván anxiously resumed his rhythmic rocking.

The footsteps receded. Were they leaving, or searching another part of the basement?

Shiván did not like the dark. Despite himself, gloomy thoughts plagued his mind. Was this the end of their time here? Would they be captured and executed before they'd even discovered why they'd been sent to this 'different place'?

No! He had to keep his eye on the silver lining, to avoid that downward slide into depression. He deliberately turned his mind to the amazing coincidence of how all four of them had separately gone to see Father Martin in England before suddenly finding themselves here. Except, he couldn't believe it was a coincidence: it had to be God's doing.

His mind went back to his own chat with the young Anglican priest...

As he sat in the Round Church of Leston discussing his dilemma in the Christian Union with Father Martin, Steve found the priest's sympathetic understanding, and his failure to rush in with clichéd advice, refreshing. The tensions between the CU and its breakaway rival organisation, Accord, would strain the wisdom of Solomon—let alone Steve's rough and ready diplomacy. Father Martin nodded ruefully as Steve described the constant infighting on the CU committee between the hawks, the hardline opponents of Accord, and the doves who urged reconciliation. The priest had no instant solutions to offer, and Steve knew he might still mess up and make a lousy President—as he had with every other leadership position that had been foisted on him. But now he felt ready to give it a go.

Father Martin echoed his thoughts. "So you feel you can hack it now, Steve?"

"Yup." He grinned. "You've done a great job — thanks. I'll give it my best shot, and leave the rest to God."

To his surprise the priest didn't smile back. "Then you'll fail," he said simply.

Steve stared at the man. All that sympathetic encouragement, and now this?

"Leadership is more than doing your best, Steve. Let me ask you something: Are you willing to serve those who follow you? To spend nights thinking and praying about their needs? To lay yourself out to get to know them, to encourage them, to bear their burdens, to suffer with them?"

Steve sat appalled, the questions hanging in the air. Father Martin said nothing, watching him with a measuring gaze.

Was he willing to go to those extremes? It came to him clearly at that moment that this was the only way he'd make a successful leader. Not by charisma, not by diplomacy, not by organising ability (which he didn't have) — but by servanthood.

He made a decision. With a dry throat he managed to rasp out, "Yes. I'm willing."

There was a blaze of light over the altar. A last ray of sun must have lit up the cross.

Father Martin gave him a broad grin. "Then it's all go! But don't get cocky. You've got a lot of learning to do. And it won't be in the Christian Union. Somewhere quite different you're going to find yourself having to lead, and learning to serve. You'll do it! And you'll strengthen many more than your fellow students in the process."

Shiván's heart lifted as he remembered. *This* was 'somewhere quite different'! Father Martin's prophetic words confirmed that he was here for a purpose. But he hadn't yet had any opportunity to lead, so that purpose was not complete. Which meant it couldn't end dismally in this dark, underground storeroom.

Suddenly they heard a low murmur of approaching voices. Shiván's heart was in his mouth, and Grildon whimpered — then someone called, "Denny!" A rapid exchange followed, and with an exclamation of relief the young man pulled the barrier away and opened the door. There was a welcome draft of fresh air. Frem stood there, his homely face creased in a smile.

* * *

They all sat at the kitchen tables sipping chass. Though he wasn't over-fond of the Dûrian beverage, Gil found himself relaxing after the tension of the past hour. Shiván relayed what he'd heard from Frem: that the enemy riders had simply looked through the ruins and left.

"Riders! So those humped animals were *horses*?" Gil exclaimed.

"I saw them the day I arrived," Danîsha said. "Half-camel, half-horse. Very peculiar."

"Not a terrestrial animal, maybe," Shiván suggested, tongue in cheek.

"Just because we can't identify it, doesn't mean it's from another planet," Gil snapped. Typical undergraduate with his head in the clouds.

Shiván shook his head. "Evidence is mounting up, Doc. One of these days you'll have to concede."

"I'll believe it when I see different constellations in the sky."

Shiván shrugged. A thought seemed to occur to him, and he pulled two objects out of his shirt pocket and laid them on the table in front of him. They looked like coins: one dark silver in colour, about an inch in diameter; the other smaller and almost black. He leant forward and peered at them; then went very still for a moment. He turned first the one over, then the other.

"What's that you've got, Shivvie?" asked Lannie.

"Two coins I found in that storeroom. They're marked 'Georgivs Rex'."

"*What?*" Gil exclaimed. "Let me see." Shiván handed them over. Gil examined them closely, and felt excitement rising within him. "A shilling and a halfpenny, I think, from the reign of George the First. The ha'penny is dated 1717." He looked at Shiván in triumph. "Now what price a different planet? English people were here three hundred years ago!"

Shiván's eyebrows were way up. "Lord love a Doc! That's a facer."

They stared at one another. "Well, thank goodness!" 'Neesh declared. "We're not all that far from home, then." Her eyes were bright.

"Let's see what else we can find in that room," Gil said.

Margay gave them a lamp, looking puzzled. They tramped back down the passage. A small crowd of curious Dûrians followed.

Gil placed the lamp on top of a cupboard inside the storeroom door. It illuminated a fascinating jumble of books and equipment, wooden chests, and hundreds of small items piled up on two tables and on the floor. They began searching.

Twenty minutes later they stood staring at their finds: a decorated mother-of-pearl case housing a tortoiseshell-rimmed lorgnette; a small, lacquered container that Gil's sneezes assured them was a snuffbox; a silver fob watch on a chain, with the hours in Roman numerals, and the name 'James Turner' inscribed on the back in flowery letters.

"I don't follow the Antiques Roadshow," Gil said hoarsely, "but I'd be prepared to bet all of these date from the early eighteenth century or thereabouts — same as the coins."

"So there really were English people here three hundred years ago!" 'Neesh exclaimed.

"There must have been. Has anyone discovered anything more modern?"

"Nope; but I found something even older." Shiván opened a polished wooden box and lifted out an ornate book whose hard, shiny cover had an irregular mottled pattern in browny-black and orange. It was about six and a half inches by four in size, and a couple of inches thick. The corners were protected by heavily decorated silver edgings. Around the spine ran a pair of similarly tooled silver hinges; and two matching clasps protected the open side of the book.

"Wow!" Lannie breathed.

Shiván patiently worked the silver clasps loose and opened the book. He lifted the lamp down to give a better light, and they all leant over to see. The first page displayed the words,

THE HOLY

BIBLE,

Containing the Old

TESTAMENT

and the New;

Newly tranflated out of the Originall
Tongues : and with the former
tranflations diligently compared and revifed.

By his Majefties fpeciall Commandment.

A fancy decoration followed. Below it stood:

Imprinted at London by ROBERT BARKER,
Printer to the Kings moft Excellent
Majefty, and by the Affignes of
JOHN BILL. Anno 1638.

"An original Authorised Version of the Bible," Lannie murmured, stroking the page lightly with her finger.

"Look at the year! Sixteen thirty-eight!" 'Neesh exclaimed.

Gil sniffed. "Oh, great. A piece of seventeenth century literature nobody can understand."

"I think we can still understand it," Shiván said. He turned to the first page of the Bible, the book of Genesis. Squinting at the small type he read, " 'In the beginning God created the heaven and the earth'. That's not so difficult, is it?"

Gil snorted. "Anyway, if we took it back to the UK with us — along with some of these other things — we might make a pretty penny out of them."

"Is that all you can think of?" Lannie said. "Making money?"

Gil took in her searing gaze and lifted an eyebrow. "Just saying, that's all. If you want to keep the pretty Bible for bedside reading, feel free."

Lannie uttered an explosive sigh and turned her back on him.

"Well, I'm just glad we have a Bible again," Danîsha said. "And what a beautiful binding, in tortoiseshell and silver."

"Is that what the cover's made of? The actual shell of a tortoise?" Lannie asked.

"A turtle, to be precise," Gil corrected.

"We so *need* to be precise," Lannie murmured.

Gil shook his head and wandered over to a table filled with odds and ends. Let them moon over their archaic volume of religious mumbo-jumbo.

Shiván was staring at the book in his hand. "I'm amazed it's so small," he said softly. "I thought books in those days were massive things. If you don't mind, I'll keep it…" It was half-statement, half-question.

"Yes, you keep it—if they'll let you," Lannie said. Danîsha nodded, her head bent over an object in her lap which was keeping her fingers busy.

"Thanks." Shiván smiled, and turned to examine his find more closely. Lannie drifted over to a different table. Out of the corner of his eye Gil saw her lift out a strangely-shaped object from between two piles of decaying books. She carefully wiped the dust off.

"This is beautiful!" she exclaimed, showing it to Shiván. He squinted in the dim light at the delicate turquoise and aquamarine swirls on the shiny, curved surface.

"Very nice. What is it?"

"A shell." She turned it over, and Gil glimpsed a long, white-edged gap underneath. The shell was an oval pinched at both ends, which filled her two hands. "It's rather like a cowry, but I've never seen one this big, or with these colours. I'll keep this."

Gil bent down and started rummaging in a chest that contained a fascinating collection of… were those scientific instruments? One looked like a telescope, while another vaguely resembled a barometer. There were some smaller items, including a double-handed magnifying glass. He picked the glass up and took it to one of the decaying books on the table. Held over the faded text, the four-inch glass gave quite a decent magnification. Not that he could read the words: they were in an attractive flowing script that he'd never seen before.

Damion was watching from the door with the Dûrians. He caught sight of Lannie with her shell. "*Hâya!*" he exclaimed. "*Bess Thrinarac siddi.*—You have a shell of Thrinar." He rattled off a long comment, and mimed holding the shell to his ear.

Lannie looked at Shiván, who shrugged. "He seems to be saying you can hold the shell to your ear and hear things that are being said a long way off."

Lannie tried it and shook her head. "*Estôr jillis.*—I hear nothing."

At that moment Damion caught sight of Gil with the magnifying glass. "*Keldon hallár!*" The old man's eyes were wide. He pointed at the two-handled instrument. "*Bleys bissilac lasa.*"

"Shiván?" Gil queried.

"He says it's a 'glass of seeing'…" Shiván asked Damion what he meant, and received a lengthy response. "Papa Damion says if you look through this, you should be able to see things a great distance away. Apparently Lannie's shell and your glass are supposed to be special. There's a prophecy about them in the Lightists' Book."

"Another load of religious claptrap," Gil muttered. He lifted the glass and peered through it. "Just a blur." He slipped it in his pocket.

Meanwhile Danîsha gave an exclamation of satisfaction as she finished assembling the object in her lap. At first glance it looked like a guitar, but Gil saw that it wasn't: it was an oval, lute-like instrument made of highly-polished red wood, with a large body and a short neck. It had seven strings.

Danîsha's face was rapt. She took a deep breath, and ran her fingers over the strings. A deep, mellow music filled the underground chamber. Everyone turned, their faces filled with amazement. There were exclamations of "Bellaril! Bellaril!", and dozens came running from the kitchen. An excited buzz of conversation broke out, but Gil felt himself shuddering. There was something profoundly unsettling about those chords.

"What a sound!" Shiván exclaimed. Lannie's eyes were wide. "Fantastic!" she breathed.

"Could do with a bit of tuning," Gil said.

"What's *wrong* with you?" Lannie snapped. "It's only *slightly* out."

"It does need tuning," Danîsha said. "But it's amazing how close it is. Someone who lived here must have been playing it not long ago. I'll work out how to fine-tune it." There was a soft light in her eyes. From the murmurs of "Mâra!" and "Bellaril!" that followed her as they left the storeroom, it seemed the locals approved.

Gil's heart sank. Now he'd have to endure who-knew-what cacophonies of religious music from that perverted guitar.

* * *

Later that afternoon Fira pronounced the surroundings free of enemy troops. Shiván went outside with Denny and a group of the older kids. The sun was shining, and it was glorious to be in the fresh air. They romped for a while on the lawn surrounding the ruins, playing universal games like 'catch' and 'hide-and-seek'. The rest of the Manor community were enjoying the coolness of the forest — and a few the comfort of their beds.

A game ended and they all collapsed panting to the ground. Denny punched Shiván lightly on the arm and said, "*Bondilaheri is veyim.* — Teach me your way of fighting." The younger ones all chimed in at once — "*Haa, Toldor! Bondilaheri anéy bissim!*"

Shiván's martial arts lessons had become a popular spectator sport in recent weeks. He hadn't meant that to happen — in fact, he hadn't intended to give lessons at all. But he so enjoyed the sport that he'd started practising whenever he had a moment of privacy. Denny had caught him at it, and before Shiván knew it, he was teaching him. He didn't find it easy. Always in the background loomed the grief of the 'accident', and the fear that it might happen again. But maybe, in this new place, he could start facing those gremlins and overcoming them.

Denny leapt up and pointed at Shiván. "Shall I kill him?"

"Yes, yes!" came the kids' eager response.

Shiván climbed resignedly to his feet. The spectators made a wide circle. Denny stood facing Shiván side-on, as he'd taught him, leaving the least body space open to attack. For a while they circled each other. Then Denny's leg whipped out in a roundhouse kick. Shiván leaned back, and the foot whistled harmlessly by. Before Denny could regain his balance, Shiván's own foot shot out, connected with the inside thigh of Denny's stable leg, and the young man went tumbling to the ground. There was a roar of approval from the kids.

Shiván swallowed. It had been a light blow, but it still brought back that sickening *crunch* so many years ago.

Fira was crossing the lawn to the forest. She stopped to watch, hands on hips, a sceptical smile on her narrow face.

Denny had regained his feet, scowling in concentration. Shiván aimed a punch at his face, which Denny easily blocked. Shiván had left himself open and Denny's own fist shot out, hitting Shiván hard on the chest. The kids shouted in delight — "*Denny! Denny!*" Shiván leapt back, kicked and missed Denny's chest (as planned), pivoted and struck out with his other foot, intending to deliver a humorous blow to the young man's backside. But the target wasn't there any more. Quick as lightning Denny had whirled round. He caught Shiván's foot with both hands and heaved. The next instant Shiván found himself lying on his back winded, while the children hooted with laughter.

Fira was shaking her head over him. "You'll never win any battles with that kind of fighting, Shiván. You should learn to use the sword." She walked on towards the trees.

Denny was crowing in triumph, and Shiván let him enjoy his moment of glory. He stood, still shaken by his own reactions, and raised Denny's arm skyward in the Dûrian high handshake. The kids drummed on their knees in applause.

Then young Bannet cried, "More hide-and-seek!" Shiván glanced at the shadow thrown by the Manor ruins. It would be a while yet before chass was served. "*Haa!*—Okay!" he said.

Denny pointed a finger at him. "You were defeated! You will seek." Shiván nodded, sat down with his eyes closed, and began counting loudly and slowly: "*Am... sen... dôr... câr... thet... lîs...*"

Through a half-open eye he saw Denny, Teynel, and a couple of others running in a bunch towards the castle.

* * *

Gil was at a loose end, unable to follow the Dûrian conversations. 'Neesh was laughing and chatting with Margay and Veynel; Shiván was reverting to type and playing with the kids; and Lannie was on chass duty.

He decided to wander down to the kitchen. Lannie would probably be with half a dozen other women and he wouldn't be welcome, but at least he could exchange a few words as he pretended to fetch something from his room.

He came down the stairs into the basement, and to his delight found Lannie sitting beside the stoves on her own.

"Gil! What brings you back?" His heart leapt. There was genuine pleasure in her voice.

"Nobody to talk to. I thought I'd have a few words with you passing through—didn't expect to find you on your own. Where's everyone else?"

"Oh... They all had other things they needed to do. I told them I'd watch the pot."

"Great. So now it's just you and me." He sat down beside her.

She looked doubtful. "I'm not sure this is wise, Gil. We'll be in big trouble if we're caught."

"Oh, I know, I know. Unauthorised hobnobbing between unmarried adults. Don't worry, I won't stay long."

They were silent for a moment. Lannie sighed. "I really enjoyed our walk this morning. Pity it ended so suddenly."

"Yes. I enjoyed being with you," he said softly, laying his hand on hers. She didn't pull it away. "It would be good if that glass of mine—or blaise, as they call it—really did let me 'see things at a distance', like Damion said," he murmured. "Then I could look into it and check if anyone was nearby."

"And I could listen in my bess shell and hear if anyone approached. But at the midmeal the Dûrians were all contradicting one another about those things."

She glanced at him. "It must be hard for you, not being able to follow everything. The arguments were about the 'Restorers' thing. The soldiers and others who don't think we're the *Atenámbaret*, also don't think the glass and the shell and 'Neesh's bellaril mean anything. But the ones who *do* think we might be the *Atenámbaret* were also arguing. Some, like Damion, said the things we found must be special 'instruments' from God to help us in our task. Others were saying there *are* shells and blaises that can capture distant sounds and images, but if ours are like that it's got nothing to do with us being Restorers. Shivvie thinks they're following different interpretations of prophecies in their holy Book..."

"Well, you know what I think about 'special instruments' and 'holy books'. But I'm keeping an open mind."

She smiled at him. "I should hope so, Dr. Denbigh. Try this on for size. Just now I *did* seem to hear something in the shell—apart from the sea-noise." She pulled her hand out from under his.

"Did you?" He longed to put an arm around her.

"Yes. I was holding the bess to my ear, thinking about Fira, when I suddenly thought I heard her voice—very distant, but it was definitely her. Then it faded again." She shook her head and gave him a rueful smile. "Probably just my imagination." He loved all her different smiles.

"Why don't you try it now?"

She gave him a sideways look. "You ought to be leaving."

"Oh, go on, it'll only take a second. This is interesting. Get the bess and have another listen. See if either of us can hear anything."

She stared at him a moment, her lips quirking. "Okay," she said, "but we'd better make it quick."

She went to her room and returned with the gleaming turquoise shell. She looked unbearably attractive to Gil, with her auburn hair done up to reveal the slender neck rising from an emerald green shift. She sat next to him and held the bess up to her ear.

"Let me see if I can hear anything," Gil said breathlessly, leaning close to the shell. He slipped his arm around her shoulders.

They heard something immediately, but not from the bess. Feet clattered on the stairs, and there was Denny with three of the children. All of them froze, their mouths round 'o's of shock at the sight of the two foreigners so close together.

Gil leapt away from Lannie, almost overturning the bench. She jumped up, clutching her shell.

"No, Denny, it's alright— It's not what you think—" she cried desperately.

But Denny and the kids had turned and run back out again.

———————

Chapter 13: *To leave but not arrive*

GIL AND SHIVÁN SAT FACING FREM, Margay's husband, across one of the kitchen tables. Fira stood nearby, leaning against one of the pillars, her eyes cold. It was the next morning, and everyone was out working. Frem's normally kind face was grim.

"Shiván, you are here to make sure Gelmion and I understand one another. Margay and I are the Keeper and Keeperess of this community, responsible for health, childcare... and decency. Since this transgression has been committed by a man, I will speak to Gelmion. Translate for him."

Shiván did so. Gil nodded. What a fuss about simply putting an arm across Lannie's shoulders! He'd been virtually ostracised since the kids' story became known yesterday. It was all *his* fault. Lannie was the injured party, though she hadn't been averse to that small amount of physical contact.

"Why Alanya not here?" he asked Frem.

The Keeper frowned. "Alanya has been dishonoured. It is not for her to answer questions. Our children have been exposed to inappropriate behaviour. It is not for them to answer questions." Shiván translated.

Gil pursed his lips and nodded. He was up against a rigid, deeply-ingrained morality like that of the Victorians. Nothing he said in his own defence would carry any weight.

"Gelmion, do you realise that what you have done is wrong in our eyes? Among your people such closeness may be acceptable for unmarried men and women. For us it is a sign of impure intentions. Do you understand this?"

Gil heaved a sigh. "I understand. I apologise," he said in English. Shiván translated.

Frem's expression softened a little. "I will convey your apologies to the parents of the children. You yourself can convey them to Alanya. Do you also understand that nothing like this can ever happen again?"

"Yes, I do."

"I hope so. We are concerned for Alanya, but even more for our children. Denny will soon be entering courtship. We will not permit him to be further exposed to inappropriate courting behaviour. Is that clear?"

"Yes, it's clear." Gil glanced towards the stairs. He wanted to get this over with.

Both Frem and Fira continued to stare at him. Irritation was building in Gil. A quick sigh of frustration escaped him.

Fira stepped forward, a cold expression on her face. "Gelmion. I'm not sure you understand this as well as you think. I shall speak as I would to a child. If you transgress again, you cannot remain among us." Frem nodded in agreement.

Gil was taken aback. No, he hadn't realised that.

Fira leaned forward and planted her hands on the table, a hard intentness in her sharp features. Suddenly she looked every inch the military officer. "And realise this, Gelmion. If you are sent away, you will leave. But you will not arrive. Do you follow me?" As Shiván translated Gil was aware of a sudden coldness within. He nodded.

"You are a stranger, and you do not share our beliefs. How do we know you will keep our whereabouts secret? I will not risk the lives of fifty people for the sake of one who cannot be trusted." She paused. There was shock in Shiván's eyes as he relayed her words in English.

"Do we understand one another?" Fira's gaze was cold and unblinking.

"Yes," Gil muttered bleakly.

"Good." Fira looked at Shiván, then at Gil. "You will not discuss this with anyone except Alanya and Danîsha." They both nodded.

She turned and stalked out.

* * *

Another day had passed, and the evening meal was over. All around the large kitchen clusters of people were sitting at the tables sipping chass and chatting. An admiring group had gathered round Danîsha, who sat with the bellaril cradled in her arms, trying out various Dûrian songs. She struck up a popular tune, and everyone began singing. Shivers ran down Shiván's back. That instrument— well, it went as far beyond a guitar as a pipe organ eclipsed a flute. There was a depth, a richness, to its music that filled the heart with delight.

He glanced round the room. Lannie was chatting with a group of women. Gil was nowhere to be seen. The poor old Doc had been ostracised since the episode in the kitchen; and the four of them were still struggling with Fira's harsh pronouncement. Lannie was keeping her distance, and Gil was taking that hard. Shiván sighed.

"*Shiván! Is fonâr*—give me a hand." He turned to see Veynel beckoning from the stoves. He walked over.

The older woman pointed to a small tray with four steaming mugs of chass. "Can you take that up to the lookouts in the ruins? All my helpers are singing with Danîsha."

"Sure thing!" He took a cloth, draped it over one arm, lifted the tray above his head with the other and began weaving his way between the tables.

Veynel's rare smile appeared, and she shook her head.

Shiván climbed the stairs and put the tray down on the top step. He pulled a lever in the wall and with a slight grinding noise the masonry door slid open. A welcome coolness wafted in. He carried the tray along the shattered passage to the central courtyard.

He glanced at the broken walls that still offered a semblance of protection. One of the lookouts usually perched way up on the least damaged of the towers. Shiván let his gaze wander up the tower to see if he could spot him. No, he was well hidden. There was the collapsed edge of the roof... His eyes were drawn up further into the night sky—

And he froze. For the first time, the sky was clear.

The tray slipped from his hands and crashed to the ground. There were questioning cries from the lookouts as he stood staring upward, mouth open. Then he turned and sprinted back into the basement, down the stairs, yelling, " *'Neesh! Lannie! Gil!*" Dûrians scattered before him, eyes wide.

Danîsha broke off in mid-chord and shot to her feet. "What is it?" Lannie hurried over. "Are you okay?"

"*Gil!*" Shiván roared. He appeared a moment later, hair tousled, eyebrows high.

"*Come!*"

Exchanging bemused glances they trotted after him as he hurried back up. The Dûrians followed en masse.

Shiván stopped in the courtyard and the others clustered round. "*Look!*" He pointed up to the sky.

"Shiván, what on earth—" Lannie began in an annoyed tone. "No, *not* on Earth," he said. Then she saw. "Oh. Oh, God." She sat down suddenly on a piece of masonry.

As 'Neesh stared up she looked older. "Dear Lord," she whispered.

Low on the southern horizon was one moon. Over to the west was a second, smaller one. In the centre of the sky, against a band of dim specks of light, was an almost perfect circle of stars.

Margay said quietly, "We call it the Ring of Orrénne. We believe the One placed it there as a promise—that the circle of his enfolding love will never be broken."

"Well, that does it," Gil muttered.

Damion came up and laid a hand on Shiván's shoulder. "You have never seen this sky before?" he asked quietly.

Shiván shook his head. "*Eshan.* —Never."

"*Atenámbaret u deylan kinnéy lassar,*" Damion announced. 'The Restorers are from a different sky.'

Fira said nothing amid the swelling murmur of comment.

* * *

A night of stunned readjustment had passed. Shiván, Lannie and Danîsha were sitting together for the dawnmeal.

"So what do we do now?" Lannie said, staring at the other two. There was a quiver in her voice.

"We can only make the best of the situation we're in," 'Neesh replied. "I think we've all secretly hoped that one day this'll be over and we'll be able to go home again." She drew a shaky breath. "We must forget that now and do our best to fit in here."

"But can't we at least... *try* and find a way back? I mean, we came here somehow—so we should be able to return the same way!"

"*If* we knew what that was," Shiván said. "But we don't. What could we do? Go round asking for the nearest interstellar space port?"

"No, but— we could at least try and do something!"

"Listen. There is no 'normal' way we could have reached this planet, and no normal way we can go home. That means *God* sent us." Shivvie emphasised each point by tapping his wooden spoon on the table. "If God sent us, he must have had a reason. Surprise,

surprise, the villagers have seen us from day one as their *Atenámba-ret* — the Restorers of the Way. Even Fira was shaken by what happened last night.

"We're in a different class now from the rebel leaders Armanet and Dôrion. How can we say this is all just a coincidence? I believe we *are* the *Atenámbaret*. We shouldn't be thinking about how to go home: we should be thinking about how to do what we were sent here to do. Father Martin told each of us we'd learn something new in a 'different place'. This is the different place, and the way we're going to learn it is by helping these people restore God's Way in their country."

Lannie was shaking her head. "How can you say that, Shiván? I mean, who are we? Just four ordinary people. We don't have what it takes to lead a national movement, or start a revolution!"

"Were any of Jesus' disciples charismatic figures in the beginning? Peter denied him; Thomas doubted him; James and John were out for their own prestige... Yet later on they turned the world upside down."

"Okay, fine, but you're still assuming that we're the fulfilment of the Dûrians' prophecies. That's a massive assumption to make. Not all the Dûrians are convinced of it, so how can we be?

"In any case, what about Gil and me? Gil doesn't even believe in God, and I'm... well, I don't know what I am right now. I used to go to church, but it never did anything for me. Then you showed how the Lightists have exactly the same religion here — and now we know that this is a different planet! That makes the whole issue of Christianity so much bigger than Earth — so much more *real*. I... don't know how to handle that yet. So how can someone like *me* be a Restorer of God's Way?"

"Do you agree that God must have brought you here? How else could you have ended up on a different planet?"

"I don't know! You could be right. I just don't know."

Shivvie smiled. "I reckon you and Gil *are* Restorers, even if neither of you feel that way right now. Saint Paul wasn't a disciple of Jesus in the beginning — he was trying to kill all his followers! Yet in the end he became one of the greatest apostles — wrote almost half the books of the New Testament. God hasn't finished with you two yet. I think he'll turn you into Restorers. Wouldn't you agree, 'Neesh?"

She nodded slowly. "I agree that God has a job for us to do in Dûrion—otherwise, why did he bring us here? I also agree that this job involves *all* of us, and that in God's time Lannie and Gil will discover their part in it. But I'm not sure that we are the Dûrians' *Atenámbaret.*

"What worries me is all the talk about war and overthrowing the government. Paul didn't start a war! He told us to obey those in authority over us. Maybe the Lightists here are wrong in thinking their Restorers will overthrow the government. Jesus said 'My kingdom is not of this world'. He wasn't a freedom fighter. Maybe what we're meant to do here is to tell people that the son of God also came to our world, and to explain what that means for both us and for them. Maybe that's how the One wants us to restore his way…"

Danîsha paused, a little breathless. Margay came and quietly collected their dishes. Denny and a girl called Ennel brought mugs of chass. The three foreigners murmured "*Len eloris.*"

Shiván took a sip of the hot beverage and glanced from one woman to the other. "Okay. We can't be sure of our exact rôle yet. Perhaps you're both right that God doesn't intend us to start some huge national campaign. But would you agree that we *might* be the Restorers—with a job description still to be supplied by God?"

Danîsha shrugged. "If we're sure it's his job description, yes." Lannie gave a slight shake of her head, her eyes lowered. "Maybe. I just don't know."

"Could we assume that is the case unless we find otherwise?"

Lannie looked up, frowning. "Why the pressure?"

"Just so we have a basis for deciding what to do. Haven't you seen the way some of the Dûrians are looking at us? Damion, Margay, Ennel and others… Expectantly. They're waiting for us to act, to do something to help *them* decide if we are who they hope we are. We can't carry on enjoying their hospitality and doing nothing. Let's accept their label of *Atenámbaret*, and trust God to show us what's involved."

There was a thoughtful silence. Then Danîsha nodded decisively. "You're right, Shiván. The worst thing would be to do nothing because we're unsure. But we can't just accept *their* assumptions. We have to find out what God wants."

"Agreed."

Lannie sighed. A glint of moisture appeared in her eyes. "We're making this decision without Gil. And I have no idea what my part will be, or if I'll even have one. But— Okay. I agree it's pointless trying to go home. We have to do something worthwhile."

"Great! Then the Restorers are officially in business. Let's pray about it."

They bowed their heads in the earthly fashion, and Danîsha and Shiván committed themselves to God and asked for his guidance. Lannie contributed a shaky "Amen".

* * *

Gil sat under the eaves of the forest, staring grimly at the ruined Manor. Resting beside him was his last food sack for the day.

He'd decided to leave. There was no future for him here. He couldn't stay with this little huddle of dissidents and become a farmer. Nor could he join Steve and co. in their crazy mission as religious freedom fighters.

He was on an alien planet. Trying to find his way home was pretty hopeless, to say the least. He had to make a new life for himself. A while back there had been some conversation in the kitchen about the capital of this backwoods nation—a city called Darthane. He'd asked through Steve if they had a place of higher learning there, and had been told they did.

He'd go to Darthane and see if he could interest this 'university' in offering him a post teaching linguistics. If they didn't have the subject, he'd create it for them. He might eventually make some guarded enquiries about travel to 'other skies', though they'd probably only laugh.

But he so much wanted Lannie to come with him. He knew she had her doubts about the freedom fighters thing. She might prefer the idea of a more normal life. *If* he could put it to her. It was a con-founded nuisance that she wasn't speaking to him. She'd overre-acted to the kitchen incident; if he knew women, she was blaming him for it. He had to speak to her.

A twig snapped. He dived into the nearest undergrowth, drag-ging his sack behind him. There was more rustling, then a sudden silence. Don't say the newcomer had stopped nearby! He'd be stuck here till he decided to move.

Then came another sound, a soft one, and Gil's eyebrows shot up. It was a woman, sobbing. Out here, alone? He crept forward through the shrubbery. His heart did a back flip when he saw who it was.

Lannie was sitting against a tree, weeping.

Something in Gil snapped, and he charged out of the bush crying "Lannie!" She leapt to her feet with a muffled scream. They stood staring at each other, a couple of feet apart. Her eyes were red, her hair mussed, her lips parted in shock. She'd never looked more desirable.

"Lannie! Oh God, I'm sorry."

Her eyes softened. "It's okay."

"Are you still upset with me?"

"Well, maybe just a little."

He took a step towards her. "Lannie, I went too far. I really am sorry. Can you forgive me?"

She stared at him for a moment. Then she nodded. A faint smile illuminated the tear-streaks on her face. "I think so. Just… be more careful next time."

Gil felt relief flood through him. The door was open, if only a crack.

"I will! Lannie, listen, we've got on well together, haven't we? I've enjoyed your company, and I think you've enjoyed mine?"

"Ye-es…" Her voice was a little doubtful.

"You're the one who's made this God-forsaken backwater bearable! I don't know how I could have managed otherwise. But now… we're on a different planet! That changes everything. I want to go to Darthane, Lannie—to the capital city. There's a university there, where I'm sure I could get a job. The thing is… Would you come with me? I care about you, Lannie; and I think you care about me, too. Am I right?"

She stared up at him, troubled. "I'm not sure, Gil. Maybe I do, but—"

"Then come with me! I can't stay here, Lannie. I have to go. I'll get a job at the university in Darthane, and you could paint, maybe open an art gallery! The standard of living would have to be higher than here."

"But Gil, you can't leave! Have you forgotten Fira's threat?"

"To heck with her threat. We'll work something out. We'll escape at night, and be long gone before they can follow us."

"Gil, you idiot, it won't be that easy! The Manor is guarded. If we did run away and got past the lookouts, Fira's soldiers know this country. They'd catch us."

" 'Us'! Then you'll come?"

She flared up. "No, Gil, I won't come! If you'll bother to listen, I'm trying to tell you something about *me*. Can you tear your attention away from yourself for a moment?"

"Ouch. I'm listening."

"Gil, I can't make a big decision like that right now. Seven weeks ago I was engaged to Matt, in Birmingham. I still love him. *And* I'm fond of you. You have to give me time."

Gil stared down at her, frustration rising. "Lannie, time is what I haven't got! I'm telling you, I can't stay on here any longer. I can't stand being close to you, and unable even to hold your hand. I've stuck it as long as I can, but we're on an alien planet, and I have to make a new life for myself. Please come with me!"

"Okay, so again it's you, you, you. What about me? My needs don't matter, I suppose."

"You matter. You matter so much to me." He moved towards her, and she sidestepped.

"Right. I'm something you need, so you just pick me up and walk off with me."

"*No!*" For a moment he clasped his head in his hands. God, how women could distort things. "I care for you Lannie, and maybe you care for me. I just want to spend time together. Is that so selfish? But here we can't!"

That calmed her a little. "If we tell them we're fond of each other, I'm sure they'll accept that. I mean, the Dûrians must have ways that men and women can 'go out together'. We just have to find out what those are."

"Yes, and I'll bet they add up to a hundred rules and regulations," Gil declared bitterly.

"I'm sorry, Gil, but I need time, okay? Besides, what about Shivvie and 'Neesh? You haven't said a word about them. The three of us talked yesterday about this *Atenámbaret* thing. We decided it's time to do something about it. Whatever you and I do needs to fit in with Shiván and Danîsha's plans."

"God, I don't care about Shiván and Danîsha!" He regretted the words the moment they left his lips.

She stared at him incredulously. "*Oh!* So it doesn't matter what happens to them, is that it? As long as we're okay. Well, *I* care what happens to them, and I'm not going anywhere without them!" She turned and marched out on to the lawn towards the Manor.

"Lannie, wait! I didn't mean that—" He dashed after her, grabbed her shoulder and swung her round. Her face was flushed and her eyes bright. Before he knew what was happening he'd clasped her in his arms and was kissing her.

She jerked away and he doubled over gasping as a small, hard fist struck him in the wind. That's a first, he thought, they normally slap your face.

When he managed to straighten himself Lannie was making a beeline for the Manor. He suddenly realised he was not alone. Margay, Denny and Teynel were staring at him in shock.

* * *

The next morning when Fira sent for Gil, he was nowhere to be found.

Chapter 14: *Sudden partings*

"SO, TROOPER DARMET, *you* were guarding the escape tunnel. Just exactly how did the foreigner slip past you?"

Fira was in a towering rage and all the soldiers wore hang-dog expressions. Darmet stood before her with his head bowed.

After the startling discovery this morning that Gil had vanished, Fira had had the whole area searched. In the eastern forest they had found broken foliage and footprints at the exit from the emergency tunnel. The trail had disappeared into a nearby stream, and the searchers had not found any tracks leading out of it. Four hours had passed and now they'd called off the hunt. A quantity of food, a sack, a robe, some firesticks and a pot of fireclay were missing.

The whole group was gathered in the kitchen after a hasty serving of chass. Shiván felt for poor Darmet as Fira faced him with arms akimbo, green eyes blazing.

"*Well*, Trooper?"

"He— I must have dropped off, Lieutenant." 'Lieutenant' was the best Shiván could make of her military rank.

"*Dropped off?* So you were asleep on duty, Trooper?"

Darmet's head sank a little lower. "Yes, Lieutenant."

"You are relieved of all duties until further notice. You will serve in the kitchen under Veynel."

Darmet's face reddened as he muttered, "Yes, Lieutenant."

"So!" Fira packed a world of frustration into the explosive word. She surveyed the assembled company. "Gelmion has passed sentence of exclusion on himself. He has left, on his own, to face dangers he knows nothing of. Only an unbalanced loner could do such a thing!" There were murmurs of shocked agreement from the Dûrians.

"He had no choice!" Lannie protested. Her eyes were red. "You forced him into it."

"I did nothing of the kind!" Fira retorted. "How dare you suggest such a thing?"

"Because you said you would kill him if he made another mistake!"

Pandemonium broke out. All the Dûrians were protesting, staring at Lannie as though she'd accused the President of belonging to the Mafia.

Lannie stood, red-faced, and marched up to Fira. "Did you or did you not tell him that he would leave here but never arrive?" she shouted above the hubbub.

"*Sit*, Alanya," the lieutenant commanded, her eyes cold.

"No, I will not sit!" There was an appalled silence. "You threatened Gelmion with death; and now you deny it?"

"Alanya. I said Gelmion would leave, but not arrive. That was not a threat to kill him. You do not understand our language. I meant that Gelmion would not arrive at *his* chosen destination. We would have escorted him elsewhere, to be kept safely under restraint as a dangerous loner."

Lannie stared at Fira, her mouth open. Shiván cast an appalled glance at Danîsha, whose eyes were wide.

"You mean— All this time— But he left because he thought you'd kill him!"

Fira's harsh voice softened a little. "I am sorry, Alanya, if Gelmion thought that. But his transgression only warranted exclusion."

Lannie sank down on to a bench. "Then what's going to happen to him now?" she demanded.

Fira's lips compressed. "I'm afraid Gelmion has put himself beyond our help. He will be far away by now. I cannot risk the lives of others in a search that has so little chance of success."

"You're just going to leave him to face all those dangers you spoke about?"

"I repeat: I cannot risk other lives."

"So what *are* all these dangers?"

"He's on his own!" Margay exclaimed.

"So what?"

"Have you not understood this yet? You cannot be alone on the roads! You'd be considered... mad! Dangerous! A criminal! An outcast!"

"Gelmion could be picked up by the army and be forced to join the Bishop's forces," Veynel said.

" —or by a Land Elder looking for an extra worker..." The dire possibilities came shooting in from all sides.

" — or by a Care House, and be locked away as a madman..."

" — or, best of all, by a group of Lightists, who would make sure he couldn't wander off again..."

" — or worst, by a Mindbender," said Fira darkly, "and become a slave for the rest of his life."

Shiván had been translating for Lannie, and by this time she was on her feet. "Then we must *do* something!" she shouted.

"Alanya, I have told you," Fira said sharply. "There is nothing we can do. I will not put the rest of this community at risk by sending out searchers."

"So you're going to sit here and do nothing?"

"No! We will not do nothing. We will pray — both for him and for ourselves."

"Oh, great, wonderful. Such initiative," Lannie muttered in English.

"But Fira," Shiván said. "When you last spoke to Gelmion, you said you could not trust him to keep our whereabouts secret. So how can you just leave him to wander free?"

Fira let out a sharp sigh. "Yes, that danger still exists. Gelmion has made things hard for us as well as himself. We cannot risk searching for him; and we cannot yet move from here. We have three invalids who can hardly walk, and two mothers nearing their time. Otherwise, I would have us all vacate the Manor and take to the forest at once." She raised her voice to address the whole group. "But this I will say! Some of you have clansfolk living within a couple of days' walk. Start preparing to go to them — and may the One go with you!"

In the buzz of conversation that followed, Fira turned to her troops. "And you, soldiers of the Light! You think you have been working hard? Your watch duties are doubled. We will guard the outlet of the escape tunnel. We will have new lookout posts in the eastern forest. ..." She continued, detailing locations, duties and schedules.

Shiván turned to Damion. "Who are these 'Mind-benders' Fira spoke of who force people to obey their commands?"

"They are workers of great evil who worship Gadesh. They take loners and others who have fallen out of their clans, and steal their wills."

"You mean, if that happened to Gelmion, he could no longer make his own decisions?"

"*Tarrathi.* — You have understood."

"He couldn't even try to escape?"

"I have not known of any Mindbender's slave who has escaped. But the greater danger is that Gelmion would reveal everything about us to the Mindbender."

"He would never do that!" Lannie protested.

"You know about Mindbenders, *Atenámbar?*"

"No, but I know Gelmion, and whatever Fira thinks, he would never betray us."

Damion stared at her a moment, then shook his head. "We can only ask the One that it will never come to that."

"So what are we going to do?" Lannie demanded of the other two.

"It's a terrible situation, Lannie, but what choice do we have?" 'Neesh said. "You heard Fira. There's nothing more that can be done."

"Well, there's something more *I* can do," Lannie muttered. She stood and marched off to her room.

* * *

She found the cream top she'd been wearing when she arrived and laid it on her bed. Her thoughts were chaotic. She was fed up with Gil for blowing it yesterday and running away; she was full of anxiety for him now; she was frustrated with this world and its weird culture — arresting people just for being on their own, for crying out loud! She wanted to return home to a normal life; she wanted to be reconciled with Matt; she wanted to find Gil and make sure he was alright. But above all, she had to leave the Manor. The others could talk and shrug their shoulders and say 'What can we do?' Not Lannie Catterick.

She'd go to Darthane. That's where Gil would be heading. Maybe she'd catch him up. She tied off the sleeves and waist of the cream top to make a bag, and shoved her meagre possessions into it. Slinging it over her shoulder she walked back to the kitchen.

Fira was still holding forth to her soldiers, and 'Neesh and Shivvie were talking to Damion. She'd miss them; and she'd no longer be one of their *Atenámbaret.* But she had her own path to follow now. She made her way round the back of the crowd and started up the stairs.

As she did so, a silence gradually descended on the kitchen. Then Shiván's voice clashed with Fira's.

"Where are you off to, Lannie?"

"Alanya, why are you leaving?"

She stopped halfway up the stairs. "I am going to Darthane," she said, "to do something about finding Gil, since no one else wants to." She turned and continued climbing. Uproar broke out below. Good. Let them try and stop her.

Predictably Fira told her to come back, then sent a posse of soldiers after her. She returned with them down the stairs, head held high. They marched her up to Fira, who stood, arms akimbo, ready to explode.

They called Shiván over to translate, though Lannie knew she could say all she needed in a few short Dûrian phrases. Dear, good-hearted Shivvie looked unhappy. Yes, she'd miss him. And 'Neesh.

"Are you a child, that you try to compel us with foolish gestures?" Fira demanded.

"No."

"Then have you heard nothing we have said this morning? Will you go out as a loner to be arrested, imprisoned, or mindbent?"

"I am going to Darthane."

"You are doing nothing of the sort!"

"How are you going to stop me?"

"I am informing you that as a member of this group you are staying here!"

"Oh? Well, I'm informing *you* that I'm going to Darthane."

"Alanya, will you stop behaving like a child?" Fira waved an arm at the roomful of people. "You have heard what was said earlier. If you leave as a loner like Gelmion you will never reach Darthane! Why do you insist on being so foolish?"

"Fira, I'm not going to keep repeating myself. It doesn't matter what you say, I am leaving for Darthane today. Will you let me go, or will you try and stop me?"

"I will stop you from needlessly throwing yourself away!"

"If that means stopping me from leaving, then you'll have to tie me to a pillar and guard me day and night. And hope the guard doesn't fall asleep."

Fira stared at her for a long moment. There was an electric silence in the room. Finally a look of recognition crossed her face. She spoke slowly. "Alanya. Are you challenging for leadership?"

Lannie blinked, taken by surprise, but the Dûrians were nodding and murmuring as though this was an expected development.

"Of course not!" she snapped. "I don't want your job. I'm leaving."

"Alanya," Damion interposed. "You are refusing Fira's command to stay here, is that right?"

"You might say so, yes."

"Then you have two choices. Either you break away like a loner—which can only result in failure. Or you challenge for leadership. That need not mean taking Fira's place here. Anyone who strongly disagrees with the leader may challenge for leadership of their own group. By her question Fira has allowed your challenge. You are therefore free to negotiate with her who will join your group."

Lannie stared at Damion; then hitched up her jaw, which had fallen. She turned back to Fira.

"Is that right? You'll allow me to lead my own 'group' to Darthane?"

Fira's lips were a thin line. "I do not think you are wise, Alanya, but you leave me no other option. Furthermore, your choice will affect me and the group here, because I am the only one who can escort you safely to Darthane. I have been there, I know the dangers. Also, you will need several other Dûrians."

"Why?" Lannie asked, puzzled.

"Because you are a foreigner," Fira responded, as though it were self-evident.

"But— How will people know that, if I'm dressed like you and keep my face hidden in my hood?"

"Because of your *shiláy!*" Fira declared impatiently.

Shivvie asked Fira what she meant, which irritated her. Damion was brought in. After a complicated exchange Shiván turned to Lannie and Danîsha.

"The best I can work out," he said, "is that it's a sort of 'aura' everyone has, which the Dûrians can 'see' or 'feel' and we apparently can't. It gives them an idea of what kind of person someone is. Apparently our auras all spell 'foreigner' pretty clearly."

"Good heavens!" Danîsha exclaimed.

Lannie stared at Shiván. "You're joking. So the Dûrians can just look at a person and tell what they're like?"

"Sort of—but not quite. I couldn't follow everything Damion said." Shivvie shrugged.

"So *that* was why the villagers treated us as Restorers right from the beginning!" Danîsha said. "I've often wondered how they were so sure."

Fira broke in. "Do you wish to challenge, Alanya?"

Lannie looked at her doubtfully. Going in a group to Darthane wasn't quite what she'd had in mind. On the other hand... she didn't even know where Darthane was.

"Let me understand this," she said. "If you came with me, Fira, you would follow *my* lead? If you felt we should take a certain route, but I wanted to go a different way, you'd go my way?"

"I am not a loner, Alanya. If I say I will follow you then I will do so. Among us, the best leader is also the best follower."

"Good enough." It suddenly occurred to Lannie that this was the best of all possible outcomes. She seized Fira's hand and raised it skyward in the Dûrian handshake. Their eyes locked, and Lannie saw her own strength mirrored in Fira's forthright gaze. "*Li eloris.*— Thank you."

There was a loud buzz of comment as people discussed this unexpected development. Shivvie and 'Neesh were following the exchanges between herself and Fira, their expressions anxious.

"*Elorestis.*—I am thanked," Fira responded formally. "But you must realise, Alanya, that this is a costly decision. I am depriving the larger group here of my experience in order to escort you on a journey I do not consider justified. Let us hope it will be worthwhile despite my doubts." Fira's sharp eyes bored into hers.

"I value what you're doing, Fira."

"But Lannie," Shiván said in English, "aren't you jumping the gun here? We still haven't worked out what we're meant to be doing as 'Restorers'. If you shoot off like this—and Gil's also gone— we'll be falling apart before we've even started."

"This is an emergency, Shiván. We can't just leave Gil to walk blindly into all those dangers."

"No, I agree. But let's see if we can kill two birds with one stone. Why don't 'Neesh and I come with you? We could make a start on what God intends us to do here, while also looking for Gil."

"You would do that?"

"Of course. What do you say, 'Neesh?"

"I'm all for it, if we're clear what our goals are."

"Right. Then let's get them clear."

Shiván stood up. "*Istar!* — Friends! It seems the One is now leading us away from the Manor, where you have cared for us for so many weeks. Danîsha and I will be going with Alanya to Darthane. We want to thank you from our hearts for everything you've done for us."

The chatter died away as all eyes turned on him.

"A few days ago we discovered that we are from a place so far away that even the sky is different. Now I must ask you: *Do you believe that we are the* Atenámbaret — *the 'strangers and loners' foretold in your Book?*"

There was a chorus of "*Haa!* — Yes!" from many, including Damion, Margay, Frem, Denny and Lannie's roommates. Others looked doubtful. Veynel spoke for them.

"I believe you may be. In some ways you fulfil what the Book says about the *Atenámbaret*. But in others you don't."

"What things do we fulfil and what do we not fulfil?"

"Your *shiláy* and your different sky tell us that you are true strangers and loners."

"Your *nestilar* — your instruments — are those foretold in the Book," Damion declared. "The Shell of Hearing, the Glass of Seeing, the Strings of Truth."

This provoked a storm of protest. "The Hearth teaches that the nestilar are not connected with the Restorers!" "The Travelling Order says they are!" "There are only three instruments, but the *Atenámbaret* are four!"

Shiván held up his hand. "We understand that there is disagreement about the instruments. Tell us now those things we definitely do not fulfil."

There was another barrage of comments. Lannie shook her head. The whole thing seemed so uncertain. She suppressed her impatience to get back to the trip to Darthane. This was important for

'Neesh and Shivvie, even if she herself was no longer part of their mission.

Three main objections to their status as *Atenámbaret* emerged. The first centred around Gil: he was from the same place as them, yet his shiláy was different. How could the Dûrians be sure any of the foreigners were the Restorers, when one of them wasn't even open to the Light? Furthermore, Gil had now disappeared.

The second objection was simply that the foreigners knew so little about Dûrion and the Lightist religion. They couldn't speak the language properly and were not even aware of the prophecies describing who they were supposed to be.

The third matter was more interesting. It seemed there was a prophecy that spoke of the Restorers wielding something called the 'Rod of Truth'. This provoked another heated debate: apparently Armanet and Dôrion, the leaders of the Rebellion, had not had this 'rod' either. Some said the prophecy was just a figurative way of declaring that the *Atenámbaret* would restore Truth to the land; others insisted that it referred to a real object, the *Ambon Sûrilac*, or Ambon of Sûrilane.

Shiván raised his hand again. When silence fell he said, "Let's assume for the moment that we *are* the Restorers of the Way. What is our task? What do you expect us to do?"

The answer to that was unanimous. *To overthrow Shambor and destroy the Mindbenders.*

'Neesh protested at once. "Why must we talk about overthrowing and destroying? Why can't we rather ask the One to so fill this country with his Light that even the Mindbenders will be touched and changed?"

The answers flooded in. Everyone in the room had some personal experience of how unthinkable that was. Relatives who'd been abducted and never seen again. The Mindbenders' utter indifference to people's welfare. The wanton brutality of their enforcers, the Bishop's Guard. Rapes, murders, the terrorisation of the whole populace. 'Neesh was looking desperately unhappy, but she was nodding. It wasn't hard to see why the Dûrians felt the way they did.

Lannie's patience came to an end. This was what Gil was walking blindly into! "Shiván!" She tugged at his shift. "Sit down for a moment and talk English. It's obvious you and 'Neesh need more time to work your goals out. I'm going to Darthane to look for Gil. That's *my* goal right now. If you come, you can make enquiries there about this 'rod' thing, and discuss the other issues as well. But I'm not waiting for everything to be sorted out beforehand. How about it? Will you join me?" She glanced from Shivvie to 'Neesh.

Shiván gave her a long look, then nodded. "I think that's the best we can do for the moment. We've got so much still to learn. And if we find Gil, all four of us can decide where we go from there."

Danîsha heaved a deep sigh. "I wish the whole thing wasn't so... bloodthirsty. I thought God had sent me here to share the good news, not to start another war! But you're right, Lannie. We need more time — *and* we need to find Gil."

Shiván stood and announced their purpose in going to Darthane. There were exclamations of support and good wishes, as well as sorrow at their departure. It hit Lannie how much she would miss these dear friends. Damion lifted his hands and all fell silent. His prayer was simple and direct: that the One would guide the Restorers of his Way into the path they should follow.

When he was finished, Fira rose to her feet. "The decision has been made. I will escort you to Darthane. Alanya, you have challenged, so you will lead. Choose now who else will accompany us. I suggest you make the group only large enough to divert suspicion — with twice as many Dûrians as strangers. Shîrinor and Cârinor have said they would like to join you."

"Oh, Shere and Khan!" Lannie was pleased. She'd always liked the twin soldiers with their cheerful efficiency.

"Troopers Tornoret and Fiminor are also willing to come. We cannot spare any more. Will you speak with these men? I need to discuss with the others who will take my place here."

She turned back to the larger group, naming Sergeant Borion as her successor. That brought the sergeant to his feet in protest, and Shiván provided a running commentary for Lannie and Danîsha. Borion declared that Fira should not leave at this crucial time with so many dangers looming; and Fira responded that since Alanya would leave anyway together with one or both of the other foreigners, she wouldn't want yet more ignorant strangers running around the countryside who might be captured and give away the community's location.

"What a vote of confidence," Lannie muttered.

Fira continued that since she knew many byways and hidden routes to and from the capital, it would be best if she went with the foreigners to guard them and keep them on the right track. In the end Borion reluctantly agreed.

The arrangements went quickly after that. For her own group Lannie accepted the four Dûrian volunteers, plus Fira—which allowed only two foreigners if their shiláy was to be adequately disguised. After some anxious discussion they decided on Shiván as the second foreigner, because he knew the language best. 'Neesh agreed to remain at the Manor, which would be helpful if Gil returned. They would miss her, but someone had to stay, and this worked out best.

* * *

Early in the afternoon Danîsha stood holding Teynel and waving as the seven set off. Margay had found them travel pouches, which they carried slung over their shoulders. They had very little to bring; their robes would serve as blankets and they would find food in the forest. Fira had a small sum of money for expenses; Lannie had her bess, and Shiván his Bible.

It was a misty day. The forest was a dim greeny-gold, and the distant lowlands were shrouded in grey. The muted colours matched Danîsha's mood. No adventures for her. Here she was, left behind to mind the house. It had all happened so quickly. First Gil gone; now Lannie and Shiván leaving. She felt more alone than she'd ever been since George died. And how did this tie in with what Father Martin had said—that she would receive her heart's desire of sharing God's truth with those who'd never heard it?

She heaved a sigh. Nevertheless. If this is what you want, Father, I'll give it my best. But it hurts, Lord. It does hurt.

Teynel seemed to feel her pain, and the little waif wrapped her arms more tightly around Danîsha. Danîsha adjusted her comb and stroked her soft hair.

Chapter 15: *Gil among the lemons*

GIL STARED DOWN AT THE ROAD. It was the first he'd seen in Dûrion, and a peculiar one it was, too.

He was sitting at the edge of a copse of trees on a hill above a small town. He'd scrambled through rough country to get to this vantage point. He knew from conversations at the Manor that the capital city, Darthane, was five days' journey to the south-east. "You follow the dawn bearing right," Shîrin had once told him.

Shere. Thinking of him reminded Gil of Lannie, who'd given the soldier that nickname. God, he was missing her. He had cursed himself a thousand times for that stupid comment. *"I don't care about Shiván and Danîsha!"* It echoed mockingly in his head, making his blood run cold every time.

The ironic thing was, it wasn't true! He was missing Shivvie and 'Neesh. He'd never felt so alone. If it hadn't been for that one comment, Lannie wouldn't have marched off back to the Manor. If she hadn't marched, he wouldn't have followed her out into the open, where others could see. If she hadn't been angry, her face wouldn't have been so flushed or her eyes so bright. If she hadn't looked so damn irresistible, he wouldn't have kissed her... His heart lurched as he remembered the first blissful milliseconds of that kiss — before she jerked back and punched him in the wind.

That was the end of it. Margay and the others were eyewitnesses — including Denny, whom they were so anxious to protect. Fira had looked like an explosion waiting to happen when she'd announced the court would sit on 'Gelmion' tomorrow morning. The verdict was a foregone conclusion. The late unlamented Gelmion would "leave, but not arrive". Dear old Shivvie had tried to encourage him, saying he'd plead as he'd never pled before; but Shivvie was the only person he'd spoken to the rest of the evening. 'Neesh was too busy comforting Lannie, and everyone else had treated him as though he were radioactive.

Well, he wasn't about to be led like a lamb to the slaughter. For a prison governor with someone on death row, Fira had been remarkably lax. He hadn't been tied up or even guarded in any way.

Before going to bed he'd collected a few necessities; then in the middle of the night he'd got up as if to visit the privy.

It was pure luck that old Darmet had been snoring his head off beside the emergency tunnel. He remembered being told that it came out in the eastern forest, which was just where he needed to go. So he'd squeezed past Darmet, and the rest had been easy. The stream near the tunnel's exit had been a gift, as had the dim moonlight through the clouds. Finding the southerly path was the biggest problem; but he'd finally struck a well-trodden track at around noon the next day and had reached the margin of the forest by evening. There he'd spent a cold, dreary night in a patch of undergrowth.

So, here he was now — facing pastures new. From the foot of his hill there was an artist's palette of fields dotted with copses and larger woods fading away into the distance. It was an overcast day; but even so, the striking feature of the fields was their vivid colours. The brilliant yellows could be rape-seed; and the bright reds might be poppies. But there were royal purples, morning-glory blues, oranges, mauves and turquoises. Even some whose colours seemed to change as the wind blew — red, then salmon-pink, then a rich yellow ochre. He shook his head, bemused. What sort of crops were these?

The fields were watered by a number of small streams; and scattered among them were many little clusters of houses. On a hill in the distance was a large two-storey building. Another manor house? Below him lay the village — or small town. He guessed it was Finien, a place he'd heard mentioned as the nearest town. He estimated it only covered about forty acres; but from his hilltop it was laid out like a map with a rectangular grid-pattern of streets.

That was what he found odd. He knew this was characteristic of American towns — but a more backward country like this? He'd have expected a haphazard jumble of primitive dwellings, with muddy tracks between them. Far from it. This was neat, clean, and carefully planned. The houses looked well-made and were strangely tall, built of yellow stone with the high-pitched roofs covered in dark green tiles or shingles. There was a glint of glass in the narrow windows. The streets were paved with closely-fitted blocks of the yellow stone; and they were bordered with lawns and flowerbeds.

In the centre of the town was an open square, on one side of which stood a circular white building with a conical green-tiled roof. At the peak of the roof was an unusual emblem. It might have been a cross, except that the horizontal bar had been replaced with a circle. It, too, was painted white. Could this be one of the churches — or 'Hearths' — Shiván had talked about?

The road that led east out of the town was advanced in its construction. This was no rutted country track. The central section was paved like the town streets. It was at least as wide as one carriageway of a modern motorway and skilfully cambered. There was a drainage ditch on either side, next to which ran footpaths for pedestrians. On this side travellers were walking east; on the far side west.

But when you looked at what was *on* the road, you suddenly found yourself back in the middle ages — or earlier. There were oval-shaped enclosed carriages with large wheels trundling along, and square carts carrying farm produce, pulled by shaggy red-brown beasts like overgrown oxen with forward-sweeping horns. Then in the centre of the road the occasional 'chariot' would flash by. That was the only word for it — an open conveyance for one or two, pulled at great speed by teams of creatures resembling large greyhounds. Also in the central fast track groups of riders would gallop past on those strange camel-horses, seated between the two small humps.

But no self-propelled vehicles passed by. No cars, buses, lorries or bicycles.

Gil shook his head to try and clear it. What was he seeing? At one moment he seemed to be in ancient Rome; the next, in the middle ages; the next, in middle America.

A detachment of green-coated infantry marched by, reminding Gil of the dangers of this rebel area. He must plan his route. Obviously he had to follow the road — how else would he find Darthane? But he couldn't slip from cover to cover alongside it, as he'd been hoping. Far too slow, with the many small streams and the hedged fields. Best to risk the road itself. He'd have to join the pedestrian footpath without attracting attention. There was a largish stream between him and the road. He could cross that at a point where it was hidden from travellers by a small copse. He'd hide among the trees and clean himself up before venturing on to the path.

All went well, except that the hem of his brown robe got wet in the stream; he hadn't tucked it up high enough. He wrung it out in the roadside copse, and brushed off dead leaves and other debris. He peered out cautiously at the footpath and the road beyond. A couple of heavily laden carts were groaning by in the nearside slow lane. Those beasts of burden were huge. He caught a whiff of their rank odour and stifled a cough.

He pulled back into the copse as a group of twelve or fifteen young people approached on the footpath, chattering and laughing. Most were carrying small bundles over their shoulders. He felt a twinge of unease at the way they were dressed—quite differently from him and the Manor community. No robes or brightly coloured shifts, but short leather jackets over sober grey or brown knee-length tunics, with leggings of the same colour running down to leather shoes. Several wore soft black hats with a small peak in the front. Gil began to worry about being conspicuous in his rustic robe.

But after the young folk another group approached, and he breathed a sigh of relief. By contrast these were all bearded men, dressed in dark purple full-length robes. As they drew nearer he saw that the robes were held in place by a wide belt, and had hoods that were thrown back. They wore sandals on their feet, and each carried a staff. They were singing a repetitious lilting song that might have been a chant. Some kind of religious order?

Then he noticed that they had the same emblem hanging about their necks as he'd seen atop the 'Hearth' in the town: the circle-and-rod. That seemed to confirm it. If he got a chance, he'd tag along behind these monks—if you could call them that, with such bushy heads of hair.

He waited as they passed, then slipped out of the copse. He had almost reached the path, when one of the monks turned and looked at him. The chant broke off raggedly and they all stopped. Gil's heart was thudding but he smiled, raised his hand in a vague salute, and made to walk past them down the footpath. The monk who'd looked at him stepped forward, however, and blocked his way. He was short and thickset, with a face like a cheerful walnut. His circle-and-rod was silver, while the others' were made of wood.

"*Neylas*, friend," he said after a brief pause. "You look lonely — and far from home. Will you join us?"

"*Neylas.* That is— kind..." Gil said awkwardly, straining his limited Dûrian. He realised how much he'd relied on Shiván at the Manor. "But I will walk... alone." Again he made to pass by, but the whole group of eight monks started moving with him, and he found himself surrounded.

The walnut was walking beside him. "*Frengor ganalestis.*—My name is Frengor," he said. "*Li?*—And you?"

Gil found the directness of Frengor's brown eyes uncomfortable. "*Gelmion ganalestis.*"

"Where are you from?"

"I am from another country."

"That much is clear. Which country?"

"England."

Frengor merely nodded. "And why are you walking alone, friend Gelmion from Inglan? Have you no one from your own country to go with you?"

"I have—three—friend, but... I want go, they want—stay." He shrugged.

Frengor's eyebrows rose. "I see. Where are they staying, these friends of yours?"

Gil frowned. A spy in monk's garb? "Over there." He waved a hand vaguely in a south-westerly direction. They wouldn't find the Manor there.

The monk nodded, a smile playing round the corners of his lips. "And where are you going, friend Gelmion?"

"To Darthane."

There was a muttering among the other monks, who had been following the conversation closely. Frengor didn't bat an eyelid.

"What are you hoping to find in Darthane?"

"The... the place where..." The word came back to him. "The university."

"Ah! You seek to increase your knowledge. But do you know the way to Darthane?"

"Er, no. I follow... road."

All the monks laughed. "This road goes to many places, Gelmion," Frengor told him. "Why not travel with those who know where to turn? But we *Baranet* are not going to Darthane. Let's see if the friends behind can help."

"No, no, I walk alone—"

But Frengor was already speaking with a crowd of brightly-dressed Dûrians who had gradually been catching them up. Next thing he was being warmly welcomed by a large patriarch in an orange jacket with a grin like a Halloween pumpkin. Frengor leaned close for a final word, his cheerful face suddenly earnest.

"*Ney mel shar*, Gelmion—go with the Light. But do not walk alone. It is dangerous. Believe me, I am helping you now." Gil blinked. The man spoke slowly so he could understand, and with intense sincerity. He continued, "Also remember this: there is only one knowledge that satisfies, and you will not find it at the University. Seek to know the truth, my friend! Search for it." The monk's sharp brown eyes bored into his. Then he grinned, raised Gil's arm skyward in the Dûrian handshake, and was gone.

Gil snorted. Mystical mumbo-jumbo, like that vicar back home. Religious professionals were the same everywhere. The first bit of advice was good, though—he didn't want to be conspicuous.

The orange pumpkin seemed to have his entire extended family with him—about thirty of them, all in different sizes and psychedelic hues. He threw an arm around Gil's waist and proceeded to introduce him to each and every one. The fixed smile on Gil's face was becoming painful by the time he'd pumped arms with the last third-cousin-twice-removed. Not that he understood the Dûrian words—he'd switched off after the wife's sister's second son.

"And now tell us about yourself, Gelmion," the pumpkin boomed. He sounded like a master of ceremonies introducing the next act.

"I from another country. I from England," he said, hoping to head off this line of questioning. Far from it. They asked where England was, and wouldn't accept his vague replies. They persisted, rattling off every country they knew, until in desperation he said England was near 'Anáricar'—a distant nation he'd heard mentioned at the Manor. It had stuck in his mind because it sounded like 'America'.

There was a shocked silence at this revelation.

"Across the *sea?*" Pumpkin asked in a near-whisper. All eyes were round.

"Yes, very, very far," Gil said wearily.

There was another silence as they digested this appalling information. Gil decided to change the subject.

"What is this plant with much... colour?" he asked, pointing at a passing field full of bright blue foliage. He'd been startled when he first saw the fields close to: the colours were not flowers, but leaves belonging to tall, reed-like plants.

"You don't have *hilminay* in your country?" Pumpkin's wife asked, amazed. A thin, colourless woman in pink. Gil groaned inwardly.

"No, we don't have. What for do you use... *hilminay*?" It irked him to sound such a fool when he spoke. He was accustomed to wielding language like a razor-sharp blade. The best he could manage here was a broken stick.

"You don't *know* this?" The wife launched into a detailed description that went way above Gil's head. It ended with a question, and Gil just stared at her with glazed eyes.

The whole group burst into laughter, and he felt irrationally annoyed. Of course to them his stupidity was hilarious; he was the first foreigner they'd met.

"Gelmion." Pumpkin was instructing him now, with exaggerated slowness. Maybe he should rejoin the monks. He looked around hopefully, but they'd disappeared. "Hilminay," Pumpkin was telling him, " — is used — to make — clothes! You see — what — we all — wear? Clothes — have — much — colour, because they — come — from hilminay, and — hilminay — has — much — colour! You understand?"

Of course not, I'm only four, not six, Gil thought, eyeing the orange twit with distaste. But he nodded and said Yes, he understood. It was actually quite fascinating. So this was where the fabric Lannie admired so much came from. Textile plants. Presumably a fibre was obtained from the leaves and spun into a thread that retained the original plant's colour — no dye required. With simple equipment lowly villagers could produce cloth that would be the envy of fashion houses back in Europe or the States. Quite remarkable.

His reflections were interrupted by a repeated question. "Gelmion!" It was the wife's sister, he thought, a square-faced lady with browny-purple hair. She was quite tall for a Dûrian — though he himself stood out above them all. "Gelmion! Tell us — about — your family." Oh, God, here we go again.

"How many — children — do you have?"

"I have no children."

The woman's hand flew to her mouth. There were murmurs of shocked sympathy. "Oh! I am so sorry. Your wife… she is unable to—?"

"I have no wife, dammit!" The last was in English.

The square lady was utterly bewildered. "No wife? Then you are not *married?*"

One of the teenage boys made a remark, and there were sniggers from the younger set. Pumpkin restored order with a heavy hand.

Suddenly Gil couldn't take any more. If this was going to continue all the way to Darthane, murder would be committed and he'd deserve Fira's death sentence.

He took a glance behind him. No monks, but there was a small group of travellers walking quietly along about twenty yards away. Their silence, and the dark, sober colours of their clothing, called to him like the dim interior of a high street church after a hectic morning's shopping.

He quickly looked at the other group again, as though doing a double take. "Aaah, *there* is my people!" he exclaimed, pointing. "I go now. Thank you, thank you. *Ney len omalend*—Light enfold you!" He held out his hand for the raised arm-shake, but Pumpkin was staring at him in horror. There were gasps of dismay, and the whole group came to a halt.

"*Those* are your people, Gelmion?"

"Er, yes. I thank you." The other group was approaching, eyeing Pumpkin's lot warily. Oh God, what now? Were these two groups mortal enemies? But he'd made his decision—and the sober group was already starting to file past. The pumpkins drew themselves aside ostentatiously, and some of the women even brushed their skirts as though contaminated.

"I thank you! Light enfold you!" he said, and tagged on behind the sober lot. There were hisses and exclamations of disgust. "Not married! *Now* we know why…" he heard the square lady say. He turned and waved, but they stood in silent disapproval.

When he turned back, his new group had hurried on ahead. He put on speed and caught them up. They closed ranks and ignored him. For a while he strode along behind, then he thought, this is ridiculous. The walnut had said being alone was dangerous, and besides, he needed help to reach Darthane. Ahead of the sobersides he could see a detachment of green-coated infantry. He didn't relish the thought of being stopped and questioned by the likes of them.

"*Neylas!*" he called. "Can I walk with you?" They hunched their shoulders and ignored him.

"Please! I am alone. Will you let me be with you?"

Finally the ranks opened, and a sour-faced man in a black tunic and grey leggings beckoned to Gil to walk beside him. He gave him a sardonic once-over. "So, you travel alone?" he said in a gravelly voice.

"Yes. I wish help for walking to Darthane." Blast this unco-operative language. Amused glances were exchanged between the other five members of the group. Again it seemed to be a family party — Pa, Ma, grown son, grown daughter, and two younger sons. They all had a strong family resemblance. A sour lot. He'd landed among the lemons.

"Where are you from?" Papa Lemon was giving him that sardonic look again.

"I am from country called England."

"Ah!" He seemed to brighten, and exchanged a significant glance with Ma. "That is far away, yes?"

"Very, very far."

Ma now spoke. She was tall, only an inch or so shorter than himself, and had a narrow face and a hooked nose. She wore a brown jacket over a dark blue blouse and matching... were those *culottes?* Good Lord. With a broomstick she'd make a passable witch.

"Do you have any family in Darthane?" the witch asked.

"No. My family is... in England. I go to Darthane to university."

"Ah." Again the pleased smile. This lot seemed positively thrilled he was alone and unattached.

"You may walk with us," Pa announced.

"I thank you. Er, my name is Gelmion."

"I am Durónne," Pa told him. No one else was introduced, to Gil's infinite relief.

An hour's walking brought them to a small river, and soon after that they turned off the east-west highway on to an unpaved road that ran roughly south-east. Gil was grateful to be with them. He might have continued east and missed Darthane altogether.

The road wound its way among the bright fields. They passed through numerous hamlets, where the houses were built of the same yellow stone as the town of Finien. However, they had wooden shutters instead of windows, and the roofs were mostly thatched. In the middle of each hamlet was a scaled-down version of the white circular building he'd seen in the town, with a wooden circle-and-rod on top. He asked the lemons about it, but their faces grew sourer and they refused to comment.

Gil was relieved when in the late afternoon they struck a well-paved road again. This brought them to a village they called Bornis. Durónne said they would spend the night at the inn, but looked very sour indeed when he discovered that Gelmion had no means to pay. After a muttered conversation with the witch, he reluctantly forked out for an extra bed. Gil discovered later that it was half a bed in a room shared with seven others.

He did not sleep well that night.

Chapter 16: *Jomel miscalculates*

JOMEL HUMMED TO HERSELF as she strolled down Bishop's Avenue after her appointment with Dhelgor, the Mindbender of Stillárre. Life could be worse. It could certainly be worse.

There was no doubt she was a big hit. To her surprise, she was attracted to him too. That was something she hadn't expected. Dhelgor was a tall, powerfully-built man with a swarthy complexion and a cynical smile. There was a single-minded ruthlessness about him that was both scary and exciting. Yet from the first meeting last week, when Priest Sarmion had introduced them, he'd focused that single-mindedness on her. He'd been attentive and considerate—a welcome change from the other senior Gadeshites, who treated her as a convenience. His love-making was passionate but not abusive. He told her he cherished their times together in his apartment—and the original one-day-a-week arrangement had already been extended to two.

This was the way forward. She'd soon have Dhelgor nicely housebroken, and then... rapid advancement to Initiation. Once she was an Initiate, her intelligence and strength of will would open the doors to the ultimate pinnacle: Mindbending.

And what fascinating insights she'd been gaining about that from Dhelgor. She could hardly believe that this one man had ultimate control over almost four hundred and fifty minds. He did not personally direct them all; but he commanded seven subordinate Mindbenders, who were his lieutenants in the Stillárre garrison of the Bishop's Guard; they had the autonomy to direct seven or eight officers each; and those each controlled *another* eight slaves—ordinary Guardsmen and informers. That was power. And she wanted it.

She came to the end of Bishop's Avenue, where it opened into the market square. On the opposite side of the wide, paved plaza—still thronged with people at this late hour—stood the imposing marble portico of the Temple of Gadesh; and to the left, the crumbling limestone of the once-proud Hearth of Stillárre. The latter was now shabby and neglected—a sign of the times.

She walked past the Hearth to a cloth merchant's stall and started idly fingering the merchandise. An assistant hovered eagerly nearby. Jomel, the wealthy devotee of Gadesh, was well known in the Stillárre market. Other merchants were closing down for the day, but this one would remain open until Jomel had finished her business. It was a satisfying feeling.

Priest Sarmion, however, was becoming a pain. He kept asking plaintively why her appointments with Dhelgor took so long, and when *they'd* be able to spend time together as planned. And she kept telling him that Dhelgor was insatiable right now, but this would wear off soon. What slimy Sarmion didn't know, of course, was that she slipped away to her own apartment after each session with the Mindbender — precisely in order to avoid spending time with him. But she couldn't carry on indefinitely like this. Once she was quite sure of her position with Dhelgor, she would tell him that Sarmion was bothering her. That would take care of the problem.

After all, being the mistress of the most powerful Gadeshite in Stillárre had to count for something.

* * *

"Ah, Jomel, my darling, at last! I've been missing you so much." Dhelgor's saturnine smile softened the severe lines of his face as, two days later, he ushered her into his luxurious apartment in the Stillárre Guardhouse.

"After such a short time?" Jomel asked archly. Her heart was thudding at the sight of him, so attentive and handsome.

"Two days feels like two years without you, my sweet."

It was a verbal game of strike-ball that they played, shooting well-worn clichés back and forth. But Jomel could see the eagerness in his eyes.

"Then you'll be glad to give me anything I want?" She looked up at him with a tremulous smile.

"Name it, my dove!"

"I want *you!*" she cried, throwing her arms around his neck.

An hour later they lay sated in each other's arms amid the tumbled bedclothes. Dhelgor twined a lock of Jomel's hair around his finger, smiling that secretive smile at her. "You are a raging *garzin* in bed, you know that?" he told her.

"If I'm such a wild bear, why haven't I killed and eaten you?"

"You have, my she-bear, you have. I am utterly devoured by your love."

Jomel gave him her misty smile; but she was considering him carefully. Could this be the moment? She wanted to take a little peek into his mind, to gauge the depth of his infatuation with her. On that would depend whether she could risk a tiny dose of mesmerism to speed her progress towards Initiation. Only a tiny dose. She knew better than to attempt the full-scale exercise of her small power on a Mindbender. But if, like Sarmion, he was totally absorbed by his feelings for her, he wouldn't notice a gentle nudge. And that might be all that was needed to launch her on the pathway to real power.

On the other hand, something within her recoiled from manipulating the first man she'd really cared for, who was so courteous and considerate. It felt like a betrayal. Shouldn't she rather wait until their relationship was better established? But it was obvious already, surely, that they were both strongly attracted to each other. Why delay, when Sarmion was yapping at her heels and she was desperate to escape the sordid life of a temple prostitute?

She made her decision. Slowly, with infinite care, she edged her way behind the outer façade and into his mind. She intended a quick look, and then out again. But she stopped, frozen, as the terrible realisation of what she was seeing dawned on her. He was fully aware of her! He was watching her every clumsy move with cynical disdain. He didn't care for her in the least. *He* had aroused love in *her*, just as she had so often done with others.

A frantic desire to leave, to scream, to run home and curl up in a ball possessed her—but she couldn't move. She was like a bird mesmerised by a snake. Why was she seeing all these horrible thoughts of his? Her power wasn't that great... He was deliberately allowing this! She had invaded his mind, and he was showing her the folly of trying to outwit a Mindbender. Now in her agony she saw that he would never have advanced her to the level of Initiate, much less Mindbender. She was slated to remain a temple prostitute until her beauty faded, and then be discarded. She had exercised her power of love-arousal too well.

Suddenly she was outside his mind and they were looking at each other in the physical world. Nothing had changed. He still had her hair twined about his finger, there was still that look of gentle devotion on his face. But his eyes: They were locked on hers, and she wondered how she could ever have seen desire in them. When he had smiled, his eyes had remained as cold and hard as they were now.

"What a fool," he murmured. "What an utter fool. Sarmion warned me, but I preferred to believe you'd have the sense to stay out of my mind. Do you realise what this means, you ambitious little bitch?"

Everything within Jomel was crying out to jump up and run, to be anywhere but here—but she seemed to be clamped in place.

"I suppose— everything's over?" she managed to whisper. She felt hot tears leaking from her eyes.

"Yes, you slut. Everything. You've blown it, do you understand? We could have had a relationship to our mutual advantage, but you chose to try and manipulate me. How stupid could you get?" His face was now scornful. "In fact, my dove, you have just signed your death warrant."

He paused to let that sink in, his black eyes still boring into hers. An overwhelming fear clenched down on Jomel's body, bile rose in her throat, and a warm trickle told her she'd wet herself.

"But—" he said, and the tiny flicker of hope helped her to keep breathing. "Because you have given me some pleasure, I will be merciful. The temple needs a human sacrifice for the autumn equinox. That sacrifice will be you, unless—" Her breathing stopped again. "Unless you can trap a suitable victim."

He looked down at her with that scornful sneer of his. It was a sneer, not a smile—how could she have imagined otherwise?

"Take careful note of what I say, little fool. Your life depends on it. The victim needs to be single and unattached. There must be no large clan lurking in the background to raise a stink when he or she is missed. Preferably an outlander—like your daddy." The sneer broadened for a moment. "The victim must not be a wealthy person—we don't want to antagonise our donors, now, do we? So, my sweet, if you can find us a poor, unattached foreigner within the next eighteen days, he can take your place at the equinox sacrifice. I think that's fair, don't you?"

"Yes," Jomel whispered, every fibre of her body screaming No! A poor, unattached foreigner? How often did those come her way? Never! There was another warm trickle. She was dead meat.

"But—" Dhelgor continued remorselessly. "For daring to invade a Mindbender's mind, your death sentence is not lifted. If you find a sacrifice for the autumn equinox, you will have to find another for the winter solstice. Then another for the spring equinox. And so on. Do I make myself clear?"

"Yes," Jomel whispered.

"Then get up and wash your stink off my bedclothes before you leave."

* * *

Jomel tried to slink unobserved into the temple that evening, but Sarmion was waiting for her. There was a malicious grin on his face as he cornered her in the entrance hall. The acolytes Chand and Guriet were lurking nearby, along with several adherents.

"So, the great Jomel returns!" he crowed. "The all-powerful devotee who thought she could mindread a Mindbender!" There were sniggers from the acolytes. The adherents stared in shock.

Sarmion took a step closer and thrust his spite-twisted face into hers. "*And* who thought she could manipulate *me!* Did you really think I was such a gullible fool? You arrogant, stuck-up little tart! I knew what you were up to all along. Did you think you mesmerised me into setting you up with Dhelgor? No! *I* put the idea of Dhelgor into your pathetic, grasping little mind, because he asked me to. And I saw your fumbling attempts to mindread and mesmerise me. But it's *you* who've been manipulated, you power-hungry whore!"

He turned to the onlookers, who now included almost the entire temple staff. Jomel cowered against a wall, wanting to die. "Let this be a lesson to you all!" Sarmion thundered. "Do—not—*ever*—try to pit your feeble wits against an Initiate! Yes, even me! I may appear a bumbling fool, but *I am an Initiate of Gadesh!* I was aware of Jomel's suppurating ambition from the start, and knew it would be her undoing. Dhelgor wanted her. So, I encouraged him, and I encouraged Jomel to think I was a doting idiot who would eat out of her hand. See the consequences!" He flung out an arm, pointing at Jomel. She cringed, her breath coming in short gasps. Her world was falling apart.

"She blew it, as I knew she would. I even warned Dhelgor, but he pooh-poohed the idea that a devotee would try and manipulate a Mindbender. Yet that is exactly what this stupid bitch did!

"So-o-o." He turned back to her, his voice dripping with vicious gloating. "Now our dear exalted Jomel will be a most beautiful and heart-wrenching sacrifice at the equinox festival." There was a general gasp from the onlookers. "Yes! That will be her fitting reward. After all, Jomel my dear, you did give your body and soul to the god, didn't you? Now he will get them a little sooner, that's all." His smile was sickening.

A flicker of pride stirred in Jomel. "Not if I can find another victim before then!" Was that hoarse croak her own voice?

"Oh, yes, to be sure." Sarmion laughed, and the others joined in, appreciating the joke. "And we all know how likely *that* is! Dream on, Jomel, my sweet. We shall watch your future progress with considerable interest."

There was another general guffaw as Sarmion turned and waddled off to his private apartment.

Chand and Guriet bore down on her, their faces glowing with malice, but Jomel fled to her cubicle and locked the door.

She sank on to the bed and buried her face in her hands. This disaster was so great, so all-encompassing, that she was beyond weeping. She knew she couldn't flee—you can't escape the Cult of Gadesh. With Initiates distance-speaking one another, she'd be caught and sent back wherever she went. She was done for—unless she could find an alternative victim. And that was all but impossible.

But she wouldn't just curl up and die. She'd go down fighting. A simple prayer from her Lightist schooldays arose unbidden in her mind — *Creator God, have mercy on me!*

Meanwhile she would spend every ounce of energy she had, every minute of her free time, scouring the streets of Stillárre for a single, unattached down-and-out who could take her place.

Map 4:
Finding Ganneret's House

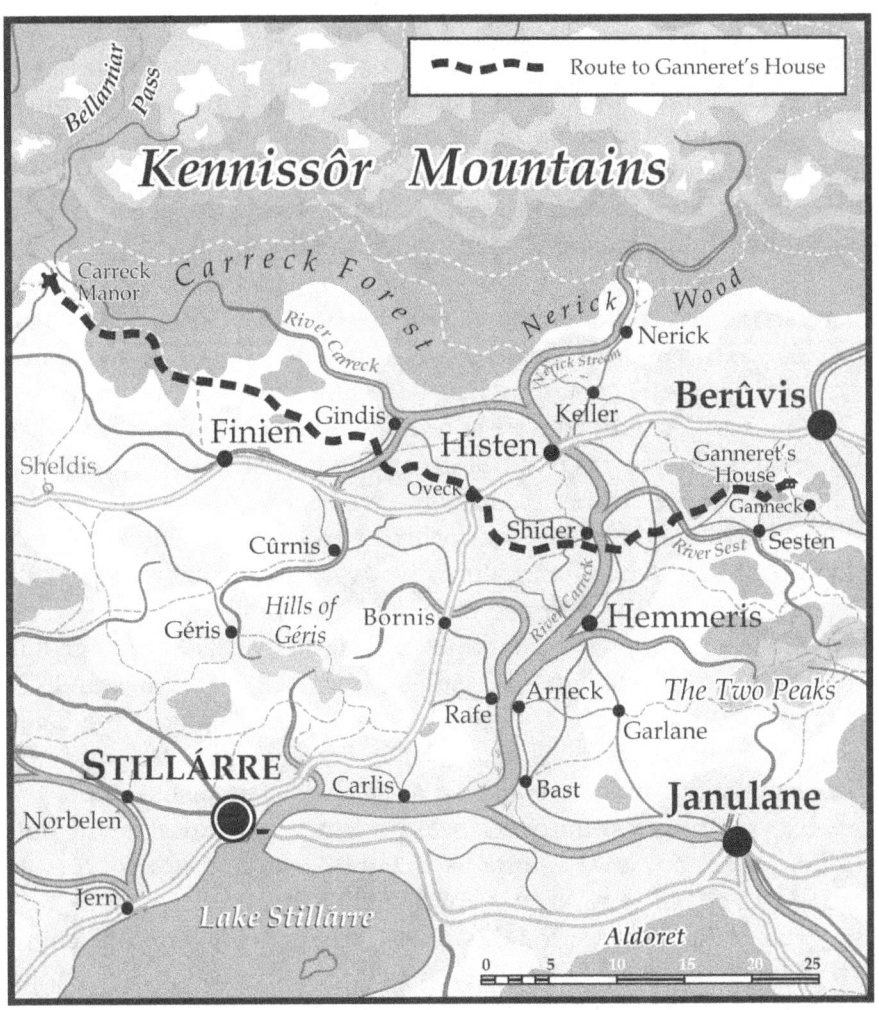

Chapter 17: *Noble welcome*

LANNIE TRUDGED WEARILY up the long hill. It was a cold, misty Saturday evening, and the lights of the house up above beckoned like the finishing tape in a gruelling cross-country marathon. It belonged to Lord Ganneret—a 'Land Elder', whatever that was; Shivvie said it sounded like a 'Duke' or 'Baron'. At any rate, a Lightist of noble birth who Fira told them might be sympathetic to their cause. He would also be certain to have heard if Gil had been arrested anywhere in the vicinity of Berûvis, the nearby town.

Lannie stumbled over a stone embedded in the darkened path, and trooper Tornoret put out a hand to steady her. The Dûrians had cats' eyes. How could she ever have imagined she could make this trip on her own? Yesterday had been like something out of a bad spy movie. They'd taken most of the day to travel about ten miles through farmland to Oveck, slipping from copse to copse, crawling along drainage ditches, scuttling with heads bent beside hedgerows. Then they'd had to wait behind a haystack, shivering in their damp clothes, while Fira found friends to take them in. A plate of thinned gruel and a cramped night had followed.

But this morning the true value of Fira's network had emerged. A large crowd of villagers had gathered outside the cottage and accompanied their party with much laughter and joking to the fields south of the village. This had got them safely across that amazing six-lane highway that stretched east and west just beyond the houses, with its fast traffic in the centre and slow traffic on the outside, pulled by those enormous shaggy oxen. *Grûnet*, the Dûrians called them. She'd never seen anything like them.

Today they had forded the River Carreck, following little country lanes; and now at last they were approaching the welcoming lights of their first safe haven since Carreck Manor.

As they drew nearer the dim outlines of a large house took shape around the misty glow of the lamplit windows. It stood high, but seemed to have only a single storey, and the walls stretched a long way in each direction. Fira led them through a well-manicured garden to an imposing door atop a wide flight of steps.

She reached for an upright prong in a hand-sized recess beside the door and plucked it. After a while they heard footsteps and the door opened. A short, pudgy figure stood silhouetted against the lamplight.

"Holy Flame, what have we here?" asked a high-pitched man's voice.

"Seven followers of the Light needing hospitality. Will you tell your master?"

"Well, I'll *tell* him. Yes, I'll *tell* him all right. Wait here." The door closed, and Lannie's heart sank.

They waited. "This Lord Ganneret," Lannie asked Fira. "You say he's sympathetic. Surely he wouldn't send us away?"

Fira sniffed. Her narrow, hawk-like face reflected scepticism in the lamplight. "We'll see," she said. "He's a good Lightist, treats his people well, but he didn't support the Rebellion."

Shîrin leaned towards her with an impish grin. "He made weapons for the other side," he murmured.

Lannie frowned. "How can he be a good Lightist if he works for the Bishop?"

Fira scowled at Shere. "He does *not* work for the Bishop. He owns an armoury. He sold weapons and armour openly to the Bishop and secretly to us."

The door suddenly opened again, and the short silhouette made way for a larger one. There was a moment of silence as the two parties assessed one another's *shiláyet*, their unseen auras. This was normal, Lannie had found. Then the tall silhouette spoke in a pleasant baritone voice.

"*Neylas.* Welcome to our home, friends. Do come in." Lannie heaved a sigh of relief.

They were ushered into a beautifully-appointed reception room. Lannie had a sudden flashback to the charred remains of elegance they'd glimpsed at Carreck Manor. This was the original. There was a thick felt floor-covering in dark burgundy, and cloth hangings on the white walls with intricate geometrical patterns in a matching burgundy and gold. Interspersed between the hangings were mirrors, bowls overflowing with dark red and ochre flowers, and, along the outer wall, windows of golden stained glass. In the centre of the room was a low circular table of pale wood surrounded by a number of chaise longues covered in what looked like dark burgundy leather.

Filling the whole room with a soft white light were four tall wooden stands from which many smaller branches curved gracefully upwards, a small lamp hanging from each branch. The lamps were the same shape as those they'd used at the Manor, but these were made of gleaming golden metal engraved with delicate filigree patterns.

Shiván summed up Lannie's reactions with a slow, murmured "Wow."

Their host gave them a quizzical look. "Do sit down," he said. He was fairly tall, dressed in a plain ochre robe bound at the waist with a cloth-of-gold cord. His brown hair had silvery highlights, and his complexion was somewhat paler than the average olive-skinned Dûrian. There was a slightly different inflection to his vowels. Cârin leaned towards Lannie and whispered, "Nobleman". She smiled.

They all perched on the edges of the chairs in their travel-stained garments. Lannie was revelling in the warmth of the house. It rose up from the floor and soaked through her clothes. This really felt like being back in civilisation again. Now if they had hot baths as well…

Their host must have heard her thoughts. He muttered something to the pudgy servant, who hurried off, throwing them all a horrified glance.

"I see that you are followers of the Light," Lord Ganneret said, "and you have clearly travelled rough to get here. Perhaps before meeting the rest of the family, you would like to wash off your travel-stains…?" His enquiring gaze was particularly focused on Lannie and Fira.

"That would be wonderful!" Lannie said, delight colouring her voice. There was a dutiful buzz of thanks from the men. She glanced at Fira, and was amazed to see her face suffused with a dark flush.

"My lord is too good," she muttered, and dropped her eyes. My gosh, that's a first! Lannie thought. It took a Dûrian nobleman to embarrass Fira.

"Not at all," his lordship said. "Here in the Manor of Sesten we give equal courtesy to all. My butler Harn will show you to the baths, and to the reclining room when you are finished." He left with a graceful nod and smile.

Fira shook her head. "I was wrong about him," she said. "He's one of the best."

Shiván stared at her with a puzzled smile. "What, just because he offered us a bath?"

"*Exactly* because he offered us a bath! You don't think Barons normally offer baths to peasants, do you?"

"Well, not to all peasants, maybe, but to special ones like us…"

The four troopers sniggered.

"It's no laughing matter," Fira snapped. "If your families had suffered half of what mine has from the pigs Shambor appointed as Land Elders, you'd appreciate this, believe me."

"So, this was a change Shambor made?" Shiván asked. "Things weren't like that before?"

"No, of course not! Shambor demoted all the village Elders and replaced them with these new *Land* Elders ruling large areas — the old baronies. We were producing more than enough food, there were no clan members starving, then *pah!* — just like that — the Land Elders started taking it all. If you want to know why I joined the Rebellion, *that's* why. Now do you understand why I appreciate being offered a bath by Lord Ganneret?"

"Um, yes, I believe I do."

They chatted for a while longer; then Butler Harn reappeared. He held out an arm to summon them, hand opening and closing. "Come this way." They followed the short, strutting figure down several passages until they reached a couple of open doorways from which wisps of steam were gently curling. Lannie's heart leapt. Hot water!

The fact that she had to share a huge, sunken tub with Fira — it was more like a small swimming pool — did nothing to lessen the sheer delight of that first bath since arriving in Dûrion. There was a flask at the side containing what Fira called 'fern oil'. She showed Lannie how to pour a little in her hand and rub it on her wet skin, where it foamed and gave off a fresh, woodland scent. Lannie soaked and rubbed and felt she was washing off seven weeks of grime and manual labour.

Sounds of splashing and raucous singing from up the passage told them the men were enjoying themselves.

Thick ochre towels and piles of clothing had been laid out on a couple of the wooden benches that surrounded the bath. There were six different sets of blouses and culottes (to Lannie's amazement), together with matching tunics, scarves, undergarments and shoes. Making their choices took some time, but finally Lannie had dressed herself in shades of pastel green, while Fira was tastefully arrayed in light and dark blue. It was startling how much more feminine she suddenly looked.

When they finally returned to the reception hall, butler Harn was tapping an impatient foot. The men were there already, looking resplendent—Shiván in a burgundy tunic and breeches, Fiminor in dark green, Tornoret in black velvet, and Shîrin and Cârin in matching outfits of russet brown and ochre. Harn told them brusquely to hurry along because Lord Ganneret was waiting. He led them down another passage to where his master stood beside a curtained archway.

The Land Elder smiled appreciatively as they approached, waving aside their thanks. He led them through the archway and they found themselves in a large, cheerful room. It had the reverse colour scheme to the entrance hall: a rich, golden ochre was the dominant colour, set off by burgundy. There were two fireplaces, one of them with a roaring blaze. Facing the flames was a semicircle of chaise longues, and others were scattered about between small tables and numerous 'light trees' like the ones in the hall.

"My dear, we have visitors," their host announced. Four figures rose up from the chaise longues around the fire: an older woman, a young man, a young woman, and a boy in his early teens. There was the usual moment of silence while the two groups assessed each other. Lannie observed with interest that the older woman's already rather mournful face lengthened further—obviously none too happy about having rebels in her home. The young man regarded them with bored indifference; and the boy's interest quickly faded.

But it was the daughter of the house—a girl of around eighteen—who caught her attention. She was about her own height, and it occurred to Lannie that it was probably her clothes she was wearing. What struck her, though, was that the girl zeroed in on herself and Shiván, and the sight of them seemed to fill her with delight. Her eyes sparkled, colour rose in her cheeks, and a joyful smile spread over her face. Good heavens, who did she think they were?

Lord Ganneret started making the introductions. "This is my wife, Nelláy. My dear, please welcome five soldiers of the Light who have made their way here with difficulty, I am sure..." The long-faced lady rather gingerly gave each of them the raised handshake.

"Lieutenant Fira en Tarrel of Histen, my lady."

"Trooper Fiminor dom Merion of Cûrnis."

"Trooper Tornoret don Hollet of Finien, your ladyship."

"Trooper Shîrinor don Danneret of Mesten, at your service."

"Cârinor don Danneret likewise."

A faint smile lessened the gloom on her ladyship's face. "I can see that you and Shîrinor are very 'likewise', Trooper."

"Um, beg your pardon, my lady, but I'm likewise. He's other-wise."

"Anyone would be otherwise to *you*, you dimwit." Shîrin shot a disgusted look at his twin. "But I'm likewise to everyone else." He smiled brightly at their hostess.

"Ah, a pair of wits, I see. You are welcome in our home."

"Then we have two strangers, who I'm sure will be telling us more about themselves in due course," Lord Ganneret said. Nelláy focused on Lannie, and her cheeks seemed to lose some of their colour. Lannie tried to be as normal as possible.

"*Neylas*. I'm Alanya."

"Alanya... ?"

Cârin nudged her. "Your mother's name," he said in a stage whisper.

"My *mother's*...? Oh, er, Brenda."

There was an expectant silence, broken by another whisper. "Where you're from."

"Oh. England." Why hadn't she been warned of all this formality? She felt like an ignorant peasant.

Her ladyship gave a nervous smile along with the raised handshake. "Welcome, Alanya em Brenda of Inglan."

Shivvie had been picking up a few tips. "Shiván em Fiona of England, at your service," he declared with a grin. It was wiped out by the roar of laughter that followed.

"What did I say?" he demanded.

Cârin was rocking with mirth, but he managed to gasp out, "Shiván, daughter of Fîyona! You give your *father's* name, not your mother's."

"Oh! Flippin' heck. Shiván em Bernard, then." There was another gale of laughter.

147

"Shiván *dom* Bernet of Inglan, you are welcome," Lady Nelláy said with a taut smile as she raised his arm.

Larion, the older son, gave each of them a perfunctory handshake before slouching off. The boy Barlet got the formalities behind him as quickly as his father's eagle eye would allow.

"And this is my daughter, Perrely."

The attractive fair-haired girl greeted the rebel soldiers warmly, but there was an excitement in her eyes when she came to Lannie and Shiván.

"Alanya." There was no attempt at the full name. "I'm so glad to see you. Welcome!"

Perrely turned to Shiván, and looked at him for a long moment. "Shiván." He smiled, and her colour deepened. Uh oh, Lannie thought. Watch that grin of yours, Shivvie boy. Perrely took his hand and raised it. "Welcome."

She turned back to Lannie. "Is it just the two of you here from Inglan?" she asked.

"No, there are four of us —" Perrely's eyes widened. " — But one is travelling alone — we are hoping to catch him up — and the other stayed behind at —"

"My Lord," Fira interrupted, "maybe we could explain our situation to you as soon as we are, ah, settled." Her eyes went significantly from Ganneret to a group of servants in the room, who were rearranging the furniture. When her glance struck Lannie it was blistering. Oh brother, she thought in dismay. I nearly blurted it all out in front of the staff.

"Of course," his lordship said. "Do find yourselves a chair." He waved an arm at the chaise longues, then murmured to the servants. They left, followed by Larion and Barlet. Everyone else settled themselves on chaise longues facing the fire. At the head of each recliner was a built-in receptacle on which stood a steaming porcelain cup of chass.

"So, what brings five rebel soldiers and two strangers to the Manor of Sesten?" Lord Ganneret asked when all were settled. His eyes, slightly narrowed, were resting on Lannie. She glanced at Fira, but everyone was looking at her. Oh, great. Something in their joint shiláy must have identified her as the leader.

"Well, as I said, there are four of us from England, but one has already left for Darthane, and one stayed behind. Have you heard of a stranger like us travelling through this area? His name is Gelmion."

"No, I have not. But are you saying he was travelling alone?"

"Er, yes. There was a, er, mistake. He left us and set off on his own. We are anxious about him."

"So you should be. That was a foolhardy thing to do."

There was a frown on Ganneret's face, but a smile on Perrely's. Lannie wondered if the girl was a little simple.

"I will make enquiries about your friend," Ganneret said. "But it would help to know where he was travelling from and how long ago he set out."

Lannie glanced at Fira, who gave a very slight nod. "He left Carreck Manor three nights ago. We ourselves set out the next morning. That's, um, Tharderil—the day before yesterday."

"Carreck Manor!" Lady Nelláy exclaimed. "I thought that was burnt down at the end of the Rebellion."

"Yes, it was, but the basement was not damaged. We've been living there."

"How many of you?" Ganneret asked.

"About fifty."

"Well, well." The Land Elder smiled. "That explains why Shambor found so few survivors. I'm glad you thought of coming to us, and that you've honoured us with your confidence. Rest assured, we shall respect it. But, tell me. Where is this place 'Inglan' that you foreigners are from? I have not heard of it."

Lannie glanced at Shiván. This was the moment of truth. It needed his command of the language.

Shivvie cleared his throat. "Our country is very far removed from Dûrion, my lord. Only this week we saw your sky at night for the first time—and all the stars were different. I believe our shiláy confirms this."

Ganneret nodded, frowning. "Your shiláyet are... extremely strange. I have never come across any like them before."

"'Strangers and loners'," Perrely quoted, her eyes bright. Lady Nelláy gasped. "*Perrely!*"

Lord Ganneret glanced sharply at his daughter before turning back to Shiván. "How did you get here if you are from so far away?"

Shiván shrugged. "We don't know, my lord. Each of us just... woke up one morning in Carreck Forest. We arrived at different times, but all within a few days of the end of the Rebellion."

Ganneret's eyes were narrowed, a doubtful frown on his face. Perrely's smile only widened. Lannie revised her opinion of the girl. She was way ahead of her parents.

"Are you suggesting, then," Lord Ganneret asked slowly, "that *you* are the true Restorers of the Way?"

"Ganneret—!" his wife exclaimed, sitting up on her recliner.

"It's all right, Nelláy. Whoever these folk are, they are not liars or deceivers. They sincerely believe what they are saying. We will hear them out. Shiván?"

"My lord, we believe we may be the *Atenámbaret* prophesied in your Book. We didn't desire this for ourselves. We didn't choose to come to Dûrion. The One brought us here. We think that must have been the reason."

Ganneret scanned the faces of the five rebel soldiers. He addressed Fira. "Do you and your men accept this, Lieutenant? Not long ago you were fighting for Armanet and Dôrion."

Fira looked uncomfortable. "I am... keeping an open mind, my lord. For a long time I did *not* believe this. But many of our group at Carreck Manor were convinced by the evidence."

"What evidence?"

"Their shiláyet, as you have noticed. Their apparently miraculous arrival. Their genuine shock at seeing our different sky. And the... 'instruments' they found in the basement of Carreck Manor: a bellaril, a shell, and a blaise. Some said, 'the Strings of Truth, the Shell of Hearing, the Glass of Seeing'."

"The Hearth does not accept any connection between that prophecy and the Restorers."

"The Hearth accepts Shambor as their Bishop," Fira shot back.

Ganneret smiled. "True. And the rest of you soldiers? Do you accept the strangers' claim?"

The four shuffled and glanced at one another. Finally Tornoret said, "I have an open mind, like the lieutenant." The others nodded. "Open mind," Cârin repeated brightly.

The Land Elder turned to Shiván and Lannie with raised eyebrows. "It seems your own escorts are not fully convinced of your claim. How do you expect to gain widespread support?"

Shiván shrugged. "We don't expect anything at the moment, my lord. We're only making the present trip to —"

Ganneret stopped him with a raised hand. He looked at Lannie. "Let the leader speak."

Taken by surprise, Lannie found herself stammering a bit. "Yes, well, we just wanted to try and find Gelmion, and also to find out about that, er, rod thing — What was it, Shivvie?"

"The Ambon of Sûrilane."

"Right. That... er... thing."

Ganneret had a quizzical smile. "That 'thing', Alanya, is possibly the most important evidence for your claim — and it seems you don't have it."

"We know we're meant to have it," Shiván said, "because of that prophecy about the 'Rod of Truth'..."

"Which definitely refers to the Restorers," Lord Ganneret added.

"Yes. So we wanted to find out about the Ambon of Sûrilane on this trip."

"What do you know about it?" Perrely asked, her smile replaced by a faint frown.

"Not much. We didn't even know what an ambon was until we saw those circle-and-rod emblems on the Hearth buildings as we came here. I suppose Sûrilane is the place where this particular ambon was kept? They said it wasn't there any more."

"No. It disappeared a couple of centuries ago."

Lannie's eyebrows shot up. "Then how are we meant to have it?"

"We'll find it," Perrely said. "I don't know how, but —"

Lady Nelláy's anguished *"Perrely!"* clashed with her husband's stern, *"'We,'* young lady?"

Perrely's hand flew to her mouth. "Oh! I didn't mean —"

Lord Ganneret's eyes were hard. "Perrely, let's get one thing clear. You are *not* going with these people. Whatever their purpose may be, it is not yours."

"But Father, the One has given me a vision —"

"Enough!"

Perrely's eyes filled with tears. She jumped up and ran from the room. Lady Nelláy hurried after her.

Ganneret heaved a deep sigh. "Overlook it, please. She's going through a difficult phase."

Chapter 18: *Death on the highway*

DANÎSHA FIRST HEARD THE WAILS as she was about to sit down for the daymeal. Everyone in the kitchen froze. Then two troopers appeared at the top of the stairs. They were supporting someone between them, a woman, whose pain-laden keening swept through the kitchen like a bitter wind.

Ennel! Danîsha dumped her plate and ran, as did Veynel and several other women. The poor girl was dirty and dishevelled, her face streaked with tears. She was trembling all over as they helped her to a bench. Danîsha sat and held her on one side, Veynel on the other. The whole community clustered round.

They got some chass into her, and slowly the wails subsided into gasping sobs. Many hands were touching her, gentle voices murmuring "Ennel", "Ennel".

Danîsha's heart was filled with foreboding. Just that morning they'd said sad farewells to Margay, Frem and Denny, along with Ennel and Lannie's roommate, the young widow Mery and her two boys. They were returning to their kinsfolk in the Géris area — the first group to follow Fira's instruction to leave the Manor. They had carefully chosen a route to avoid towns and villages.

Ennel's story came out incoherently between sobs. It was only later with Veynel and Damion's help that Danîsha managed to get the overall picture. She sat now drinking a final cup of *chass* trying to digest it all, with Teynel snuggled up against her. Thank God Teynel had chosen to stay with her substitute granny! She gently stroked the girl's shoulder.

The kitchen was almost empty; Ennel had been tended and cleaned and tucked up in bed with a sleeping draught. As far as Danîsha understood her story, the group had reached the point where they needed to cross the main road that went to Finien. Ennel had gone across first when there was a gap between groups of walkers, slipping into a small copse to wait for the others. Then Mery and her children had crossed, closely followed by Frem, Margay and Denny — who had dodged behind a group of five cloaked men walking along the road. They had just been approaching the copse when there was a shout, and the five men had hurried over to them. Ennel had heard and seen everything from the shelter of the trees.

Two of the men were evidently informers for a Mindbender, and they had recognised the group's *shiláy*, their aura, as that of rebels against the Bishop. The men began questioning Frem and Margay.

Danîsha shivered as she remembered the utter silence that had fallen on the Manor community at those words. Was this the end for them all? And not through Gelmion, as everyone had feared, but through their own Frem and Margay?

But Ennel had gone on to say that those dear people had not uttered a word about the community sheltering under the burnt-out Manor. They'd admitted that they'd been with the rebels in Carreck Manor before it was destroyed, and that they'd escaped into Carreck Forest. When asked if there were others with them, they'd replied that they'd lived with a group of refugees for a while, but that all were now trying to return to their kin.

The informers seemed to accept this, but had ordered Frem, Margay and the others to accompany them to Finien. Danîsha heaved a deep sigh as she recalled what had followed. Shiván, Shiván, what possessed you to start teaching Denny your martial arts? Seeing his family threatened, Denny had decided to play the hero. He'd kicked one of the informers in the stomach and lashed out at the other with his hand — before discovering that their three companions had drawn swords. Even then the foolish boy hadn't stopped — he'd tried to kick the sword out of one of his attacker's hands. Unfortunately he'd kicked the sword itself. He'd gone down, and the three had quickly finished him off.

Oh, Denny. Again Danîsha found tears trickling down her face, and she impatiently brushed them away. So young, so full of life; and now dead.

Ennel, horror-struck, had choked back her screams as she watched Denny being killed only a few yards from her hiding place. But Mery's little ones must have been making enough noise to cover any sound of hers.

They'd left Denny lying on the road, groaning and bleeding his life away, and marched Frem, Margay, Mery and her children down the road towards Finien.

When they were out of sight Ennel had dragged Denny's body into the copse and, trembling with shock and terror, had dug a shallow grave for him with her hands in some soft soil. A fresh outburst of weeping had followed before she could tell them how she'd pulled his body there, covered it over, and sobbed out a prayer to the One Creator God. Then she'd somehow managed to cross the road and stumble home to the Manor.

Danîsha heaved a deep sigh.

Well, from tonight the Manor was both home and prison. A haven they couldn't leave. Their new leader, Sergeant Borion — an older man, gruff but fair — had announced bluntly that all other travel plans were suspended. The lookout points Fira had set up were to be manned day and night: the troopers were down to five hours' sleep. Work outside the basement was reduced to bare essentials, only to be undertaken when the all-clear had been given.

Teynel whimpered, and Danîsha tightened her arm around the doubly-bereaved child. She would defend this innocent waif to her last breath.

* * *

"And thus, my friends, I invite you to restore your hearts at the wellspring of the One's great goodness. He has opened the way —"

"Mindruler."

The Bishop's rolling phrases continued, but a separate compartment of his mind registered annoyance. What was Dhelgor doing, distance-speaking him now? In the middle of dawn hearthtime at the Cathedral?

"Mindbender of Stillárre, make it quick."

"My apologies, but you asked to be informed if more rebels were caught." Shambor felt a sudden glow of pleasure. More rebels in the net? Yes, that was worth the interruption.

"I will mindspeak you in a moment. Wait."

The Bishop brought his remarks to an early close. There might be some disappointment among the worshippers, but he only undertook these ecclesiastical duties for the sake of appearances. A few of those crowding the great circular sanctuary of Darthane Cathedral — the High Hearth — would be regular attendees; but the majority were visitors who had come to see him, the head of Hearth and State, and to gawk at the vast, beautifully appointed edifice.

Mind you, it was worth gawking at. Majestic columns rose to support the central dome, the ceiling of which glowed with an intricate geometric design in red, blue, gold and silver. The delicate lines and arcs constantly recreated the ambon, the symbol of the Lightist religion. Scores of light trees hung suspended with little lamps on the end of every branch, illuminating both the sanctuary and its magnificent roof.

Then there were the wide circular windows, filled with coloured glass repeating the ambon motif. Everywhere was the glitter of gold and silver among the rich reds and blues of the furnishings. And at the focus of the semi-circular ranks of chairs stood the raised 'empty altar', with a gem-encrusted ambon high on the plain white wall behind it.

Well, he himself preferred an altar that was used for its original purpose. But if all these glittering baubles kept the people happy for now, so much the better. Little did they realise that one day, not far off, this monument of oppressive Lightist dogma would at last be put to its proper use — the worship of Worldruler Gadesh.

Shambor stepped down from the lectern below the altar, and made an impressive, slow progress in his flowing blue-and-silver robe to the Bishop's Chair at the side, where he turned and sat facing the congregation. The Kindler-Director came fussing up to take his place at the lectern, his russet vestments flapping. He lifted his hands, and the choir in the gallery burst into song. The congregation joined in sporadically.

Finally at leisure to pay attention to Dhelgor, Shambor mindspoke him. "Yes, Mindbender." He could see that Dhelgor was at ease in his luxurious apartment adjoining the Stillárre Guardhouse — with a pretty girl on his lap. Lucky fellow.

"*A group of rebel sympathisers have been caught by my informers near Finien, Mindruler, and I —*"

"*Rebel* sympathisers? *It's rebel soldiers I'm after, you dolt! Have you interrupted my hearthtime just to tell me about a few backward peasants?*"

"*No, Mindruler. I remembered your desire to teach the people of Berûvis a lesson — after their insolence in offering allegiance to Armanet. I thought perhaps —*"

"*Ah. Yes, that is a thought. We're out of plausible local victims. Who are these people?*"

"*Three adults and two children whom my informers detected crossing the Carreckis to Finien road. There was a fourth adult, a young man who tried to fight my men with his bare hands and feet. He was left dead at the roadside. We have learnt that there were a number of small groups like this—refugees from Carreckis and other destroyed villages—who were with the rebels. They escaped just before Carreck Manor was destroyed. They have been living rough in the forest, but are now seeking refuge with kinsfolk. I have doubled my patrols in the area.*"

"*Good. Yes, this sounds promising, Dhelgor.*" Shambor made a mental note to reward him for his forethought. "*And they're just peasants, you say? No rebel troops among them?*"

"*Just ordinary villagers, your Dominance.*"

"*Where were they heading?*"

"*For Géris, Mindruler. At first they wouldn't say, but a little persuasion was applied via the children.*"

"*Right. You will ensure their clansfolk in Géris learn the consequences of failing to report rebel sympathisers?*"

"*Already in hand, Mindruler.*"

"*You have done well.*"

"*Thank you, your Dominance.*"

Another quick mind-contact, and all was arranged. Legate Yonistor of the army garrison in Finien would organise immediate transport for the prisoners to Berûvis. It was market day there tomorrow—ideal for the executions. Yonistor would also triple his patrols in Carreck Forest. Between his patrols and Dhelgor's informers, the remaining sympathisers would soon be rounded up.

The songs were ended, and Shambor made his stately way back to the lectern to pronounce the benediction.

"Now, dear brothers and sisters," he intoned, solemnly raising a hand on high, "may the Light, Joy and Peace of the One Creator God enfold and fill you, and move you to deeds of love toward both friend and foe. Amen."

Map 5:
Gil's Wanderings

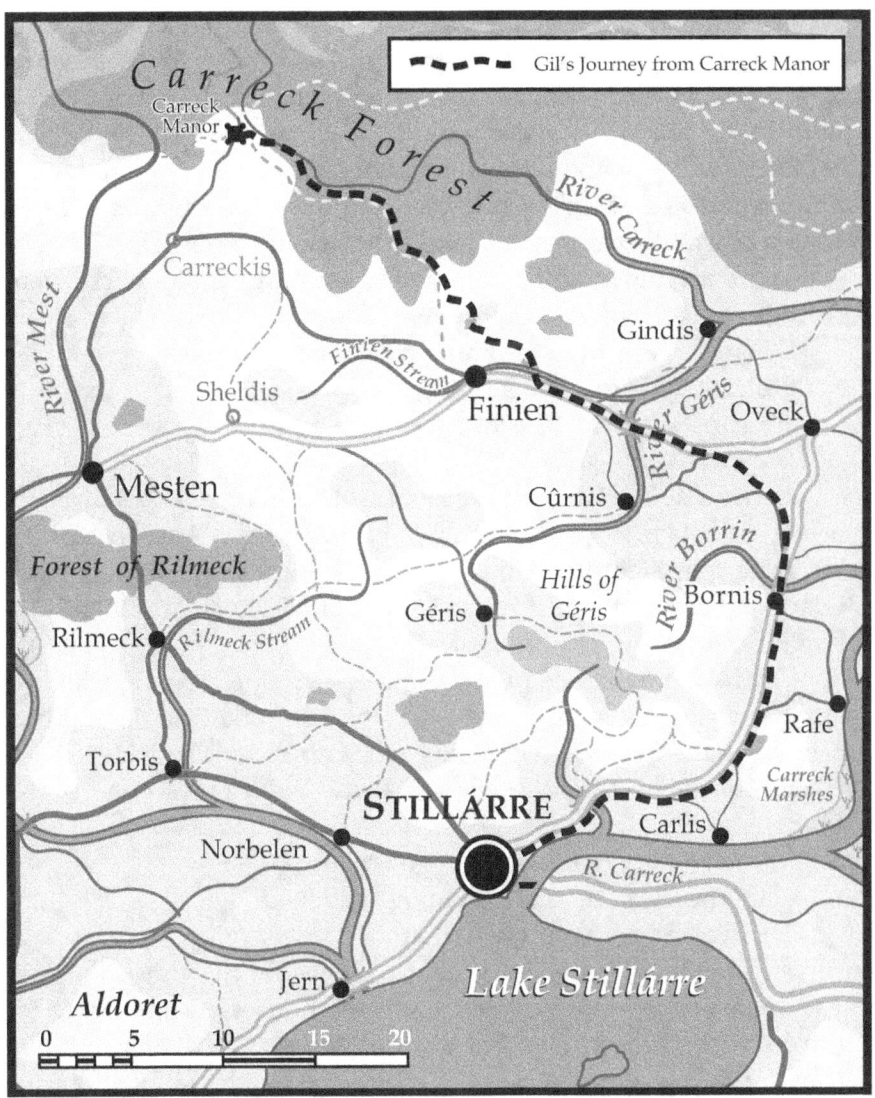

Chapter 19: *Victim found*

GIL PLODDED SLOWLY up the rise. They'd been walking for about seven hours solid. After a broken night at that wretched inn, he could scarcely put one foot in front of the other. His back ached from the rock-hard bed, his feet were blistered, and there was a dull throb behind his eyebrows. My gosh, what he'd give for his comfortable BMW and a six-lane motorway!

They crested the rise and there in the distance was a large walled city on the shores of a lake. "Darthane!" he exclaimed.

Papa Durónne looked at him with a sardonic smile. There were faint grins on the other lemons' faces.

"Stillárre," he said in his gravelly voice.

"Stillárre?" Gil queried stupidly.

The grins widened. The joke was on him.

"But I think you go Darthane!"

There was open laughter now. Gil seethed with helpless fury. So, he'd been taken, not for a ride (which might have been bearable), but for a long, foot-breaking walk to the wrong destination. God, what he'd say to them if he had the words! He swore fluently in English, provoking more laughter.

Why hadn't he noticed the change in direction? When he looked at the sun now he realised they were heading south-west, and had been for some time. He could only put it down to lack of sleep.

Durónne said, "Stillárre is a large city. You can also find scholars here."

"But why you not tell me you go Stillárre?"

Again the sardonic smile. "You never asked."

There wasn't much to say to that.

They plodded on, and Gil kept his eyes on the city up ahead. The yellowstone wall snaked around the houses, disappearing towards green fields in the west. To their left a wide river wound its way to the city, flowing into the lake right beside the wall on this side. He could make out a wharf with a number of ships tied up to it. The lake was a large one, stretching to the horizon; but clearly not a sea: no breakers along the shoreline.

After another hour of weary trudging, a massive gatehouse loomed before them. Gil estimated the well-fitted stone wall on either side must be twenty-four or twenty-five feet high. There was a solid traffic jam in all lanes. It took them a quarter of an hour to reach the gatehouse and shuffle their way through the twenty-foot-deep tunnel under the walls. Heavy metal-bound gates flanked the sides of the tunnel at the outer entrance.

Eventually they were through and into the city. Tall yellow-stone houses lined the street, with high wooden doors and narrow windows. There were paved pedestrian walkways on both sides. Near the gate these were occupied by dozens of little stalls where hawkers sold everything from wine flasks to shoes.

Blast those lemons! This might be a city, but it wasn't Darthane. He dismissed Durónne's vague mention of 'scholars'. Shiván had said there was only one university, and that was in Darthane. Now he'd have to find another group to take him.

He'd stick with the lemons for tonight, though; hopefully they'd fork out for another bed in an inn. He didn't care how many he shared it with; he'd sleep like the dead.

They walked on until the road opened out into a wide, well-paved square. Various imposing buildings fronted on it, so he assumed this must be the city centre. All around it were poles from which clusters of little lamps hung, and workers were right now climbing ladders and lighting them.

The lemons entered a large inn, and before long Gil was eating ravenously. There were actual lumps of meat in the stew! He hadn't tasted meat since arriving in Dûrion. That made him think of Lannie and her relief that the Manor community were vegetarians. The old ache resurfaced.

As they were finishing their meal sounds of revelry began to float in from the square. There was music with a rhythmic beat—unlike the cloying sweetness of the Lightist songs—along with laughter, shouts, clapping, and the stamp of feet in time to the rhythm.

"Our people celebrate tonight, Gelmion. Do you wish to join us?" Durónne said.

Suddenly that was just what Gil wanted to do: to let his hair down and enjoy himself. He didn't know who "our people" were, but their kind of celebration was exactly what he needed right now. The only thing was, his feet were covered in blisters and he could hardly walk.

"I watch!" he declared.

The lemons all smiled their secretive smiles again as though the joke were on him; but that was their way. Now he wanted to be friends with everyone.

Soon he was sitting at a table out in the square where a vigorous folk dance was in progress, to the accompaniment of flutes, drums and smaller versions of Danîsha's bellaril. The imposing marble portico of one of the buildings was lit up and decorated—presumably the headquarters of "our people". Attendants were placing flasks of wine on the tables. Gil grabbed one and swallowed deeply. Near him a row of men were prancing to and fro. Opposite was a line of pretty girls. Just what the doctor ordered.

* * *

Jomel stood in the temple portico looking wanly out at the celebration. They had these once a month to attract adherents. She supposed she'd have to go out there and do her bit, or the others would tattle to Sarmion. She should also continue her hunt for a substitute victim to take her place at the equinox festival; but two days of scouring the streets of Stillárre had left her discouraged and deeply weary.

All the seemingly homeless beggars she'd spoken to had local clansfolk who'd rejected them—but who would be up in arms if they simply disappeared. Probably some of their kin were still secretly helping them. That was the way the Dûrian clan system worked. The spaced-out 'stinkies' she'd found propped against walls were all locally known, and some of them were even prominent socialites from the best families when they weren't high on the drug teméyn. Which her own Cult of Gadesh provided, she thought with disgust.

How did the temple *ever* find victims for their quarterly human sacrifices? Well, they milked the prisons for condemned loners— which she couldn't do; and of course they had the whole mind-bending network to draw on. She knew that the poor victim at the summer solstice—the only human sacrifice she'd seen—had been brought in from elsewhere.

She shivered at the memory. *Then,* of course, it had been a high point in all the exciting new experiences she was having: that pathetic young man, screaming his lungs out until they mercifully slit his throat before carving him up. It had horrified her at the time with a kind of impersonal, delighted horror. It was amazing how your perspective changed when it was due to be *you* up there next time.

She pulled herself together with an effort and walked slowly down the broad marble steps to mingle with the crowd. She was supposed to keep her eyes open for likely prospects and entice them with her charms — or with tantalising whispers of 'personal powers'. Just as she herself had been lured into the Cult. Her heart wasn't in it.

At the bottom of the steps she was intercepted by a sour-faced man in a black tunic and grey leggings. Beside him was a tall woman in culottes. They had a travel-worn look about them.

"Ah, excuse me, Devotee," the man said in a gravelly voice. He must be an adherent to have recognised her grey tunic and white skirt.

"Yes?" she replied brusquely.

"May we speak to the priest, please?"

"The priest is busy preparing for worship. Why do you want to see him?"

The woman spoke with matching sharpness. "We have a commodity for sale. Fetch him at once."

"What is this commodity?"

"That is for the priest to hear."

Jomel looked at them scornfully. Where were they from, these arrogant adherents? Probably some district shrine where they had no idea of the proper relationship between the ranks.

"Listen," she said. "I don't know who you are, but here in Stillárre the priest is not disturbed by any and every *adherent*" — she extracted the maximum scorn from the word — "who wants to see him. Unless you tell me what he is to be disturbed *for,* I shall not do so, and neither will you."

The woman flushed darkly, but the man laid his hand on her arm.

"We have a, er, possible victim for the equinox sacrifice."

Jomel stood rooted to the spot. Did she really hear that? A long moment passed. The woman stirred impatiently. "Well, are you going to call the priest, or not?"

"I— er, yes. Yes. Just a minute. Wait right here."

She turned and hurried back up the stairs, her thoughts whirling. A possible victim! Falling into her hands just like that! A huge load rolled off her shoulders. She was free!

But wait. She couldn't hand this over to Sarmion. His hatred of her was so blatant he'd find any way to cheat her of the reprieve Dhelgor had promised. He'd hide the victim till the next sacrifice and simply not tell Dhelgor. No question of it, he wanted *her* up there on the altar. How could she bypass him?

She scurried into her cubicle to think. Money! That's what those scumbags out there were after. If she came out loaded with cash… Yes! That was it. Pretend to be acting on Sarmion's behalf, and the colour of her money would do the rest. She would lure the victim into her cubicle, and then inform Dhelgor herself. Sarmion needn't come into it at all.

With trembling hands she pulled out the little chest from under her bed, fumbled with the key, and opened it. Thank the god her patrons were lavish with their gifts! She grabbed a leather bag of jewellery and emptied it on the bed, then scrabbled in the chest and filled the bag with every coin she had. This was her life's savings, but the extravagance would impress them. She threw the jewellery back in the chest, locked it, and shoved it under the bed again. Then, tucking the bag under her tunic, she hurried out, suddenly fearful that the 'sellers' might have grown tired of waiting, or— Gadesh forbid! — have started dealing with someone else.

Relief poured over her when she saw them still standing there, the woman tapping her foot. Jomel slowed to an imperious saunter. The square was full of noise and laughter as the revelry hotted up. That was good — no one would overhear their conversation.

"Well?" the woman demanded.

"Priest Sarmion is interested. He has empowered me to deal on his behalf."

"Now, wait a minute —" The man's protest clashed with his wife's "Fiddlesticks!"

Jomel pulled out the money bag and let it jingle. "Tell me about this possible victim," she said.

Two pairs of eyes were focussed on the bag. She idly poured a little pile of gold coins into her hand. The eyes widened.

The man licked his lips. "Er, well, this foreigner joined our group on the way here, you see — " A foreigner! Oh, thank the god! " — and we know your people sometimes come searching for suitable sacrifices, so we thought — "

"Was he alone?"

"Entirely alone." The wife nodded emphatically. "He comes from far away; that's where his family is."

Jomel's eyes closed in a moment of pure bliss.

"And how will I know that what you are saying is true?"

The woman bridled. "His shiláy, of course! You can't be near him without feeling his foreignness."

"And the way he speaks," the man added. "Baby talk. He hardly knows the language."

"Right. Here's my offer. I will give you what is in my hand now. You introduce me to this foreigner, and if he's as suitable as you claim, you get the same again. Is that a deal?"

There was a moment of silence as the two looked, first at the coins in her hand, then at each other. Their thoughts were transparent. Their instinct was to bargain, but the money in her hand alone was worth a year's wages.

"Done," the man said hoarsely and held out his hand. She poured the glittering coins into it and he hurriedly stuffed them into a pocket.

"I'll show him to you." The woman actually managed a smile.

A few minutes later she was approaching an enormous fellow in a rustic robe who was sitting at a table watching the dance. His shiláy struck Jomel with an almost physical blow. *So* foreign! Not Marûvian, Thrinari, Pandian, Selmian — not even Gnarthrog. She'd never come across anyone who felt as utterly alien as this large stranger.

"Gelmion," said the woman, "this is one of our people, and she'd like to meet you." Jomel gazed yearningly into that strange, square face with its thatch of black hair. She projected her love-arousal at full strength, and was rewarded by a dawning appreciation in his eyes. Yes. This could work.

"Gelmion, my name's Jomel," she said, with just the right blend of diffidence and eagerness. "I wondered — I mean, I saw you, and I thought — could we dance together? Just you and me, I mean."

His eyes widened. "Juss' you, me? Dance? No, feet too sore. Sit!" He thumped the chair beside him. His breath smelled of wine. She sat down opposite him, in the process allowing her tunic to slip off one shoulder. His eyes became glued to that little island of bare skin. She beckoned, and an adherent refilled the wine flask.

"Where are you from, Gelmion?" she asked shyly.

"I from England," he said, his gaze switching between her face and her shoulder.

"Inglan! I don't know that country. Do you have any family?"

"No wife. Family in England." He gave her a meaningful look.

"Poor man, you seem so alone! Don't you have any friends?"

"Yes, I have friends." Uh oh.

"Are they here, with you? Can I meet them?"

"No, they not here. In Dûrion, other place." Ah.

"Are they also from Inglan?"

"Yes."

"And are they like you — all alone? Or do they have their families with them?"

"They like me. Also no family."

"Oh, how sad. How many of these friends from Inglan are with you in Dûrion?"

"Three." Three more single, unattached foreigners! She could live for a whole year.

"Will they come and join you in Stillárre, do you think?"

"Yes, maybe. I don't know." He was fidgeting impatiently. Better shelve these delightful friends for future reference. Right now Gelmion himself satisfied all Dhelgor's requirements.

There was one final test. She put out her thoughts to mindread him — but they recoiled, unable to enter. She tried again — no success. This was unheard of! She tried a third time, but the access-point simply was not there.

"You have — problem?" Gelmion was looking at her strangely.

"No! No problem. I'm just not used to being with such a big, handsome foreigner." She smiled coyly, hoping she wasn't laying it on too thick. But his brow cleared and there was a look in his eye that she knew only too well. Her victim was hooked and ready to be reeled in — as soon as the preliminaries were attended to.

"Gelmion, I'm sorry, I need to... you know? I'll be back soon."

After a moment he got it, and nodded vigorously. "I wait!"

She slipped off into the crowds. As she'd suspected, the 'sellers' had been watching every move, and met her halfway. She said, "Did you know he has three more friends here, just like himself?" The two adherents' eyebrows rose. They shook their heads.

"Well, he has! If you can find them in time for the winter solstice, there will be more where this came from. Ask for me — Jomel. Have you got that?"

The man muttered a brief "Yes," but there was a gleam in his eye. She dropped the second pile of coins into his greasy, outstretched paw; then the two of them vanished into the night. She returned to her sacrificial victim, eager and slightly out of breath.

She held out her hand. "Gelmion, come! I have a place near here..." He was on his feet at once, holding her small hand in his large one. A tremble ran through her. This tall bear was rather attractive... *No!* She pushed the thought aside. There was no way she was getting emotionally entangled with a sacrificial victim! But she could have a little fun with him first. She took the half-full wine flask from the table, and they made their way to the temple, Gelmion limping at her side. She led him to her cubicle.

There the progress of events was predictable and ordinary — to her, at least. He took a lot of satisfying, but that, too, was to be expected when she'd exercised her power. She was glad she'd given him some pleasure before... She felt a pang of guilt, but suppressed it. It was either him or her, and he'd been dropped in her lap by the god.

She looked at him as she pulled on her clothes. He lay sprawled on the bed, snoring. No need for the wine after all. She draped his brown robe over him.

"Sweet dreams," she murmured as she slipped out of the cubicle to find Dhelgor.

* * *

Gil awoke on a hard floor with a splitting headache. There was a deafening racket all around him. Bellows, moos, bleats, whinnies — where was he, on a farm or something? There was a farmyard stink in the air. He pushed himself up on an elbow and tried to take in his surroundings. They meant nothing to him. A floor of rough flagstones, wooden walls on three sides, a half door with a trough attached, and a yellowstone wall at the back. Above were unsmoothed beams supporting a tiled roof.

What was this, an animal stall? He staggered to his feet and yelped as the broken blisters made themselves felt. He tried to hobble to the half-door, but something held him back. He looked down, and his eyes widened at the sight of a chain clamped to his right ankle. It ran to a solid-looking metal ring in the rear wall. My God, he was a prisoner! He sat down and tried to prise the clamp off, but it seemed to be welded on.

Panic flooded him and at the same time memory returned. That whore Jomel! How could he have been so unbelievably stupid? Apart from the agony of having betrayed Lannie, he'd apparently allowed that bitch to imprison him! A dim voice echoed in his mind: *Do not walk alone. It is dangerous. Believe me, I am helping you now.* That monk—the walnut—on the Finien road. If only he'd accepted his help, stuck with the pumpkins, endured their barrage of questions! He might be safely in Darthane now, instead of... wherever *this* was.

It was impossible! He could not be imprisoned like this for absolutely nothing. Certainly not for rape—it was Jomel who'd seduced *him*. And what about Papa Durónne and his lemons? Where were they when he needed them?

"Help!" he shouted. He dragged the chain across the floor to where he could just get a view over the half-door. It looked like a courtyard outside—and, yes! There was one of those huge oxen in the stall opposite, staring blankly at him; another further along, and then one of the camel-horses. Noises from the other stalls showed that they were occupied by smaller beasts. Was he just another animal now?

"Help, somebody! Make me free!"

A door creaked and an old Dûrian man with white hair and a tattered black cloak stomped into the courtyard. One of his eyes was missing, but the other fixed Gil with a baleful glare.

"Shut yer noise! You'll get the rest of 'em going."

"But why I here? What I do wrong?"

"You? Nothin'. You been given a special *callénne*, you have."

"What is *callénne*?"

"Ah, you stupid foreigner! A gift, that's what."

"This is gift? Tied like animal?"

"Ah, well, that's juss in case yer don't want the gift."

"*Which* gift? Tell me!"

There was a malicious gleam in the old man's eye. He spoke slowly and carefully, so Gil could follow every word.

"The gift of havin' yer body cut up and offered in the fire to Gadesh."

"*What!*"

"You're dead meat, mate, juss like all these animals here. Only you're a person, see, so that makes it special. You'll be well fed. They like 'em plump—more fat for the fire."

Gil's knees buckled and he collapsed to the floor.

"Mebbe that'll shut yer noise," the old man muttered as he stomped off.

Chapter 20: *Disaster in Berûvis*

THE DAY AFTER THEIR ARRIVAL at Lord Ganneret's house Lannie and Shiván enjoyed a leisurely dawnmeal. It was Anderil—the One's day. Soon afterwards the whole party set out for the Berûvis Hearth. Lannie was pleased Lord Ganneret had invited them to the morning worship. So far she and Shivvie had only experienced the Manor community's informal hearthtimes led by Elder Damion.

Of course, Fira had raised objections. It was too dangerous; they shouldn't show themselves in public; what if the Bishop had informers at the Hearth? Ganneret had replied that his whole household would be attending—some twenty people. That should be enough to mask the presence of two foreigners—even, he'd added apologetically, with a shiláy as strong as theirs. Lannie had said that would be fine, and was pleased to see the iron lieutenant bite her tongue.

Half the party travelled by coach, while the rest rode the strange camel-horses. The two carriages, painted in the family's burgundy and ochre colours, were each drawn by three pairs of tall, sandy-brown animals vaguely like overgrown greyhounds with powerful shoulders and hindquarters. They were called *sinélle*. Lannie had seen them before, streaking along the central fast lanes of the highway pulling two-person chariots and larger vehicles. This morning, however, they travelled at a sedate pace down a long, winding driveway. This joined the highway not far from the western entrance to Berûvis.

It was a neat little town with well-laid out streets, flowerbeds, and green-roofed buildings. The Hearth was a circular white building on the market square. Its green-tiled dome was crowned with the usual white ambon.

The carriages pulled up behind others waiting to drop their distinguished occupants at the main door of the Hearth, after which they were driven off and parked in side streets. The Baron's servants tied the horses to one of the many hitching rails that lined the square. By the time Lannie and Shiván made their regal arrival, the entire household was standing ready. Lord Ganneret and Lady Nelláy led the way into the Hearth, followed by butler Harn, while

Perrely and her two brothers accompanied the two of them amidst a crowd of servants to disguise their shiláy.

They entered the rounded arch of the door and found themselves in a large circular auditorium. There was a thick blue floor cloth, and the white walls had many windows with rich yellow glass that let in a warm light. Rows of chairs were set in a three-quarter-circle facing an alcove at the front. In the alcove, on a low dais, stood a flat slab of carved stone. Above it was a white wall with a tall silver ambon in the centre. Indirect light lit up the alcove from windows on either side, making the ambon glow. To the right of the dais was a wooden lectern on which a heavy, black-bound book rested. On the left were two rows of half a dozen chairs.

Perrely seemed to have recovered from her father's rebuke the previous night. "That's the empty altar," she told them, gesturing towards the stone slab. "Nothing is ever placed on it because we don't believe—"

"Good grief." Lannie had stopped cold. Shiván, too. There were exclamations from behind as some of the servants bumped into them.

"What's the matter? Keep moving," Perrely said anxiously, taking Lannie's hand. Lannie started walking again, her eyes wide as she took in the familiar details.

"Seen this before?" Shivvie spoke English in an undertone beside her.

"Yes!"

"The Round Church at Leston, right?"

"Right. Where each of us met Father Martin, before coming here!"

"I thought that was an unusual church. Now we know it wasn't. It was a Dûrian Hearth."

"That's stretching it a bit, but the similarities are amazing! Remember the Irish cross above the altar? Take away the horizontal bar, and you'd have an ambon!"

"Stop talking your language!" Perrely's brother Larion hissed from behind. "Do you want to get us in trouble?"

Lannie gave him a dark look, but he was right. They fell silent. Lord Ganneret led them halfway down one of the aisles where they seated themselves in three rows, the guests safely surrounded in the middle.

Musicians filed into the chairs to the left of the dais, and soon after that worship began. Lannie found herself vaguely disappointed. The general outline was the same as the hearthtimes they'd had with Damion at the Manor, but there the similarity ended. This was a ritual, part of a time-honoured tradition. The heart had gone out of it. She remembered the longing, the outpouring of love, the naked adoration in the faces of her Manor friends as they sang their Hearthsong to the One Creator God. There was none of that here. Many looked bored. Some were not even singing. Oh, well. What's new? Organised religion is the same everywhere. Patches of fresh, new growth among masses of dead wood.

Eventually an elderly man in a white robe went to the lectern and began to read. "Kindler Dorlion," Perrely whispered to her. She gathered he was the equivalent of the priest or vicar. He had the rather tired, kindly expression she'd seen on other elderly clerics; and his shoulders were stooped.

Kindler Dorlion was reading in a high, bleating voice. Lord Ganneret's servants were shuffling in their seats, but Shivvie was drinking it in. Lannie wished she understood Dûrian as well as he did. This was difficult stuff—far removed from everyday speech. She supposed she was feeling how a foreigner would when hearing the King James version of the Bible being read in English.

The reading was followed by more singing, then a short homily from the Kindler on the topic of loving one another. How clichéd could you get?

Finally the *Limmeris Narac*, the Remembrance of Flame. Here at last the hearthtime came alive. All sat in silence as a shallow metal dish with glowing coals was carried on rods down the central aisle and placed on a tripod in front of the altar. When the orange-robed attendants had withdrawn, everyone stood.

The musicians began to play a haunting melody very softly. The ladies of the choir chimed in with a gentle lament. Women in the congregation joined them. There was a sudden change of key, and the men of the choir added fullness to the song. Men in the congregation followed, as the hymn swelled to a growing crescendo. There were no bored faces now. It was obvious that this was what people had come here for.

The music built in thrilling stages to a resounding climax, every voice at full stretch—then, suddenly, there was silence. Into it fell like soft rain the ladies' voices, singing a reprise of the lament they had begun with. Everyone stood with their hands stretched out towards the ambon above the altar.

As the music faded Kindler Dorlion cried out, "He has burned for you! Will you shine for him?"

"*We will shine!*" the people roared back.

"Flame turns the Dark to Light!"

"*We will shine!*"

Then, suddenly, worship was over. People began laughing and chatting together, but Lord Ganneret quickly herded his party out to the waiting carriages. This was one hearthtime when socialising would not be appropriate.

* * *

Perrely sat on her own in the reclining room, thinking. The family was back from the Hearth, chass had been served, and everyone was filling in time until the midmeal. Father was deep in conversation with the rebel lieutenant, and Mums was being dutifully polite to Lannie. The twin soldiers Shîrin and Cârin were regaling her brothers with tales of derring-do, while the other two troopers heckled from the sidelines. Shiván had disappeared somewhere.

When Shiván and Alanya arrived yesterday it had been so amazing to see the vision the Prince had given her coming to life before her very eyes! There they were, just as they'd appeared to her — Alanya, the red-haired lady with the aggressive walk; and Shiván, the stocky young man with fair hair and a friendly smile. They looked different in the Dûrian clothes Father had given them; and their faces were so much more vivid in real life.

Could she have been deceived, seeing what she wanted to see? No, surely not! Red hair and blond — that had definitely been in her vision. And their shiláy was overwhelmingly foreign! So full of individuality and self-assertion. No one she had ever met could more aptly be called a 'stranger and loner'. Everything they'd said matched that description. Their miraculous arrival in Dûrion from a foreign sky; their instruments; the other man, Gelmion, setting off on his own — what was that, if not the action of a loner?

She'd been mortified by that slip she'd made, and Father's instant ban on joining the Restorers. She'd meant to break it to her parents gently, telling them about her vision, enlisting their sympathy and understanding. That was off, now. Having made his decision, Father wouldn't back down. It was a shame the Restorers themselves, and their escorts, had been so tentative about their purpose here. That hadn't exactly won Father's confidence. Plus the unfortunate fact that they didn't yet have the *Ambon Sûrilac*, the Ambon of Sûrilane...

But, come what may, she would obey the Prince's command: *To be with the ones he had sent; to encourage them, and pray for them.* No matter what Father said, that was her job now. Why, she had even asked the One to bring the Restorers to *her*, since she couldn't go to them—and he'd led them right to her doorstep! The message couldn't be clearer.

* * *

Next morning the guests resumed their journey to Darthane. They set out early, dressed in their old clothes, which had been cleaned and pressed. Shiván was sorry to leave. He was also disappointed that Perrely was not there to see them off. He couldn't understand it. She'd seemed quite happy all of yesterday—completely over her father's ban on joining them. Strange.

Lord Ganneret, with typical generosity, had offered them an escort of his servants. It would be difficult and time-consuming, he said, for them to find their way round the town from this side, with the river and many fields to cross; but if they went through Berûvis with a large group of servants to dilute their shiláy, they shouldn't have any trouble.

The walk to Berûvis was uneventful. But when they entered the town they found all the inhabitants streaming towards the market square. Fira wanted to take side streets, but the servants became panicky, saying they'd be too conspicuous. So they followed the crowd.

As they drew closer to the square, there was a commotion among the servants—and suddenly Perrely appeared among them, wearing a bright smile. She was dressed in old, travel-worn clothes and had a small leather pouch attached to her girdle. "I told you it would all come right, didn't I?" she said to Shiván.

"Perrely, what are you doing here?" Lannie demanded. The servants were clamouring that she should be taken home. "*Foolish* girl!" Fira snapped.

Perrely's face set in an obstinate expression. "The One told me my place is with you. My father can't forbid that. The Book tells us to obey God rather than men."

"Alanya, send her home at once," Fira hissed.

But matters were already out of Lannie's hands. The press of people was now so tight that none of them could have fought their way out. They were carried along by the crowd into the square, hemmed in on all sides by other groups craning their necks, who pushed back when they were shoved.

There was an excited buzz of rumour all around them, and the servants almost had a joint heart attack when they heard that some important rebel leaders were to be publicly executed. To add to the confusion, today was market day. The square was crowded with traders' tables, animal pens, and country folk. But up near the Hearth building a wide platform had been raised. On one side was a low wooden stand next to which a muscular man stood, holding a shaft in gloved hands. At the front was an ambon, symbol of the Bishop's authority.

As more people entered the square, Lannie's group was pushed further forward. Fira struggled to head them to the right where the main road exited; but there was no hope of reaching it. They ended up beside a wooden pen with deer for sale. The animals were milling about, adding their deep bellows and rich aroma to the general chaos.

A trumpet brayed off to the left and silence spread rapidly over the large gathering. A squadron of grey-cloaked, silver-helmeted cavalry entered the square. Fira stiffened and her mouth puckered. "*Dimanar Steylanac!*—Bishop's Guards!" she hissed. For the first time since Shiván had known them, Shîrin and Cârin looked grim.

"These are the Mindbenders' soldiers?" he asked Perrely, who had ended up beside him.

"And their slaves. They're terrible." She shot him an anxious glance.

The Guardsmen began clearing space round the platform, and shifting currents in the crowd forced them closer. The riders dismounted and formed a grey barrier, holding the mob back.

A few minutes later the trumpet sounded again and more mounted Guardsmen entered the square, preceding a lone rider in a dark blue cloak trimmed with grey.

"The Mindbender of Berûvis," Perrely whispered in Shiván's ear. He passed the information on to Lannie, who was on his other side. She shot him a horrified glance.

The Mindbender dismounted and climbed the steps to the platform: a grey-haired man with a deeply-lined face and steely black eyes under bushy eyebrows. A hush settled on the crowd as he came to the front and grasped the ambon with one hand. He let his eyes wander over the packed mass of people, waiting for complete silence.

"People of Berûvis." His baritone voice rang out clearly. "Eleven days ago, in this square, you were shown a traitor. You know who I mean!" The steely eyes seemed to penetrate Shiván's, and a shiver went down his spine. "Armanet, his name was. A coward who has since recanted publicly of his treason and paid the penalty for it. *How did you greet him?*" The sudden force of his words was like a slap in the face. There were gasps, and then silence.

"Ye-e-es." The Mindbender nodded slowly. "You welcomed him, didn't you? You bowed the knee to him. You sang the Song of Allegiance — *to a traitor!*" This time it was a whiplash, and Shiván jumped with everyone else.

"Your ringleaders have received their just reward for that act of defiance against our radiant Bishop. And we have searched tirelessly for all who still dare to oppose him. For those so-called 'rebels' who cling to their pathetic illusions. Who still imagine that Armanet and Dôrion were 'Restorers of the Way'!" He flung an arm out. "*Where are they now?* Where are their armies, those glorious Restorers?" The arm thrust downward, pointing to the ground. "*Rotting where they belong!* That's where they are. And that's where *you'll* be, my friends, if you ever again show sympathy to those who defy our Lord Bishop.

"Today this will be demonstrated beyond any possibility of misunderstanding. You will see justice done on five deluded fools who supported the rebel cause. *Not soldiers!* No. These are common people, like yourselves. Ordinary, everyday folk who *betrayed their Bishop.*"

He paused to let his words sink in. "Prince's blood," Cârin murmured. Shiván glanced at him. His face was pale, like his brother's. Fira's fists were clenching and unclenching. In the midst of his own horror Shiván felt a surge of commiseration. These might be people their friends knew personally.

"Pay special attention to this," the Mindbender continued. "Two who will die today are children."

There was a concerted groan. "Oh, dear God," Lannie muttered. "I don't need to see this. Can't we get *out* of here?" She looked round desperately, but they were solidly packed in. Perrely's face was white.

"Yes! Innocent children. *Are they?* What lies, what deceptions have already been planted in their young minds? If you find a nest of snakes, do you kill only the adults? No! In the same way *your* children will die if you bite the hand that guards you."

He paused to let his eyes roam over the market square. There was a deathly hush, broken only by the grunts and bleats of the animals. The Mindbender raised a clenched fist. "Now see the justice of your Bishop!" he declared.

He strode off the platform, and the muscular man beside the stand hefted the implement he was holding to his shoulder. For the first time they saw that it was a broad-bladed axe.

"Oh, shit, I think I'm going to be sick," Lannie said. Shiván didn't feel so good himself. "Prince, have mercy on them," Perrely murmured, her face contorted with anguish.

A group of grey-cloaked Guardsmen began mounting the platform stairs, escorting the prisoners. People craned their necks to see. Three of the bound figures were adults in dishevelled peasant shifts; and there were two smaller forms. The soft sound of the children's weeping floated over the square. As they reached the top, one of the adults turned for a moment toward the crowd.

Shiván felt the blood drain from his face; his knees were suddenly weak. "Oh no. Oh no. Oh God, no."

"What? What is it?" Lannie asked, her voice filled with alarm. She hadn't seen. But she would. Because the prisoners were being turned to face the crowd.

Lannie looked away from him back to the platform. She saw Margay. And she screamed.

"*MAARGAAY!*"

* * *

175

The silence of the crowd was shattered. Uproar broke out, and as in a dream Shiván saw Lannie surging forward with some insane notion of rescuing Margay. The entire front line of Guardsmen turned and began forcing the mob aside to reach the troublemaker. People pushed and fell in their desperation to get out of the way. Fira was shouting above the din, trying to rally their group. He couldn't see Lannie any more. Ganneret's servants had vanished, and so had Perrely.

Shiván was cut off from the others; the foremost wedge of Guardsmen was coming towards him. He tacked himself on to a group of frantic farmers and helped them bulldoze their way to the left-hand side of the square. Others eddied in behind them, and the last he saw before dodging into an alleyway was the grey-coats heading in the opposite direction, the way Fira had gone. There was no sign of Lannie.

"Oh God, please protect them," he breathed.

Things were quieting down now and no one was looking towards him. He found that from the mouth of the alley he had a good view of the platform. The Mindbender was assuring the crowd that the sympathiser who had given herself away would be caught and dealt with. He stepped aside; and with a sick feeling in the pit of his stomach Shiván realised that the show would go on.

Well, the trip to Darthane was done for; the least he could do was to stay right there and pray for his friends. Pray through to the end. Dear gentle Frem and kind, efficient Margay, standing there so calmly. A lump the size of an egg was stuck in his throat, and warm tears were streaming down his cheeks. The third adult was Mery, Lannie's roommate at the Manor, with her two sons Bannet and Grildon. About nine and six, he thought. They were wailing louder now after all the commotion, each in the grip of a grey-cloaked Guardsman. Poor Mery couldn't even comfort them in their last moments.

Any second now he expected Lannie to join death row.

Frem was executed first. He was led over to the wooden structure, made to kneel, and his neck stretched over it. His forehead rested on a lower block. The executioner raised the axe above his head and stood poised for a long moment. Shiván's prayers tumbled through his mind incoherently; he hardly knew what he was saying as he pleaded desperately for God somehow to intervene…

Then the axe fell.

Shiván closed his eyes in sickened horror. There was no breath left in his lungs. "Oh Lord. Oh Lord," he gasped. Mery's two boys started screaming their lungs out, till they were muzzled by the Guardsmen's gloved hands.

He forced himself to watch as Margay was led to the block. His heart unclenched a little at the serenity on her face. There was a woman who knew where she was going. He closed his eyes as the axe fell; but he knew in that moment that Margay had reached a place of peace beyond the brutality of this world.

The boys were killed before their mother. Was that merciful or not? There were groans and sounds of weeping from the crowd at the sight of those two pathetic little figures, forced to kneel on a raised step, screaming till their shrill young voices were cut short.

"Oh God, have mercy, have mercy." It was all he could find to say. As he spoke, Mery collapsed. The Guardsmen dragged her to the block, and she was unconscious when the axe fell.

They began clearing up the mess. Still no sign of Lannie. That at least was a relief.

Shiván sank to the ground and leant against the alley wall. His whole body was trembling. He felt a hundred years old. "God, have mercy," he whispered.

Chapter 21: *Gil joins the Bishop's Guard*

GIL STARED LISTLESSLY at the heaped platter of fatty grûn meat, *cayet* tubers and crunchy purple *tilnet* beans. There were no utensils. They weren't even trusting him with a wooden spoon. But the old one-eyed stockman had been right—he was getting plenty of food. Not that he was eating it.

He'd been through the whole gamut of emotions yesterday. Shock, horror, despair, rage... He'd yelled, wept, cursed and hammered at the sturdy walls of his stall. It had achieved nothing more than an answering uproar from the animals and a rich stream of invective from the old man. He wished he'd been able to answer in kind.

But now the rage had burned out and his mind was numb. What was there to think of, when all options were gone? He'd tried to approach the problem logically, but had got nowhere. Breaking out was physically impossible. He had no money to offer as a bribe. He could throw the slop bucket or the wooden platter at the old fool, but what good would that do? His foot shackle felt as if it had been welded on—endless prying with his fingers had found only a couple of ridges; no sign of a keyhole.

He sat on the wooden bench that ran along the side wall, toying with his robe, which was bundled up beside him. For some reason they'd tossed that into the stall as well. Worth nothing, he supposed, though it was a heavy, durable fabric. He idly lifted it up, and the lower part fell to the ground with a muffled *thunk*. He felt in the pockets, and was surprised to find his two-handled glass—the blaise from the Manor storeroom. He'd brought that with him, he couldn't think why. Nor could he imagine why it hadn't been removed.

Anyway, a fat lot of good it would do him! He pulled it out and held it by one handle to examine the plate of food. The grain of the meat showed up in close detail. Great. Fantastic. He glanced around the stall, but he already knew no sunlight found its way in. No chance of starting a fire. He slipped the blaise back in the robe pocket.

Well, it seemed he was destined to die here in Dûrion to satisfy religious superstition. If not at the hands of the Lightists for offending their 'One Creator God', then to appease this bloodthirsty 'Gadesh' — who if Shivvie were right, was the Dûrian Satan. The two opposites. And he didn't believe in either of them. So much for Father Martin's babblings about 'learning to see the truth'.

A black despair settled over him. From being a person of some account in Britain, he'd fallen all the way to having no value at all. He was worthless in Dûrion. Good for the fire, nothing more. Was this what his whole life amounted to? Years of study, years of striving for excellence, all to end in ashes on a primitive altar. What had been the point of it? How had he ever imagined that studying reams of academic papers justified his existence? He might as well have stayed home and played tiddlywinks. To think that he'd argued vehemently with other linguists about whether the sentences "He considered him a fool" and "He considered him *to be* a fool" were the same grammatical construction!

He was the fool. It was all empty, worthless, meaningless. The Dûrians had valued his life accurately.

Yet Lannie had cared for him. Just a little. And how had he repaid her? By pressurising her, forcing the issue, then running off without her. At the first opportunity after that he'd betrayed her to gratify his lust with that slut Jomel. A fiery death was all he deserved.

The thought of how he was to die had its usual effect of turning his knees to jelly and his bowels to water. To be burnt alive! It was the sort of thing one read of in history books, shuddered at briefly, and passed on. The stockman had spoken of him being 'cut up' and offered to the god! Were they going to carve him like a joint of beef? He leant forward for another dry retch. Or would they have the decency to kill him first? He'd asked One-eye, and the malicious old sod had laughed and said, "Sometimes they do, sometimes they don't."

Gil's meditations were mercifully interrupted by the tramp of boots in the courtyard outside. He leapt up as One-eye threw the door open for two heavyset men in grey workers' tunics. One was holding a dagger.

"Stand still," he growled, clasping Gil in a bear-like grip with the dagger pressed to his throat. Gil froze. This couldn't be *it*, though. One-eye had taken pleasure in informing him he had two weeks to anticipate the great event.

The other man knelt down and started doing something with his shackle. A wild hope sprang up in Gil. Was he being released? Had someone realised it was all a mistake? He felt a cold sliver of metal moving about between the shackle and his leg—then there was a *click*, and the shackle was off. Good Lord! So there was a lock on the inside. A clever piece of workmanship.

He was released, and both men stood before him with daggers drawn. "Put your robe on," came the curt command. "You're seeing the Mindbender."

The Mindbender? What was this, then? Gil had vaguely heard talk of Mindbenders at the Manor; all he knew was that they were bad. Very bad. His excitement at being set free suddenly cooled. This was not so good. But why would the Mindbender want to see him? Why not just order whatever it was to be done? Such a summons could only mean he had something the Mindbender wanted—impossible though that seemed. Which gave him bargaining power. Hope raised its head cautiously.

He pulled his robe on and the two musclemen grabbed an arm each and escorted him out of the stall. One-eye stood by with a sour expression.

"I thank you, you such big friend to me," Gil told him as he passed by. The old man spat on the ground.

Gil was escorted through various passages to a lavishly appointed room in the temple itself. He gaped at the wall hangings and soft floor cover, all in shades of blue and grey. In a corner, reclining on chaise longues, were a powerfully-built man in a blue robe, who watched him with cold eyes; and a young woman in grey and white. He immediately recognised her: *Jomel*. She had the gall to give him a demure smile. He pointedly ignored her and bowed to the Mindbender, who indicated a low stool facing the two chairs. He sat rather uncomfortably on the small surface. The two henchmen left, closing the door.

"So this is Gelmion." The Mindbender spoke lazily, looking him over. "The foreign loner who has come to grace our temple."

There was a silence. Gil said nothing, but looked the Mindbender steadily in the eye. He knew the politics of power. The man was trying to make him feel uneasy, to provoke a servile response.

The sardonic smile widened slightly. "You have spirit, I see." Suddenly he became businesslike. "Jomel here told me about your three companions. Where are they now?"

So that's what he wanted. Gil's heart sank. Was it his life in exchange for the other three? If so, it would be a lie: they'd kill him anyway. Was he going to be tortured to give the information? Oh, God. He'd betrayed Lannie once, he didn't want to betray her again — nor Shiván and Danîsha. He'd have to play for time.

"I not know," he said. It was partly true.

"Where were they when you left them?"

He did his best. "I, uh, I not know Dûrion. I go east. They stay."

"Were you four on your own, or with other Dûrians?"

Trick question. He glanced at Jomel. What had she found out from the lemons? She was still smiling that damn smile. Best to mix in a little truth.

"We stay with Dûrians. Then I want to go Darthane. I leave."

"Where were these Dûrians?"

He shrugged. "I not know. I still learn language."

"Why did you come to Stillárre instead of Darthane?"

"I try go Darthane. But people trick me, bring me here."

"And your friends stayed behind with the Dûrians?"

"Yes."

"Were they staying in a village?"

"No."

"In a town?"

"No." He licked his lips. Better seem a bit more forthcoming. "They stay in forest."

"Ah. In the forest. A large forest?"

"Yes."

"With tall trees?"

"Yes." Oh God, he hoped he wasn't locating them too accurately. But the forest covered a pretty wide area. Just let them not think of the Manor.

"Mmmm. We'll find out in due course whether you're telling the truth, Gelmion." Cold black eyes bored into him. He wondered uneasily what that might mean. "Now, tell me: Why did you leave your friends?"

"I want to find work. They want to stay."

"They were happy living in the forest?"

He began to sweat. "They like Dûrians. Make friends."

"Is that how you live in your country—in caves in the forest?"

"No, we live in house. But some people, they like outside. Forest. Mountain." Jomel's smile was wider. She was enjoying this, the bitch.

Dhelgor raised one eyebrow quizzically. "*Do* they? A strange people. But tell me, were your friends happy that you left?"

"I go at night. They not see."

"And now that you are gone—will they try and find you, do you think?"

Gil's head began to ache with the pressure of double-guessing the man. The truth was, of course, that they *would* try and find him if they could. He knew that, and it shamed him. He didn't deserve such friends. But what should he say to the Mindbender? If he told him the others would *not* come after him, that might seal his own fate. If he told him the others *would* come after him, he might be preserved as bait. But the others probably couldn't leave the Manor, even if they wanted to. Commandant Fira ruled with an iron rod. So the second answer would buy him a little time, and do the others no harm. Probably. But the alternative... he shuddered at the thought of going back to that stall.

"Yes, I think they try find me."

"Mmmm. You think they would come to Stillárre and start asking for you?"

"Yes, I think they try that." He was glad to see the smile wiped off Jomel's face. She was suddenly looking anxiously at the Mindbender.

"Then you'd better be here to greet them, not so?"

Relief welled up. He smiled. "Yes, I think."

Jomel was up on one elbow. "But Dhelgor, the adherents who brought Gelmion are already looking for the others—"

He gave her a cold glance. "Not reliable." He turned back to Gil. "Gelmion, I am offering you a choice. You may join the Bishop's Guard here in Stillárre to help find your friends; or you may be sacrificed to the god Gadesh. Think quickly."

Oh my God, what's the Bishop's Guard? What should I do? he thought desperately. Jomel bought him some time. There was anguish on her face, and she was clasping and unclasping her hands.

"Dhelgor!" she burst out. "I told you about him! You *can't...*" Her voice faded away.

Dhelgor rounded on her. "Now you're telling a Mindbender what he can and cannot do?"

She was almost in tears. "*Try* it, Dhelgor! He's different—you can't!"

The Mindbender looked at Gil with those steely eyes; an expression of bafflement briefly crossed his face. He was silent for a moment.

"This will take time," he said meditatively. "But it can be done. It *will* be."

"*No*, Dhelgor—!"

He turned to her. "Jomel, my sweet, *if* with Gelmion's help we find his friends before the sacrifice, you have nothing to worry about. If not... the sentence stands, and you will take his place."

"*No-o-o-o!*" She hurled herself at his feet, sobbing. "I did everything you wanted! I found an unattached foreigner, a loner—*and* three others! You can't break your promise!"

He took her head in his hands and turned her face up to his. "Jomel, my dove," he said softly with his sardonic smile, "I can do *anything.*"

The two henchmen had materialised beside the chaise longue. Without a word spoken, one of them hoisted the sobbing woman over his shoulder and left the room. The other stationed himself against the wall.

Gil sat appalled. He'd hated Jomel for what she'd done to him, but he'd never realised... Now it was her life against his and his friends'. Whatever he did, someone would die.

"Well, Gelmion, I'd say justice was done, wouldn't you? Jomel betrayed you; now she herself has been betrayed. You must be glad."

"No."

"No? How noble. In which case, of course, you will be anxious to save Jomel's life by offering yourself for sacrifice. Is that your answer to my offer? Or do you choose the Bishop's Guard?"

Gil swallowed. "What is Bishop's Guard?"

"Soldiers, Gelmion. The guardians of the Bishop's peace. I am their Captain in Stillárre. Will you join us, or die?"

Soldiers. So he was being press-ganged into the army. Well, there were worse fates than that. Such as being burnt alive. On the other hand, he hadn't liked all that ominous stuff about what Dhelgor could or could not do to him. He'd obviously tried something and failed. His mind went back to that moment when he was sitting with Jomel at the celebration, and she'd seemed disconcerted. Maybe she'd tried the same trick, and that's how she knew it didn't work. If two had tried and failed — But Dhelgor was obviously more powerful, and he'd said it was just a matter of time…

"Answer quickly, Gelmion, or I will make the choice for you."

Well, it was a question of life or death, really, wasn't it? "I join Guard."

The Mindbender smiled gently. "How wise," he murmured. "Just what I would have chosen for you myself."

* * *

Dhelgor stared at the sleeping man in baffled rage. A whole day had gone by since Gelmion joined the Bishop's Guard, and he *still* wasn't mindbent!

This should have been easy. By the dark flame, it was how he himself taught Mindbender candidates! Work on the subject when he was asleep, with no disruptive thoughts or emotions to get in the way. But for once that bitch Jomel had been right: the access points were simply not there. Gelmion's mind was so alien, so differently constructed, that he could not find a way in even when he was asleep.

Split the man! Dhelgor was *not* going to hand him over to Shambor. It was what he ought to do, of course. The Mindruler would be livid if he ever discovered that Dhelgor had handled such an alien mind on his own. But what Shambor didn't know wouldn't hurt him.

Dhelgor intended to net these four foreigners solely for the glory of the Cult in Stillárre — and himself, of course. The rumour that innocents were being sacrificed to the Worldruler — shrieking for mercy, protesting their blamelessness — would draw foreign merchants and wealthy patrons to the Temple like ants to honey. It would boost not only the temple's prestige, but also his own as leader of the Gadeshite community in the city. Such was the power of innocent blood. Far better than the offscourings of the prisons that they usually had to make do with.

Dhelgor returned to the task with renewed vigour. He *had* to have access to this man's mind and memories. It was obvious that Gelmion had been telling only half the truth during questioning yesterday. He intended to extract the full truth from his mind, and track down those companions of his wherever they were. Lone foreigners like these might only cross one's path once in a lifetime.

The Mindbender sat hunched over Gelmion's sleeping form on a stool beside his narrow bed. Gelmion had been given teméyn both last night and this morning. The dose had been higher than usual. Yet when Dhelgor had tried to penetrate this alien mind at various moments during the day, he'd failed every time. This evening since Gelmion had fallen asleep, Dhelgor had been probing him for an hour to no effect. But now he was going to examine this mind minutely. He was going to go over every little knot and wrinkle of the tangled thought-patterns, and *somewhere* he'd find a crevice through which he could worm his way in.

At least Gelmion didn't have the shining barrier that made Lightists so hard to mindbend. Only Shambor could handle those with ease — and even he couldn't break through the barrier, he could only work around it.

Two hours later Dhelgor was still looking for a crevice, muttering under his breath.

An hour after that he straightened slowly, and stretched. There was a faint smile on his face. He'd found it. Almost invisible, hidden under an intricate knot of memory. But it was there. He hunched over again and slipped into Gelmion's mind.

* * *

Gelmion was riding one of those camel-horses to the town of Mesten. It was the sort of thing Gelmion knew how to do. He was cantering in the fast lane of the paved highway with nineteen other Guardsmen in grey cloaks. That's what Gelmion was — a Guardsman.

Gil, on the other hand, did not know how to ride a camel-horse. He did not want to go to Mesten. Gil heartily disliked the Guardsmen, who swaggered about bullying innocent citizens. Gil was just an ordinary Englishman who wanted a decent job.

But what Gil wanted had ceased to matter. Gil was a prisoner in Gelmion's mind. Gil could want, but he could do nothing. He couldn't stand up or sit down if his master didn't wish it. He could only seethe with rage while Gelmion—his body—did whatever it was told.

Now he knew what it was that Jomel thought Dhelgor could not do. And Dhelgor had done it. Now, when it was too late, he understood what *mindbending* was. It was the ultimate slavery. He was a prisoner in his own body. He could think, he could feel, he could react—but he couldn't move a muscle.

He imagined this must be what total paralysis was like—only far worse, because now someone else controlled his muscles. He hadn't wanted to turn out at the crack of dawn this morning—but he'd done it. He hadn't wanted to climb on this camel-horse—he'd been terrified—but he'd done it, and somehow his body knew what to do. If it hadn't been *his* body they were manipulating, he'd have marvelled that they could transfer a physical skill so effortlessly. As it was, his mind blazed with helpless fury.

It was worst when he heard the voice, cold and contemptuous, speaking in full confidence of instant obedience. *Report to Lieutenant Falmenor.* That was it. And his limbs leapt to obey, while his mind screamed obscenities. But he'd quickly learned to moderate those reactions. His master didn't like them. And his master had ways of inflicting mental pain that Stalin and Hitler would have envied. The whole of yesterday he'd been broken in like a horse or dog—punished when he rebelled, rewarded when he did not.

They crested a rise, and there in a valley beside a river he saw the town of Mesten. He blinked a couple of times, and noted absently that he seemed to be doing that a lot now. The town was larger than Finien—the little place he'd seen after leaving the Manor—but it had the same neat houses, green roofs, and well-laid streets. They'd be staying the night there, he'd been told.

He found himself wondering if the physical agony of being burnt alive would have been more bearable than the mental agony of mindbending. But there'd never really been any choice, had there? Dhelgor would have mindbent him regardless. He wanted to find the other three. Then they'd all grace the altar of Gadesh. This posse of Guards was no doubt a search party, and he'd been included to identify the others if they found them. Well, there was a lot of forest to search. He only hoped the Manor lookouts were more alert than Trooper Darmet had been, the night he'd escaped.

His mind heaved a shuddering sigh, though his face remained impassive — apart from the blinking — and his body sat straight in the saddle. The perfect, well-disciplined Guardsman, he thought bitterly. But his mind was tormented by the inevitability of what would happen if they did come across the other three. He would recognise them — even from a distance — and Dhelgor would know at once. That would be it. The end. Curtains. Not only for them, but for all the other poor innocents at the Manor. The inner Gil wept. Iron-faced Fira had been right; it would have been better for him to "leave, but not arrive". Now he had thrown the lives of all those good people into jeopardy.

They rode into Mesten, and the townsfolk scurried away in fear, clutching their children. At the Town Elder's house on the market square they were reluctantly admitted and given a passable meal. It was afterwards that the blow fell.

The patrol's commander, Lieutenant Falmenor, had been chatting affably with his unwilling host, but now he turned to Gil.

"Tomorrow, Trooper Gelmion, you will lead."

"I, sir?" Gil felt as if he were stammering, and his eyelids fluttered in a flurry of blinks. For some reason the conversation was taking place out loud. All the Guardsmen turned to listen.

"Yes, you," Falmenor said impatiently. "You know the best way to approach the Manor unseen — and you also know how to open the hidden masonry door, and where the escape tunnel comes out. You will receive a full briefing on our strategy in the morning." He glanced round at the other Guardsmen. "All dismissed. We need our rest."

Gelmion's body stood, bowed, and walked calmly out. Gil's mind was screaming.

Chapter 22: *Enter Gwargif*

PERRELY SAT IN THE KITCHEN peeling cayet. She attacked the large tubers with a sharp knife, while Cook and the maids kept throwing her anxious glances. Perrely ignored them. Right now she needed self-expression. Never mind if she sliced a finger off.

Yesterday had been a disaster. She'd obeyed her Prince's command to join the Restorers — and the whole venture had gone no further than Berûvis market square! How could Alanya have been so undisciplined as to scream like that? Had she never attended a public execution before?

Yes, it was tragic — especially with children involved... Perrely's knife was still for a moment, sorrow welling up at the memory of those two small figures mounting the steps. But Alanya could surely have restrained herself! What good had her outburst done? It had simply scattered their group and destroyed the trip to Darthane. The last she saw was Fira yelling to a couple of her soldiers. Shiván and Alanya had disappeared — she could only hope they'd escaped. She herself had been hustled out of the square by the servants.

Then the dismal walk home, and Father's wrath on her arrival. She hadn't seen him so angry since Lari had set fire to the stables a couple of years back. The upshot was that she was grounded until further notice. No more lone trips into Berûvis, nor to the Wayside Chapel. Her attempts to explain about her vision had been swept aside. Never mind what God had said, she'd disobeyed her father, and that seemed to be all that mattered in this house.

So, what was she supposed to do? She couldn't go anywhere, let alone try and rejoin the Restorers. And how could she do that, even if she were able? They'd been scattered. One or both of them might have been captured. In which case it was all over. Yet again she'd pinned her hopes on a lost cause. *Dear Prince, don't let that be so! Shiván and Alanya* must *have escaped! You showed them to me. They are your Restorers! Please watch over them...* Her knife stilled and tears began dripping on the cayet.

Cook came and gently eased the knife from her fingers. "You go upstairs, m'lady, and have a good cry. You ain't helpin' yourself nor us down here."

Perrely glanced at the mutilated cayet and nodded. She stood and walked slowly to the stairs, her hands clasping and unclasping. Oh, how she needed a visit from Brother Frengor now! From time to time he and a junior brother would come to the house to talk and pray with her. He would at least understand about her vision, even if he didn't agree with how she'd interpreted it.

As she trudged up the stairs she pleaded desperately with the One to send Frengor soon. She really needed help sorting this mess out.

* * *

Danîsha plucked the berries selectively, a few here and a few there, as birds would eat them. The bushes and vines in the forest were laden with autumn fruit, but none must look as though they had been deliberately stripped. It was part of their new stringent measures for concealment. The planted areas had been covered with leaves and debris, and the herd of milk deer moved further from the Manor. They were gathering food only as needed now, and over a wider area.

Suddenly a volley of loud wails broke out to the north, accompanied by shouts and the *thwack* of a heavy stick being brought down with force. Feet thudded as other gatherers ran to the sound. Danîsha joined them, her heart hammering. What was this? An enemy spy captured?

What she found was one of the villagers standing red-faced with a broken branch in his hand. Cowering before him was a strange creature, something like a huge wolf or vastly overgrown dog, covered with shaggy grey-white hair. It was this that was emitting the human-sounding wails.

"*Dorbian!*" a woman exclaimed, packing a wealth of disgust into the word. She was carrying a hooked pole for snagging fruit from the upper branches, and started beating the creature with it. The squeals increased in intensity as the wolf—or whatever it was— tried to wriggle out of range. It was making no effort to defend itself or to run away. Other Dûrians were joining in as well now, sticks and feet raining down on the creature as it huddled against a tree.

Fury welled up in Danîsha. She couldn't abide cruelty to animals. "*Jedas! – Stop that!*" she bellowed at the top of her lungs. The whole group froze in amazement. She strode over, grabbed the woman's pole and threw it to the ground.

"What do you think you're doing, attacking that innocent creature? It's doing nothing to you!"

"*Nothing?*" the woman protested. "It was stripping our fruit from this vine!"

"It's a filthy Dorbian," a man added, as though that explained everything. He raised his stick.

At that moment a throaty baritone rang through the glade.

"*Light!* Gwargif smell light!"

Did that come from the *creature?*

It scrambled to its feet, and everyone jumped back. It walked through the crowd of dumbstruck Dûrians to Danîsha, who stood immobilised, goose pimples running down her arms. The massive creature gazed at her, its head at chest height, an expression of amazed delight on its dark, intelligent face. Its wolf-like features were surrounded by what looked like a helmet of long, thick hair.

"Lady of Light!" it exclaimed in a snuffly accent, its brown eyes gleaming with excitement. "I am coming so far! I am coming over mountain to come to *you.* Lady of Light, receive me! They hit me, and, Lady, I come from my people, I come to Light, and you are Lady of Light. Please, I talk with you."

Danîsha gaped at the wolf-like creature, thoughts whirling crazily through her mind. A performing animal? A well-trained pet? But look at the eyes! They were too intelligent, too alive! Was it a costume, with a person inside? No! You'd be able to see a gap round the eye-holes. But then... that could only mean... Her mind threatened to close down. *A different intelligent species.* That was *impossible.*

It—he—was looking at her anxiously. "Lady, I stay? I come far, I find you, you receive me, Lady of Light?"

The others were also astonished. "By the flame, it speaks Dûrian!" the woman gasped, wide-eyed. There was a general rumble of amazement.

The Dûrians marvelled that it spoke their language. Danîsha was overwhelmed that it spoke at all. Suddenly her knees couldn't hold her, and she sat down abruptly. A warm, dog-like scent wafted into her nostrils.

There was a sadness in the brown eyes. "Gwargif smell fear," he said softly. He squatted down and leant over her, earnestness in that startlingly intelligent face. "Not be afraid, Lady of Light. Gwargif not hurt any person with Light. Gwargif *never* hurt *Lady* of Light." He lifted a large, five-fingered paw and placed it on her hand.

"Will you look at that!" one of the villagers exclaimed.

"Lady receive Gwargif?" the Dorbian asked again.

Danîsha drew a deep breath. She had to deal with this. No matter what his shape, he had a name, he was intelligent, he spoke Dûrian... and he was asking her a question.

"Yes," she gasped. "Lady receive Gwar– gif. If he tells me who he is and what this is all about."

The long white tail thumped on the ground, and a warm smile lit up his face. "Lady of Light make Gwargif happy," he said.

There was a buzz of animated conversation as the villagers drifted back to their work, leaving Gwargif with Danîsha. Apparently he was her problem now.

Danîsha stared up at the wolf-like animal, still not quite believing this was happening. She took a deep breath and spoke to it—him.

"Who are you?"

"I Gwargif. I lead *hrarakh*—warriors—for clan *Dirkhas*. I from Dorbai. My people Dorbi."

"Is that the same as what the Dûrians called you? You're a 'Dorbian'?"

He blew sharply through his large nose and bobbed his head. She jumped. Then she realised he must be saying 'yes'. His brown eyes were fixed earnestly on hers.

"Why were they so angry? Why did they beat you?"

"They think Gwargif dark Dorbi. Is stealing is dark Dorbi do, is kill animal, is bad thing. Gwargif not dark Dorbi. Is from Dorbi of Light."

"Oh, um, I see. That's good."

Another snort and bob of the head.

"And do all Dorbians, er, talk, like you?"

A slow smile spread over his face. "Yes, Lady, we talk. Is people is say we talk too much."

Danîsha chuckled, and Gwargif joined in with an odd, coughing laugh which set Danîsha off even more. Soon she was wiping her eyes.

"Lady think is strange, Dorbi talk?"

"Well, you see, in my country we have, er, creatures like you who don't talk." For a moment she was embarrassed, thinking she might have offended him. But he nodded gravely.

"Gwargif know Lady of Light is from different place."

Danîsha felt a growing bewilderment. How did he know? What was this "Lady of Light" business? Where did you begin with someone *so* different—an intelligent person in the body of a wolf?

"So you came looking for me?"

"Yes, my people send me, Lady. They send me for Light—to come, because we know that Light coming." His eyes glowed with eagerness. "We see Darkness—and we need Light; and we come, because our great Leader, he say, We fight Darkness, and we fight Darkness with Light—and we know that people come, and they are with Light, and we come and fight, because we not want Darkness in our place. And now Gwargif find Lady of Light, and is happy." His face beamed as he again laid a heavy, five-fingered paw on her hand.

Danîsha tried to sort something out from this jumble. "You're looking for people of Light who are fighting the darkness? And you want to help them?"

Snort-and-bob. "Leader send me and two others, find Warriors of Light—I find *you!*" Delighted smile.

"'Warriors of Light'... You mean *Atenámbaret*—Restorers of the Way?"

Snort-and-bob.

Danîsha stared at the intelligent wolf-like creature. He knew about the Dûrians' *Atenámbaret*—he'd crossed mountains to find them. And he'd recognised her immediately as one of them!

She shook her head in wonder. He snorted-and-bobbed. They both laughed.

* * *

Sergeant Borion, their new leader, refused to allow the Dorbian into the basement, but Gwargif took the decision in his stride. He slept outside, and gathered his own food in the forest, careful not to strip entire bushes. But each midmeal break Danîsha and Teynel would join him with a bowl of food, eating their midmeal at the edge of the forest.

He told them about his home in the far north, near the 'white lands'; and spoke with wistful longing of his wife Hishray, and his cubs. He explained that he was still young, so only had five children. He asked her in turn about her foreign companions, and seemed especially pleased that there were men as well. He referred to Shiván and Gil as 'Fathers of Light', which Danîsha found rather funny.

This morning Gwargif was waiting eagerly for her in the ruined courtyard.

"Lady!" he exclaimed. "Is night, is Gwargif hear sweet sound! Sound bring smell of Light! What is sound Gwargif hear?"

Danîsha explained that she'd played her bellaril for the Dûrians last night.

Gwargif went very still. "Lady of *Light* make this sound?" he whispered.

Danîsha felt herself blushing. "Well, the bellaril really made the sound, you know — it's a beautiful instrument, I just play it."

"Lady bring bella–, berral–... sound-maker, play for Gwargif this noon?"

Danîsha agreed.

Later when everyone sat down for the midmeal, Danîsha took the bellaril and her bowl of food, and walked up the stairs to join Gwargif. They went to their usual spot under the trees at the edge of the forest. Teynel was on kitchen duty, staying behind under protest.

Danîsha sighed with contentment. It was a bright early autumn day, the trees starting to enter their full glory. The hollow of land in which the Manor sat was enclosed in an open torc of gold. Above them to the north towered the purple heights of the Kennissôr Mountains; they seemed to be holding up the thin layer of cloud through which the sun's radiance filtered.

When she'd finished eating Gwargif said eagerly, "Lady make sound?" He looked at the bellaril, his tail thumping.

"Oh, alright, I'll play for you." She grinned at him, picked up the instrument, and started strumming a much-loved song.

As the mellow tones filled the air, Gwargif's eyes grew huge. He began to tremble, then exclaimed with awe and growing excitement, "You are Mylendel. You are *Mylendel*! Warrior of Light, singer of truth! *Mylendel*, Lady of Song!"

He could no longer contain himself, and rose up to a startling height on his hind legs. He began leaping and twisting in the air in a wild dance of joy as Danîsha played, laughing at his exuberance.

Without warning Gwargif dropped from mid-leap to all fours. A deep rumbling sound began. It took a moment for Danîsha to recognise it as a growl rising from the Dorbian's chest. She faltered and stopped playing. Gwargif's hackles were up, and he was staring alternately at the Manor and at the gap beyond it, where the hills fell away to the lowlands.

Danîsha stared at the Dorbian, her heart beating an uncomfortable tattoo. "Gwargif, what's the matter? What do you smell?"

"Gwargif smell deep Darkness," he said, the growl still reverberating through his voice. "Dark of people hate Light. Dark coming to kill."

Just then two of the lookouts appeared a hundred yards off at the edge of the forest. They saw Danîsha and gestured urgently at the Manor before pelting towards it themselves.

"A patrol!" she exclaimed. "We must run!" She scrambled to her feet clutching the bellaril and the food bowl. But Gwargif leapt in front of her.

"Not go!" he barked. "Darkness at house already. Gwargif not smell soon enough. *Not go!*" he barked again, as Danîsha made to run to the Manor.

Danîsha twisted her hands. This was a nightmare. Every instinct screamed at her to run for safety in the hidden basement. But Gwargif seemed to be saying the enemy were already there. How could they be? The lookouts would have given warning long before that.

Gwargif stood growling in front of Danîsha as another noise made itself heard. The drumming of horses' hooves.

A moment later a squadron of grey-cloaked cavalry burst into the Manor clearing and fanned out to surround the building. Danîsha gasped. They'd all be trapped inside! Oh, dear God.

Other riders appeared from inside the ruined building, guarding every doorway. Gwargif had been right—they were there already. Then one rider spurred his horse directly towards her, sword drawn. Gwargif began to rumble like a volcano, the hair standing vertical on his back.

"Run, Lady!" he shouted between the rumbles. "Run to forest! Gwargif follow!"

But Danîsha stood rooted to the spot. She had recognised the rider's face above his grey cloak.

It was Gil.

Map 6:
Gil's Return to Carreck Manor

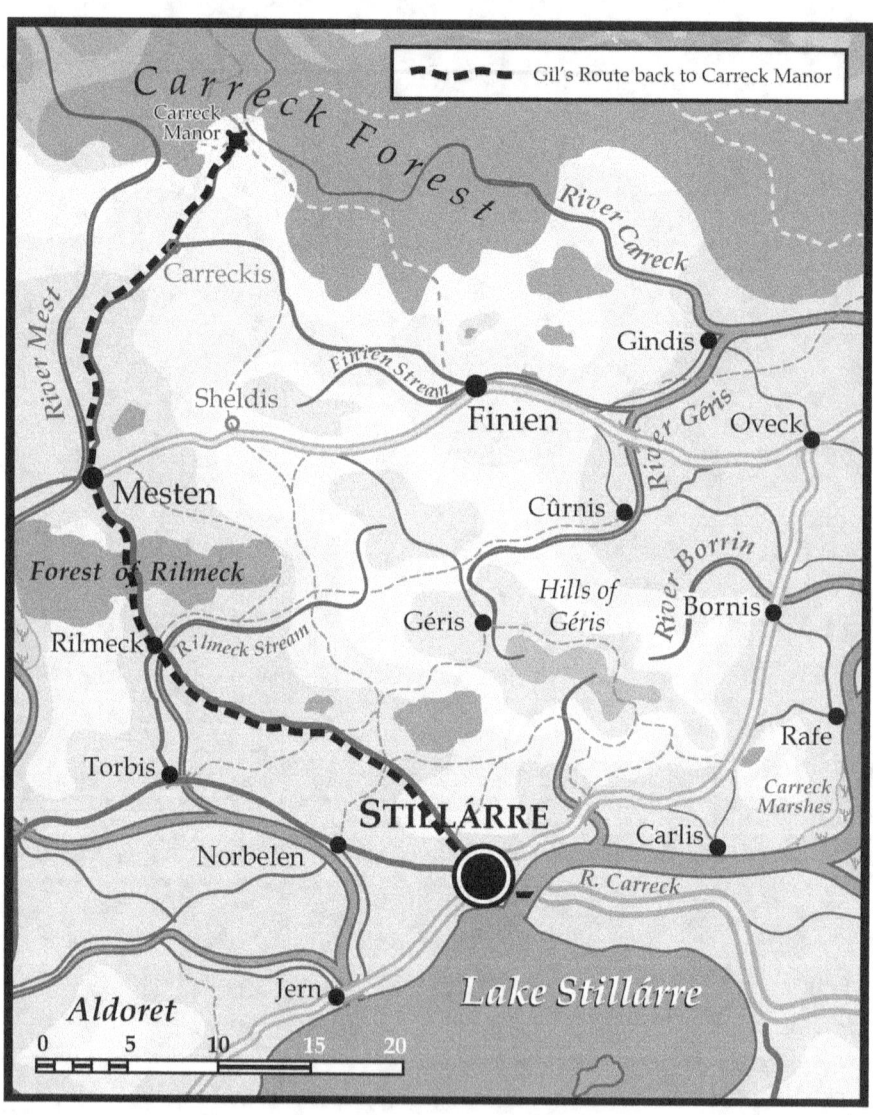

Chapter 23: *Darkness falls at Carreck Manor*

GELMION SPURRED HIS HORSE into the Manor clearing at the head of the patrol. He saw the unmistakable grey-haired figure of Danîsha standing at the forest edge beside a large, grey-white… was that a *wolf*? But first things first. He had to show Lieutenant Falmenor the door to the basement.

Within him Gil was crying out in agony, as he had been since last night. He'd never known pain like this. Dhelgor had plundered his mind. He'd ransacked his memory and dragged out every detail about the Manor and its inhabitants. Thanks to him, Gil Denbigh, the Dûrians who had sheltered him and taught him the language would be slaughtered. Somehow the fact that they had sentenced him to death had faded into insignificance. That had been for a reason. This slaughter was mindless savagery.

And thanks to him, his three English friends would be captured. He blinked furiously. They would all be sacrificed on the altar fire, he was sure of that now. Whether together or one by one, he didn't know. Dhelgor had discovered his feelings for Lannie, and was twisting a knife in the wound. *"I'll have her first, Gelmie. If you're very good I might give you a go later. Better make sure you co-operate."*

Co-operate! That was a joke. His body would perform the required actions, whether his mind consented or not. That fiend Dhelgor would get hold of Lannie and do with her whatever he liked — with or without the kind 'co-operation' of Trooper Gelmion.

But the Manor community was finished, thanks to the actions his body had already performed. Earlier he'd led the first squad of nine Guardsmen by a roundabout route to the eastern forest. Wood scouts had silently located the Manor lookouts — and sharp-shooting bowmen had killed them. Not one had escaped to give the alarm. Then Gelmion had shown them the outlet of the escape tunnel. They were even now advancing up it towards the kitchen. There was no escape for those in the basement.

Trooper Gelmion found the section of wall in the Manor passage, and with a face of stone showed Lieutenant Falmenor the hidden lever that opened it. Then he was summoned elsewhere.

Gil's mind detected a note of eager anticipation in Dhelgor's command to go and fetch Danîsha. Of course, it *would* be Trooper Gelmion who was selected for this task.

"Ah, but she's your friend," his master's voice pointed out reasonably.

"You're sick."

A sudden bolt of pure pain convulsed him, and he almost fell out of the saddle.

"Get Danîsha!"

He spurred his horse to a gallop. She was still standing at the edge of the forest, with that wolf-thing in front of her. He drew his sword. 'Neesh was staring at him, her mouth open — she'd recognised him. Gil's mind cringed; Dhelgor chuckled, watching through his eyes.

Then there was a blood-curdling roar and the wolf exploded in his face. His horse screamed and jerked out from under him. Trees and grass flashed across the sky, his sword shot from his hand, and he landed with a juddering crash on his back. The next instant the wolf was on top of him and he was staring into a dark, intelligent face that was snarling in a most wolf-like way. It made a lunge for his throat and he clamped his eyes shut.

"No, Gwargif!" Danîsha screamed, and he'd never agreed with her more.

"Is servant of Darkness, Gwargif kill," the wolf snarled, and Gil's mind reared back in shock — more at the voice than the threat.

"He's a friend, Gwargif."

"He want bad for you."

"It's a Dorbian — a Lightist one." There was wonder in Dhelgor's tone.

'Neesh was now bending over him. The Dorbian wolf — or whatever — continued to snarl in his face.

"Gil, *why?*" she demanded, her red-rimmed eyes blazing. "Why are you part of this?"

He desperately wanted to speak, but his lips would not open. His eyelids kept blinking. *Wait,* Dhelgor said. *Reinforcements are on their way.*

"Did you do this? Did you lead them here?"

He stared at her dumbly, crying out helplessly in his mind, *No! They tricked me! I did everything I could to keep the truth from them, but they stole my memories!*

Danîsha's lips tightened.

No, 'Neesh, I'm not being stubborn. What you're seeing is not me, *I'm a prisoner inside…*

"If you're trying to get revenge for the death sentence they passed on you, you're wrong — we all were. It wasn't a death sentence. 'Leave and not arrive' is a Dûrian way of saying they would take you somewhere else, not where *you* wanted to go, but somewhere safe. They wouldn't have killed you, Gil. But now —" Suddenly her eyes filled with tears, which flowed down her blotched cheeks. "Now they're *all* going to die, because of you…"

Gil wept with her. He should have known the Manor community wouldn't kill him. They were too caring for that. What a mess. What a waste. All these good people dying because of one small misunderstanding and his reactions to it. His heart felt as though it were tearing apart. Then — maybe Dhelgor's attention was elsewhere — he felt a warm tear escape his eye. 'Neesh was still staring at him, anger and grief in her face — was that a momentary flicker of surprise? Had she seen?

* * *

Danîsha saw the tear trickling from Gil's eye, and realised that he was doing this against his will. She was about to urge him to escape with her and Gwargif into the forest, when a drumming of hooves and a deepened rumbling from the Dorbian brought her head up sharply. She gave a gasp of dismay. Three riders were galloping towards them from the Manor. They would be there any moment.

"Gwargif, leave him! We must run!" She scrambled to her feet.

"Lady, we run, they kill. Make sound, Lady of Song!"

Danîsha was already stumbling toward the forest. What was Gwargif talking about? Why wasn't he coming? She looked back, her legs trembling. The leading horseman was only a couple of hundred yards away.

"*Gwargif!*" she shouted desperately.

"Lady!" It was between a bark and an agonised yelp. "Make song! Quick!"

Had he taken leave of his senses? He wanted music — *now?* This delay had finished them, she saw with despair. The riders were a mere hundred yards off and closing in; there was no escape. They had drawn their swords.

She collapsed beside the bellaril and the overturned food bowl. Well, she might as well die to the sound of this beautiful instrument. She picked it up and fumbled to position it correctly.

"*Mylendel!* Sing!" Gwargif barked. With a corner of her mind she saw that he was trying to move himself round to face their attackers, but Gil was struggling under him.

A sudden peace descended on Danîsha. It had been a good life, all told, and she was ready to meet her God. She was so glad she'd seen Dûrion — and she was sure she'd be reunited with many of her Dûrian friends who died today. She positioned her fingers and started to play one of the few English songs she'd practised on the bellaril.

"*Amazing grace, how sweet the sound —*"

The first mellow notes of the instrument brought the oncoming horses to a sudden, shuddering stop. The third rider, furthest from them, went sailing over his mount's head. He hit the ground with a sickening thud and lay still. Danîsha's playing faltered, but she continued, her mind dazed by what was happening.

"*— that saved a wretch like me!*"

Gil had stopped struggling, but his hand was clenched in a fist, the knuckles white.

"*I once was lost, but now am found —*"

The other two riders sat frozen in their saddles, bound by the web of music. She could see sweat on both their foreheads; their faces were masks of pain.

"*Was blind, but now I see.*"

Gwargif had left Gil. He came over and gently snuffled her shoulder.

"See, Lady of Song," he murmured. "Shining One touch your sound. You are *Mylendel*. We walk, you sing. They not follow."

"*Through many dangers, toils and snares, I have already come.*"

Danîsha got to her feet, still playing. She went over and squatted down by Gil. His eyes were squeezed shut; there was anguish on his face. You didn't enjoy the bellaril, did you, Gil? Maybe this is why; the Shining One sings through it, and you are not ready to hear his song.

"*'Tis grace that brought me safe thus far —*"

Goodbye, Gil. I know you can't come with us now; I hope one day you will.

She walked into the forest, her fingers still strumming, her voice singing softly as Gwargif padded behind her.

"And grace will lead me home."

* * *

Dhelgor was enjoying his midmeal entertainment. He lay on a recliner in his comfortable Stillárre apartment, popping grapes into his mouth. There was a faraway look in his eye as he directed his slaves and subordinates at Carreck Manor.

He had savoured Gelmion's shock at discovering that the carefully-guarded secret of his friends' whereabouts had already been filched from his memory. This was ultimate power—control over the minds of others. But it would be short-lived with Gelmion if he carried on fighting him like this. He'd seldom come across such implacable opposition. When Dûrians found their inner stronghold taken, they suffered shock and grief, but they soon realised it was pointless to resist (apart from Lightists, of course—but they never lasted long anyway). Gelmion was not a Lightist—but his mind resisted control every step of the way.

Like that offensive *"You're sick"* comment a few minutes ago. Dhelgor's lips tightened in displeasure. If it hadn't been so urgent for Gelmion to go after Danîsha, he'd have given him a lot more than a brief jolt of pain for that. He'd still suffer for it, though. Oh, yes. Dhelgor knew very well how to make a squeamish mind like Gelmion's suffer.

Meanwhile he was enjoying seeing him trembling with a Dorbian in his face. The view from his eyes was quite chilling. But he'd better send reinforcements. His mind swooped back to the Manor basement, where he found Lieutenant Falmenor, his subordinate Mindbender, rounding up the prisoners. Gesh! What a sorry lot. They'd be sorrier soon. Then they'd be beyond sorrow—but Gelmion would delay that moment as long as possible. Dhelgor rubbed his hands in anticipation.

The only grit in the gruel was Falmenor's report that there was no sign of Gelmion's other two companions, Alanya and Shiván. He hoped his subordinate had picked up the second-hand mental images correctly. He'd look through Falmenor's eyes and double-check later.

Dhelgor ordered Falmenor to assign him three Guardsmen, and sent them clattering upstairs and on to their horses. He watched through the leading rider's eyes as he approached the little group by the forest's edge. This would be interesting. He had them all draw their swords.

First Danîsha leapt up to leave, then she came back. The Dorbian squirmed around to face them, still pinning Gelmion down. Dhelgor allowed the foreigner's body to struggle, but that Dorbian was heavy.

Now Danîsha had sat down. She was picking something up. Did the old woman have a weapon? He laughed incredulously. No—it was a bellaril! Great Powers of Darkness, she was going to give them a song while they captured her! This entertainment became more amusing by the moment.

They were almost there now. He could see the foreign woman's lined face filled with a quite unwarranted peacefulness. She began to play...

...and all heaven broke loose. Power stopped. Control was gone. The horses shuddered to a halt. With each note of the bellaril a blinding pulse of light invaded Dhelgor's eyes and beat upon his mind. He tried to scream, but nothing came out. The rider whose mind he was using became a direct conduit of light and sound. He tried to make him turn around, to escape, but his feeble mental energies were drowned out by the light. He clasped his arms over his head.

Still the unrelenting, razor-sharp notes continued, each one releasing a brilliant shaft that slashed through every layer of deception to the very core of his being. He rolled off the recliner to the floor, curled up in a foetal position, his mouth wide in a voiceless scream. The light blazed brighter, exposing him pitilessly, till he could take no more. His mind shut down, and blessed darkness fell.

* * *

Dhelgor woke up to find himself lying on the floor. How by the six portals had *that* happened? He must have dropped off—literally. Late night with that new adherent. It was a good thing Falmenor was competent enough to keep things going. He took his place again on the recliner and had a grape. Now, what were those four Guardsmen doing milling around at the forest edge? He frowned. He hadn't sent them out there! One of them was nursing a broken arm, and another was Gelmion. Gelmion was supposed to be in the basement!

All the Guardsmen seemed genuinely bewildered, not knowing how they'd reached the forest. He angrily ordered them back to the Manor.

* * *

As Gelmion trotted dutifully with the others toward the ruined building, the mind of Gil within him was quivering in the aftermath of a powerful experience — but it kept slipping from his grasp. Dhelgor's attention was elsewhere for the moment, leaving him free to think about it. Something had happened out there at the edge of the forest. Something important. He remembered shedding a tear. A tear Dhelgor hadn't known about. What could have caused that? It must have been an agony even greater than his normal condition these days, to have forced an actual tear past the Mindbender's iron control. His mind wrestled with the elusive memory, but could not pin it down.

They entered the Manor ruins, and screams and shouts came floating up from the basement. Panic gripped Gil's mind. This was what he'd been desperately afraid of all along. He'd be forced to take part in it! His mind cried out in horror, but his body calmly dismounted from his horse in the central courtyard, tethered it, and walked with the others to the open door. At Dhelgor's command he drew his dagger. The screams were piercing now, set against a continuous background of sobbing, groans and whimpers.

He walked down the stairs into a scene from a horror movie. The lamps were lit and the kitchen looked normal — except for the figures strapped to tables, chairs and columns. They were being subjected to every torture imaginable. A choking sensation filled him. He wanted to look away, but could not.

"Here he is!" cried Lieutenant Falmenor. "Now we can *really* begin. Look at your betrayer, all you miserable rebel filth! Who is he?"

There was a silence as thirty or more pairs of eyes stared at him. His friends. He wanted to cry out to them that it was all a lie, but his face was set in concrete.

"I asked a question. Answer me!" Falmenor's dagger flashed downwards and Trooper Darmet screamed as his left hand was nailed to the table. The poor man gurgled and mercifully passed out. Gil's mind whimpered.

"Who is he?"

"Gelmion," came the ragged response.

"Yes, Gelmion! Look at him. What is he now?"

A dull chorus intoned variants of "A Bishop's Guard."

"A man who's seen the error of his ways! A man who serves the Bishop. A man who's come to stamp out vermin like you. But if anyone wants to live, they have only to tell us where the other foreigners are. *Where are Shiván, Alanya and Danîsha?* Come now, let us know where they're hiding, and you'll be spared!"

A wild relief bloomed in Gil's heart. Lannie and the others had escaped! That was fantastic. Then he saw the hopelessness in his friends' eyes, and knew that the Dûrians would die, whether they betrayed the foreigners or not. His heart clenched. There sat the small, bound forms of Lary and Hald, Delmy, Jemmy — and Teynel. Children, whose innocent lives were ending in this horrific way thanks to him. He wanted to raise his hand and plunge the dagger it held into his own heart; but he could not. His tearless eyes kept blinking.

"Sorry for them, are you?" came Dhelgor's sardonic voice. *"You seem to have mistaken your rôle here, Gelmion. You're their torturer and executioner, not their bleeding-heart rescuer. I think we need to get that clear right away..."*

"Gelmion!" exclaimed Falmenor, struck with a happy thought. "Why don't you apply a little persuasion?" His arm swept round the bound figures.

Gil felt Dhelgor's compulsion taking hold of his body. *"No! No! I won't –"* He struggled with all that was in him, straining to seize back control as his arm rose to hurt his friends.

"Oh yes you will."

Gil screamed inside his head, willing his hand to stop, straining against his own muscles, clenching them, pulling them back...

But they kept moving implacably towards their target.

Gil's mind darkened and became lost in a black mist as despite all his efforts he lifted the dagger and began performing the most barbaric acts he had ever committed. His Dûrian friends screamed under his knife. They went on and on. They would never stop. They would scream in his mind forever.

In the mist he felt himself carrying out other atrocities, each worse than the last. They all died at his hands, all his friends, while his comrades of the Bishop's Guard laughed and applauded. As his body performed actions he could never have dreamed of in his worst nightmare, his inner mind closed down. Gil could no longer stand by and watch. He surrendered Gelmion to Dhelgor.

Finally there was silence as Gelmion stood staring into Teynel's dead eyes. But the screams echoed on in Gil's mind.

* * *

Mindbender Dhelgor was frustrated as he picked at his midmeal. So near, yet so far! True, a nest of rebels had been wiped out, and one day he might be able to claim credit for that. True, Gelmion had been subdued. His mind was in shock, and would be weighed down with guilt when it recovered. From there it would be an easy matter to blur the distinction between his, Dhelgor's, mental suggestions, and Gelmion's own despairing thoughts. He would come to the conclusion that it had been his own evil desires that had led him to behave as he had; then the battle was almost won.

And he still needed Gelmion. That was part of the frustration. Because despite the achievements on the credit side, the raid had failed in its main aim — to capture the other three foreigners. Before Gelmion completed the executions Lieutenant Falmenor had found out that Alanya and Shiván had set out for Darthane some nine days ago; and that Danîsha had last been seen going to the forest before the raid yesterday. Maybe that was why he'd found Gelmion and three other Guardsmen at the forest's edge? He shook his head. That little episode bothered him.

Be that as it might, he'd failed to catch the foreigners Shiván and Alanya. He couldn't embark on a search towards Darthane without Bishop Shambor, the Mindruler, becoming aware of it; and that was the last thing he wanted. He knew very well that the Mindruler would look with extreme displeasure on his attempts at empire-building in Stillárre. And those on whom Shambor looked with displeasure didn't last long. He shivered. No, the Mindruler must never know about this. Fortunately the autonomy Shambor had given him as a senior Mindbender meant that his memories were his own. Later, when time had blurred the facts, he might be able to refer casually to the nest of rebels he'd cleared out at the Manor, and gain some credit for it. But not yet.

Meanwhile, though, Danîsha had vanished into the forest and they were hunting high and low for her. That was another complication he hadn't anticipated. Legate Yonistor of Finien was also sending patrols into the forest to hunt for rebels—at Shambor's command. His greatest fear was that his men would encounter Yonistor's, and a report would find its way back to Shambor. He'd be hard-put to explain—

"Mindbender."

Shambor! It took all Dhelgor's control not to choke on his soup.

"Yes, Mindruler." Iron discipline prevailed. There was no quaver in his mental voice; he presented a calm front to his master.

"A report on those northern informers of yours. Caught any more rebel sympathisers?"

"No, Mindruler. We're patrolling the roads between Mesten and Berûvis."

"Have the relatives of those peasants who were executed been dealt with—in Géris, wasn't it?"

"They have, sir. Two put to death as an example to the others."

"Good. Keep up those informer patrols. I have ordered Yonistor at Finien to send more men into the forests. I want every last rebel rounded up! Is that clear?"

"Yes, Mindruler. I will spare no effort."

"You'd better not."

The presence departed, and Dhelgor heaved a sigh of relief. Then panic struck. More patrols from Finien! He had to withdraw his men at once. He issued the order to Falmenor.

It all came down to Gelmion now. The information Falmenor had gained from the Manor rebels was that Alanya and Shiván were looking for Gelmion, thinking he'd gone to Darthane. When they found he hadn't—maybe they would come looking in Stillárre. And maybe they'd bring Danîsha with them. That signed Gelmion's reprieve. Dhelgor was unwilling to rely on the mental pictures of the other three foreigners that he'd picked up from Gelmion's mind. Such second-hand images were not very accurate. And a person's shiláy only became apparent at close quarters. No, Gelmion's friends needed to find *him*. Then the jaws of the trap would close.

* * *

For a day and a half Danîsha and Gwargif had lain low in the forest while the Bishop's Guard searched for them. They'd found a
cave that had been prepared long ago as a temporary shelter, with
a few basic provisions for emergencies. Gwargif had silently shad-
owed the searching riders until he saw them regrouping yesterday
near the Manor and setting off to the lowlands. He'd followed
them till he was satisfied they were truly leaving. This morning
he'd sniffed all round the Manor to make sure none had remained
behind as an ambush. Only then had he given Danîsha the all-
clear.

Even so, he pleaded with her not to go down into the basement.
But she had to know. Teynel, the young waif who'd adopted her,
who'd clung to her as the granny she'd lost. She had been on
kitchen duty that terrible day. Could she have escaped? Hidden in
a dark corner? Might she even now be cowering down there, afraid
to come out?

Danîsha stood at the top of the basement stairs. Her knees were
trembling, her stomach threatening to void itself at the nauseous
stench that wafted out of the black doorway to the basement.
Gwargif stood growling at her side. Taking that first step was the
bravest thing she'd ever done. The Dorbian brushed past and pre-
ceded her down the stairway into the darkness. The rumble from
his chest deepened, and in the gloom Danîsha could see the grey
hair on his back standing up. She was carrying a firestick already
daubed with fireclay. She felt along the wall till her hand found the
first lamp. She broke the firestick and lit it.

Danîsha forced herself to look at what the lamp's glow revealed.
Her heart almost stopped at the scene from hell that met her eyes.
She sank down on the stairs. "Oh Lord. Oh Lord," she gasped.
Then she was violently sick.

But she had to know. She pulled herself to her feet, then slowly,
like an old woman, felt her way down one step at a time. All
around were her friends—her Dûrian family. Slaughtered in the
most barbaric way imaginable. Was Teynel among them?

She lit more lamps. She walked among the carnage on a stone
floor black with congealed blood. Jannel and Remmy... Darmet...
Tears streamed down her cheeks as she murmured their names.

Little Hald… Veynel… Damion… She had to sit on a bloody bench and close her eyes to avoid fainting. But where was Teynel?

Clinging to a last glimmer of hope she made her way towards one of the passages off the kitchen. Maybe Teynel had escaped down there, into one of the storerooms…

But before she reached the passage she almost stumbled over a small body lying on the floor. A wail of anguish burst from her heart as she saw Teynel's sweet face. Her lifeless eyes held a bewildered look. *Why?*

Danîsha sank down beside her. Her eyes went over the matted hair she'd brushed and stroked so often. Teynel's comb was entangled, and she gently pried it free as waves of grief shook her body. She took the comb and squeezed it between her hands until the prongs pierced her skin.

Her mind overwhelmed, she prayed to die.

———————————————

Chapter 24: *Home sweet home*

GIL WOKE UP SCREAMING. He hadn't heard such a high-pitched sound issuing from his own lips since childhood. He sat panting. His eyes were clenched shut. He was shivering, both from cold and from terror.

Had it finally ended? Did he have enough blood on his hands now? He opened his eyes and looked down. His hands were surprisingly clean—but he started at what else he saw. He was stark naked! Then he remembered: they'd returned to Mesten last night, and in his state of shock he'd pulled all his bloodstained clothing off, thrown it as far from him as he could, and collapsed on to the bed.

But this wasn't the Guardhouse in Mesten! He leapt up, looking around wildly. What had they done to him? Was he a prisoner again?

The room he found himself in was comfortably, even luxuriously furnished. He'd been sitting in a well-padded armchair. The floor was covered with a fuzzy brown cloth that felt warm underfoot. To one side there was a wide, oddly-proportioned table and a too-broad chair made of matching sandy-coloured wood. The table was littered with papers. Facing the armchair was a recess in the wall in which sat a wide, flat basket made of blackened metal strips...

With an almost-audible 'click' his dislocated mind suddenly snapped back into focus. A fireplace! This was his flat in London. He was back home—in England! Relief overwhelmed him like a tidal wave and he collapsed into the armchair again. His eyes wandered over the familiar furniture, savouring every stain and blemish. He could hardly take it in. He'd thought he was condemned to a lifetime of exile on an alien planet, and now, suddenly—he was home!

No, wait a minute. He shook himself. He'd had a dream, that was all. A nightmare—the worst he could remember. He frowned. But that was the problem—he did remember. Everything. In pitiless detail. He shuddered. And that was unlike most dreams, surely? You woke up remembering the emotions that prompted the dream, but the actual details were hard to reconstruct. You felt dissatisfied when you tried to tell it to someone else, because it no longer made sense, and you found yourself filling in gaps and rationalising in order to make a coherent story out of it.

This dream was different. He remembered the details all too vividly.

Meanwhile here he was without a stitch of clothing, shivering! *That* didn't make sense, if it was a dream. Why would he have stripped, sat himself down in an armchair, and fallen asleep? Well, he couldn't remember now, but all the other stuff in his mind was too fantastic to be true. It had to be a dream, for God's sake.

He glanced at his left wrist to check the date on his watch—but there was no watch. Of course! It had stopped working just before he left the Manor, and he'd… He crushed the thought. It must be somewhere. He went to the bedroom and looked on the bedside table, in the top drawer of his chest of drawers, under the bed… but it wasn't in any of those places. He did find his dressing gown and slippers, and put them on. He felt a lot better wearing them.

As he was leaving the room, he caught sight of himself in the large mirror above the dressing table, and stopped to look. A tanned, weather-beaten face stared back at him. That was odd. He hadn't gone abroad this summer. In which case… He shook his head. Dûrion kept coming back to haunt him, but it had to be a dream. He'd caught more sun than he'd realised during that weekend in Cornwall, that was all.

Back in the living room he hunted for yesterday's newspaper and found it under the coffee table. It was dated September 14th. Now for the acid test. He turned the computer on. As it booted up he watched anxiously for the date and time to appear on the screen. Eventually it came up—September 15th, 07:11. He heaved a sigh of relief. No time lost! It *was* a dream.

He stretched luxuriously. Now he was going to have a good, hot bath. He normally showered, but today for some reason his whole being craved full immersion in hot, soapy water. He took pleasure running the bath, testing the water, and then the crowning moment when he lowered himself into its clean, invigorating warmth.

As he soaped himself, though, his euphoria began to fade. Dûrion was thrusting itself on his attention again. He held up his hands and stared at them. There were calluses on them. These were not the soft hands of an academic. They were the hands of someone who for many weeks had been doing manual labour. He examined his feet — the same story. There were scabs, bruises and welts on his arms and legs that spoke of a rough, outdoor life.

Worst of all, now that he looked closely, he found many small, brown stains spattered on the backs of his hands and on his arms. They didn't come off easily in the hot water.

Grief welled up in him. It was true, then. It had really happened. All of it. Tears ran down his face as he desperately scrubbed every last stain away.

He dressed in a daze, pulling on clean underwear, fresh-smelling grey trousers and a crisp shirt with faint pink stripes, topped off with his trademark navy corduroy jacket. The sleek fabrics felt too good to be true. Then he made breakfast, still on autopilot. Percolated coffee, toast and poached eggs ought to have tasted glorious after weeks of foreign food; but he scarcely noticed them. His mind was struggling to come to terms with two different realities.

So he had really been in Dûrion for... what? Seven weeks? Must be at least that. Yet here he was, back in his flat, the morning after he'd left. The newspaper and computer proved it. He shook his head. That didn't add up. Or rather, it added up if Dûrion was a dream. Not if Dûrion was real. But if Dûrion was a dream, too many other things didn't add up: his missing clothes, missing watch, weather-beaten face, callused hands, scarred body — and above all, those... stains. He couldn't bring himself to say the *b*-word.

He absently took another sip of coffee as he sat at the kitchen table, staring blankly at the toaster. So what was he to make of this? He'd spent seven weeks elsewhere while only seven hours had passed here. He couldn't get around that. The evidence was in his mind, as well as his body. 'Yesterday' was a distant memory — just as it would be after seven weeks. He could remember its major event — the confrontation with his colleagues over that article he'd plagiarised — but that was all. He had no recollection of what he'd eaten for breakfast or lunch, or even where he'd eaten. He couldn't remember what classes he'd taught, or which individuals he'd tutored.

So. Between yesterday evening and this morning his memory had been overlaid by seven weeks of experience in a different reality. How could that have happened? Well, maybe it did work like a dream. Dreams might seem to take hours or days, but actually only lasted a second or less in real time. In which case seven hours of real time would account for a hefty chunk of alternate reality.

A more immediate question sprang to mind: Was he home for good now? Or would he have the Dûrian 'dream' again? He shuddered at the thought of falling asleep and finding himself back in the body of Gelmion the Guardsman. And yet... Not everything in Dûrion had been bad. There was Lannie. His heart lurched at the thought of her. Would he ever see her again? Would it be worth going back to Dûrion (supposing he could choose), just to see her and apologise for his stupidity and say goodbye? No. Not if he was to be the bait that lured her to a fiery death.

The chimes of the living room clock recalled him to the present. Eight-thirty! He ought to be leaving for work. But what was he supposed to be doing today? He went to the living room and rummaged through drawers till he found a dog-eared departmental timetable. Wednesday. Third-year syntax class. Second-year reading group in types of linguistic theory. Scribbled note—weekly session in the afternoon with Pete Stanton. Pete Stanton? Oh, yes—one of the doctoral students he was supervising. What was his thesis about again? He couldn't for the life of him recall. Nor could he remember where he'd reached in those other two classes.

Oh well. Nothing for it. He'd have to call in sick—for the first time in five years.

Jean Overton, the crusty, beak-nosed departmental secretary, was terse on the phone. Of course she knew via the grapevine of his current difficulties over the plagiarism charge, and it didn't take a genius to work out what she attributed his 'illness' to. His status in the department was rapidly slipping. Yesterday this in itself would have been a major disaster. Today it was about as important as losing a child's plastic penny.

After staring into space for a while longer he decided to buy a newspaper. He'd eventually have to deal with his crumbling career here in England; for now his mind was too busy recovering from the battering it had received in Dûrion.

He came back to the flat with his paper, comforted by the sights and sounds of traffic, of the familiar urban landscape, of people dressed normally and speaking English. He made more coffee and settled himself on the sofa. It must be decades since he'd had a quiet morning like this.

The headlines were predictably all about the latest political scandal — who had said what to whom, who was blaming whom, and who was really to blame. The other front page items were about equally fatuous non-issues. How had he ever devoured this stuff so avidly? He turned to the middle section.

The pictures hit him first: piles of black bodies; desolate faces; bewildered children. Suddenly he was back in a dim basement, raising his dagger over a screaming child. Through a mist of tears he read the article that went with the pictures. An association of African war widows was holding a march in London to bring their plight to the attention of an indifferent world. Victims of rape, mutilation, torture and horrific acts of barbarism — conveniently forgotten now the crisis had passed. They had no social welfare, no insurance policies, no compensation from their bankrupt government. No one cared whether they lived or died.

At the end of the article was the name of an aid agency, and a phone number. He fumbled in the desk drawer for his credit card. His voice was not entirely steady as he spoke to the volunteer who took his call. Maybe she was used to that. What she wasn't used to was the amount. There was a short silence, then a hesitant query.

"Er, was that... two *thousand* pounds?"

"Yes."

"Well, thank you, sir; thank you very much indeed."

"Don't thank me. I'm giving it to you because I can't give it to — the relatives of — Never mind. Believe me, this is the least I can do."

He gave the card details, then put the phone down on her enthusiastic appreciation.

In the afternoon he took his BMW out of London for a drive on the M40 motorway, remembering how he'd longed for the car on that endless walk to Stillárre. It gave him a melancholy pleasure to think that in half an hour he easily covered a distance that had cost him eight hours of painful foot-slogging in Dûrion.

He branched off the motorway on to a local road, then a country lane, meandering through the Oxfordshire countryside. Before he realised where he was going a faded notice reading 'Leston' floated past his car window.

Leston! Father Martin. The Round Church, where this had all begun. And there it was, just as he remembered it, standing white and peaceful on the village green with its circular tower.

Panic hit him. This was the last place he wanted to be! What on earth was he thinking? He accelerated past the church and on through the village, breaking the thirty-mile-an-hour limit in his haste to get away.

Several miles out of Leston there was a lay-by. He pulled over and stopped the car to allow his jangled nerves to settle.

But try as he might, he couldn't stop his mind from going back to that fateful day.

"Dr. Denbigh! How good to see you." There was a warmth in Father Martin's greeting that made it more than a polite cliché. Gil was impressed that Dr. Martin Fellowes remembered his name from the one previous occasion they'd met, when the priest-cum-linguist had given a guest lecture at the university. They shook hands.

"I'm glad you were in," Gil said. "I was passing this way, so I thought I'd drop by..." It had a false ring. Whoever passed through Leston?

Father Martin smiled and ushered Gil to the lounge area in the nave of the unconventional church. "Take a seat. Can I get you some coffee?"

As they chatted about linguistics and other inconsequential matters, Gil began to relax for the first time since the ultimatum that morning. The coffee was good. So was the company. Indirect lighting provided a dim, warm ambience – except for a spotlight on the Irish cross above the altar. The golden bars and silver circle gleamed in the light. Gil noticed two sections of well-worn brown leather inset into the vertical bar towards the lower end. Handgrips for when it was carried aloft in processions?

"So, what's troubling you, Dr. Denbigh?"

Gil started. He felt himself colouring at the man's perceptiveness. He deliberately put his coffee mug down on the circular pine table, then looked the priest in the eye.

"I'm not in the habit of confessing my sins," he said. "But I've got myself into rather a tight spot. I need to talk it through with someone – and I ... thought of you. If you wouldn't mind."

"Not at all. I'll gladly listen. But no advice!"

Gil smiled. "That's fine with me."

He told the priest how badly he'd needed to publish more academic articles in his bid for the Chair of Linguistics. How he'd plagiarised a younger lecturer's work, adapting a paper of his and publishing it as his own in an obscure periodical. How this had come to light. The ultimatum from two colleagues this morning: either a public apology from him, or public exposure by them. A week to 'consider his position'.

Father Martin listened intently. When Gil had finished, the wide-set turquoise eyes considered him gravely. There was no condemnation in the priest's gaze: rather, Gil felt he was weighing him up, considering how much he could handle.

"I suppose the answer's obvious," Gil muttered, examining his hands. "'Fess up and take the consequences."

"No."

Gil looked up, startled.

"Can you see the truth?" the young priest asked earnestly. "Can you see how both you and your colleagues have been in the wrong?"

Gil stared at him. "I – No, I'm sure they were in the right, but – "

"Which is more important: truth, or its consequences?"

"Truth, I suppose." Gil was starting to feel uncomfortable.

"Dr. Denbigh – " Father Martin glanced down for a moment, as though unsure whether to continue. "Forgive me if this sounds presumptuous, but... Are you willing to see the truth?"

Suddenly the strange question assumed a deep importance in Gil's mind. He himself would not have expressed it that way, but it seemed to go to the very heart of his dilemma. If he could only get a handle on the truth, there would be no dilemma. He had somehow become entangled in a web of deceit. He'd been blinded. He needed to see the truth; then he'd see everything clearly.

He looked the priest in the eye. "Yes," he said quietly. He glanced up. Had the cross over the altar brightened for an instant? Imagination.

A smile tugged the corners of Father Martin's lips. "Then let me assure you, you're in for a rough ride! Truth doesn't come cheap." He sobered. Laying a hand on Gil's shoulder he said, "I won't advise, but I'll say this: you won't see the truth in your present situation. You'll see it in a com-pletely different place. You might not like what you see – and things will probably get worse before they get better. But you will see the truth. And as someone once said, the truth will set you free."

Gil gave a bitter laugh as he remembered those words. Yes, he had seen the truth in a different place. But had it set him free? No, just the opposite! It had revealed him for what he truly was: not just an amoral academic, but a fool, a betrayer, a worthless piece of human driftwood good only for the fire, whose so-called learning counted for less than nothing. The truth had enslaved him, turning him into a mutilator and murderer of innocent men, women... and children.

He buried his head in his hands.

After a while he sat up, heaved a shuddering sigh, and restarted the BMW. As he navigated the country roads following signs to civilisation, he was conscious only of a deep fear and longing: never to see that 'different place' again. *Dear God, don't send me back to Dûrion. I've learnt enough truth to last a lifetime. I'll build a new life here, away from the university. I'll devote myself to charitable causes. Just don't put me back in the Bishop's Guard...*

He finally reached the flat around five after battling through the early rush-hour traffic. He was bombed out. He ate the sandwich he'd bought at a filling station, then walked wearily to the bedroom and pulled off his clothes. He was exhausted. He sat on the edge of the bed, then keeled over on to the pillow and let his eyes close. He mustn't sleep, though. Just rest for a moment. There was a reason, an important one, why he mustn't sleep... he couldn't remember what it was. He slowly drifted off.

———————————————————

Chapter 25: *Shiván on the run*

SHIVÁN HAD BEEN ON THE RUN for two and a half days. Now he squatted miserably in the mist beside a little farmhouse. He wished the unwelcome guests on the doorstep would leave, but he had no idea what to do or where to go when they did.

The beheadings in Berûvis were still a ghastly backdrop to all his thoughts. Stranded on his own in the Dûrian countryside, with the trip to Darthane a total bust and the Restorers scattered to the four winds, Shiván felt himself teetering on the brink of the slippery slide down into depression.

After the executions he'd tagged along with the group of farmers whom he'd earlier helped bulldoze a path through the crowd. Dressed in brightly-coloured shifts and robes like his own, they seemed to offer the best chance of escaping Berûvis unnoticed.

But that small measure of security hadn't lasted long. After walking quite a distance from the town he'd discovered that the farmers were regarding him as a welcome addition to their harvest work force, and soon after that he'd given them the slip. He'd set off along country lanes in the hope of making his way back to Lord Ganneret's house. That had seemed the best option, and for several hours there had been light at the end of the tunnel. Lannie and the others might have returned to the Baron's house, expecting him to do likewise. Or Ganneret might have heard something. At the very least he would provide him with another escort through Berûvis and set him on the Darthane road.

Then that hope, too, had faded. As the country lanes meandered back towards Berûvis they became roads, and the roads became increasingly well-populated with people and wagons. The first couple of groups he'd passed had looked at him strangely and muttered among themselves. The third had demanded he join them, giving chase when he hadn't. He'd only managed to shake them off by charging across a field. After that he'd hidden in a copse or under a hedge each time he heard other travellers — until the roads were so busy that there was no point continuing his journey. He'd spent a miserable night huddled in a pile of leaves under a tree.

During the next couple of days his spirits sank lower, and posi-tive thinking became harder. He was only able to travel in the early morning and late evening when the roads were almost empty. As usual the sky was overcast, hiding the two moons; so walking at night was out of the question. Then, to make things worse, a fine autumn mist had settled over the countryside.

He'd soon become completely lost. He had no idea whether he was still heading towards Ganneret's house. He'd reached a high, imposing stone structure with many tall arches reaching up into the mist. He could only guess that it was an aqueduct, bringing fresh water to Berûvis. He'd spent a night huddled under one of the arches.

In his desolation he'd pleaded with God to show him the way—in a very immediate and obvious sense. During the solitary day-light hours he'd read his antique King James Bible with the tor-toiseshell covers. A familiar passage from the book of Proverbs had provided some comfort: *Trust in the* LORD *with all thine heart; and lean not unto thine own understanding. In all thy ways acknowledge him, and he shall direct thy paths.* He told God he'd take the final promise literally; but he was drifting into apathy, and couldn't rouse him-self to believe it would really happen.

Last night he'd reached this farmhouse. He'd crept into the at-tached barn, where he'd spent the warmest night so far in the hay beside a shaggy ox and a couple of bovine deer. He'd been so ex-hausted that he'd completely overslept. The hay must have hidden him when the farmer took the animals out this morning. But now he had to go. He didn't know where, he just had to go—if only these purple-robed guests chatting to the farmer's wife would re-move themselves. They were blocking his line of escape.

"Thank you for your prayers, Reverend," the woman was say-ing. "Our Garny is so much better! The Keeperess does what she can, but she has to work in the fields like the rest of us these days..."

From his hiding place Shiván could see the visitors' leader, though the robed figures behind him were shrouded by the mist. The leader had a friendly face, deeply wrinkled and surrounded by a luxuriant black beard. "Light be thanked!" he exclaimed. "It's the One Creator God who has healed him—not our prayers."

As it dawned on Shiván what he was hearing, he felt the first faint stirrings of hope. This had to be a genuine Lightist! Could he… dare he…?

Crinkle-face was holding up a small silver ambon. "The One bless you and keep you," he intoned, and the other bearded purple-robes joined in. "The One make his Light shine upon you, and be gracious to you. The One smile upon you, and give you peace."

Shiván sat, stunned. It was the priestly blessing from the Old Testament! Slightly changed, but essentially the same. Yet the Lightists' Book was *not* the Bible. He'd heard enough other quotations to know that it was a book of this world, written by people of this world. But here its words were almost identical! Proof, if he'd needed it, that God's message was the same across the universe.

The purple-robes were leaving now. Suddenly the most important thing in the world was to speak to them, never mind the consequences. He quivered to jump up and run after them, but hard-earned caution made him wait until he heard the cottage door close. Then he slipped through the narrow gap and hurried down the lane. He almost ran into the last of the purple robes as the figure loomed up suddenly in the mist.

The eight or so men all turned when he reached them. He stood facing them nervously while they tested his shiláy, poised to flee and wondering if he'd made a bad mistake. Then to his huge relief, smiles broke out all around.

Crinkle-face came forward. "*Isset, mel anéy nalest* — welcome, friend! Welcome in the name of our Prince. We see you are his servant — and you're alone, and in need. My name is Frengor, and these are my brother priests of the Travelling Order. How can we help you?"

Joy broke through into Shiván's darkness. *In all thy ways acknowledge him, and he shall direct thy paths.*

"I'm Shiván, er, dom Bernet — I'm a foreigner, and I'm trying to find my friends, who are travelling to Darthane…"

He stopped, puzzled. A buzz of excited comment had broken out among the priests, and Frengor was grinning broadly and nodding.

"Alanya and a group of rebel soldiers. Am I right?"

"I — Yes! But how — ?"

"Shiván, you are doubly welcome!" The next moment, to his amazement, he was clasped in a bear hug by the priest, and all the others crowded round to raise his hand and clap him on the back.

"How do you know who I am?" he gasped when the exuberant greetings had finally died down.

"Brother Ongaret can tell you that story in a moment. But first— let's sit by the road here and share a meal, and you can tell us how you've managed to lose your companions."

Shiván sat, bemused, his despair slowly evaporating in the warmth of the priests' friendship as they sat in a little group co- cooned by the mist, eating dark bread and farm cheese. He told them his story. Their faces grew solemn when he described the exe- cutions in Berûvis. They'd heard what happened, but had not been there themselves. Frengor muttered angrily about darkness in high places.

When he'd finished his tale there was silence. Frengor sat with his arms on his knees, fingering his silver ambon. Then he turned to Shiván with a broad grin.

"God is good!" he exclaimed.

"The Creator is all goodness," his fellow priests responded.

The sudden change in mood took Shiván by surprise; but he no- ticed the other priests were looking at Frengor expectantly.

"Does Alanya have red hair?"

Shiván blinked. "Yes, she does."

"Then let's share our first piece of good news. Brother Ongaret, tell Shiván what you heard in Berûvis on Marneril, after those un- godly executions."

The thin-faced young priest described how he and a couple of his companions had bumped into a group of rather puzzled townsfolk who'd sought their advice. In a nearby alleyway they'd encountered the strangest bunch of people: three Dûrians whose auras reeked of rebel sympathies; and a red-haired woman who had the most dis- turbingly foreign shiláy they'd ever come across.

"Which is exactly how I'd describe *your* aura," Frengor inter- posed, looking at Shiván with a twinkle in his eye.

"That must have been Alanya!" Shiván exclaimed. "And our friends were rebel soldiers. But there were five of them."

Frengor's eyebrows shot up. "I'm sorry to hear that. You're sure they said three, Ongaret?"

The young priest nodded. "That was the number."

Frengor looked at Shiván sympathetically. "Perhaps the other two became separated during the disturbance—like yourself."

Shiván nodded. It would be too much to hope that they'd all escaped. He just hoped Lord Ganneret's servants had got Perrely home safely.

Ongaret continued his story, describing how the red-haired woman had asked the townsfolk if they'd come across another foreigner like herself—a man with the unusual name of 'Shiván'. They said no, they hadn't—then the strange group had hurried off.

The townsfolk had asked Ongaret and his companions whether they should report this to the authorities. Ongaret had advised them to ignore what they'd seen. Enough innocent blood had already been shed.

Their story filled Shiván with relief. He thanked Ongaret for saving his friends' lives. "Did the townsfolk say in which direction those people were heading?"

Ongaret thought for a bit. "No, but we were on the eastern side of the town. I would guess they were trying to get out that way, towards Lômack and the Darthane road."

"Oh, right. Thanks." So they were still making for Darthane. That was a blow. He suddenly realised how much he'd been looking forward to recovering, mentally and emotionally, in the comfort of Ganneret's home. But these priests were already doing a great job of hauling him out of the depths.

"Now to our other piece of good news, Shiván," Frengor said, beard bristling and every crinkle in his face grinning. "You and Alanya are not the first we've met with this disturbingly foreign shiláy."

It took him a moment to get it. Then his jaw dropped. "Gelmion!" he exclaimed.

The priests all laughed. "Gelmion it was," Frengor declared. "We met him just outside Finien, oh—about a week ago. And a good thing we did, too. He was all set to walk to Darthane on his own—not a good idea, as I'm sure you've found out. We got him fixed up with a farmer and his family—good Lightists—who were travelling to Berûvis. They said they'd find another group to take him on to Darthane. He should have arrived by now. If you go there yourself, you may even meet him coming back. *If* he hasn't found what he was looking for at the university." His eyes held a quizzical look.

Shiván was too relieved to notice. "That's really great!" he exclaimed. "We were worried sick about Gelmion. There was an, er, argument, and he left without telling us."

"So we gathered," Frengor said dryly. "I suppose now you'll be wanting to follow your two friends to Darthane, young Shiván?"

"I, er— Well, yes… if someone can point me in the right direction."

Frengor's expression softened. "You have been alone and adrift," he said softly, "and there is a deep pain that has threatened to overcome you. But in the One's strength you will face the pain, and he will banish it. Do you believe that, Shiván?"

In an unsteady voice he replied, "I have to."

Frengor smiled. "Keep holding on to that. Meanwhile, why don't you come with us to Lômack—the next town on the highway? We'll find a Lightist group there who can take you on to Darthane."

Shiván was profuse in his thanks, but Frengor brushed them aside. "Let's all thank the One Creator God." They raised their hands and looked upward in the familiar Lightist attitude of prayer, while Frengor spoke simply, thanking their Father in the Light for bringing about this meeting and looking after Shiván and his friends. Shiván was moved by the down-to-earth directness of the prayer. These were the straightforward words of a son to a father he loved and respected. If this man wasn't a Christian, he didn't know who was. Tears started in his eyes simply from the realisation that he was no longer alone.

The priests packed the leftover food in their belt pouches, and Shiván slung his travel pack over his shoulder. They set off again through the thinning mist, and soon reached the six-lane highway. He walked in the centre of the group of priests, filled with relief that he no longer needed to be poised for flight at the slightest glance from other travellers.

"So, Shiván, you are also from Inglan, like Gelmion?" Frengor asked as they walked down the pedestrian lane of the highway.

"Yes, we're all from the same country—Alanya and Danîsha, too."

"Danîsha?"

"Oh, I forgot I hadn't mentioned her. She stayed behind in… where we were living, in case Gelmion returned there."

Frengor gave him a lopsided smile. "You are wise to be cautious." He was sunk in thought for a while as he walked, absently rubbing the silver ambon that hung around his neck. "And why did you come to Dûrion?" His gaze was intent.

"Well, none of us actually *chose* to come to Dûrion. It's hard to explain — we can't explain it ourselves — but we just woke up here one morning."

Frengor's eyes twinkled. "I hardly think your arrival was an accident, my brother — I hardly think so. You — you are different from Gelmion. You, I can call brother; Gelmion, I could not. I sense strongly in you the Light of the One Creator God — he is your father, just as he is my father. That makes us brothers. Am I right?"

"Yes!" Shiván exclaimed. "I believe that's true."

Shiván felt a strong urge to share with Frengor the real purpose he believed God had for them in Dûrion; but after Lord Ganneret's reaction he wasn't sure that was wise.

"We have a different 'Book' from yours," he said. "But some passages are almost identical." He took the King James Bible out of his bag. They stopped at the side of the road, and all the priests crowded round as Shiván undid the clasps and opened the tortoiseshell cover. A babble of surprise broke out at the strange writing. Shiván turned to the Old Testament passage containing the priestly blessing Frengor had given the woman at the farmhouse. There were murmurs of astonishment as he translated it into Dûrian. One of the priests thrust forward an open copy of their Book, and they all intoned the parallel statement. Shiván stared fascinated at the attractive, flowing script.

"Well, my young brother," Frengor said, "we have the same Father, and the same truths given in these two Books. Even if there are differences, what we share is greater than those differences. The shiláy cannot lie — we *know* you are our brother in the Light." At that they all stood and embraced him, murmuring "Brother Shiván". He found himself choked up by their open-hearted acceptance.

As they continued walking Frengor remarked, "That's a beautiful copy of your Book, Shiván. Do you or your friends have any other items that you feel the One may have given you for a special purpose?"

They exchanged a glance of complete understanding. "Yes, we do," Shiván said quietly. "Gelmion has a glass; Alanya has a shell; and Danîsha has a bellaril."

"The Prince be thanked," Frengor murmured, his eyes bright. "I believe the One has indeed caused our paths to cross today. They need to cross again—after your trip to Darthane. The earliest you would be back would be in... what, about five days? Very well, we'll be waiting for you in the Berûvis area. Lady Perrely will send word when you reach her home.

"Until then—only be true to him in everything, and he will guide your steps."

In all thy ways acknowledge him, and he shall direct thy paths. Shiván walked on with wonder in his heart. The mist was clearing, both within and without.

* * *

They took lodgings at an inn in Lômack—a small town rather like Berûvis—where Frengor quickly found a Lightist group travelling to Darthane. He explained Shiván's situation to their leader Kindler Tondor, a slender man in a white robe with short purple hair parted down the middle. He agreed to let Shiván join his party, which included the Kindlers of several Hearths in Berûvis, Lômack and the surrounding villages, along with many of their flock. There were forty-five of them all told—they filled four of the tables in the common room. They were a friendly bunch, who welcomed Shiván like a long-lost cousin despite his foreign shiláy. Shiván felt the last of his inner darkness fading away.

Frengor told him the group was travelling to Darthane to protest to Bishop Shambor about the Festival of Unity now taking place there. The priest shook his head. "A futile gesture. Futile," he muttered. "The Festival is a celebration of the 'oneness of all faiths', and these devout Lightists from northern Dûrion are hoping to see the Bishop and protest that it blurs the distinction between their faith and the evil practices of the Lightless cults. Which might have been a fine idea if it were not Shambor himself who's doing most of the blurring!"

Next morning Shiván said a regretful farewell to Frengor and the priests, and set off with his new group towards Darthane.

He could only trust that God would direct his paths to intersect with Lannie's.

Map 7:
Journeys to Darthane

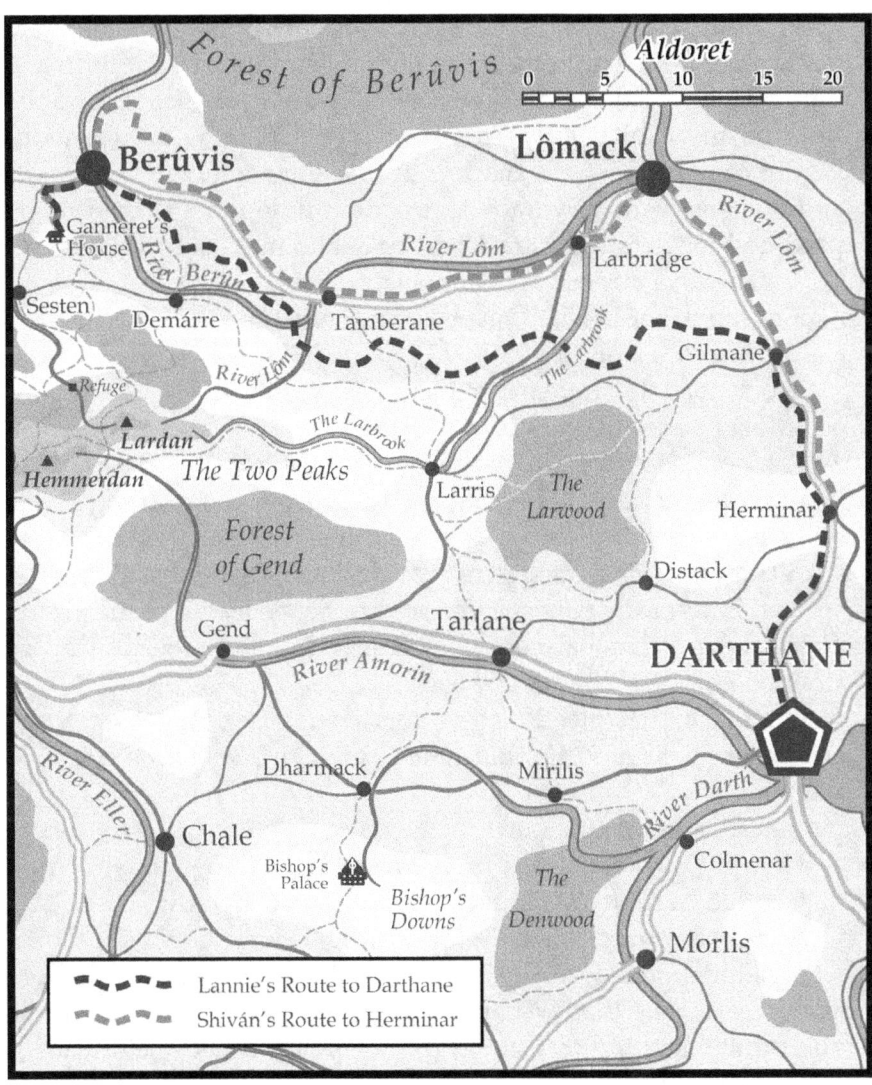

Chapter 26: *Welcome to Darthane*

THE DARTHANE ROAD was swarming with travellers. Lannie gazed down on it from the crest of a hill overlooking the village of Gilmane. Alongside her in the grass lay Fira and the twins, Shîrin and Cârin. They could see that most of the traffic was heading south, towards the capital city. The inner, fast lane was a continuous stream of horsemen and chariots. In the slow lane, carriages, carts and wagons were moving nose to tail at little more than walking pace; and the pedestrian track was one solid mass of travellers.

"Is it always this busy?" Lannie wondered.

Fira shook her head. "Must be some cultist festival."

"Why a cultist one?"

"Look at all the dull-coloured clothes," Shîr said.

"Must be a pretty big do," Câr added.

Fira nodded. "It's just what we need right now. If we can slip in between a couple of those big cultist groups, their strong shiláy will help mask ours." She looked at Lannie.

"Okay, how do you suggest we do that?" Lannie said. She respected Fira for the way she deferred to her as leader of the group. There were occasional compressed lips, but the rebel officer restrained herself. It couldn't be easy.

Fira's eyes narrowed as she surveyed the scene. "Best to go around the village," she said after a moment. "We'll be less conspicuous."

"Let's do it," Lannie said.

They got up and slipped from cover to cover down the hill until they entered a narrow country path between hedgerows.

As they continued Lannie found herself worrying again about what had happened to Shiván. How could she have been so stupid as to scream like that? What if Shivvie had been captured...? She pushed the dreadful thought aside. She *had* to believe he'd made it out of there somehow.

Her own escape had been something of a miracle. As she'd pushed through the crowd mindlessly with some wild idea of rescuing Margay, she'd suddenly seen that the entire front line of the Bishop's Guard were pushing their way towards *her*. In a panic she'd scuttled into the only hiding place available—the nearby pen full of deer for sale, where she'd crouched down among the warm, grey bodies. The deer had been startled, and began milling about. Thank God their agitation had gone unnoticed by the Bishop's Guard—but not by the eagle-eyed twins.

She'd huddled between the deer's legs, breathing in their rank smell and weeping silently through the terrible executions. When the square at last began to clear the twins and Fira had softly called her name. She'd rejoined them, and they'd left the square with the rest of the crowd. Guards were stopping people at random, but by the One's gift they'd slipped through unnoticed.

Sadly there had been no sign of the other two troopers, Fiminor and Tornoret; and she assumed that foolish girl Perrely had been dragged home by Ganneret's servants. But Shivvie... If he *had* escaped he was on his own now, and she could only hope that he'd somehow find his way either to Lord Ganneret's house, or back to the Manor.

One thing was for sure, she'd be following Fira's advice from now on. The veteran rebel officer had led them safely through a maze of side streets in Berûvis until they'd come out in the countryside. Lannie had asked some townsfolk if they'd seen Shiván—earning a sharp rebuke afterwards.

Since then it had been walking, crawling and running along country lanes, beside hedgerows, over streams, avoiding all villages, and sleeping rough in the woods—until this morning, when they'd reached the Darthane highway at Gilmane, far enough from Berûvis to risk rejoining it. Her feet were blistered; her arms and lower legs red with scratches and itchy from insect bites and stinging plants.

They approached the highway and hid in a copse of trees. There they straightened their hair and brushed off their robes. They watched the throngs passing up and down, waiting for the right opportunity.

Fira spotted a couple of pedestrian groups in drab clothes heading south. "There! Between those two," she said.

They hurried across the highway and pushed forward on the walkway until they were sandwiched between the two groups. The one in front was in blacks and greys. "Gadeshites!" Shîr hissed, a look of disgust on his face. The group behind wore a wider variety of colours—dark greens, maroons, greys and muted blues. Câr guessed they were probably worshippers of Minórre, the god of the harvest. They were singing a mournful song with strange cadences.

"So, are they *both* having festivals in Darthane?" Lannie asked, still picking dirt from her hair.

"There are groups from almost every cult here," Fira said sourly. "Look at those standards up ahead." She pointed to where a group of people dressed in varying shades of blue were holding banners aloft painted in wavy stripes of light and dark blue. Bells were attached to the ends of the poles and tinkled as they walked. "Votaries of Sharn, the river goddess," she muttered. "The second most powerful cult after Gadesh."

"Whoa, and behind them! Look at that lot bouncing up and down only half-dressed!" Shîr exclaimed. "They'll be devotees of Borlaze."

"The god of love," Câr said. He gave Lannie a wicked grin.

Fira scowled at him. "It must be one of these 'all-faith celebrations' our beloved Bishop is so fond of," she declared angrily, keeping her voice low. "He's not satisfied with pretending to be the Restorer of the One's true Way. Oh, no. He wants us to believe that the dark cults are also 'true ways' to the God of Light! Did you ever hear anything so ridiculous?"

Lannie shook her head. She had, in her own world. They walked on in silence, taking in the cacophony of sounds, smells and sights that surrounded them.

At noon they stopped for the midmeal with crowds of others in the village of Herminar, near the crest of a small ridge of hills. The inn there was doing a roaring trade. They managed to order a meal of nut-and-bean stew with only a puzzled glance from the overworked waiter. They finished their meal as quickly as possible and resumed their journey.

As they came over the crest of the hill above Herminar, Lannie gasped. There in the distance lay the great capital city of Dûrion—Darthane itself. Shîrin, Cârin and many of their fellow-travellers were also seeing it for the first time. They joined a small crowd that had stepped off the road and were pointing and exclaiming.

The city looked like a vast golden ring filled with rubies and crowned with a glistening diamond. The ring was the high wall of smooth yellow stone. Inside were many imposing yellowstone buildings amidst a sea of whitewashed homes tiled with terracotta. The acres of red roofs seemed to swell upward toward the central hill. There at the heart of the city, drawing every eye, stood the great Cathedral. Its white domes and tall, cylindrical towers mounted up towards a gleaming ambon at the highest peak. The whole structure seemed to point upward, drawing the hearts of all who saw it to the One above, who was Ruler of all.

"The 'Jewel of Dûrion'," Fira murmured. "Once it stood for something."

They continued down the hill with the crowds of fellow-travellers to the wide plain that lay before the city.

As they drew closer, Lannie marvelled at the towering wall of yellow stone. It must be thirty feet high, and seemed in good repair. High above among the battlements small, red-cloaked figures were pacing to and fro.

"The City Guards," Shîr murmured.

Ahead of them the six-lane highway was swallowed up by a dark tunnel at the foot of a massive gatehouse. Its tower rose high above the wall itself, and more red-cloaked Guards could be seen patrolling the gatehouse battlements.

"Has anyone even *tried* to break in here?" Lannie wondered.

"Never!" Cârin declared, shocked.

"Nonsense!" Fira retorted.

Câr raised his hands in mock surrender. "Just joking, Lieutenant! The Founders besieged Darthane, and the Gnarthrog Tyrant and all his troops surrendered."

"Who were these 'Founders'?" Lannie asked.

"They're the people who first drove the cults out of Dûrion," Shîrin replied. "They established... everything!" He threw his arms wide in an all-inclusive gesture. "The Hearth, the Kindlers, the Bishop—"

"They made Dûrion a Lightist nation," Fira said, "ruled by the laws of the Book. And now Shambor's doing all he can to make us cultists again."

"So that's how you came to be ruled by a Bishop," Lannie said.

"No, *not* by the Bishop. He simply administered *God's* laws. For centuries Dûrion was a great example to all the nations around us. We followed the One's laws, and we prospered. We had surplus food, which we used to trade with the surrounding nations. Everybody produced enough for themselves, *and* more. The extra was kept in great storehouses in Darthane, not only for trade, but also to be distributed to our own people when the harvest was poor."

"Now Shambor has those storehouses," Cârin added, "and he sells the surplus at a handsome profit to foreign merchants."

"Now Shambor has *everything*," Fira said, keeping her voice low and glancing around. "All the food goes to these new 'Land Elders', and from them to Shambor. Ordinary people have to make do with whatever's left over."

"So — the poor get poorer, and the rich get richer," Shîr concluded with a shrug.

Lannie sniffed. "That sounds familiar."

By the time they reached the towering gatehouse they were shuffling along in a solid mass of humanity all waiting to enter the city. To while away the time, people began creating their own impromptu entertainments. Up ahead the devotees of Borlaze, the god of love, began a wild dance, accompanied by drums and flutes. Half-naked men and women leapt into the air and twirled around in a frenzy of excitement. Others in the crowd urged them on with rhythmic clapping and cries of encouragement. Shîrin and Cârin's eyes were wide with appreciation.

"Now, *there's* something worth watching!" Shîr exclaimed, as a large-breasted woman leapt high above the others.

"You keep your eyes to yourself, Trooper!" Fira snapped.

"Have a heart, Lieutenant — were you never a young man?"

"No, Light be thanked. You control your wandering eyes, because once we get inside the city, it's going to be worse. I know these cultist festivals," she muttered darkly.

Fira's words were prophetic. No sooner had they come out at the other end of the long, dark gate tunnel, than they found themselves plunged into an exuberant, all-inclusive street party. The noise was deafening. Despite the fact that the light was fading at the end of the day, the open space in front of the gate was filled with merchant stalls doing a brisk business. Several different bands were competing to make music, and the celebrants of Borlaze immediately added theirs to the cacophony. Everywhere people were dancing in a greater or lesser degree of undress. The twins' eyes were wide.

Lannie was appalled at what she was seeing. "Is this what they call a religious festival?" she exclaimed.

"Cultists!" Fira snapped.

"We'd better get out of here fast," Lannie decided.

They pushed forward among the writhing bodies. A man in a long, grey robe barred their way, hands raised as if in blessing. "Join the Oneness of the Infinite, my children!" he cried.

"The Oneness of Lust, you mean," Lannie retorted, pushing past him.

Her words were borne out as a young woman sidled up to Cârin with a shapely breast on display. "Have some fun, sweetheart?" she purred, smiling into his bulging eyes.

"*Cârinor!*" Fira's voice was a whiplash. Sheepishly Câr turned and followed his brother and the two women as they forced their way up the street.

Everywhere it was the same story. The whole city was celebrating—both cultists and so-called Lightists. As they approached another group Fira gave a gasp of horror, and pointed out to Lannie a Lightist Kindler with the distinctive short hair and centre parting. He was leaping about enthusiastically with the rest of them.

"*That's* what Shambor has brought us down to," she hissed.

After pushing their way through more drunken revellers, prostitutes of both sexes, and drug peddlers, they found an inn in a relatively quiet side street. The innkeeper welcomed them in the spirit of the festival.

"Wise people, wise people!" he cried. "Coming in early before the crowd! *Ney'n silmen'!* Five beds, is it?"

"Four," Lannie said.

He peered at them through bloodshot eyes. "Four, of course. Two and two, yes?" He gave them a grotesque leer. "And then you go out and celebrate our glorious victory!"

"What victory?" Fira snapped, bristling.

"Why, our Lord Bishop's great vittry over those cursed Lightiss fanatiss... fanassick... rebels. Thass why we're having this Fess'val of Unity, dincha know? No more rebels! We're all one, now. Lightiss, Gadeshice, Minórriss—we're all one in the Unicy of the Infinite!" The innkeeper's luxuriantly moustached face glowed with wine and enthusiasm.

A leather-jacketed student shouted out, "You've been enjoying too much of your own wine, innkeeper—pass a pitcher over here!" His companions began banging on the table.

Before the befuddled man could comply, Fira caught his attention by slapping a couple of coins down on the counter.

"Four beds... Yes, yes, two and two..." he muttered. He gave Fira change and pointed vaguely to the stairs, before turning to fill a pitcher with wine.

Lannie, Fira and the twins climbed the stairs and searched along a corridor with many doors until they found two that were unlocked. Shîrin and Cârin settled themselves in one, while the women took the other.

"Are we going to eat?" Lannie asked. "I'm not hungry, but the twins—"

"Oh, everything will have meat in it here," Fira said with a grimace. "And if we ask for anything different, we draw attention to ourselves. We can look for a market stall tomorrow and buy some proper food. It was a good thing that innkeeper was drunk, though."

"Why do you say that?"

"Because otherwise he might have noticed our shiláy—or yours, at least. As it was, I don't think he noticed anything except the wine fumes coming out of his own mouth. In fact this whole despicable 'Festival of Unity' has made things a lot easier for us. To tell you the truth, I hadn't even expected we'd get into the city without being captured or reported. But here we are, at an inn, and probably safe for a couple of nights. I wouldn't want to risk longer than that, though—even if our cash wasn't running out. Do you agree?" she asked with a sardonic lift of the eyebrows.

"Those are my thoughts exactly," Lannie declared. They laughed. Lannie could no longer think of Fira as the hard, soulless taskmaster she'd seemed at the Manor. The hawk-faced rebel officer might be a bit short on humour, but she was strong-minded, intelligent, and as good a follower as she'd been a leader.

"Now I'd better go and see that those two light-wits next door don't get up to any mischief," Fira muttered. Lannie heard her haranguing the two men through the open door, interspersed with their perky replies.

As she lay on the hard, lumpy mattress, sleep didn't come easily. Tomorrow she would visit this so-called university, and ask if Gil was there—or if he'd come looking for a job. If he hadn't... Well, they'd start enquiring at inns all along the route. She wasn't going to give up. But as for their other aim in coming to Darthane—enquiring about that prophetic 'rod', the Ambon of Sûrilane—she wouldn't do that all on her own. She'd ask a few questions, that was all. Then she'd head back to Carreck Manor in the hope of finding Shivvie there, with 'Neesh—and maybe Gil.

Oh, she so much hoped Gil would be here, at the university! She was tired of being the odd one out in their little group. She needed someone to talk English to. Especially Gil.

The next morning the whole city was hung over after a wild night on the tiles. They made their way through the sparsely-populated streets to the foot of Cathedral Hill. All Fira knew was that the university was either part of, or attached to, the Cathedral.

It would be a high risk actually entering the building, and Lannie had determined to do that alone, despite fierce objections from Fira. She wasn't going to risk her friends' lives as well. Her foreign shiláy would stand out like a sore thumb—but she could only hope that the scholars at the university would be too hung over to notice, or that they'd simply regard her as an intriguing phenomenon to be studied.

"Okay, let's find the university," she declared briskly. Shîr and Câr snapped to attention and saluted. They fell in behind her and Fira as they headed up the hill.

The avenue was beginning to fill up now; there were many people heading in the same direction. Fira worked her usual magic of finding them a place between two groups with strong auras of their own. As they wound their way up the hill they kept catching tantalising glimpses of the turrets and central dome of the Cathedral, growing ever more massive the nearer they came.

At last they reached the crest of the hill, where the road opened out into a broad plaza—and they all stopped, awe-struck. Before them rose the High Hearth of Dûrion in all its splendour. The vast building covered the entire hilltop, spreading out in every direction. Their eyes were drawn upwards, past the great dome that dominated the skyline, to the graceful columns of white stone mounting ever higher towards the clouds. On the very topmost turret stood the silver ambon, glittering in the morning light.

Lannie uttered a long, drawn-out "Wo-o-ow." She hadn't seen a cathedral in England that was half as big or a quarter as beautiful.

"I've never seen it this close," Fira muttered. There were tears in her eyes. "It took thousands of workmen a hundred years to build this Cathedral for the glory of the One Creator God. It glorifies him still, even if men of darkness defile it now."

After a long moment they moved on with the crowds. Fira risked a question to a young student in his short leather jacket and brown knee-length tunic. He looked at her oddly, but said, "The university? That's where we're going. Just follow our group."

They did so, and found themselves at the back of the Cathedral, behind the great circular sanctuary. The students all streamed into a wide doorway at the head of a flight of stairs, which led into a three-storey building adjoined at right angles to the Cathedral proper. Its roof was still only half the height of the Cathedral itself. Six storeys! But then Fira had explained that this was not only a place of worship, but the parliament building and government offices of the nation of Dûrion.

The four of them stopped at the foot of the entrance steps. Lannie took a deep breath. "Well, here's where I leave you."

All three Dûrians looked unusually solemn. Lannie realised afresh how precarious her mission to Darthane had always been; how amazing it was that they'd got this far; and what courage her rebel friends had shown in accompanying her.

"I trust we'll see you again," Fira said, a blend of command and entreaty in her voice. "Can you find your way back to the inn?"

Lannie swallowed the sudden lump in her throat. "Yes, don't wait for me here. I'll find my own way back. And thank you all. Thanks for everything."

"*Ney mel shar.* — Go with the Light," they said in unison.

"*Ney mel sharras,*" Lannie replied.

They lifted their right hands, palms open, in the farewell gesture. Then she turned and walked alone up the university steps.

———

Chapter 27: *Danîsha finds her purpose*

DANÎSHA AWOKE to an appetising aroma of bean and carrot stew wafting through the cave. Gwargif was squatting beside her make-shift bed, holding out a bowl and spoon. Her tired mind was amazed again at how human he could sometimes be. His five-fingered paws turned quickly into hands when he needed them. This morning he must have gathered firewood, lit the fire, and cooked the stew.

"Mylendel must eat," he said anxiously, offering her the bowl. She struggled into a sitting position and took it, more to please him than because she was hungry.

"Thank you Gwargif," she murmured. Then, as she tasted the contents of her spoon, "This is delicious!" she added.

"Is good," he said with a broad smile. His eyes followed each mouthful to make sure she ate it all.

When she'd finished Danîsha put the bowl down with a sigh. Then her eyes filled with tears. "I keep seeing Teynel's face, Gwargif. They killed her — for nothing!"

"Gwargif see," he said gently. Then in a hard voice he growled, "Gwargif see work of great darkness, Gwargif see men not care about Light, Gwargif see deep blackness here."

Danîsha broke down and wept. A warm, wet tongue licked her hand. She looked up and saw the compassion in his eyes.

"Teynel in Shining Place now."

"I know, Gwargif, I know." She reached for Teynel's small wooden comb that always lay beside her bed. She turned it over in her hands, feeling it with her fingers, unable to see through the blur of tears. "It just... hurts so much—"

Gwargif sat close beside her; she put her arm around him and buried her head in his fur.

That night as before, the Dorbian built up the fire, and then went and lay at the entrance of the cave, keeping watch. He assured her that he did sleep, but only lightly. And, as before, Danîsha had the nightmare. When she woke up crying out, Gwargif was there. He sat with her until she had calmed down and was able to drop off once more.

Back in England, Father Martin had asked her if she was willing to suffer to proclaim the truth of God to those who didn't know it. She'd never realised it could cost so much.

The next day passed in a blur. She kept reliving that terrible scene in the Manor basement. Seeing Teynel's dead face. Extracting the comb from her tangled hair. Falling into the overwhelming despair of knowing that Teynel had entrusted herself to Danîsha, and she'd failed her.

Without Gwargif she would have given herself up to the greycoats, who had returned and were combing the forest.

As they fled ahead of the patrols to a new hiding-place, Gwargif comforted her—sometimes by his quiet words, sometimes merely by his presence, sometimes by his prayers. The way he prayed surprised Danîsha: they were Old Testament prayers—stark and uncompromising. Prayers that the Light would take vengeance on the powers of darkness which had triumphed here in Dûrion. That the Shining One would pour the terrible blaze of his wrath upon those who had committed this unspeakable evil.

As the immediate pain began to recede, a grim determination took root in Danîsha. She would not rest, she would not turn back, she would not even think of anything else, until she had spent every last drop of her strength bringing God's justice down upon those who had done this to Teynel and her beloved Dûrian friends. She remembered as a distant dream her abhorrence of violence in the discussions they'd had at the Manor, her well-meant desire that the powers who controlled this nation might be brought to see the error of their ways. How naïve she'd been. Those who committed atrocities like these needed to be *stopped*. And if that took fighting... so be it.

When she told this to Gwargif, his tail thumped and his eyes glowed. "*Now* you are Warrior of Light. *Now* you are Mylendel!" he barked.

As she spoke to the One about it in the days that followed, she felt the desire for personal revenge ebb away. *Vengeance is mine*, God had said. *He* would avenge Teynel. But she had not a shadow of a doubt that she would be an instrument in wreaking that vengeance. God had brought her to Dûrion for a purpose, and *this* was that purpose. *This* was how she would reveal God's truth to those who didn't know it. She would pursue justice with every fibre of her being and with every drop of energy God gave her. Deep within she declared war on the powers of darkness that treated human life with such contempt, and forced others to do the same. She thought of the tear in Gil's eye.

In the first flush of determination, Danîsha burned to set out at once with Gwargif and track down those who had committed the slaughter at the Manor. She would freeze them with the bellaril, and Gwargif would kill them. But the Dorbian counselled patience.

"Is not just you, Mylendel," he said. "Is *all* Warriors of Light. You say is three more. At home is Dorbi *Varlezagh*—holy men—is tell us Shining One send *Warriors* of Light. Not just one Warrior."

"But the others are gone, Gwargif," protested Danîsha. "Alanya and Shiván have gone to Darthane—I don't know if they'll come back..."

"They come, Mylendel," the Dorbian said softly. "You wait, they come. Shining One not make mistake, they come. When you all together, then you go, you break down darkness, you bring Light again."

"And Gelmion? What about him, when he doesn't even believe? He's on their side now—he's been captured by those... monsters, and forced to obey them!"

"He Warrior of Light, but not yet. Shining One free him, open his eyes, *then* he see, then he believe. You wait, you will see."

Though not convinced, Danîsha had to accept that there was no point dashing off on a one-woman crusade. She had to wait at least until Lannie and Shiván came back. And then, if Gwargif was right, they had to find Gelmion. But on one thing she was utterly determined: they would not rest until these powers of darkness were overthrown.

"And Mylendel, listen!" Gwargif's eyes were bright with enthusiasm. "Shining One not leave Warriors of Light alone. He tell Dorbi holy men, holy men tell our great leader, and great leader tell Gwargif come find Warriors of Light—then we *all* come, all Dorbi warriors. We come soon, we come five thousand, Mylendel—five thousand Dorbi warriors, we all come to help Warriors of Light."

Danîsha stared at Gwargif, her mind trying to grapple with what he was telling her.

"You mean, your people will send all these warriors—five thousand!—just to come and fight for us?" she said.

"We fight for Shining One," Gwargif replied, his eyes glowing, "but you, you are leaders, Warriors of Light, you tell us where to go, where to fight; we fight for you and for Shining One, we drive darkness out."

Danîsha gaped at him. Suddenly this was far bigger than her personal vendetta against those who had murdered Teynel. These were plans that the One had laid far in advance, and for which he had summoned not only her, Denise Thompson, to carry out—but also Lannie Catterick, Steve Harston, and maybe even Gil Denbigh. They were all utterly unprepared, but *he* was not. He had brought them to Dûrion to lead his assault on the powers of darkness here—*and quite independently he'd summoned the Dorbians to support them.* She was stunned. She raised her heart up to God in awe and gratitude. Gwargif's tail thumped on the floor of the cave.

Chapter 28: *Priest and Scholar*

TO PERRELY'S GREAT RELIEF, Frengor and Brother Ongaret arrived at
the door of her house five days after the executions in Berûvis. She
didn't know how much longer she could have survived her father's
grounding order. When Butler Harn told her, she hurried at once to
the door, thanking the One and ignoring Harn's sour face. The butler, like the rest of her family, did not approve of the travelling
priests. Never mind, *she* did.

She led the two men eagerly to the reclining room, throwing out
a command en route to Harn—"Chass and cakes!" Frengor grinned.
"And the One bless you, Harn," he said to the man's outraged face.

Perrely pulled three recliners to face each other, and the priests
settled themselves on the plush burgundy fabric. They did look
out of place with their beards and rough, homespun robes. Harn
will have those recliners thoroughly cleaned afterwards, Perrely
thought ruefully.

They chatted about this and that until Harn returned with two
servants carrying the refreshments. Once the butler's stiff back had
left the room and Perrely had given each man a cup of chass, she
could hold herself back no longer. She poured out to Frengor and
Ongaret all the ups and downs of recent days.

That led into the story of her vision, and Frengor kept nodding,
his smile widening with each new detail. When she'd finished, he
thumped his knee.

"Thanks be to the One!" he exclaimed. "This confirms what he
has been saying in my own heart since the day we met Gelmion!"

"You've met Gelmion?" Perrely exclaimed. The fourth foreigner—the one who'd gone missing!

"Yes, we met him eight days ago just outside Finien. The ultimate 'stranger and loner'! I've never met anyone who so perfectly
filled that description."

"That's just what I felt about Shiván and Alanya!"

"Yes, indeed." The priest shook his head sadly. "Gelmion confused us, though, didn't he, Ongaret?"

Brother Ongaret was a young priest with a thin, earnest face. His
adam's apple bobbed up and down as he spoke. "Gelmion's only

aim was to go to the university in Darthane. He was not following the Way of the One."

Perrely shook her head. That was a problem she'd been wrestling with.

"But he was the strangest stranger I'd ever met on the roads," Frengor said, "and obviously a loner, all by himself like that—but his story showed that he'd come with three others. We didn't know quite what to make of it, did we Ongaret?" The young priest nodded. "Until yesterday. That was when we met Shiván."

"He escaped?" Perrely gasped.

"Yes, by the One's gift. And so did Alanya. Tell Lady Perrely your story, Ongaret." Ongaret did so, adam's apple bobbing as he described the meeting between the Berûvis townsfolk and Alanya's group.

"Oh, I'm *so* relieved," Perrely's eyes were moist. The past five days had been agony.

"Well," Frengor continued, "Alanya and Shiván are now travelling separately to Darthane, and we must pray that they find each other. But after meeting both Gelmion and Shiván—and now hearing your vision—I no longer have any doubt that these four foreigners are indeed the 'strangers and loners' that the One Creator God was speaking of when he said: '*I will send strangers and loners to rebuild the broken path and restore the Way and cleanse my rescued people.*'"

Perrely's heart filled with joy, and tears welled over.

"And have you thought of the other prophecies of the Restorers?" Frengor asked, his voice bubbling with enthusiasm.

"There's the one about the Overguardian: *The Overguardian will uphold and guide them with the Sword of Light.*" Perrely hesitated. "Could Shiván be the Overguardian, do you think? He's rather young."

"Nevertheless, I believe that is what your vision revealed. Shiván was holding the Book. The Book is the Word of God, and the Word of God is described as the Sword of Light. But he'll need to grow into the leader God intends him to be."

Perrely shook her head, overcome again by amazement. "And the three things the others were holding—they're mentioned in the prophecy of the Instruments…"

"Exactly!" Frengor rattled off the passage, a finger raised in the air:

"The Glass of Seeing shall sear the evils that blemish my Way.
The Shell of Hearing shall destroy the lies that pervert my Way.
The Strings of Truth shall proclaim the words that restore my Way.

"Scholars have thrown doubt on this, trying to make out that it's all just 'poetic language'. Yet in your vision you saw Gelmion with a glass, Alanya with a shell, and Danîsha with a bellaril—and Shiván told me yesterday that they actually *have* those instruments."

He paused and uttered a sigh of pure delight. "The Prince be thanked that I have lived to see this day."

Perrely's mind had jumped to another matter. "What about the 'Rod of Truth'—the Ambon of Sûrilane? In *The Return of the Prince* it says, *They will hold high the Rod of Truth to summon the faithful; they will raise it above the altar of darkness, and release my captive people.* Shiván said they don't have the Ambon. And so many people—like my father—say that's the most important mark of the Restorers of the Way."

Frengor smiled at her. "Nowhere is it stated, younger sister, that the *Atenámbaret* will be fully equipped when they first arrive. For me it is enough that these foreigners arrived miraculously from a different sky—that they have already found the instruments—and that their shilávet mark them unmistakably as strangers and loners. The leaders of the recent Rebellion claimed to be the Restorers, yet they had none of those marks. And your vision provides the final evidence that puts their status beyond doubt. In the vision, you saw them with the Ambon. They will find it."

Perrely nodded, finding comfort in Frengor's certainty. "But what about Gelmion? He's not a follower of the Way. Yet he has the Glass of Seeing. How can he be both a Restorer and not a Restorer at the same time?"

Both Frengor and Ongaret laughed. "You've said it yourself," Frengor told her. "Right now he's neither the one nor the other. But I believe he will become the Restorer the One intends him to be. The One brought him here in the same way as the others, and gave him the glass. He clearly has a purpose for him. We can leave it to the One to prepare Gelmion for that purpose."

Perrely nodded again, and looked down at her hands. The hardest question remained. "And what about me, Frengor? I did a very stupid thing, running off to join the Restorers against my father's wishes. Now I can't go anywhere. How can I obey the One's command to be with them? Even if I could leave, how would I find them?"

Frengor's smile broadened. "That's all taken care of, younger sister. When I spoke to Shiván, I arranged to meet him — and Alanya, if they find each other — here at your father's house when they return from Darthane."

"You *did?*" Hope blossomed in Perrely's heart. "But will my father agree? He's very doubtful about the Restorers now — and he's forbidden me to join them."

Frengor looked at her with narrowed eyes. "Do you think he might change his mind if requested by the Visionary of our Order?"

"The Visionary!" Perrely exclaimed. "Does *he* know about this?"

"Certainly. In fact, he's in Berûvis at the moment. He believes, like me, that these foreigners are the true Restorers, and I know he'll be in favour of your joining them once he hears about your vision."

"Would you really ask him to speak to my father?"

"Consider it done." Both Frengor and Ongaret were smiling broadly. "Now, let's lift this up to our Father in the Light."

They all raised their hands and faces heavenward. Perrely's heart was full of thankfulness.

* * *

At the University in Darthane, Lannie had at last been conducted to someone who might be able to answer her questions.

"Come in, my dear, come in!" the scholar piped in a squeaky, old man's voice. His face was rather indistinct under a large hood, but Lannie was aware of laughter-lines and two smiling blue eyes. He was lying on a recliner amid piles of books and papers. "Do take a seat," he said, a gnarled hand appearing from the sleeve of his scholar's white robe to indicate the empty recliner facing him across a small table.

He swept aside the books piled on the table, and they vanished among the general clutter of the room. Lannie found herself lying comfortably on the recliner opposite him. The room's one circular window was open, and a distant hum of human voices chanting in unison wafted in on the sweet-smelling breeze. The table was mottled with watery colours from the window's stained glass panels.

"Bring chass!" the scholar cried to an unseen servant. A moment later there were two steaming mugs in front of them.

"Sweeting?" the scholar asked, holding up a small pouch of soft leather.

"Oh! I haven't had that before. You mean to put in the chass?"

"Yes, that's right. A bit decadent, I know, but it does improve the flavour." He gave a wheezy chuckle, eyebrows raised and eyes twinkling as he awaited her reply.

"Yes, thank you, I'd like that." A hot, sweet drink at last! She'd so missed her one spoon of sugar here in Dûrion.

"Good, good." He pulled open the drawstrings of the bag and poured about a teaspoonful of dark grey powder into her mug, then stirred it. She sipped the chass, and her eyes widened.

"Why, that does taste nice."

The scholar pointed a bony finger at her. "There, you see, you've learnt something new. I always say, no one can enter this room without doing that." He gave an infectious chuckle. Lannie found herself joining in.

"Now, this is really quite an event for me, you know," he continued, his eyes beaming at Lannie from under the hood as he sipped his drink. "I've studied foreign languages, but I've seldom met anyone who *speaks* them! But you're trying to find a friend of yours, I understand?"

"Yes. His name is Gelmion. He was coming to Darthane to look for a job at the university. Have you seen him, by any chance?"

"No, my dear, I haven't."

Lannie struggled to control her emotions. So Gil hadn't made it to Darthane!

"Oh dear, I *am* sorry to disappoint you," the scholar continued, his eyes wide and sympathetic. "What, er, subject was he hoping to teach?"

"Languages. That's what he taught at university in our country. He's highly qualified."

"Oh, then he would definitely have been sent to me. I am the High Preceptor of Languages. I personally select everyone who teaches languages here." The large eyes surveyed her mournfully.

"Oh, well, we'll just have to— keep looking for him." She attempted a bright smile.

The rise and fall of the distant chanting grew louder. It had a strangely soothing effect. She'd find Gil somehow. She knew it.

"When you do, come and visit me again. It would be good to have a genuine speaker of a foreign language among our preceptors." The old scholar smiled at her as he took another sip of chass. "Now, is there anything else I can do for you?"

"Well, my friends and I were interested to hear about the Ambon of Sûrilane, and how it just disappeared a couple of centuries ago. You must know a lot about it here at the university. Do you have any idea what happened to it?"

The old man's eyebrows rose and he nodded sagely. "Indeed we do. I'm impressed that you've taken an interest in our great national mystery." He leant forward and lowered his voice. "The thing is, you see, what *really* happened to the Ambon is not something we can make generally known. It would cause far too much alarm and upset. But since you and your friends are foreigners— How many of you are there, by the way?"

"Four—including Gelmion."

"Right. We could tell you what we know—if you promise not to spread it about. In fact... how about this for an idea?" His eyes gleamed with enthusiasm, like a schoolboy suggesting a bit of mischief. "Why don't you go and find this Gelmion—and your other friends—and come back together? When you're all here, you can give us a demonstration of your very interesting foreign language, and I can also see if Gelmion would be suitable for a preceptorship. In return we'll satisfy your curiosity about the Ambon of Sûrilane! How does that sound?"

Lannie found herself infected by his enthusiasm. She was keen to agree. But the proposal was a little odd. "Why can't you just ask *me* about our language, and tell *me* about the Ambon?"

"A–ha!" Up came the finger again. "But if Gelmion wants a job, he'll have to come here anyway. And I need all four of you to carry out the necessary language experiments. One is too few. Please indulge an old man for seeking a little insurance, but you see, you might just go away and not come back." His eyes gazed at her woefully. "I'm getting on in years, and it would be a major achievement for me to publish findings about such a *very* foreign language! You do understand?"

Lannie felt bad that she'd made him plead. "Of course. We'll be glad to come back together."

"Wonderful!" he exclaimed in relief. "Oh, I do thank you for humouring me."

Lannie smiled back at the old scholar. There was a Dickensian charm about him—she'd stumbled across a Cheeryble brother in this cluttered Dûrian office.

"So, you'll really tell us about the Ambon and give Gelmion a job—if he's suitable?"

"Of course, my dear, of course! Just come back with the other three, and we'll help you in any way we can. And by the way—" He leant across the table holding out the small leather bag of sweetening powder. "Take this."

"Oh, that's very kind of you, but I really can't—"

"Of course you can! I can always get more—and I want you to enjoy this, as a memento of our chat together today." His voice dropped to a conspiratorial whisper. "If you want to make it last longer, just keep it as your own little secret! It's got a metal chain: hang it round your neck under your shift. Then when no one's watching, you can take it out and indulge yourself!" He gave a saucy grin, making her chuckle. "It's very good on its own, too," he told her. "Doesn't have to be added to chass. You want my prescription?"

"Yes, please." She hung the bag around her neck, tucking it into the top of her shift.

The finger was raised again. "A quarter of a handful every morning!"

Lannie laughed. "Thank you, doctor, I'll do that," she said. "And thank you for all your help."

"Not at all, not at all. I wish you success finding your friends—and come back soon!" The door opened and a servant stood ready to escort her back through the labyrinth of passages. She turned and waved to her Cheeryble scholar on the threshold.

Bishop Shambor watched grimly as the red-haired foreigner walked away.

———————————

Chapter 29: *Mindlock*

GIL WOKE THINKING OF COFFEE. Someone was disturbing him, wanting him to go somewhere, but he needed coffee first. He'd brew a cup in the kitchen—

"Gelmion. Out front. Full dress uniform."

Gil's eyes shot open. Reality crashed in. The Mesten Guardhouse! *No! Dear God, no! Not Dûrion again... I can't—! No, no, no, no, no, no, no, no-o-o-o...*

"Get dressed—now!"

A bolt of pure, unadulterated pain blasted him to the floor screaming in agony. Whimpering, he staggered to his feet and started fumbling for his tunic and leggings.

The ride to Stillárre took place in a haze of misery and disbelief. *Why?* Why that one, tantalising reprieve? What had jerked him back to this living hell?

In the days that followed, as he found himself once more an impotent spectator of the brave exploits of Gelmion the Guardsman, his thoughts went back time and again to that one idyllic day of freedom. It appeared in his mind as an ancient black-and-white movie on a tiny TV screen. He replayed it, longed for it, wept over it a hundred times.

Gelmion, apparently, had carried on as usual here in Dûrion while he, Gil, had been back in England. No one had noticed his absence. Had his body been in two places at once? Or was he suffering mental delusions? Multiple personality disorder? Had he created an elaborate 'alternate reality' for himself? If so, it was not to escape, but to punish himself. Why? What was he trying to compensate for?

Oh, God. When would this nightmare end?

* * *

Today the sky was bright but overcast, as usual. Gil would have felt more in sympathy with a torrential downpour. He was with a detachment of the Guard that had been sent by Mindbender Dhelgor to deal with a 'troublemaker'. The six of them were riding through the streets two abreast on their black horses. What a fine sight they must make, their grey cloaks with the dark blue trim rippling as they rode, their high, shell-shaped helmets gleaming silver to match their buttons, the metal toe caps and heel guards of their blue leather boots shining in the stirrups. People scurried out of their way, then watched them pass with sullen faces.

And what dread enemy were they setting out to defeat? A widow with four children—whose crime was that her house abutted on the Stillárre Guardhouse just where Mindbender Dhelgor wished to expand his luxury apartment. Gil's imprisoned mind felt sick.

It went about as badly as he'd expected. The woman screamed when they burst in. When they ordered her to leave her own home, her eyes blazed, and for a moment he thought she would defy them. Then she was frantically gathering together her children and a few possessions. She left the house, turned, and faced them. Her face worked, and there was a 'plop' as a gob of spittle landed on the toe guard of Gelmion's boot.

She scurried away at once, her meagre belongings tucked under one arm, the other clutching the youngest child. But Gil felt his body galvanised into action, and knew she couldn't escape. He reached her in four long strides. The first kick sent her sprawling to the ground, pots and bundles scattering, children screaming. The second two with the sharp end of the toe guard broke a couple of ribs and probably punctured a lung.

"Let that be a lesson to those who defy my lord Dhelgor!" his voice proclaimed to the hidden neighbours. Doors and windows remained firmly shut. The woman lay gasping and moaning in the mud, the children huddled beside her, terrified and silent. A grand victory for Dhelgor, Gil thought bitterly.

The patrol left to find other victims, and Gil closed his mind to the woman's sufferings, as he was learning to do. But how much longer could he endure the hypocrisy and brutality of the Bishop's Guard?

A desperate plan had been growing in his mind recently. Maybe he could play along. Suppress his horrified reactions, as he had with the widow. The Mindbender had his own twisted system of rewards. If he saw Gelmion apparently embracing the thuggery, he might eventually promote him. And with promotion, he knew, came a degree of independence. Not total; but officers in the Bishop's Guard were not subject to their master's constant presence in their minds and could to a large extent decide for themselves how they carried out their instructions. That way he might at least mitigate some of the worst excesses…

Nothing, though, could wipe out the horror of the Manor. Every night he relived the unspeakable crimes his own hands had committed, and woke drenched with sweat. *What! will these hands ne'er be clean?* He found no melodrama in Lady Macbeth's words. His own hands bore the indelible stain of atrocities he could never undo.

* * *

Fira was relieved that Alanya had returned safely to the inn. That was more than she'd expected. As an experienced officer, she'd gone into this whole Darthane mission with strong misgivings. Alanya was a foreigner, and hadn't an inkling of the dangers she was exposing them all to. Nevertheless somehow, by the Prince's gift, they had entered the city without being captured.

But when she'd said farewell to Alanya earlier today she hadn't expected to see her again. This saddened her, because despite her headstrong ways, she'd grown fond of the red-haired foreigner. Her own plans had been carefully laid: they would wait at the inn until the following noon. If there was no sign of Alanya by then, she and the twins would leave. It was too dangerous to spend a third night in the same place. They would make their way back to Carreck Manor along byroads already mapped out in her mind.

However, against all expectation, Alanya had returned. That was good. But there was a frown on Fira's face as she lay on the hard bed with Alanya snoring gently across the room from her.

What was not good was that there was a subtle difference in Alanya's manner: an unexpected secretiveness that made her gloss over what had happened at the University with a laugh and a few superficial comments. "Oh, I met this funny old scholar, and we had such a good chat together—he made me laugh! No, he hasn't seen Gelmion, but we're bound to find him. If we all come back together and give him examples of Inglish, he'll tell us about the Ambon of Sûrilane." Any further questions were brushed aside.

Alright, it was fine by Fira if Alanya wanted to keep that conversation private—and she'd been perfectly friendly about it, not the least defensive as though there were anything to hide. But it was unlike her. She'd always been open and straightforward. Also, she'd started biting her fingernails: a nervous mannerism that was out of character.

Then there was the urgency to round up the other three foreigners and bring them to Darthane. That had to be done *now*, immediately, no time to be lost. Out of Darthane and back on the north road first thing in the morning. How do we find Gelmion and Shiván? No clear answer. Apparently we just go out and look, and there they'll be.

Fira's frown deepened and she ran a hand through her hair. That happy, unshakeable confidence was at variance with the nail-biting. There was an unreality there. Never mind the details, 'the scholar' has said everything will be fine, therefore it will be.

It was the 'bargain' — information about Inglish in return for information about the Ambon — that was the clincher. Why couldn't they have exchanged information there and then? It would strike anyone as an obvious ruse to get all four foreigners to Darthane. Why was Alanya so unsuspicious?

No, something was amiss, and Fira had a growing, deeply unsettling suspicion of what that something might be.

* * *

Bishop Shambor paced up and down in his office, hands clasped behind his back. He had sent his secretary Estaron away; he was seriously disturbed.

He'd barely managed to mindbend the red-haired foreigner. He had never encountered such difficulty before. Her mind had been virtually impenetrable — to *him*, the Mindruler of Dûrion!

She'd worked her way up to him. The reception clerk at the University had foolishly taken her to the High Preceptor of Languages. The scholar had hastily sent her over to the Cathedral. The senior Kindler on duty had dropped her like a hot stone in the lap of one of the subordinate Mindbenders. He had tried to mindread her — failed totally — and taken her to his master.

Realising he faced censure for incompetence, Mindbender Threndor had let the foreigner precede him into Shambor's office. Wise of him. One whiff of the woman's shiláy, and Shambor had known he was up against something new. Something threatening. A mind he *had* to control.

He had succeeded. But only just.

He wiped a hand over his mouth before re-clasping them both behind his back. The speed of his pacing increased.

It wasn't as if he'd never mindbent foreigners before. Selmians, Marûvians, Thrinaris, Pandians—even a Khrell and several Gnarthrog. But *this* mind...! 'Foreign' didn't even begin to describe it. Simply finding the access point had been a nightmare. And the shining barrier within that protected all Lightist minds had sprawled everywhere, obscuring the voluntary neural connections. He'd felt like a man blundering about at the foot of a vast mountain of Light, searching with dazzled eyes for the single screw that needed undoing.

In the end he'd found that narrowest point in the nexus of linkages, and had performed the disconnection that could, at his command, separate Alanya's will from her voluntary actions. In Alanya's case he wanted her to continue acting under her own volition for as long as possible.

For the moment she was quite unaware she was his slave. But when she found herself doing things without her own consent—things she would not normally have done—that would be the moment of truth. Then she would become aware of his overriding control and realise she was a prisoner inside her own mind.

Even before that happened, anyone who knew her well would see subtle differences in her behaviour—small ways in which she was acting out of character. Left to themselves, many mindbent slaves developed nervous tics, or fell back into childish mannerisms. With no time for progressive conditioning he could not prevent that. But he would be seeing through her eyes and hearing through her ears. He could deal with any who showed themselves too observant...

It was a good thing she'd taken so easily to the 'sweeting' powder in the soft leather bag. As always, that was crucial.

He rubbed his hand over his mouth again. These were just the mechanics. It was what he had discovered as he probed her memory that had truly appalled him. It was *that* that had lent her mindbending such urgency.

Her words, which might have been lies, were not. There were three other foreigners, just like herself. And they were starting to believe that they might be the *Atenámbaret*—the Restorers of the Way. Hence their interest in the Ambon of Sûrilane.

Unlike most of his Mindbenders, Shambor had grown up in a Lightist family. He knew their traditions, their precepts, their 'Book', intimately. Threndor, Dhelgor of Stillárre, Hollet of Berûvis—they would all have treated Alanya and her friends like any other loners, snapping them up for their own private use. He doubted they would have seen anything untoward in the presence of foreign loners in Dûrion. He did.

He lifted a large tome off one of the bookshelves and carried it to his blackwood desk. The Book—the cursed Lightist scriptures. His Mindbenders mocked it; but he knew better. He feared it. With hands that were not quite steady he turned to a well-thumbed passage. *I will send strangers and loners to rebuild the broken path and restore the Way and cleanse my rescued people...*

Armanet and Dôrion, leaders of the recent Rebellion, had clearly been neither strangers nor loners. But *these* four... If anyone satisfied that description, they did. And it had to be more than one. Alanya, alone, he could have ignored. Not four of them.

He took a deep breath. He'd done all he could. He'd imposed the mindlock on Alanya. He'd given her the soft leather bag. And he'd had that hypnotic 'conversation' with her in which he'd planted a necessary deception in her mind—the memory of a kindly old scholar. Alanya had provided the rest herself. He saw in her mind that she did not want to continue searching for the Ambon on her own. She intended to return north, in the hope that all four of them would meet again at Carreck Manor. That suited him well. Let her lead him to her friends. He'd struck the scholar's 'bargain' with her... and had added *an overriding imperative to bring all her companions back to Darthane.*

His hands bunched into fists. He had to have them. All four. And crush them.

Chapter 30: *Hijack*

DANÎSHA SAT BESIDE GWARGIF at the entrance of their latest cave, fingering Teynel's comb. They'd been dodging from one hidey-hole to another to avoid the grey-coats, and she was heartily tired of it. When would those monsters finally give up? They had been searching every cave and clump of undergrowth for days now. She had wanted to blast them with the bellaril, but Gwargif had cautioned against it.

"Mylendel, wait till song-maker needed. Wait for other Warriors of Light. Too many men of darkness. Kill some now, then many more come."

Danîsha sighed. He was right, though she couldn't abide leaving those... *psychopaths* to roam free. And how would Lannie and Shiván find her if she was constantly on the run in the forest? "We need to be closer to the Manor, Gwargif. We must watch out for the other Warriors of Light. We may have to help them when they get here."

Gwargif did his snort-and-bob. He looked at Danîsha with a twinkle in his eye. "Lady of Song is impatient. But yes! We leave." He turned and sniffed the air to the south. "Child-killers go now. Come, Mylendel."

He set off cautiously eastward, towards the Manor.

* * *

"That's the ridge where we first saw Darthane, isn't it?" Alanya said. She stopped chewing a fingernail to point at the hills looming ahead. Fira nodded. She was relieved that they'd finally reached the Herm Downs.

God knew they'd taken long enough to get out of Darthane this morning. First oversleeping; then the twins demanding a proper dawnmeal—"You can't expect us to walk on empty legs, Lieutenant!"—and the hunt for a stall selling fresh food; then the struggle to avoid being dragged into the ongoing celebrations of the Festival of Unity; and finally having to wait while a military column marched through the North Gate.

Two hours just to get out of the city! And she'd hoped to reach Lômack in enough time this evening to hunt through the inns.

Alanya was insisting on searching in every town and village on the route from Darthane to Carreck Manor, to try and find Shiván and Gelmion. So much for her own idea of an unobtrusive journey back along the byways! But if her private suspicions about Alanya were correct, all plans would have to be changed anyway. She was still trying to work out how.

They reached the village of Herminar half an hour later, and decided to stop at the inn for their midmeal. They were walking between two parties of foreign merchants, who fortunately made the same decision. Fira felt unobtrusively in the leather money bag at her waist. It was a lot lighter than when they'd left the Manor. If they ate frugally they might just have enough to see them to Ganneret's house…

The inn was so busy they had to sit on the nearby village green with a hundred others. Fortunately, though overcast, it was not raining. Several groups had finished eating and were singing a well-known Dûrian song before setting off again. Their group was settling down on the grass, each with a freshly-baked bun and a bowl of watery bean and cay stew, when Alanya's eyes widened. Her jaw dropped. Fira's stew leapt from its bowl as Alanya shrieked, "*Shiván!*"

Alanya jumped up — and there through the crowd, frozen in the act of lifting a spoon to his mouth, was Shiván.

His whole face lit up when he saw them. He came charging over. The twins raised his hand and clapped him on the back, while Fira frantically wiped stew from her tunic. She and Alanya both received a rib-cracking hug. Fira felt a surge of annoyance at this unseemly public display — but Alanya seemed to take it in her stride. What strange customs these foreigners had. But she was delighted to see that Shiván had survived the executions in Berûvis.

By the time their first incoherent greetings and questions were over, many of Shiván's group had gathered behind him. Their shiláy was a strong, clear Lightist one, to Fira's relief. Shiván made the introductions. The leader was Kindler Tondor; she'd heard of him.

When the introductions were over they sat down together and shared their experiences. Alanya described how she'd escaped capture in Berûvis, and though Shiván was clearly delighted to hear it, Fira felt she recited it rather mechanically, like someone else's story that she'd learned. And whenever she thought people weren't watching, up came the fingernails to be chewed. Fira shook her head. Alanya worried her.

Shiván had noticed the nail-biting as well. He was looking at Alanya with a puzzled frown. Alanya quickly changed the subject, asking how he himself had managed to escape. Shiván's story was typical of him, Fira thought—humorous and understated. He was a young man of great ability who didn't value himself at his proper worth.

Then Alanya told Shiván about her interview with the scholar. It was the same superficial account, majoring on the scholar's person-ality and glossing over the details. A frown gathered on Shiván's face. He asked a question in their own language. Alanya laughed as she said a few words in reply. Still frowning, Shiván asked several other questions, receiving similar brief responses. He raised his eyebrows and shrugged. *I must talk to Shiván later*, Fira thought.

The rest of the midmeal passed quickly. Shiván went off for a while to chat with Kindler Tondor and members of the other group, which he would now be leaving.

After all the farewells had been said, the five of them crossed the highway and followed the northern pedestrian lane towards Lômack. Fira and Shiván walked behind Alanya and the twins, who were joking together.

"What do you think of Alanya's story?" Fira asked quietly.

Shiván turned a puzzled face to her. "Unconvincing. How long has she been like this? All airy and confident, I mean, and chewing her fingernails?"

"Since she saw that scholar at the Cathedral."

"Hmmm." He stared unhappily at the ground as they walked along.

"You asked her some questions about that, in Inglish. What did she say?"

"She just avoided them. Didn't give any proper answers at all."

"The scholar said everything will be fine, so it will be. Don't worry about the details."

"Exactly! It seems so strange. I mean—it's not like her. She never just accepts what others tell her."

"That's what I felt, Shiván. I'm glad you confirm it."

"Also, here's a scholar of languages talking to a foreigner, and apparently he didn't even ask her what language she spoke! Or get her to say a few words. I've studied with language scholars in our own country, and I can tell you, that's totally unbelievable. And biting her nails all the time! That also started after she saw this scholar?"

"Yes."

Shiván ran a hand through his tangled blond thatch. "What's got *into* her?"

Fira gave Shiván a long look. "I think the answer to that is... a Mindbender."

"*What?*"

"We learnt in the Rebellion that nervous mannerisms like nail-biting, blinking, constantly scratching oneself... are a clear sign of mindbending. Alanya has been mindbent. We have a Mindbender among us right now."

Shiván stared at her, appalled. "What do you mean?"

"If Alanya's mindbent, then her Mindbender sees everything she sees and hears everything she hears. He knows exactly who we are, and where we're going."

Shiván face was a study in shock. "They can do *that*? I thought they just controlled what their victims did..." His voice dropped to an incredulous undertone. "You mean we're being watched all the time? *Why?* The Mindbender can't know we're the Restorers of the Way — can he?"

"They read minds, Shiván. The Mindbender knows everything Alanya knows."

"So he's following us — through Alanya — because we're the *Atenámbaret?*"

"I don't know. Possibly. Or he may just be hunting for loners — people who can safely be enslaved, without causing an outcry from their relatives. He'll know from Alanya's mind that there are three others like her. He's letting her lead him to them."

"So all that stuff about going back and getting information about the Ambon of Sûrilane — "

"Is a load of *grûn* manure." She saw Shiván wrinkle his nose. They'd just passed a fresh pile of reeking dung left by the huge beasts pulling the carts.

Shiván was running a hand through his tousled hair again. It was sticking out in every direction. "So we're being hunted. God help us. Is Alanya — " He paused. "Does the Mindbender somehow fix his commands in Alanya's mind, so she does what he wants without realising it?"

"No, it's worse than that. The Mindbender is *in* her mind constantly, controlling what she does. Don't ask me how it works, but from what I've seen, sometimes the slave is left free to behave as they would normally, while at other times the Mindbender directly controls them."

"We've got to do something!" Shiván exclaimed — then glanced anxiously at Alanya and the twins. Thankfully their voices were raised in argument about something. In a lower tone he continued, "We can't just carry on, leading the Mindbender to Gelmion and Danîsha!"

"I agree. But what *can* we do? The minute we try anything, the Mindbender will know through Alanya. In any case, she's the group leader. She decides where we go and what we do. One of us would have to challenge for leadership — which the Mindbender would immediately be aware of."

"Maybe we'll just have to risk that." Shiván's expression had hardened. "We have to disappear — to follow a completely different route the Mindbender wouldn't expect."

"But he'll be able to see and hear everything through Alanya."

"*Haa.* Let me think about it…"

* * *

Bishop Shambor smiled thinly at the Thrinari ambassador facing him across the blackwood table. Secretary Estaron stood nearby at his table, taking notes. Shambor could have done without this interview, because it distracted him from following Alanya's progress north. But diplomacy followed its own immutable timetable.

He tuned out the conversation Alanya was having with the twin rebel soldiers, and focused instead on the current tensions between Thrinar and Dûrion concerning the newly-imposed traffic tolls on the Thrinar Pass…

* * *

Lannie's group reached the village of Gilmane, where enquiries about Gelmion at the single inn produced no result. As they walked on past fields of wheat-like *farn* grain, Shiván and Lannie were in the lead while Fira followed with Shîrin and Cârin. For a while he and Lannie chatted in English, enjoying the ease of their own language. Lannie didn't seem particularly disappointed by the lack of news about Gil. "We'll find him," she repeated confidently a number of times. Shiván forbore to ask what she based her optimism on.

He glanced back at Fira and the twins. Fira gave him a nod. Shîr and Câr's eyes were wide.

Just off the road up ahead was a small copse. He pointed it out to Lannie. "Why don't we take a break? We've been going for some time now."

Lannie shook her head. "It'll be dark in a couple of hours. We need to reach Lômack and make enquiries at the inns there. I want to keep going."

"Ah, come on, Commander, just a short break? My group started *early* this morning, and I'm pretty whacked. Ten minutes under those trees — away from the crowd — relax a bit — then we'll be all set for the final push."

Lannie gave him a long look. "Since when have *you* needed a break? You've got twice the energy of the rest of us put together."

"Alanya!" Fira called from behind. "I think it's time for a rest."

Lannie turned and stared at her. "*You* want to rest?"

"Us too, great leader!" Shîrin chimed in. He looked at Cârin, who nodded.

Lannie threw up her hands. "*All* of you? I didn't know I was with such a bunch of wimps. All right, but only for a few minutes."

Lannie turned off the highway towards the copse. As she entered the trees, Shiván grabbed her from behind, pinning her arms to her sides. She let out one startled scream before Fira clapped a hand over her mouth, pushing her head back hard against Shiván's shoulder. Lannie began struggling fiercely, and it was all Shiván could do to hold her. He backed against a tree trunk and clung on for dear life, groaning as she kicked his shins. Fira somehow kept her hand clamped over Lannie's mouth. Shîr grabbed her feet.

"Câr," Shiván gasped, "the fireclay!"

"And a loose cloth from my bag," Fira added.

As Lannie drew breath to scream, Fira deftly thrust the cloth between her jaws. Lannie coughed and spluttered, and as she was doing so, Fira yanked the cloth out and wound it around her mouth several times before tying it firmly at the back of her head.

"Now the fireclay, Cârin."

Câr passed her the pot, and she dug out a lump of the thick red clay. Kneading it with her fingers she made a little ball. Shîr held Lannie's head to one side and she pushed it gently but firmly into the right ear, tamping it down. They repeated the process with the left ear. Then Fira took a heavy scarf and bound it tightly round Lannie's eyes and ears, leaving only her nose visible.

"Cârin, get the binding cord," Shiván said. He did so. "Now we must take her outer robe off." It was a struggle, but they managed, tumbling her to the ground in the process. The three men held Lannie down while Fira wrapped more cloths round her hands and feet to prevent chafing before tying them tightly with the cord. Finally she strapped Lannie's bound arms to her body.

They stepped back and surveyed their handiwork. Lannie was jerking on the ground, making muffled sounds, and a wave of shame washed over Shiván. Had he really done this to *Lannie?* No, not to Lannie. To a Mindbender's spy.

Shîrin was looking at him with raised eyebrows. "I think you've won your challenge for leadership, Shiván. We've silenced Alanya. But now…"

Cârin was nodding. "The Mindbender will be after us with galloping Guardsmen."

"Which is why there isn't a moment to lose," Fira cut in. "Shiván, we should leave here at once."

They all seemed to be looking to him for leadership, which made him uncomfortable. "Fira, this may have been my idea, but I'm not qualified to lead. You—"

She was shaking her head. "Oh no, Shiván. You are qualified to lead *because* it was your idea. You challenged—you won—you're in charge. That's how it works."

He looked at the twins. They were nodding. "But I never wanted—"

"You're the boss now," Cârin said, saluting smartly. "You speak, we obey."

There was no time for argument. He took a deep breath. "Right." Maybe this was where the leadership lessons Father Martin had predicted back in England began. "We'll take it in turns to carry Alanya. I'll start. Fira, can you cover her with her robe to hide the bindings? She's sick—we're taking her home. But first—" He gestured to the others and walked a little way away. "Even though her ears have been plugged," he said in an undertone, "we must avoid saying anything about our plans when we're near her, just in case. We're going to make for that forest to the west — the, er, ..."

"Larwood," Fira supplied.

"We'll hide there tonight, then cross the Two Peaks to Ganneret's house."

"That's quite a climb," Cârin commented.

"Exactly why it's a good way to go," Fira said. "It'll be a while before the Mindbender thinks of looking there."

"But he'll be sending riders to look *here*," Shiván added, "so let's get moving!"

* * *

"Your Serenity must understand that despite the goodwill in my country towards —"

The Thrinari ambassador was in full flood, but Shambor could no longer ignore the insistent nagging at the back of his mind. He nodded sympathetically, then tuned in once more to Alanya.

What he heard had him leaping to his feet. "Forgive me, your Diplomacy — a matter of the utmost importance — we will have to resume this discussion later."

The eyebrows rose on the ambassador's heavy, warty face. "As you wish." He rose. "If other matters are more important than relations between our two nations, they must take precedence. I shall of course make this known to my government." He bowed and walked towards the door with ponderous dignity. Secretary Estaron, his expression neutral, went ahead and opened the door, bowing with steepled fingers as the ambassador left.

Shambor was already mindspeaking his Guardsmen.

* * *

Lannie couldn't believe they were doing this to her. What had come over Shiván? Normally inoffensive and friendly, now *tying her up* like a dangerous criminal! Had he gone crazy? In her outrage she struggled and jerked and screamed ineffectually through the gag. She felt a faint satisfaction when Shiván had to readjust his grip. She wasn't going to give him an easy ride.

She was shut in on herself. Outside sounds were an indistinct rumble, and only a dim light filtered through the blindfold. But the more she struggled, the more the thin binding cord bit through the cloths into her wrists and ankles. The knot of the gag tightened on her neck, and the fireclay made uncomfortable lumps in her ears that hurt when she bumped them.

She decided there was no point wasting energy making herself even more uncomfortable than she already was. She'd conserve her strength until they had to feed her. *Then* she'd give them what-for.

She relaxed—but almost instantly her body resumed its jerking, her voice its inarticulate shouting. *What?* She'd decided *not* to struggle. Must be a reflex reaction. She made a deliberate decision to stop. Her body carried on regardless. Panic crashed in on her. She was having a seizure of some kind—*she couldn't control her actions!* Her body was writhing, her voice was yelling, and her mind was screaming in terror. Was she… *possessed* by something? Was this why Shiván had trussed her up?

Horror engulfed her mind in a black flood.

* * *

"Get Legate Derlion in here at once!" Shambor barked.

"Yes, your Radiance."

Secretary Estaron made an unhurried exit, but the Bishop hardly noticed. His slave—*his* slave!—was being carried off bound, gagged and blindfolded.

He paced up and down in front of the blackwood desk, hands clasped behind his back, the blue and silver robe swishing against the floor cloth. He'd anticipated everything except foreigners with original ideas. He'd even had them followed by four Guardsmen—but he burned with frustration that he himself had ordered the Guards to await reinforcements at Herminar after the reunion with Shiván. Even then he'd sensed a threat in that young man. He'd felt it would be wise to put some distance between the group and the pursuing Guardsmen. After all, he himself could follow their route through Alanya…

Well, now he was paying for his folly. All he had from Alanya was a dim light and muffled noises. That young snake Shiván could hardly have chosen his moment better. When he'd done his vanishing act the Guards were still in Herminar. He'd instantly sent three of them galloping up the road to the spot beyond Gilmane where he'd last seen the group, but that had taken over an hour and the fugitives had been long gone by the time they arrived.

He wiped a hand over his mouth. They wouldn't stay lost for long. He'd mobilised every Guardsman in both Darthane and Lômack, and Legate Derlion would send mounted regular soldiers as well. They would flood the countryside around Gilmane in all directions. But even on horseback it would take three hours to deploy those forces from Darthane. He was hoping desperately for a sighting before then. And Alanya was going to help with that, despite being bound like a deer for the slaughter. He'd taken direct control. She was going to struggle, and keep on struggling, in the hope of attracting attention.

It would take only one passer-by to remember someone carrying a struggling woman, and he'd have them.

* * *

Shiván and his group hurried along the winding country road towards Larris. Ahead and slightly to the south lay the dark shadow of the Larwood, where they planned to spend the night. Behind it, silhouetted against the glowing clouds that shrouded the sunset, loomed the ominous mass of Lardan, easternmost of the Two Peaks. It wasn't high enough for permanent snow, but it was high enough, as Shîrin put it.

Shîr led the way and Fira brought up the rear. She kept glancing anxiously behind them. Cârin walked in the middle grasping Lannie's writhing form. Shiván hovered nearby to help. Several times she'd seemed almost to go into convulsions. Shiván was appalled at her determination and stamina. Fira thought it was the Mindbender, trying to attract the attention of passers-by; they had twice dodged behind hedges or into copses to avoid other travellers. Fortunately there were few of them at this time of day.

Fira suddenly grabbed Shiván's arm. Her narrow face was tense, her mouth a thin line. She pointed in the distance behind them. A small cloud of dust was growing where the road met the eastern horizon. The sound of thudding hooves came faintly on the still evening air.

Riders seldom galloped on these country roads. It could mean only one thing. Shiván called to the others to stop and looked round urgently. There were no copses nearby. The road at this point was raised slightly above the bare, harvested fields around it. It fell off steeply on the northern side into a drainage ditch.

"Quick! Down there," he said.

They tumbled down the bank into the ditch. Lannie almost jerked herself free of Cârin's grasp. She was convulsing violently now, her muffled shouts and screams redoubled. Câr lay on his back holding her face-down on top of him, and Shiván crouched with his arm raised, hesitating. At last he delivered a sharp blow to the back of Lannie's neck. She collapsed and lay still. With a slightly shaky hand Shiván checked her pulse. It was the first time since the... accident that he'd used his martial arts for real, and everything within him shuddered. Lannie's pulse was rapid but strong. Thank the One.

"Pull your hoods over your heads. Hide your hands!" Fira hissed. Shiván pulled up Lannie's hood as well as his own. He thanked God for the dark robes they wore. They all settled into stillness. Shiván felt his heart pounding.

The hoof beats drew nearer. The noise swelled to a crescendo and the ground vibrated. For a moment the riders seemed to be slowing down — then relief flooded over Shiván as they thundered past.

They waited till the sound faded into the distance. Finally Shiván lifted his head, and found the others doing likewise. Lannie lay like a limp doll in Cârin's arms. She'd be out for a while longer.

Slowly Shiván and Fira stood up — and found themselves staring into the startled faces of a couple of farm workers on the road.

"What...?" one exclaimed — then Cârin rose up like a muddy apparition from the ditch, clasping a body in his arms. The farmer workers yelled and fled down the road towards Larris.

"*Flisht!*" Fira swore.

"Where did they pop up from?" Shiván exclaimed.

Fira pointed across the road. A small path ran back through the fields towards the south-east. "They must have come that way. Prince's blood! If we'd tried to attract attention we couldn't have done better."

"Something tells me we'd better get off this road soon," Cârin muttered. "If those riders were Bishop's Guards, and they question those two fools..." He let the sentence tail off.

They set off at a brisk pace, looking for a path that would take them south-west to the Larwood. After a few minutes they found one and turned off along it in single file, Shîrin carrying Lannie.

The wood drew steadily closer. They had been walking for half an hour, and Shiván estimated they would reach the trees in another ten minutes, when Cârin, in the lead, gave a cry.

"The riders!" He was pointing ahead and slightly to the north.

They all stopped and squinted against the evening light. Shiván's heart sank as he saw three distant figures galloping along a track that would intercept theirs. Their grey cloaks billowed out behind them.

"They're trying to cut us off!" Cârin looked anxiously at Shiván.

Flisht. The swearword popped out of his subconscious. He had to lead—but Fira was so much better at it. He met her level stare. No help there. Oh God, please guide me… Well, come to think of it, there was only one hope—to reach the forest first. They had to escape those Guards. They couldn't fight. *He* couldn't fight. Not for real…

"Run for it!"

They started sprinting for the dark shelter of the Larwood. Fira had told him earlier that it was a dense forest, with thick evergreens growing under the taller deciduous trees. If they could disappear in the undergrowth they might stand a chance.

For about five minutes it was touch and go. Despite his burden Shîr kept up with them, his face red from the effort. But the Guardsmen were travelling faster. Slowly but surely they were gaining in the race for the point where the two tracks crossed near the edge of the forest. Shiván felt panic rise and his knees go weak as he realised they weren't going to make it.

"Shiván!" Fira gasped. "Stop—make a circle!"

He shouted to the others. In the midst of a green meadow they took their stand. Shîr put Lannie on the grass, and they formed a ring around her, the three rebel soldiers with their swords drawn, Shiván standing empty-handed, his thoughts chaotic.

The grey-cloaked horsemen closed in, forming a moving circle around the defenders. The leader barked a command, and there was a ring of metal as they swept out their longswords. His dark face creased in a sneer of triumph. Shiván's throat went dry. He prayed for a quick death.

Map 8:
Escaping the Mindbender

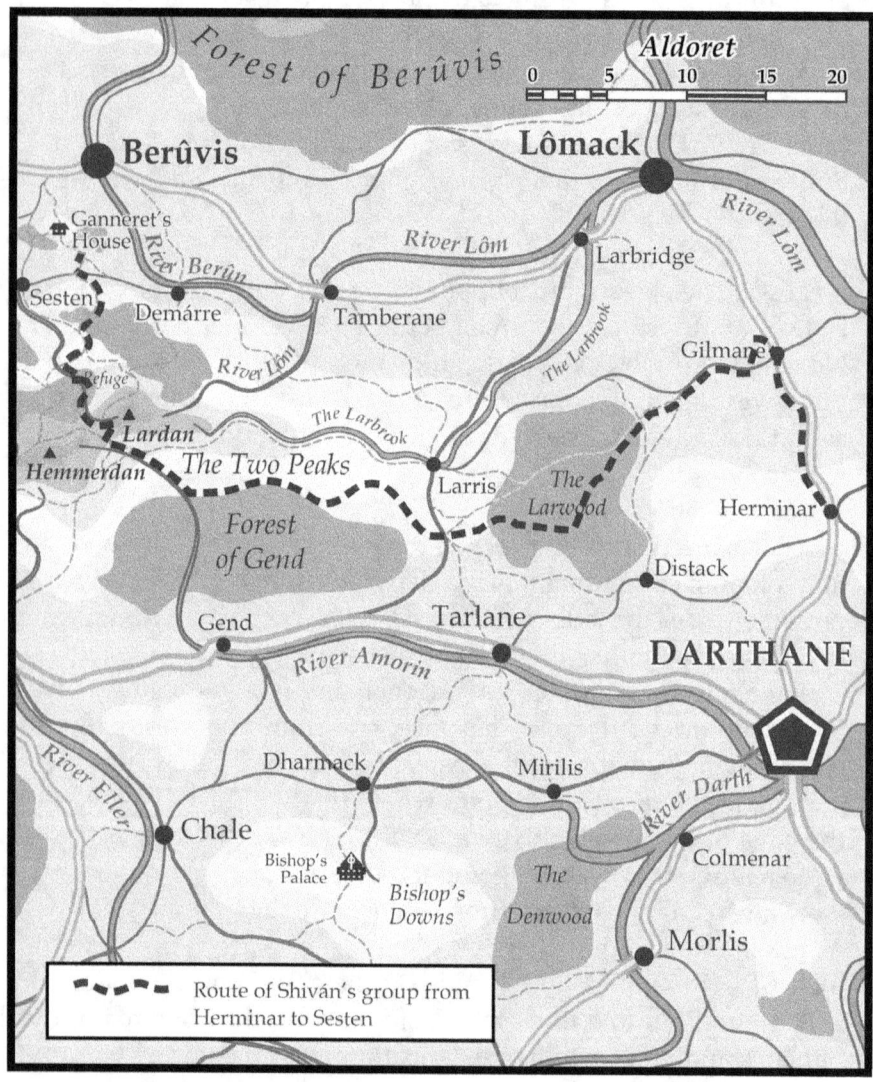

Chapter 31: *Encounters*

JOMEL STARED LISTLESSLY at the piled tray. Roast game bird with a variety of stewed roots, boiled peas and carrots, all topped with a sprinkling of *ganáy*—the crunchy aromatic seasoning imported from the tropics. One clove of *ganáy* cost more than she earned in a month. Beside the heaped platter of food was a carafe of wine, a matching crystal goblet, and a bowl full of mixed fruits and nuts. They weren't stinting her.

In fact they were trying to tempt her. She'd eaten hardly anything since Dhelgor's betrayal five days ago, and her mirror told her she was losing weight rapidly. If she carried on this way, they'd start force-feeding her: the Cult frowned on sacrificing emaciated victims. She could imagine what delight the acolytes Chand and Guriet would take in pouring thick, greasy pap down her throat, and she wasn't going to give them the pleasure. She picked at the meal, making herself swallow at least half of it.

It was Chand and Guriet who'd brought the tray, then lingered to mock her. They'd bowed low as they presented it, asked unctuously after her health, wondered whether she needed any 'trimming' with the meal, and regretted that the game bird's head had been cut off, as it should really have been left in one piece before dismemberment... But maybe it was better to do it in stages. Would she like a leg or two cut off now, to save trouble later? She'd ignored them, staring silently at the wall of her cubicle. Eventually they'd left, offering flowery condolences on the tears trickling down her cheeks.

A deep shuddering sigh escaped her as she lifted the wine goblet to her lips. In a few moments she'd add a liberal dose of the sleeping draught she kept for troublesome patrons. It was the only way she could get through her empty days. The nights, of course, were as busy as usual. Priest Sarmion was wringing all the profit he could out of her body before it was chopped up and burnt on the altar.

And only two weeks ago—it seemed a lifetime!—she'd been at the height of her career. Mistress of the Mindbender of Stillárre. Bowed and scraped to by the merchants in the market square. A force in the temple whose will was not lightly crossed. How exciting and important that had seemed at the time! How empty it seemed now. She'd admired Dhelgor, who was above her, and despised Sarmion, who she'd thought was below her. And wasn't that how everything in the Cult of Gadesh worked? Everyone scrambling for higher position; grovelling to those above, trampling on those below. How small and petty and self-absorbed.

Today was Anderil—the Lightists' day of worship; their 'Oneday'. Her mind slipped back to those childhood years at the Hearth school with Perrely. After a busy week, Anderil had been an oasis of rest. Yes, there were the obligatory hearthtimes, but they hadn't been much of a burden. In fact, there'd been a comfort and a joy about the singing and the words of encouragement from the Lightist Book that with hindsight seemed idyllic—although of course she hadn't appreciated them at the time.

Snippets of sermons long forgotten came back to her. *The last will be first, and the first will be last.* Just the opposite of the Cult of Gadesh. The Lightists talked a lot about humility, didn't they? To be truly great you had to seek the lower place, not the higher. You had to serve, not rule. And the example was Prince Orrénne himself, who though rightfully king, had died an outcast to save his people. He had cared more for them than for his own power and position.

Suddenly that unselfish approach to life—which had always seemed laughably naïve—took on a new validity. There was a purity and a wholesomeness to it that exposed the Cult of Gadesh as a seething cesspit of blind, self-absorbed maggots, frantically writhing over one another to devour a rotten prize that stank in the nostrils.

Words from the Lightist Book floated into her mind: *Ask, and you will receive. Seek, and you will find.* Not power, or position, or wealth. But what you *really* needed.

Right now, she was as low as she could go. Her heart was numb, all pride and ambition gone. Striving for status in the Cult of Gadesh had brought her to a dead end—literally. She had nothing left to lose.

Ask, and you will receive.

Jomel slipped to the marble floor and lay flat on her face, hands clasped over her head. This wasn't how the Hearth school had taught her to pray to the One Creator God, but somehow now it seemed appropriate.

"Creator God," she whispered, "I don't know how someone like me can even say your name. You know I've given myself to your enemy, Gadesh. But you said *Ask*. So I'm asking. I don't want to belong to Gadesh any more. I don't want to be sacrificed to him. If I can be of any use to you at all, please rescue me." She paused, tears flowing freely. It was probably hopeless, but she had nowhere else to turn.

How did you end a prayer to the One? A phrase came to her from those long-distant schooldays: "In the name of the Father, and of the Son, and of the Unshadowed Light."

She lay motionless on the floor, her joints becoming stiff and her body chilled by the cold marble. She hardly noticed these things, because there was a new presence in the cubicle. She might have been imagining it, but he seemed to be standing just in front of her. A deep sense of awe filled her, unlike anything she'd felt in the Temple of Gadesh.

This was God.

She kept her hands tightly clasped over her head, not daring to move before the absolute purity and majesty now confronting her.

It was as though a voice said softly, "Your request has been heard."

"Thank you," she whispered.

* * *

The Guardsmen on their small camel-horses were circling Shiván and his companions swiftly. Their longswords pointed skyward — more of a symbolic threat at the moment as they revelled in their superiority over this ragged band on foot. The leader's swarthy face wore a sneer.

"Put your swords down and we'll spare your lives."

Shiván didn't believe it for a moment. No, this was fight and die, or die anyway. His heart sank. His comrades' lives hung on his response. But if they fought, he would have to fight too — using his martial arts, since he had no weapon. He couldn't stand idly by. Yet after the event that had blighted his teenage years, he'd sworn never again to attack with intent to do harm. Knocking Lannie out had been bad enough; but deliberately attempting to maim or kill…? He stood paralysed.

"Shiván!" Fira prompted urgently.

The others deserved a chance to live. By a supreme effort of will he called out, "*Attack!*"

Shîr and Câr stood poised for the command like arrows in a bow. As one they shot towards the Guard leader like high-powered projectiles, taking him by surprise. They moved so fast that the next thing Shiván knew, both the leader and his horse were down with the twins on top of them. The horse screamed, legs pedalling furiously as it tried to break free. The rider behind struggled to control his own plunging mount. Shiván shot a quick look round: Fira was going hammer and tongs with the third Guard. Lannie lay huddled on the ground with her hands over her head.

But now the second rider had regained command of his horse and was poising his longsword to strike at the twins, who were still busy with the leader. Steeling himself, Shiván loosed a rapid kick at the Guard's elbow. By some miracle it connected, and the longsword flew from the Guard's hand.

Ignoring a wave of nausea, Shiván launched himself at the man and dragged him from his horse. They tumbled to the ground, the Guard landing on top. He knelt forward over Shiván, straddling him. One hand pinned Shiván's neck while the other reached for the dagger on his belt. Shiván kneed him sharply in the groin. The Guard gasped and jerked forward. Shiván drew back his hand and hardened his knuckles to deliver a killing punch to the throat with all the strength he could muster ...

And froze. A picture flashed on his mind. Himself at the age of fourteen, an alien from Africa surrounded by a ring of jeering school kids. Dave Garner, leader of the 'townies', circling him, dabbing at him playfully, smacking his face, taunting him. His own fury rising. Why should he put up with this? He'd been Junior Taekwondo Champion at his club in Kenya! Caution was swept away on a flood of wrath. Shiván jumped back, launched himself into the air and packed every ounce of force into a roundhouse kick at his tormentor's chest.

His foot connected with a sickening *crunch*. The school hero shot back into the crowd and collapsed on the ground. The roar of excitement died as he lay there making horrible gasping noises. A numb horror descended on young Steve Harston as he realised what he'd done.

And with that, his alienation at school was complete. Garner was in and out of hospital for two months with a punctured lung, while Steve went from one panel of grim-faced adults to the next—

parents, teachers, lawyers, social workers—sliding all the while into a deep depression. It had taken him the rest of his schooldays to struggle out of it. And he'd sworn never, *ever*, to attack like that again.

Shiván snapped back to reality as the snarling Guard raised his knife to strike. He heaved desperately, but the man was heavy. He seized the Guard's left hand as it went for his throat, and fumbled for the knife arm, but it was coming down—

Suddenly the Guard stiffened, eyes widened in surprise. The knife in his falling hand grazed Shiván's wrist; then he slowly keeled over.

As he subsided to the ground, Fira pulled her sword from his back.

Shiván struggled to his knees and looked at the still figure beside him. A red stain was spreading across the centre of the grey cloak. The man's lifeless eyes stared into the grass. Shiván felt sick.

"Shiván!" Fira's harsh voice recalled him. "Shiván, we've won." Her hand reached down to haul him to his feet. As he stood, dazed and weak at the knees, she clapped him on the back. "That was a tremendous thing you did—kicking the Guard's sword out of his hand! I've never seen anything like it."

"But you killed him."

"Of course I did! You'd have done the same."

"No, I— Thanks. You saved my life."

"That's what comrades do." She patted his shoulder and went off to see to Lannie, still curled up in a foetal position.

Shiván looked around. Fira's own opponent lay sprawled on his back, very still, while Shîrin and Cârin walked up with wide grins, a huddled grey form on the ground behind them. Câr cradled a blood-soaked arm. The three horses had disappeared.

Shiván felt empty. Fira didn't know he'd failed in the end. He tried to remind himself that the Bishop's Guards were instruments of evil who murdered innocent people. It made no difference. He could not have killed that Guard.

The twins swaggered up. "So much for *them* and their loud talk!" Shîr said. Câr glanced from Shiván to the body at his feet. "Well fought, great leader!"

Shiván shook his head. "Fira killed him. Otherwise it would be me lying there."

Câr's grin faded. He shrugged, and opened his mouth to speak when Fira came up carrying Lannie. "Shiván, the One has given us victory, but we need to move on."

"Right. Câr, your arm…"

"Will survive. Just a cut. The Lieutenant, I'm sure, will be delighted to bind it up like Alanya's mouth once we're in the forest." He grinned at Fira, who snorted.

"Then let's get there before more grey-coats arrive."

* * *

"*Send them! Now!*"

Shambor had half-risen from his seat to bellow at the half-wit.

Legate Derlion paled and took a step backwards. "Y–yes, my Lord Marshal. I shall instruct the —"

"*Get out!*"

The man turned and fled through the door Secretary Estaron was already holding open for him.

Shambor clenched his fists as he stood leaning forward on the blackwood desk. He was breathing heavily. Incompetents, the lot of them. All that drivel about the dangers of night riding, the lack of local facilities, and Gadesh knew what else. He needed Derlion's mounted detachment at the Larwood *now*, not next week or whenever the idiot had been pompously informing him they could manage it.

Three of his Guardsmen killed. *Gesh!* He could scarcely credit it. By an unarmed civilian and a few rebel scum on foot. A deepseated fear trembled behind his outrage. "*Strangers and loners … will restore the Way and cleanse his rescued people.*" No one could stop them. You could throw everything you had at them, and they'd still succeed. Because they came in the power of the One Creator God.

No! That was pure superstition. The stale old dogmas of his youth coming back to haunt him. Amazing how childhood fears could linger. But he was the Mindruler of Dûrion now. Controlling men's minds — *that* was ultimate power. He could take care of this pathetic band of would-be supplanters. As he had with Armanet.

In fact, even if Derlion's mounted infantry never made it to the Larwood, he knew how to snare these deer. He sank back on to his chair, his face relaxing in a grim smile. Sadly for them, he had inside information. He'd be prepared to wager they had no idea of all the nuggets he'd plucked from Alanya's mind.

Ah, they were untying her. Time to glean a few more titbits...

* * *

Deep in the Larwood, Shîrin held Lannie while Fira undid her blindfold and removed the fireclay from her ears. Lannie shook her head, winced, and blinked in the dim light of the single lamp Cârin was holding. Shiván stared at her, nervous of what might follow. Would Lannie try to make a bolt for it? Or scream to attract attention? At least the Mindbender couldn't find out where they were; the centre of a thicket looked the same everywhere.

He squatted, facing her. Even though this wasn't the old Lannie, he found it difficult to meet her accusing gaze. "We'll untie your hands and remove the gag so you can eat if you promise not to make a fuss, Lannie."

She stared at him a moment longer, then nodded her head briefly.

After he and Fira worked the knots free, Lannie groaned and stretched. "I need something to drink," she croaked, rubbing her wrists. Fira helped arrange her legs, which were still bound, so she could sit upright. Cârin poured water into a mug and handed it to Lannie. She sipped eagerly, then sat cradling it in her hands. Her eyes surveyed them coldly.

"Well, what are you all staring at? Your prisoner is not making a fuss."

"We had to do this, Lannie," Shiván said unhappily. "I'm sure you know why."

"Strangely enough, I don't, but I'm dying to find out. After all, it's not every day your so-called friends tie you up, knock you out, and carry you around like a sack of potatoes."

"Lannie, you're not yourself. You've been mindbent."

"Mindbent! Oh, I see. I'm suddenly a public menace, am I? And since when have you been an expert on mindbending, Steve Harston?"

"I'm not an expert, Lannie, but—"

Fira laid a hand on his shoulder. "Shiván, this is not Alanya speaking. There's no point getting into a discussion with a Mindbender. He'll tie you up in knots, and learn things you don't even realise you're telling him."

"My word, yes, you'd better be careful, Shivvie—I might say a spell, or put the evil eye on you. Come *on*, get *real*." Lannie spoke in English, and her glance was scornful.

Shiván sighed. It was a good attempt, but he wasn't convinced. Fira was right. Least said, soonest mended. "Do you want anything to eat?"

Lannie's eyes glittered for a moment, then she seemed to relax. "Thought you'd never ask," she drawled. Shiván nodded to Cârin, who passed her some fruit.

They all shared what the twins had foraged in the forest. Shiván was about to suggest they get some sleep when Fira exclaimed, "What have you got there?" Lannie was trying to push a small brown object down the front of her dress, but Fira's hand shot out and grabbed it. Lannie screamed and fought to pull it away from her.

"It's private!" she shrilled. "Shiván, tell her to let go. It's mine! Ow!"

"I want to see what it is," Fira said. "Hold her hands, someone!"

Shîr grabbed one hand and Shiván the other. Lannie screamed non-stop, struggling to break free. Câr scrabbled for a cloth and slapped it over her mouth.

Fira had hold of a small bag, made of soft leather and attached to a chain around Lannie's neck. While the three men held Lannie still, Fira opened it and poured a dark grey powder into her hand. She sniffed it, and her face puckered with disgust.

"Teméyn!" she exclaimed.

"Prince's blood!" The twins stared, horrified.

"What is it?" Shiván asked.

"Only the most dangerous drug in Dûrion," Fira told him grimly. "Mindbenders use it. Alanya was trying to pour it into her water."

* * *

A *drug!*

Lannie seethed in the prison of her mind. 'Sweeting in your chass?' the old scholar had asked. 'You mean, to sweeten it?' she'd said, poor innocent. 'Yes, that's right... it improves the flavour.' So she'd swallowed it—literally—hook, line, and sinker. *Now* she finds it's the drug Mindbenders use!

Shiván was right. That was no scholar, it was a Mindbender. She'd been well and truly duped. All that stuff about giving them the information they wanted when she brought her friends—*lies!* Well, he was having a bit of difficulty now, wasn't he? The swee—, the *drug*, had been taken away. He'd been trying to get her addicted, but he'd failed. She'd had, what, three teaspoons of the stuff so far? That couldn't cause an addiction—could it?

"*You'd be surprised what it has already caused.*"

Lannie recoiled mentally at the alien voice in her mind. Her body lay still, bound and gagged again.

She found herself responding in the same way. "*Who are you, you bastard?*"

"*Your master.*" A cold laughter echoed through the voice.

"*You're not my master.*"

"*Oh, but for all practical purposes, I am. Was it* you *who put up that little fight just now?*"

Lannie had no answer.

"*The time will come, my poor fool, when you'll wish someone would animate your body. Are you happy they've taken the drug away? You should be trembling. You know why?*"

She lay fuming. She was *no one's* slave, and she refused to play his games. Without warning, a bolt of pure pain lashed through her. Her mind screamed while her body remained motionless.

"*I asked you a question, slave.*"

Lannie stubbornly clamped her mental lips shut. This time the agony was so intense she thought she would die.

"*Tell me why you should be trembling at the loss of the teméyn, you pathetic would-be Restorer!*"

"*Because you w–won't … be able to c–control me any more?*"

He laughed scornfully. "*I hardly imagine that would cause you any sorrow. No, you fool, you should be trembling because you will be unable to control* yourself. *Do you think when the drug wears off, everything will return to normal? Sorry to disappoint you. I have imposed a mindlock. You will be able to do nothing, do you understand? Your body will be paralysed. You will think, you will feel, but you will be unable to move, you will be unable to talk; you will be unable to do anything. You will depend on others to carry you, to feed you, to dress you, to clean you when you soil yourself. How does that sound?*"

"*Not – so good.*"

"Not so good is right. You will remain helpless until I recapture you. But that won't take long, my miserable little Atenámbar. *Then your body will move again — at* my *command. So will your friends'. Believe me, you will suffer for your defiance. Oh, yes. You'll have many long years to suffer at my leisure."* A final bolt of pain left Lannie gasping.

"Now are you trembling?"

"Y–yes."

* * *

A short night passed, followed by a long day. By the end of it Shiván was exhausted. He glanced up at the high peak of the Lardan, a pointing finger of bare, reddish-brown rock towering above them. Away to the west the Hemmerdan sat like a hunched bear silhouetted against the sunset. In the four miles between stretched the Saddle, a barren ridge of tumbled rock and heather. The land fell away sharply to the south — the side they were toiling up now. Fortunately their path wound between rocky outcrops and clumps of hardy bushes clinging to the mountainside, so they could not easily be seen from below.

This had been the most physically testing day Shiván could remember since arriving in Dûrion. They'd been walking, crawling and running for about eleven hours now. He could barely keep pushing one leg after the other up the steep incline; but the three rebel soldiers climbed tirelessly. It was Shîrin's turn to carry Lannie, trussed up and struggling.

Fira kept urging them on — and he was grateful to her. She'd woken them at an ungodly hour this morning, long before dawn, answering the twins' complaints with a sharp retort that the Mindbender's troops would be starting early, too. And by heaven, she'd been right! They'd made their way westward to the edge of the forest, moving from thicket to thicket, and had then waited in hiding while Guardsmen and soldiers entered in a steady stream along paths to the north and south. Shiván had had to knock Lannie out again to stop her attracting attention.

But after a number of heart-stopping close-calls they'd made it out of the forest and across a road to the south of Larris. Then came the long, slow trudge up the ever-rising foothills towards the Lardan peak. At first they'd dodged from cover to cover, but after a while they were alone on the high hills. Shiván had wished there

274

were time to appreciate the magnificent view of central Dûrion — the autumn woods and fields glowing in the mellow light, and the glint of many rivers. But Fira was constantly glancing behind and urging them on.

Now they'd almost reached their goal — the Saddle, and the jumble of rocks at the foot of the Lardan where they'd look for a corner to shelter in for the night. A cold wind was sifting through Shiván's robe, and he shivered. They couldn't risk a fire. It was a bleak prospect.

Just then Shîr, ahead of him, stumbled and nearly fell. Lannie was jerking in his arms. "Be still, or we'll both fall," he growled. But Lannie's movements became more violent, her whole body arching against Shîr's restraint. He stopped to get a firmer grip, and almost lost his balance as another spasm stretched Lannie in an arc of tension. A long, agonised "Aaaaah!" filtered through her gag.

"Fira! Câr! Help Shîr!" Shiván shouted. He himself struggled up from below to support the rebel soldier. The other two hurried back down the path, and Cârin was just in time to grab Shîr's arm as Lannie arched again, almost sending him tumbling.

Shîrin sat down, and they all helped hold Lannie. "We'll have to wait till this eases off," Shiván said.

Fira was looking anxiously around them. "The Mindbender's trying to attract attention. He must have people nearby. We can't wait long."

But the violent spasms continued, and the muffled cries became more desperate. Shiván frowned. "Sounds like she's really in pain."

Fira shook her head. "This is some kind of trick. I don't like it. If we all carry her..."

"That would mean untying her arms," Cârin said doubtfully. "We can't get a grip on her top half while they're strapped to her body."

"She's stopping," Shîrin said. Sure enough, the archings were becoming less intense and more sporadic. The cries dwindled to whimpers. There was a final spasm, a gasp of pain — and Lannie collapsed limp in Shîr's arms. Her head lolled to one side, and Fira moved it back on to Shîr's shoulder.

Sudden alarm clenched Shiván's heart. "Is she dead?"

"No, she's still breathing." Fira was holding the back of her hand against Lannie's nose. She looked sharply at Shiván. "This is a trick.

The Mindbender wants us to think Alanya's desperately ill. Then we'll take her to a Care House or a Keeper — and he'll catch us."

Shiván shrugged. "You may be right. At any rate, she seems to be unconscious now."

"That could be part of the trick! We think she can't hear because she's unconscious and has ear plugs, so we start talking freely in her presence. Like mentioning where we are. Don't do it!" She turned her hawk-like gaze on each of them in turn.

Shiván smiled briefly. "Okay, we won't. Now I think we'd better get moving."

Shîrin shouldered his limp burden, and they went on up the path and over the crest on to the Saddle. After some searching they found a narrow crevice at the base of a rocky outcrop that gave a little protection from the icy breeze. They ate the last of the berries and nuts the twins had gathered in the Larwood, and settled down for an uncomfortable night. Cârin took the first watch.

Lannie remained unconscious, and Shiván worried about that as he lay on the hard ground trying to sleep. Fira could be right; maybe this was just one of the Mindbender's tricks. But what if she was wrong, and Lannie *was* ill? Could that teméyn — that drug — have poisoned her? He'd find it hard to forgive himself if he just left it and she got worse. On the other hand, Fira had been right about many things. If it weren't for her, they would never have escaped the Larwood this morning.

Yes, they had much to be thankful for. And he was bone weary… He slowly drifted into a light sleep.

* * *

Shiván was not reassured the next morning when they tried to rouse Lannie and found her still limp and unresponsive. He and Fira knelt over her anxiously. She was breathing slowly but steadily, her temperature and pulse seemed normal, and she flinched when he scratched the back of her hand with a stone. Otherwise she might have been a hundred miles away for all the notice she took of them.

Fira stood, a grim frown on her narrow face. "I don't like this. Fireclay ear plugs are not always effective. She could be hearing everything we say, but the Mindbender's preventing her from responding to make us careless."

"If so, why did she jerk her hand away when I scratched it? And why doesn't he make her seem more sick, to draw us to one of the towns, as you suggested?"

"I don't know, Shiván." She jerked her head towards Shîrin and Cârin, who were standing a little distance away. Shiván and Fira joined them, and out of Lannie's hearing she continued in a low voice. "We need to disappear. The Mindbender may have troops up here already. And we don't know for sure what's happening with Alanya. My guess is that if this is a trick of the Mindbender's, he'll adopt a different tactic once we stop moving. He'll make Alanya struggle again to attract attention."

"Sounds great, Lieutenant," said Cârin. "Just one question. How do we disappear?" He gestured at the barren landscape of the Saddle, grey and desolate in the cold pre-dawn light.

Fira smiled. "You didn't learn everything in the Rebellion, Cârinor don Danneret. There is a refuge up here, prepared long ago for exactly this kind of emergency. I think I can find it—if you agree, Shiván?"

"You mean, somewhere we can hide?"

"For several days, if need be."

"A refuge! Aha, so *that* was the real reason we toiled all the way up here. Accept my humble tribute, Lieutenant." Cârin swept her an elaborate bow.

Shiván was not convinced. Lannie's condition alarmed him, and he wanted to get her to Lord Ganneret's house as soon as possible. But before he could speak Shîrin suddenly raised a hand, staring towards the southern ridge.

They all froze and listened. In the dawn silence they heard it— the distant clink of metal and rustle of movement up the southern path. Motioning to the rest to wait, Shîr crept to the edge of the Saddle and took a discreet look. He returned with a sombre expression. "An infantry patrol—ten men on foot with swords," he explained for Shiván's benefit. "Thank the One they can't get horses up that path."

They stuffed their few belongings in their travel bags, hoisted Lannie on to Cârin's shoulder, and set off at a run.

Fira led them to a small stream, which they followed downhill. Faint cries behind them and the distant thud of feet showed they'd been seen. The stream soon grew to a young river, and after a while, to Shiván's relief, they charged into a belt of evergreen trees hugging the river's edge. He noted briefly that they were like conifers; a thick carpet of flat, reed-like 'needles' lay on the ground. Fira led them in a weaving path among the trunks, now nearer, now further from the river. The thudding of feet behind them became muffled.

Then Fira swerved toward the water, and leapt on to a rock in mid-stream. She jumped across to the other bank, and waited while the others followed, passing Lannie from hand to hand. As soon as they'd all made it she set off rapidly through the trees, away from the water. When they paused to catch their breath they heard their pursuers running by on the opposite bank.

Fira gave them little time for rest, however. They scurried on down through the pine woods across several tributary streams, the roar of the main river growing steadily more substantial. Not so easy to cross now, Shiván thought with satisfaction. Then suddenly they came out on to a promontory overlooking a deep channel. The river frothed and roared over rocks below them, the air moist with spray. There was neither sight nor sound of their pursuers.

Fira pointed downstream. "That's where we'll stay."

Shiván stared in disbelief at a small, tree-covered island rising on rocky cliffs out of the torrent. It was nearest to this shore, and its cliffs rose to about the same height out of the water. But between the grass on the near-shore cliffs, and the grass on the island, was a chasm some fifteen feet wide above foaming rapids. Nothing to an athlete with a good, long run-up—but there was no run-up: the trees came almost to the edge of the cliff.

"Ah, that's a good one, Lieutenant. Very good, ha-ha." Shîr shook his head as though the joke were on him. "But come on now, where have you hidden them?"

"Hidden what?"

"Our wings." He stared at Fira with raised eyebrows, hands on hips.

She smiled mysteriously. "You're nearer the truth than you think, Shîrin. There *is* something hidden. You can help me fetch it."

'It' turned out to be a broad, thick plank about twenty feet in length. Wrapped in oilcloth for protection, it had been hidden under a low bank in the woods opposite the island. Inside the oilcloth was also a length of rope. They dragged it to the edge of the cliff, and used the rope to haul it upright against one of the trees. Then they carefully lowered it across the chasm. Shiván laughed in delight. Their own drawbridge. They'd hide it on the other side after they crossed, and no one would suspect its existence. Searchers wouldn't give the inaccessible island a second glance.

Shîrin and Cârin, the most agile, took Lannie across between them, her top end strapped to Câr's back, Shîr carrying her legs. Fira and Shiván followed, and hauled the plank across after them.

A belt of woodland enclosed the island's up-thrust rocky head, at the base of which, hidden by trees, was a small hollow and a cave. A stream chattered nearby. In the cave they found firesticks and a pot of fireclay, plus a quantity of dried fruit, hard biscuits, nuts and grain in earthenware jars. After the Larwood it seemed the lap of luxury. They all sank down on the grass outside with sighs of relief.

Yes, they needed this respite, Shiván thought. The patrol they had evaded today would be followed by others. Best to wait till the hue and cry died down.

But he found himself thinking wistfully of Lord Ganneret's comfortable home.

Map 9:
Crossing the Two Peaks

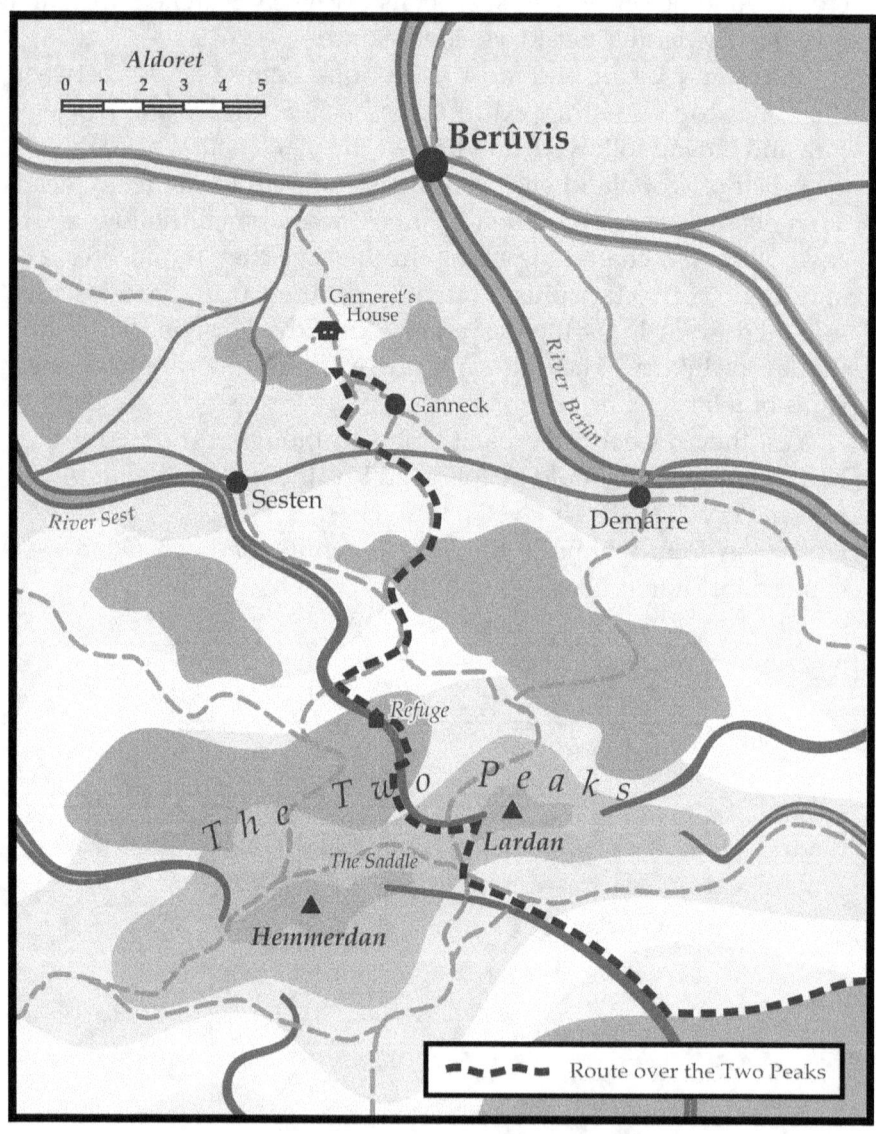

Chapter 32: *Paralysis*

LANNIE WOKE SLOWLY. There was a feeling of warmth on her face. She seemed to be lying on grass, in the open. Leaves were softly rustling around her; there was the rumble of a river in the background, and the murmur of human voices nearby. The air was full of fresh forest scents.

Then a new realisation came crashing in: the presence in her mind was gone. She was free! The darkness that had enveloped all her thoughts since leaving the Cathedral had vanished. Joy welled up within her, but her cry of triumph was silent. Her vocal cords were still.

She tried to open her eyes, but nothing happened.

Relief battled with growing anxiety. She was free, but she couldn't do anything. The raging pain and convulsions she'd suffered before passing out were gone — leaving her body limp and unresponsive.

The warmth on her face was becoming uncomfortable. She must be lying in the sun. Something sharp was sticking into her back. She struggled to open her eyes, move her head, turn over, call for help — nothing happened.

Memory of the Mindbender's voice returned. *I have imposed a mindlock. You will be able to do* nothing, *do you understand? Your body will be paralysed. You will think, you will feel, but you will be unable to move, you will be unable to talk; you will be unable to do anything.*

Her joy switched off like a light. He was out of her mind, but he'd locked her body and kept the key. Icy panic filled her, and her throat went dry. Paralysed! The horror of three years ago came crashing back. But this was worse — she couldn't even open her eyes! To her friends she would appear unconscious — even brain-dead. They wouldn't know there was a living mind inside the limp body. How long could she survive like this? Unable even to turn her head from the sunlight, or shift herself off a sharp stone...

A feeling of nausea swept over her. She *couldn't* go through all that again. She just couldn't! She'd go mad.

No! She *had* to keep a grip on her thoughts. God. She had to start thinking of God again. *God, I've been avoiding you, but can you still hear me? Why have you allowed this? Help me — Oh God, please help me!*

Her voice echoed down the empty corridors of her mind.

* * *

At first light the next morning they lowered the plank across the stream and left the island. It was Shiván's decision, in the light of Alanya's 'illness'. Fira was unhappy about it, but she honoured his leadership.

Yesterday Alanya had continued to lie, limp and unresisting, wherever they'd placed her. At one point Shiván had noticed that her face was turning red from the sunshine falling on it. Fira had never heard of people blushing because of the sun, but apparently for the foreigners this was a bad thing. They had moved her into the shade. Alanya hadn't roused for food or drink—they'd had to force a watery bean broth into her mouth, but the One be thanked, she'd gulped it down reflexively. Shiván was anxious to get her to Lord Ganneret's house, where medical help could be summoned.

Fira walked warily down the forest path, leading the way to the lowlands. Her eyes flicked everywhere; her ears caught every breath of wind, every rustle of leaf or snap of twig. She was as taut as a drawn bowstring. A total of five patrols had passed the island yesterday. She saw no reason to believe they would be absent today. The Mindbender knew they were here, and he would not give them up easily. She did not expect to reach the road between Sesten and Demárre, which was their first objective.

Yet they did.

Maybe the steady drizzle helped, blanketing the hills with a grey mist. But when Shîrin and Cârin, who were scouting ahead, returned to say the road was clear, she could hardly believe it.

"Four hours, Shiván!" she said in a fierce undertone as they huddled under the dripping eaves of the woods. "We've walked for four hours without seeing a single patrol. Yesterday three of them passed the island in that time. And now the twins come and tell us there are no troops on the road! It's not possible. The Mindbender *can't* have given up this soon. It's a trap. It must be."

"Oh come, Fira. I think you're a better pathfinder than you're admitting. You've led us by a devious route and avoided the patrols." Shiván stood holding Alanya's limp form over his shoulder, ignoring the drips that fell steadily on their sodden robes.

"It wasn't *that* devious."

"And the empty road may not stay empty for long," Cârin put in. "We should get moving."

Alanya gave a sudden shiver—the first sign of life in two days.

This seemed to decide Shivàn. "Let's go, guys," he said. Fira sighed as she led the way again. They had no choice, really. Going back was not an option. But she mistrusted the ease with which they'd escaped the Two Peaks. It had been a pushover. And her years in the Rebellion had taught her that Mindbenders were no pushover.

Half an hour later they slipped across the narrow country road. Westward, to their left, they could see the thatched roofs of the village of Sesten through the drizzle. Ahead, across a belt of farmland, stood the wooded hill they would climb to reach Sesten Manor, Lord Ganneret's home.

* * *

Lannie was in a waking nightmare. She was slung over someone's shoulder, outwardly limp and silent, inwardly weeping uncontrollably. This was worse, far worse, than what she'd endured during the Guillain-Barré paralysis. That had come on gradually, for no known reason—which was horrible—and there'd been a lot more pain; but at least she'd still been able to open her eyes and to speak. Now she couldn't so much as twitch a muscle of her own free will.

Lannie wept in helplessness and gut-wrenching fear.

Guillain-Barré had persisted for about three months, if you included the slow recovery period when she'd endured endless therapy sessions re-training her in the simple activities of daily living. How long would this paralysis last?

Until she had another dose of the drug teméyn; which would only happen if they were captured by the Mindbender—her 'Master'. Then they'd all be mindbent by that sadistic psychopath. His words, spoken with chilling certainty, struck terror into her soul: *You'll have many long years to suffer at my leisure.*

And if by some miracle they escaped the Mindbender? Then all she could look forward to was a lifetime of *this*.

Again Lannie wept.

At last, emotionally drained, her inner sobbing slowed and stopped. She reached an empty peace devoid of hope.

Her mind drifted apathetically to her brief 'religious phase', which had started during the Guillain-Barré paralysis. She'd found peace then, too. But not this present numbness. That had been a peace vibrant with hope. It had centred on an unseen person: Jesus Christ—known here as Prince Orrénne.

How had she ever allowed that peace to slip through her fingers? It had happened so gradually she'd hardly noticed. It must have started during therapy, as the paralysis slackened its grip and the prospect of returning to a normal life grew stronger. Church had been a sad disappointment. She'd stuck it out for just over a year after regaining full movement, but she'd become increasingly irregular. Then she'd decided it was doing nothing for her and stopped going, telling herself she could get more out of reading the Bible and talking to God on her own. Which, of course, hadn't lasted long. So she'd ended up exactly as she'd been before the paralysis.

Her thoughts were interrupted as she felt herself bumping up and down. Whoever was carrying her was running! Terror flooded in. Had they been found? Were the Mindbender's men after them? Then they slowed to a walk again and her fear subsided.

In recent years she'd written off her 'religious phase' as a temporary emotional prop to keep her going during that terrible time. But what if she'd thrown the baby out with the bath water? What if the peace she'd experienced was based on fact, not fiction? The discovery that the Dûrians had the same religion on a *different planet* had shattered all her comfortable assumptions.

So here she was, again paralysed; but now with even less hope. She'd thrown away her only lifeline. There was no way God would accept her back. The tears inner flowed again.

Then a memory came: Shivvie, 'Neesh and herself sitting on a log in the forest, quizzing old Damion about Prince Orrénne. Damion had said that the three of them were children of the One Creator God. He'd *included* her. So had all the Dûrians at the Manor. They had felt it in her shiláy. But the Elder had excluded Gil, saying that he saw "not by the Light, but by his own understanding".

She had asked, "And me? How do *I* see?"

She remembered Damion's answer: "You have seen the Light, and the Light has claimed you. But you have closed your eyes. Light is shining all around you. Open your eyes."

Was that true? Could it possibly be that God still accepted her? That she only had to open the eyes of her mind, and she would see that Light and know that peace again?

Words from the Bible came back to her that she'd memorised when she first turned to Jesus Christ. He had said, *I will never leave you; I will never forsake you. I will never drive away anyone who comes to me.* And St. Paul's assurance to his young helper Timothy: *If we are unfaithful, He will remain faithful, because He cannot deny who He is.*

Her anguish turned to tears of renewed hope. A window opened in the dark prison of her mind, and Light shone in. Words from one of the Psalms, which she couldn't even remember learning, flowed into her mind:

Where can I go from your Spirit? Where can I run from your presence?
If I go up to the heavens, you are there; if I make my bed in the depths,
     you are there...
If I say, "The darkness will hide me and the light will become night
     around me" –
even the darkness will not be dark to you; the night will shine like
     the day,
for darkness and light are the same to you.

Suddenly it was as if she had never turned away from God. His love and acceptance enfolded her, as fresh and unconditional as the first day she'd come to him. She could hardly believe it: he was there, because he'd never left.

Her 'bearer' started climbing, and there were more bumps and jolts. Drips and sudden sprays of water fell on her face and trickled inside her robe from the damp trees they were walking under. But Lannie hardly noticed. She was revelling in a long-forgotten presence, and rediscovering the peace that came from God, not circumstances.

Time passed, and it was as if God gently led her thoughts back to the Mindbender who had caused her present paralysis. When she'd heard his voice in her head, it had seemed like a distillation of pure evil. As though she were talking to the devil himself. A preacher in church had once quoted a description of the devil as a roaring lion, prowling around in search of someone to devour. Well, he'd found *her.* But he'd overlooked the fact that God was with her.

The preacher had gone on to say that the devil's roaring was just for show: he had no real power over those who trusted God.

They only needed to stand up to him, and he'd slink away. At the time it had all sounded rather childish. Now she found herself wondering whether the simplistic imagery covered a more profound truth.

Resist the devil. Could that voice have been lying? It had told her she'd be permanently paralysed without teméyn. But the devil was 'the father of lies'. Therefore—assume that was *not* true.

The preacher had told them to talk to the devil—to call him a liar to his face; and she'd yawned. Now she began speaking to the voice. She knew that the physical person who had done this to her, the Mindbender, could no longer hear her. But if the Bible was right, he'd only been representing someone else—the father of lies. *He* would hear.

"You're a liar," she told him. "*You say I'll always be paralysed. That's not true.*"

Her mind reared back in shock as she heard the voice again. "*But you can't move,*" it said.

"*I don't believe that!*" she snapped back. "*I will move, and you can't stop me.*"

"*Just try it, then,*" the voice snarled. It sounded deeper and more malevolent than before.

God, help me! she cried out in her mind, and willed her arm to move.

It remained where it was, dangling down someone's back. But she felt the muscles tense in her upper arm. They had *tried* to obey her! She willed her eyes to open, and felt her eyelids quivering.

The voice roared in rage, but Lannie's heart was exultant. *Thank You, God!* She *would* break through. She *would* regain control of her body.

"LIAR!" she yelled at the voice. *With God* all *things are possible.*

* * *

Shîrin and Cârin were scouting ahead and Fira was bringing up the rear as the group plodded through the dripping trees towards Lord Ganneret's house. It was the middle of a dreary afternoon. Shiván remembered the last time he'd walked up this hill. How long ago it seemed, and how innocent he'd been then! Just a hanger-on, accompanying Lannie to Darthane because of his language skills. Now he was the leader, he'd survived a whole raft of dangers, and Lannie was an inert body hanging over his shoulder...

But he was so looking forward to reaching the warmth and safety of Ganneret's home. The good baron, surely, would know a doctor or someone who could help Lannie discreetly. Fira had been vague about the possibility of medical aid—just spoke of Keepers, ordinary folk with a little practical skill like Frem and Margay; and of Care Houses in the towns, which they couldn't risk visiting.

The twins had just rejoined them when there was a sudden sound from behind. Had that been a muffled shout? They all whipped round. Fira was missing! Distant noises came from a thicket some way down the hill. Its branches were jerking with violent movement.

Shîr and Câr charged back down the path. Shiván, carrying Lannie, had a moment of agonised indecision. As the twins arrived at the thicket Fira came crashing out, wrestling with an infantryman in a green cape. *An ambush!* Shiván quickly put Lannie down at the foot of a tree and ran to help. He saw Shîrin seize the young soldier from behind; and in a moment the infantryman was standing still in Shîr's grasp, squinting down his nose at a sharp sword. Cârin emerged holding a second young trooper by the scruff of his neck, a dagger at his throat.

All three of them turned to Shiván as he came up. "What now, boss?" Shîr said. "Finish them off?"

"I wouldn't, Shiván," Fira said. "They were only doing their duty—watching for us, I think. Am I right?" she demanded of the two troopers. They both muttered "Yes," their eyes on the ground. "They'll get punishment enough if they're found bound and gagged. Do you agree?"

Shiván grinned. "I agree. Let's tie them up in the thicket."

Cârin began rummaging in his pack for a length of cord—but they all turned at the sound of running footsteps from further up the hill. "Backups coming!" Fira hissed. She hustled them all into the thicket.

"We must ambush them," Fira whispered. "There'll be two—they normally work in doubled pairs. They mustn't get away to report they've seen us."

The footsteps approached, then slowed down. "Caldet! Efferon!" a voice called in an intense undertone. The bushes parted, and Fira and Shîr leapt forward, grabbing the two new arrivals from behind.

"Rookies," Fira remarked tersely. After removing the four young soldiers' weapons they bound their hands and feet, then roped them securely together against a sturdy trunk inside the thicket. Shiván felt a stab of pity for them. They did not look happy.

Fira touched him on the arm. "We'd better get going—we must find a different path. There'll be other troops about. The sooner we get to Ganneret's house the better. Where's Alanya?" She looked round the party, then all eyes turned to Shiván.

"Oh, gadzooks!" he exclaimed. "I left her up the hill." They set off at a rapid trot.

They reached the spot where they'd heard Fira's scream. "She's behind this tree—" Shiván said, then stood stock still. They all looked behind the tree.

Lannie was not there.

———————————————

Chapter 33: *Closing net*

PERRELY SAT ON THE CREST OF THE HILL above her house. It was Anderil—the One's day—but she hadn't attended either Hearth or Travelmeet. She sat in her favourite spot under a wind-twisted *ginésse* tree, hugging her knees in the chill breeze. She needed to be alone sometimes. Most people found that very strange, and whispered sorrowfully to one another that she was rather a *loner*, poor girl. But it didn't bother her—Prince Orrénne had been a loner, too.

Beside her in a drawstring bag lay her precious copy of the Book. The world was spread out before her, and the sun was shining—a rare privilege in this season of raingold. It would cloud over again tonight. She was looking forward to goldshine—that final burst of crisp, bright sunlight and clear skies before winter set in.

Below was the manor house on its shelf of level ground halfway down the hill. The green roof tiles showed darker patches—father still hadn't had the moss cleared. The fountain sparkled in its square courtyard, surrounded on all sides by wings of the house. Beyond, the hill descended through woodland to the Sest valley. The village of Sesten, from which the manor took its name, was a distant cluster of thatched roofs beside a shimmering blue curve of the river. South of the village the majestic heights of the Two Peaks towered up, gleaming brown, purple and green in the sunshine. She thought again how much she loved this place, and how she'd miss it when she joined the Restorers.

Brother Frengor had promised to get the Visionary of the Travelling Order himself to speak to Father. He must have kept his promise, because not long afterwards Father had taken her aside and actually apologised for not listening when she'd tried to explain. He said the Visionary had described her 'dream' (as Father called it), and had spoken so eloquently on her behalf that Father felt he could not hold her back from following the One's vision. There had been tears—especially when Mums joined them—and they'd prayed together as a family, committing her to the Prince's keeping. It had been so wonderful; she could still feel the inner glow.

Meanwhile her family's unwonted involvement with the Travelling Order had even extended to lending Brother Frengor a horse! He urgently needed to fetch something for Shiván—who he believed was the Overguardian, the leader of the Restorers—and had set off yesterday at a gallop for the Order's headquarters in Stillárre. He expected to be back this afternoon. Any day now Alanya and Shiván might arrive at their house from Darthane, probably with Gelmion.

Which brought her back to her reason for being here. She'd felt strongly moved to pray this morning for Alanya, Shiván and their companions—and for her cousin Jomel. All of them, she felt, were in special need. As she looked across the valley at the twin peaks Lardan and Hemmerdan, she had the strangest feeling that Shiván and Alanya were somewhere up there, needing her prayers—though she couldn't imagine what would have made them choose such a difficult route home. She poured out her heart to the Prince of Peace, pleading with him to keep them safe, and to enable her to join them soon. She asked him to protect Gelmion and Danîsha as well, though she'd never met them. And Jomel…

As she spoke her cousin's name to the Prince, a wave of sorrow swept over her. She was filled with a deep, heart-rending anguish, and her words dissolved into pain-wracked sobs. Jomel, poor beloved Jomel—what were they doing to her? God was letting her feel her cousin's hurt. Which could only mean that Jomel was facing some terrible disaster! *Oh my Prince,* she cried through her tears, *help her! Show yourself to her, rescue her…*

The anguish gradually faded and peace descended. The Prince had heard her. He was with Jomel at that very moment. Relief filled her heart.

Then she heard the hoof beats.

She looked down at the tree-lined avenue that led up to the manor house from the direction of Berûvis. She caught glimpses of horsemen through the branches—quite a number, riding in single file. No carriage, though. Not likely to be any of the Berûvis gentry paying Father a neighbourly visit.

The first few riders entered an open stretch of the avenue. They were all wearing grey cloaks. Perrely's heart leapt into her mouth. *Bishop's Guards!*

She counted them—ten.

Ten Guardsmen arriving together could only mean serious trouble. Shiván and Alanya—had they been caught? Had the Bishop discovered that these were the prophesied Restorers—and learned that Lord Ganneret of Berûvis had entertained them? She broke out in a cold sweat. *Dear Prince, help us!*

She jumped to her feet and instinctively slipped behind the *ginésse* tree, though a single person would hardly be noticed from below. Her family—what would happen to them? Her mind shot this way and that trying to decide what to do. Returning to the house would only mean she'd be caught as well. But where could she go? How could she help them? Father and Mums, Larion and Barlet—

The Guardsmen had reached the gravelled space before the front door and were hitching their mounts to the rail. Butler Harn appeared briefly then scuttled back inside. Perrely watched drymouthed as the Guards crowded into the house.

She knew she should run for it, but she couldn't make herself leave. She had to see what happened. For a long time nothing did. She began to wonder if the Guards were there to stay. Were her family being held captive? *Shiván and Alanya!* They would be coming here! Was this a trap? *Frengor*—due to arrive any time now! She must warn him—they must both warn Shiván—

She looked down into the valley. Her heart chilled as she saw a company of green-coated infantrymen marching along the Demárre road. It was an obscure country lane—the military never came there. Until now.

She committed her family to the Prince's protection. She had to intercept Frengor. *Please guide my steps!*

Grabbing her bag with the Book, Perrely scrambled as fast as she could down the far side of the hill.

* * *

Lannie heard a muffled exclamation, and felt the vibration of two pairs of feet running back the way they'd come. There was silence for a moment, then she was carefully placed on the ground. Her bearer's feet followed the other two. *What were they doing?*

A minute passed, and she was still lying there. Had they abandoned her? Why? Was there an attack? What would happen if they didn't come back? *Oh God, please help me!*

She had to break this paralysis. A few minutes ago she'd succeeded in moving her left index finger a fraction of an inch. It was possible! She had to keep on contradicting the lies that whispered Fluke! Or, Those tiny movements don't count. You'll never lift your arms or legs. She had to believe her recovery now would be immediate. Not spread over two months, like last time. The peace of God still calmed her fears. She knew he could do it.

She needed to see where she was. She concentrated all her attention on opening her eyes.

"In your dreams!" the voice hissed.

"Liar!" she replied.

She felt the small muscles in her eyelids quivering. Open!

"They won't."

God, you gave me eyes to see!

A surge of effort pulsed through her—and she felt her eyelids moving. But something was pressing on them, stopping them from opening... Then she remembered the blindfold. She had to get it off!

She tried lifting her arm—and it moved. "Thank you, God!" she exclaimed, and heard a muffled voice croaking the words. Of course. She was gagged as well. That could wait...

Slowly, with agonising difficulty, she raised both hands and hooked her thumbs under the blindfold on both sides. Then she started pushing at the tight cloth with short, sharp jerks, gaining more strength as she did so. Suddenly the blindfold shot up over her forehead, her eyes opened, and light dazzled her.

Her focus adjusted, and there above her was an ordinary tree— but the Grand Canyon or Taj Mahal couldn't have looked more beautiful. She heard—or imagined—her captor's vicious snarl, and her lips widened in a smile of pure joy.

With more effort she pulled the gag off her mouth.

She lay on her back catching her breath, looking up at the tracery of leaves, moving her eyes, lifting her fingers, delighting in the renewed contact with her body.

She wondered what the muffled sounds were in the background; and then remembered the clay that had been pushed into her ears. She eased the earplugs out, and gasped as a volley of grunts and cries burst in on her from some distance away. A fight! Had the Mindbender caught up with them?

She became aware of boots thudding along the path towards her from the opposite direction. They would see her, capture her; take her back to the Mindbender!

The thought lent a desperate strength to her sluggish muscles. Summoning all her mental energy and praying urgently, she strained to turn herself over, to roll toward the nearby bushes. At last she rocked over on to her stomach. Two more turns and she'd be hidden under the foliage. The thud of feet was drawing rapidly closer. She strained for all she was worth and managed one more roll — but now the boots were almost here. She was in the open between the tree and the undergrowth — they'd see her! In a desperate frenzy she jerked herself under the foliage just before two pairs of booted feet clattered by.

They hadn't seen her. She sank back on the leaf mould, and the world faded away.

When she came to, she heard voices.

"She can't have gone off on her own — someone must have taken her!"

It took her a moment to recognise the voice. Shiván! They were back. Were they all safe? She forced her eyes open. She could only see the leaves of the undergrowth.

Fira was speaking. She was low down, near the ground. "Look at the way the grass is flattened. She's been rolled over..." The voice moved closer. "Here are her ear plugs!" Lannie's muscles were too tired to move again. She willed Fira to find her.

"But then it's hard ground. I don't see any more signs. They must have picked her up."

"But why would they take off her blindfold and earplugs?"

"I don't know, Shiván. We can only hope they were Lord Ganneret's people. But in any case, she's been taken away."

No! She tried to shout "I'm here!" but nothing came. She began to panic as she heard Fira and Shiván giving instructions to search the nearby paths. They wouldn't think to look in the undergrowth!

"Here!" she shouted, and this time her voice worked — but it was muffled by the gag. They didn't hear.

Summoning all her faith she shouted at the top of her lungs, "Shiván!"

What came through the gag sounded more like "Hawaa!" — but Shivvie uttered a startled "What was that?" Relief flooded over her.

Soon afterwards she passed out again, but not before she was once more hanging over Shiván's shoulder. She'd never thought she'd appreciate that undignified position.

* * *

"*Another* bunch of leaves on the ground!" Fira muttered. She was trained to notice anything out of the ordinary, and these unnatural tree droppings set an alarm tolling in her mind. She pointed out to the others the sprig of golden foliage lying at the foot of a tree beside the path.

"Birds getting violent?" Shiván hazarded.

Shîrin bent and picked the sprig up. He examined it then passed it to Fira. "Not birds. It's been cut."

She looked at the smoothly-sliced wood, then at Shiván. "This is a warning. We must not go to the house."

He frowned. "How do you make that out?"

She sighed. This foreigner. "Because people do not idly cut leaves from trees and drop them on the ground!"

"But how can you be sure it's a warning? Maybe someone was collecting the leaves—for decoration or something—and they accidentally dropped a few bunches—"

She shook her head. He was determined to get to Lord Ganneret's house and wouldn't listen to reason. "Trust me, Shiván. In this country people do not decorate themselves with leaves. And did you notice that each of the three bunches we've seen has been placed exactly at the foot of a tree? No, this is a deliberate warning. We must turn back."

"And go where?" he demanded. "We've come all this way to get to Ganneret's house because it's the only safe place, and you're saying we must turn back now?"

It was the end of a long, difficult day and everyone's nerves were frayed. With an effort Fira bit back a sharp retort.

"I'm saying Lord Ganneret's house is *not* safe any more, Shiván. That's what I believe these leaves are telling us."

Shiván looked round at the others. The twins both nodded.

A bitter expression crossed Shiván's face. "All right, then. Lead back, Macduff."

That last word sounded like an Inglish expletive, but he was telling her to lead, so she led.

They'd gone a short distance back down the path when Cârin called out softly, "Listen!" They all stopped and heard it: footsteps behind them. They hurried on in the gathering gloom, the twins bringing up the rear with drawn swords. The footsteps swelled in number and began to run towards them. They ran away. Shouts broke out behind. Suddenly a single figure appeared on the path in front. Fira swept out her sword, but a girl's voice called out unsteadily, "This way! Quick!"

Fira sheathed her sword and followed. Ganneret's daughter! What was she doing here?

"Perrely!" Shiván exclaimed.

"Here!" the girl hissed, and they dived into the undergrowth after her.

Chapter 34: *Restorers of the Way*

A COUPLE OF NAIL-BITING HOURS passed before they could breathe freely again. When the hunt moved on Perrely guided them from the little cave where she'd hidden them to a cottage belonging to a Lightist family in the nearby village of Ganneck. But when they entered, instead of the householders, they found themselves surrounded by a sea of purple robes. The travelling priests! In a moment Frengor was thumping him on the back and raising his hand high in the Dûrian greeting. Relief and joy flooded over Shiván.

Frengor had arranged with the family that they would move out and stay with friends while the priests temporarily took over their home. Now they set about turning the fugitives into members of their order. Shiván was soon struggling with strange clothing. Around him stood a crowd of purple-robed priests. They chuckled as Brother Lannet knelt at his feet fastening the criss-crossed straps around his soft chamois leggings. They found it amusing that he couldn't do such a simple task for himself. But at least once the leggings were done he should be able to manage the socks, sandals and robe...

He glanced around. The kitchen of the cottage was full to bursting. Two of the priests were his former travelling companions. Shîrin and Cârin looked every inch the eager young novitiates in their purple robes. Lannie, Perrely and Fira were upstairs in the family bedroom, also converting themselves into priests. Lannie would be a sick priest, the reason they were all having to bed down here in the village of Ganneck. They could only leave once 'he' was well enough to walk.

But Shiván was thrilled that Lannie had improved so rapidly. She'd woken up in the little cave where they'd been hiding. She'd still been very weak, but was clearly making rapid strides in regaining control of her own body. She'd told them in jerky, stammering sentences how she'd started overcoming her paralysis by listening to God and resisting the Mindbender's lies. She was still in the process of doing that. Shiván was amazed and delighted. Was this the same Lannie Catterick as the sceptic who'd stopped going to church because she had better uses for her time? The doubter who wasn't even sure if she still believed in God? Wonders would never cease.

Perrely, too, had impressed him. She'd told them of the Bishop's Guards lying in wait in her house, holding her family hostage; but without tears. Only a tightness around her eyes and mouth revealed the emotion she felt. And she'd calmly gone ahead and made all the arrangements for *them* to escape—though it might mean death for the rest of her family. She was the one who had intercepted Frengor and his party before the priests reached the manor. She was the one who had flitted around all the approaches to the house cutting sprigs of leaves to catch their attention. She was the one who had found hiding places for herself and many of the priests, and waited to guide them to safety. What a girl!

Shiván shook his head slightly as Brother Lannet started on the second set of leggings. It wasn't only Perrely's courageous behaviour. Frengor had brought these spare sets of priestly vestments with him. He'd *expected* them to be on the run and in need of a disguise. When he'd spoken with Frengor after the incident at Berûvis, nothing had been said openly about him and his friends being Restorers of the Way. But Frengor had obviously drawn his own conclusions. Well, he was grateful. The priestly robes seemed likely to get them out of rather a tight spot.

Lannet had finished now. Shiván thanked him and quickly pulled on the coarse socks and sandals. A bit loose, but they'd do. Then he slipped the robe over his head.

"Behold our latest novice!" Lannet exclaimed. There was a patter of laughter and table-banging.

"A fine one, too," Frengor declared in his resonant baritone. "Any time you want to join us permanently, Shiván, just say so. Now, attention everyone! We're going to speak to the One. Ongaret, ask the ladies to come down."

While solemn, thin-faced Ongaret climbed the stairs—just a sturdily-built ladder with flat boards for rungs—Frengor explained that they could expect visitors before long. The whole area was crawling with troops. At first they would hunt for the fugitives on the paths leading away from the area, but when they failed to find them they would check here. A Mindbender was behind this—and Mindbenders were thorough. Shiván's heart sank. As if in answer the priest punched a finger in the air and exclaimed, *"But the One who is with us is greater than those who are against us!"* There was a muted roar of approval. His heart rose again.

Then silence fell. Everyone was looking at the stairs. Lannie was coming down! In priestly robe and all, slowly, one step at a time — but she was doing it! There was an enthusiastic drumming of hands on tables. "Go, Lannie!" he cried in English. She shot him a brief smile before her face closed in concentration again. Thank God!

When Lannie had made it down and been helped to a chair by many solicitous hands, Frengor thrust an arm out towards her. "Here we have one miracle," he cried. "Now we must ask the Prince for another! Our two foreign friends look just like ourselves. If we have visitors, how will the visitors know that they are different?"

"By their shiláy," several voices answered.

"Exactly. I want us to ask the Prince to hide their shiláy. To make it blend with ours. Will you join me?"

There was a chorus of assent, and Frengor asked God exactly that, with no fuss or fancy words. As when he'd first met the priest, Shiván was touched by the simplicity of his faith.

Soon afterwards a meal of bean loaf and cayet was served. The priests had brought their own food, and cooked it themselves. Shiván sat next to Lannie and Perrely. Frengor and Fira came to join them. All three of the women could have passed without a second glance as young novices of the Travelling Order.

"Well, now we know why we got down from the Two Peaks so easily," Fira remarked. "They were deliberately letting us through, to lure us to Lord Ganneret's house."

"What about those four we tied up?" Shiván asked.

Fira grimaced. "Oh, they were young recruits. I think the first two were trying to get out of our way, but one of them cracked a twig and I went after him."

"Why?"

"*Why?* Because they would have reported seeing us to the Mindbender."

Shiván frowned. "But surely the Mindbender would know about it anyway?"

"How would he know? They weren't able to report back."

"Why would they need to? He was in their minds, wasn't he?"

Understanding dawned on Fira's face. "*Oh!* You think they were mindbent? No, Shiván. They were ordinary Dûrian soldiers."

"Then how come they were working for the Mindbender?"

"They weren't. The only troops the Mindbenders command are the Bishop's Guard. But they are powerful. Alanya's Mindbender is very anxious to recapture her, so he's called in the help of the Berûvis garrison—the regular army."

"And if they capture us—by searching this cottage, for instance—they'll just hand us over to the Mindbender?"

"Exactly. Which would be worse than killing us. Am I right, Alanya?"

She nodded, her eyes dark.

"Far worse," Frengor added gently. "What you suffered, Alanya, was only the beginning. I have dealt with people who have been Mindbenders' slaves for years. Can you imagine how *their* spirits were warped?"

"I—can," Lannie ground out.

"The Mindbenders use their drug-enhanced mental powers to make a small, physical alteration in a person's brain. This is called the 'mindlock', which, when the person is under the influence of teméyn, cuts off the mind's commands to the body. But it is temporary, and *can* be overcome by the mind itself. That happens naturally after two to four weeks when the victim has escaped the Mindbender and the effects of the teméyn have worn off.

"But the lies the Mindbender has planted in his victim's *thinking* work against recovery. That is where special help and strong determination come in—to fight those lies. When they are overcome, the mind is set free to break down the mindlock. That is why Alanya's recovery in just two days is so—"

There was a loud banging on the door. Sudden silence fell. Frengor went over and opened the door. Two infantrymen in dripping green capes stood revealed in the lamplight. These were not youngsters, but veterans with a hard-bitten look about them. They swaggered in, crowding the priests back, and announced they were searching the house for missing prisoners.

There wasn't much to search. They walked round the kitchen, shouldering priests aside. They looked under the table. They passed right by Shிván and Lannie without a second glance. They looked into the adjoining stable and prodded the straw. They climbed up to the bedroom. Finally they left without a word.

There was a collective sigh of relief. Then the priests raised their arms heavenward for a moment of silent thanksgiving before laughter and excited chatter broke out on all sides. The younger priests started singing a song praising the One, and everyone joined in. Then a fresh round of chass was poured. Shiván felt bathed in warmth. God was with them.

Frengor was smiling at Shiván and Lannie. "Well, now, you two strangers and loners. Perrely tells me you didn't seem quite sure whether you were the *Atenámbaret*. But this past week you've seen God doing some amazing things. How do you feel now? *Are* you the ones prophesied in our scriptures? *Have* you been sent to restore the Way of the One?"

Shiván looked at Lannie. She shrugged. "I've been sure for some time," Shiván said. "Alanya not so much; nor Fira and the others. What do you think?"

"I think you need to hear the vision God gave Perrely—before she ever met you." Everyone looked at the girl, who flushed at the sudden attention. She turned to Shiván and Lannie with eyes that were bright in the flickering firelight.

"I didn't manage to tell you this when you were with us," she said. "But it's why I was quite sure you were the Restorers of the Way. About a month ago, while I was talking to him, the Prince gave me a vision of four very strange-looking people. They were in a mountain forest. One was a red-haired lady wearing black culottes and a cream blouse, carrying a turquoise shell—she looked just like you, Alanya." Lannie blinked, her eyebrows high. "Another was an older lady wearing a grey three-quarter-length tunic with vertical folds, and a soft blue jacket—she was carrying a bellaril."

"Danîsha!" Shiván, Lannie and Fira exclaimed simultaneously. "Those—were—the clothes she wore!" Lannie croaked in English. "Grey pleated—skirt, blue—cardigan!"

Perrely's smile widened. "Then there was an older, very tall man. He wore a dark blue corded jacket, a narrow blue scarf around his neck, a white blouse, and grey ankle-length breeches."

"*Exactly* what Gil had on when he arrived," Shiván muttered. "Corduroy jacket, white shirt, blue tie, grey trousers."

"He had a two-handled glass—a blaise—in his hands. Then I saw you, Shiván. You were wearing a white, short-sleeved blouse and a pair of blue ankle-length breeches. And you were carrying your Book."

"T-shirt, jeans, Bible. Wow."

"But that's not all. After that I saw all of you in a glade, and Alanya, you were holding up a tall silver and gold ambon that caught the sunlight. It was beautiful."

"The Ambon of Sûrilane!" Shiván exclaimed.

"Yes. You all turned to me, and you, Shiván, beckoned me to join you. So… I think that's why I'm here right now." Her voice tailed off, and a trace of uncertainty clouded her eyes as she looked at them.

Frengor surveyed the rest of the group, his face solemn. "You've heard how exact Perrely's vision was. You've felt the foreigners' shiláy — you know they are 'strangers and loners'. You've seen that they have the instruments foretold in the prophecy of the Restorers. You've understood from Perrely's vision that they *will* have the Ambon of Sûrilane. And you know how they escaped in Berûvis, how they defeated three armed Guardsmen, how Alanya miraculously broke free of mindbending, how they escaped the Bishop's trap here. Does anyone still doubt that Shiván, Alanya and their two friends are the *Atenámbaret* foretold in the Book?"

"*No!*" the priests exclaimed as one.

Fira and the twins exchanged wide-eyed glances. "Perrely's vision is— amazing," Fira said, looking from the girl to Shiván and Lannie. "It… almost convinces me that they *are* the Restorers of the Way. I never thought I'd say that." Shîrin and Cârin were nodding, their faces solemn.

"Only one thing still troubles me," Fira continued, "and that's Gelmion. He's not a follower of the Light. How can he be a Restorer?"

"Remember Forlion," Frengor said quietly. "When Prince Orrénne first began his work, Forlion was a priest of Gadesh in Orselm. But he became a follower of the Prince and wrote *The King They Could Not Kill*, one of the best-loved Accounts in the Book."

Fira nodded. "You think Gelmion will find the Light, and then become the *Atenámbar* God intends him to be?"

"That is what I believe. The One's plans seldom spring into being all complete. They are laid far in advance and develop gradually, like everything he brings to life. The Restorers of the Way are *becoming* what they will be. Gelmion is not yet open to the Light—but he will be. Our Restorers do not yet have the Ambon of Sûri-lane—but they will have it."

"Something else," Lannie said. All eyes turned to her. They waited while she gathered her strength. "Evidence from—the enemy. The Mindbender spoke—to me. Called me a ... 'pathetic little *Atenámbar.*' "

There was a shocked silence. Then Frengor spoke in a hushed voice. "Only one Mindbender in Dûrion could have called you that: and that is Shambor dom Beldet."

"The *Bishop?*" Shiván exclaimed.

"Yes. He alone of all the Mindbenders in Dûrion had a Lightist upbringing. That's how he rose to become Bishop, while all the time in secret he was an Initiate of the Cult of Gadesh."

"You mean—" Lannie exclaimed, horror in her eyes, "I was mindbent—by Shambor himself?"

"So it seems," Frengor said solemnly. "He alone would have recognised you as a Restorer of the Way. And therefore a threat to his power."

"So it's *Shambor* who's after us," Shiván muttered. The ruler of Dûrion. What had they got themselves into?

But there was a soft light of joy in Frengor's eyes. "Shambor knew who you were. *That* is why he's pursuing the four of you. You are the only enemies he truly fears. All thanks to the One Creator God," he murmured. "All thanks to the Prince. All thanks to the Unshadowed Light. Welcome to Dûrion, Restorers of his Way."

"All thanks," the priests echoed. There was awe on their faces.

Fira was staring at Shiván and Lannie as though seeing them for the first time. "Then it *is* true," she murmured. "Shambor himself has recognised you." The twins were nodding, their customary smiles absent.

Tears of joy trickled down Perrely's cheeks.

Shiván swept his hand over his hair, trying not to meet all those awe-filled eyes. He didn't know where to look or what to say. He'd always believed they were the *Atenámbaret*—but having it publicly confirmed took the whole thing to a new level. How did you respond when people suddenly boosted you up on a hero's pedestal? He glanced at Lannie. She, too, looked shaken by the speed at which things were developing.

Frengor turned to the two of them. "We accept you as our Restorers. Can you do the same?"

Lannie's eyes were full. She nodded. Shiván swallowed. "Yes, we accept. Though we haven't a clue what we're supposed to do, or how…"

Frengor smiled. "You needn't worry about that. Only be true to him in everything, and he will guide your steps." *In all thy ways acknowledge him, and he shall direct thy paths.*

"But as you have accepted, I declare you the Restorers of the Way, to whom all Dûrians who follow the Light owe allegiance.

"You, Alanya, are the bearer of the shell of hearing. I name you *Atémban*, Restorer of Hearing. You will listen and seek out the truth. You will be slow to speak. You will penetrate to the heart of the matter. Then your words will strip away the subtle webs of darkness and deceit."

"Wow," Lannie murmured.

"If Danîsha accepts the One's task for her — and the Light tells me she already has — I name her *Atémbellar*, Restorer of Song. She will play the strings of truth, and let the Song of the One be heard again in the land.

"If Gelmion accepts the One's task for him — and the Light tells me he will — I name him *Atémbis*, Restorer of Sight. He will carry the glass of seeing. He will root out all that defiles the eyes — cultism, immorality, ostentation, greed.

"And you, Shiván, I name *Aténnelor*, the Overguardian. You are the sustainer and servant-leader. You will strengthen those who restore the Way. You will lead — by finding the right path, and enabling others to follow it with you. You will banish the darkness that envelops the Way. Against inner darkness you will wield the Sword of Light, the Word of the One. Against outer darkness you will wield — this."

The priest pulled aside his robe to reveal a belt on which hung a leather scabbard decorated with intricate curlicues. From it he drew a two-edged broadsword. The hilt end of the gleaming, silver blade was engraved with the flowing script Shiván had seen in the Lightist Book. The grip was covered in red leather bound with crossed silver threads. The pommel was an intricately patterned hemisphere of silver, matched by a large, cup-shaped hand guard. Linking the guard to the pommel were two silver arcs of metal on either side of the grip, within which the hand fitted. Together they made a circle — which, crossed by the long, straight blade, formed an ambon.

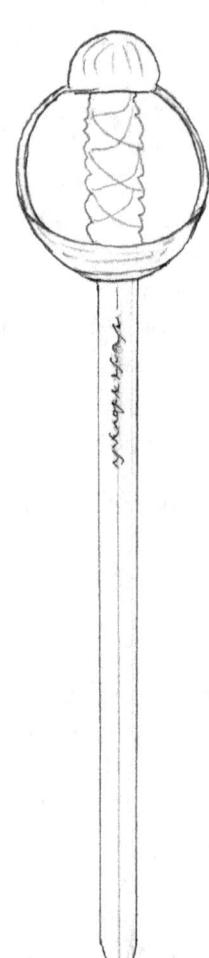

"This is the Blade of Darthane," Frengor said softly. There was an intake of breath all round the room. "Prince's Blood!" Shîr exclaimed. Resting the sword on his open palms, the priest held it out to Shiván. "It belonged to one of the Founders of Dûrion, Garion don Lûcas, three hundred and sixty years ago. He wielded it against the evil powers that then oppressed our people. Before his death he left it with the Travelling Order — and I have fetched it for you from our Domicile in Stillárre.

"Garion said that a time would come when it would again strike terror into the forces of darkness. I believe that time is now. I believe that you, Shiván *Aténnelor*, are the one to wield this blade. And with this gift the Travelling Order pledges its allegiance to the One's Restorers."

Shiván's heart sank as he gingerly took the weapon from Frengor's outstretched hands. It was surprisingly light. This Garion-whoever was obviously a famous character in Dûrian history. It was as if he were being handed the sword of Oliver Cromwell or George Washington. He felt unworthy, embarrassed and unhappy. After that episode years ago with the school bully he'd sworn never again to attack with the intent of doing harm. When they'd fought the Bishop's Guards beside the Larwood he'd been unable to kill his opponent. Now a great honour was being bestowed on him for that exact purpose.

Every purple-robed priest in the room was kneeling with head bowed. Fira and the twins were staring with wide eyes. He swallowed.

"Thank you. Please— do get up." There was a loud rustling as the priests resumed their seats. "This is a... fantastic gift," Shiván stammered, "but... I can't... I mean, I wouldn't know how..."

"I'll teach you, Shiván," Fira said quietly.

Frengor was smiling again. "All thanks to the One Creator God! Let's remember his Son, whose Way of sacrificial love these servants of his are restoring." He raised his hands and eyes heavenward, and all followed suit as together they joyfully celebrated the *Limmeris Narac*, the Remembrance of Flame.

When the priests' deep-throated harmony died away and the final resounding declaration had been made, they came one by one to Shiván and Lannie, offering words of affirmation and support.

Fira spoke for herself and the solemn-faced twins. "Our allegiance is no longer to Armanet and Dôrion. Our swords are yours now." She knelt and offered her weapon hilt-first to Shiván.

"You take it and give it back," Frengor murmured.

Shiván did so. He could only nod to Fira, the lump in his throat too large for speech.

Shîrin and Cârin followed suit. "Now you're *really* the boss," Câr murmured with the hint of a grin.

When everyone had returned to their seats and a hubbub of conversation arose, Shiván sat staring at the Blade on the table in front of him. He turned to Lannie.

"How do you feel about being a Restorer of the Way?"

Her eyes were dark. "Frightened."

He nodded sombrely. "Me, too."

His only comfort was that his rôle seemed to be mainly about leadership, not fighting. Father Martin had been right all those weeks ago. It was here, in Dûrion, that he would learn servant-leadership. Not at the University of London. Not in planning Christian Union meetings for a timid student minority. But in combating the forces of darkness that controlled this land.

The prospect made his blood run cold.

* * *

They were settling for the night. Perrely was about to climb the steps to the "lady priests' bedroom", as Shîr described it, when Frengor called her over. His face was wreathed in a warm smile.

"Well, my lady, it's thanks to your vision that the One's Restorers have been accepted tonight. What a special part he's given you to play!"

She smiled back at him, though tears still lurked near the surface. "I can't tell you what this means to me. All my life I've wanted only one thing, to serve the Prince with my whole heart. I've longed to see him restore his Way in Dûrion, and I've dared to hope I might be involved. But *this* is beyond my wildest dreams!"

The priest nodded. Then the smile faded from his face. "Even though it might cost you your family?"

Perrely dropped her eyes and wrestled for a moment with her feelings. Then she looked up at Frengor. "I made the choice between God and family long ago," she said quietly. "The thought of what might happen to them torments me. But it must not prevent me from doing what is right."

"The One comfort and keep you, younger sister. We will commit your family every day into his safe keeping. But your special part in restoring the Way is far from over. You'll leave with Shiván and Alanya tomorrow?"

"Yes, if they'll have me. I've nowhere else to go."

Frengor's grin reappeared. "Of course they'll have you! You not only confirmed the One's purpose for them today, but you saved their lives!"

She looked at him soberly. "I hope I can serve them well. I'm not much use at fighting — not like Fira, Shîrin and Cârin."

"Younger sister, you didn't mention your own rôle earlier on. I believe the Prince has summoned you to pray. One prayer warrior is worth a thousand swordsmen. Our God delights in using the weak to defeat the strong — *because* they pray! And the One's Restorers can do with a lot of prayer right now. They need to grow into their rôle. Shiván particularly. He's still too unsure of himself. You will help him with that."

She felt her face colouring. "Me?"

Frengor grinned. "Yes, you."

Map 10:
Back to Carreck Manor

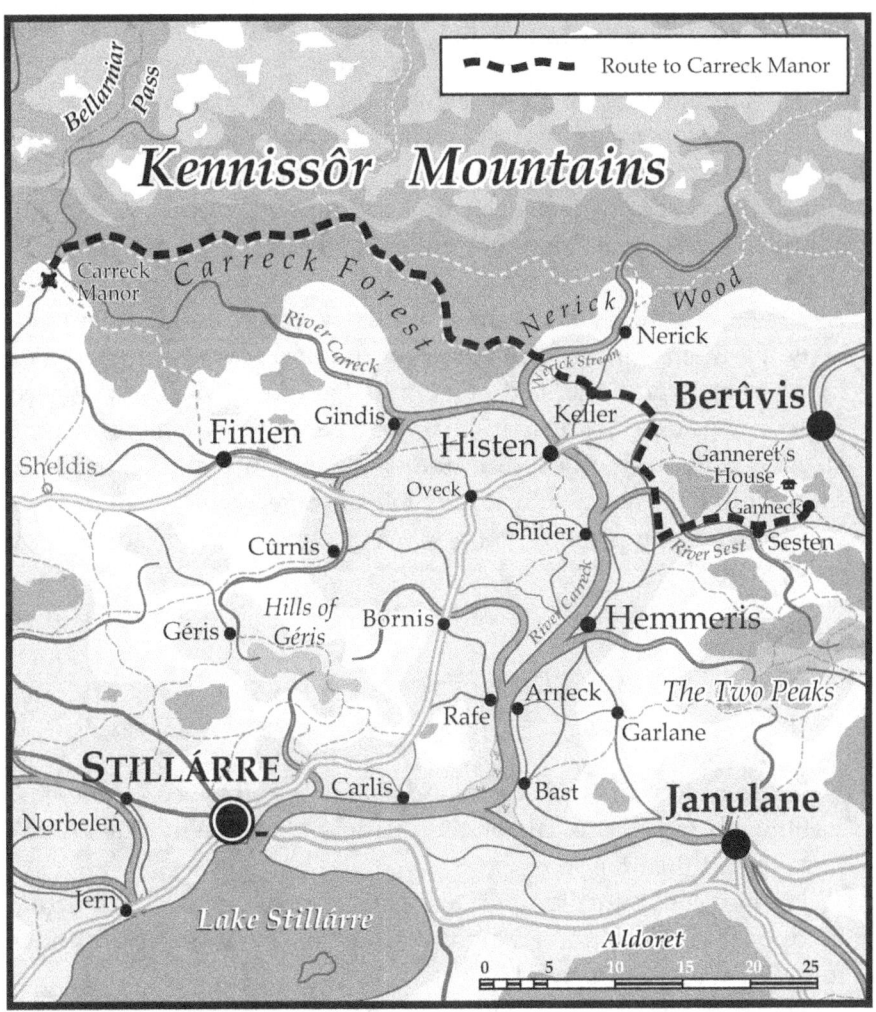

Chapter 35: *Of Bess and Blade*

FRENGOR WOKE THEM IN THE GREY DAWN. To the priests' amusement Shiván had slept in his harness and leggings. He felt stiff and uncomfortable. Before long the three lady priests came down the steps – Lannie moving more easily, he was glad to see.

While others made chass and a simple dawnmeal, Frengor called the Restorers, along with Fira and Perrely, into conference. First he had Lannie walk for them. She paraded up and down – slowly, but confidently. They decided they could leave the cottage that day.

Frengor's next question was whether they were happy for Perrely to join them. Of course they were! The girl seemed rather overcome by their warm acceptance. Fira did ask how she'd cope with living rough, and she said she could handle it. Well, they'd see. Shiván considered privately that this pampered rich girl would struggle without her beautiful home, her servants, and all the trimmings. But he continued to admire her courage.

"The final question," Frengor was saying, "is – where do you want to go?"

"Carreck Manor. We need to find Danîsha and see if Gelmion has returned."

Frengor nodded. "I thought you'd say that. There's a problem, though."

"What's that?"

"Carreck Manor is where Bishop Shambor will expect you to go."

Shiván's frown was mirrored on Lannie's face. "Why? He doesn't know about the Manor."

Frengor looked at Lannie, his eyes compassionate. "I'm afraid he does. You told him, Alanya, without realising it. He will have found out from your mind."

She stared at him in shock. "You mean... He didn't just – control me, he was able to – read my mind? Search my memory? Find out *everything*?"

"I'm afraid so."

"Oh, God," Lannie croaked in English, burying her face in her hands. Shiván felt for her. The thought made even him queasy. But the wider implications were more frightening.

"So… he'll know about Carreck Manor? That we stayed there?"

"Yes."

A growing horror gripped his mind. "Then he knows about all of us — the rebels — the basement refuge… We must leave at once! We must warn them —"

Frengor gently clasped his arm. "Slow down, Shiván. He let Alanya go, remember. He wanted her to lead him to the other three — and she did lead him to you. That suggests to me that he has not done anything yet about Danîsha and Gelmion. Since Alanya escaped, he's been too busy trying to recapture her to worry about a few rebels up at Carreck Manor. If you can escape his net now, he may spend another couple of days searching this area while you are well on your way up north. You may yet be in time to warn your friends.

"So, once more!" the priest said. "Where do you want to go? If it's still Carreck Manor, I would suggest you avoid the most obvious route, via Finien. That's the first direction Shambor will start searching when he suspects you've slipped through his fingers. But perhaps you'd rather go somewhere completely different — the last place he'd expect?"

Shiván shook his head, only partly reassured. "No. We must still go to Carreck Manor. Danîsha is there, with our friends; and Gelmion may have found his way back as well. Even if Shambor's forces reach the Manor before us, they may escape into the forest, and we can look for them there."

Frengor inclined his head. "A wise decision, *Aténnelor*. Very well. Carreck Manor it is! You can travel with us as novitiate priests for the first part of the journey."

Before leaving the cottage, they asked the One to bring them safely through the net of Guards and soldiers that Shambor had thrown over the whole area.

* * *

Lannie walked slowly but steadily with her companions, overjoyed that she could control her body again. They'd left the cottage six hours ago, and she had kept going, taking one step after another — except during the midmeal and several shorter rests. Now they were passing through the grain lands between Histen and Nerick, following country lanes to the little hamlet of Keller. The fields were brown and empty now, the harvest almost done; though here and there workers were still loading sheaves on to wagons. As a backdrop the trees of Carreck Forest flamed like red-gold fire lapping at the feet of the snow-capped Kennissôr Mountains that towered against the northern sky.

The dark lies still kept whispering in her mind. *You can't keep this up much longer, you know. Sooner or later you'll lose co-ordination and stumble...* Or, *What an effort this is. It would be so much easier just to lie down and be carried.* To every insidious suggestion she shouted Liar! — and the voice was silenced. *Resist the devil, and he will flee from you.* Her heart swelled with joy as she realised it was literally true. Every step was a miracle.

She was seeing more answers to her prayers now than at any time since inviting Jesus Christ into her life three years ago. The wonderful rediscovery of God's acceptance; her escape from the mindlock; Frengor's answered prayers to let her and Shiván pass undetected... She knew that to the Dûrians their foreign shiláy was as obvious as a different skin colour — yet those soldiers who'd searched the cottage last night hadn't noticed anything unusual.

This morning they'd set out bold as brass: a party of travelling priests in the familiar purple robes; and they'd passed any number of military patrols and checkpoints — the area was bristling with them. Yet they were waved on without question. She shook her head. It was still hard to believe.

But then... there was the other side of the coin. With privilege came responsibility. There was no longer any doubt — she was a Restorer of the Way. What this would mean in practical terms she didn't know. The possibilities scared her. But she knew who she was up against.

A burning core of righteous anger had been kindled in her by the callous cruelty of Shambor's voice. He had enjoyed taunting her. He would enjoy making her and her companions "suffer at his leisure" if ever he recaptured them. And if that pleasure palled, he would snuff out their lives without a second thought. Shambor was the personification of evil, and she would gladly take part in any endeavour to end his reign of terror. What had happened had changed her. She had a job to do now. And they had to find Gil because he had a job too, though he might not yet realise it.

Frengor's words last night echoed in her mind. *You, Alanya, will listen and seek out the truth.* Amazing how closely that echoed Father Martin's words to her back in England: to learn how to listen and discover the truth about people. Previously she'd understood that entirely selfishly, as a way to avoid messing up her friendships, as had happened with both Matt and Gil. But now it had a wider meaning, which resonated with something deep within her. She would hear both truth and untruth, listen to it, and sort out what was true. She'd have no mercy on lies.

It all started with listening—that was why she had her beautiful shell, her bess. Frengor had said the instruments symbolised—and maybe assisted—each Restorer's special task. Her hand slipped into the pocket of her robe. The feel of the bess was comforting. She took it out and cradled it in her hands. She remembered that time at the Manor when she'd thought she heard Fira while listening to the shell. With an effort she lifted the bess to her ear, still cradled in both hands. Her thoughts went to dear, kindly Danîsha, her motherliness, her strong sense of duty...

And there was Danîsha's voice—faint, but unmistakable! It was coming from the bess. She stumbled and almost fell. 'Neesh seemed to be talking to someone called 'Hargift'. She had a strange certainty that the voice was coming from the direction of Carreck Manor—though that was many miles distant. She couldn't make out the words clearly—

She'd stopped without realising it. The rest of the group came to a halt and stared at her, as she listened with rapt face to the shell.

"... have to move again. Why ... all these soldiers ... Manor ..."

A strange voice spoke in an almost unintelligible accent. "... smell darkness. Come, mile and dell..." It faded into gibberish. Then the voices were silent. Only scuffling sounds, as of objects being lifted, with the occasional grunt or sigh.

"Lannie, what is it?" Shiván's voice broke in on her thoughts.

She looked up, suddenly aware that they were standing still and all eyes were on her. "I've just heard Danîsha," she said, her voice tinged with amazement.

"'Neesh!"

"Yes, and someone else—near Carreck Manor."

"You heard that in the *shell?* ... Lannie, are you feeling okay?"

"Just a moment, Shiván." Frengor was looking at her intently. "Is that what you're saying, Alanya? That you heard Danîsha speaking in the bess?"

"Yes. It was very distant and unclear, but I know it was Danîsha."

"Shiván, this may be the first true use of a Restorer's instrument. Alanya does not have a bess of Thrinar just for decoration. What did Danîsha say, Alanya?"

She repeated the broken fragments of conversation.

"That—is—amazing!" Shiván breathed, shaking his head. Perrely's eyes were bright.

"Did you say Danîsha and this—'Hargift'—were at Carreck Manor?" Fira asked.

"Ummm… Not *at* Carreck Manor. Nearby."

"How can you be sure of that?"

"I— don't know. I just am. It's like— when you hear a voice, you—turn your head in the right—direction. I just *knew* they were there."

Fira turned to Shiván. She looked anxious. "I don't like this. Danîsha spoke of 'all these soldiers', and the 'Manor'. Also that she and her friend would have to move. Alanya says they weren't *at* the Manor. That sounds as though the Manor has been taken over by soldiers already, and Danîsha—with a stranger—has escaped into the forest." She looked at Lannie again. "Did she mention any of the others?"

Lannie shook her head. "They might have been with her. I only heard—two voices."

They asked Lannie if she could hear anything more. She lifted the bess to her right ear with one hand, while the other covered her left ear to block out the surrounding voices. She heard only the shell's soothing rumble, like distant surf. As she shifted its position to hear better, she instinctively used both hands on the bess to get a better grip. Instantly the sound changed to the swish of leaves in a forest and the muffled tread of feet. Her eyes widened. *That* was why it hadn't always worked! It needed *both* hands—like completing a circuit.

But there was no more to be heard from Danîsha. Now, could she hear Gil as well…? Her heart speeded in anticipation. But there was nothing—only the sound of the sea. She slipped the bess back into her pocket. She was disappointed and anxious about the situation at the Manor—yet strangely elated. This 'Restorer' business was real.

She walked the rest of the way past Keller to Nerick Stream without stumbling. They crossed at a ford Fira knew, and followed a narrow path into the mellow autumn forest. The trees were smaller and closer together here, and there was more undergrowth. The path was a tunnel through a golden mist of leaves. At last they reached a wide glade with a brook running through it where they decided to make camp for the night. Lannie sank down gratefully on a fallen tree trunk. To her surprise, Perrely showed herself quite competent, mucking in with the priests to collect wood, lay a fire, and build a lean-to. Before long she brought Lannie a steaming mug of chass.

* * *

After the evening meal, Frengor led the Remembrance of Flame in his usual exuberant fashion. That merged into community singing, filling the forest with harmony. Then everyone leant back and began chatting, or just relaxing. Perrely glanced round the campfire circle. This was by no means the first time she'd stayed overnight with the Travellers at their waymeets and midsummer festivals. She loved their freewheeling, joyous style of worshipping the One.

But tonight was special. She was with her new family. Shiván, his blond hair shaggy and tousled, sharing a joke with Cârin and Shîrin. Fira talking earnestly to Frengor. Alanya beside her, leaning against a log and resting—as she had every right to do. These were the brothers and sisters the One had placed her with. She looked forward to meeting Danîsha and Gelmion, the other two Restorers. Their faces, as she'd seen them in her vision, had grown dim. They would be so much more vivid in real life.

Thoughts of her own family never stopped running through her mind. The sudden parting from Father, Mums and her brothers—and the fear of what might happen to them—was an aching wound that was wrapped in God's peace. Despite the pain, she was where her Prince wanted her to be, and those dear to her were safe in his care. But if only she knew where they were...

A sudden thought struck her. Alanya's bess! *Could* she...? She turned eagerly to the foreign woman. "Alanya! You heard Danîsha this afternoon with your bess. Do you think you could also hear my parents, if you listened for them?"

Alanya turned to her, and Perrely saw the dark shadows under her eyes. "I— I'm sorry," Perrely said. "You look so tired. Maybe tomorrow…"

"No," Alanya said in her hoarse voice. "You're right. You need to know. And I need to—practise doing it." She took the bess from the pocket of her robe. Perrely's heart quickened as she lifted it with both hands to her right ear.

"I'm thinking of your father…" Alanya murmured. Her eyes narrowed and her face tightened in concentration. Perrely held her breath.

Time stopped.

Then Alanya was shaking her head. "Sorry. Nothing. Let me try your mother…"

Another long, heart-stopping moment.

But again Alanya was shaking her head. Perrely felt her eyes fill with tears.

Alanya leant towards her and laid a hand on her knee. "That doesn't mean— they weren't there. I don't know them as well as I know Danîsha. Maybe I failed. Or maybe they just— weren't talking right now."

"It's all right," Perrely said, taking herself firmly in hand. "Thank you for trying."

Frengor broke the awkward moment. "Alanya!" he called from the opposite side of the circle. "You did very well today." There was a general murmur of agreement. "How are you feeling?"

"Tired." Everyone laughed. "But glad—to be free."

"So you should be. All thanks to the Prince! Only two days off the drug, and you've completed an eight-hour walk!"

There was a thudding of knees being slapped in appreciation. Alanya smiled and nodded her thanks.

"It's pretty amazing how you've broken free," Shiván said. "I mean, that wasn't any old Mindbender, it was Shambor himself!" He paused, then continued in a musing tone, "The Bishop certainly spared no effort to find you, with all those troops and Guards around Berûvis this morning. What I don't get is how he could have organised it from way down there in Darthane."

"Oh, but Shambor would have called on the Mindbender of Berûvis," Frengor told him. "That's how all those troops arrived so quickly. Mindbenders distance-speak one another, you know. No need to send a messenger. They themselves use the drug teméyn, just like their slaves, and that enables them to talk to one another over long distances."

"Yikes! I see."

Alanya was lying back on her elbows. She roused herself to ask a question. "Is taking away that — drug — the only way a — slave can be freed? I found it — rather unpleasant."

Frengor grinned ruefully. "I'll bet you did! But, believe me, there is no pleasant way to break free of a Mindbender. Yours has been the least unpleasant escape I've come across — because of the battle you yourself fought and won. The only other way is by death — either of the slave or the Mindbender himself."

"What happens — when a Mindbender dies?"

"If the death is expected, he will normally transfer his slaves to another Mindbender beforehand. They can do that, you know. But if not — Well, I once heard of a Mindbender who was killed. Not in this country. The relatives of an enslaved man ambushed the Mindbender when he was travelling. That's why they normally avoid having slaves with local family connections."

"Did his slaves — escape when he was killed?"

"No, they froze."

"Froze? Couldn't move — like me?"

"Not quite the same as you. They were still on the drug. Their bodies' freedom to act was dependent on the Mindbender — and he was dead. So they froze in whatever position they happened to be in when he died."

"Hah!" Shiván's laugh was incredulous. Perrely, too, was amazed, and there was a grunt from Fira.

"What — happened to them?" Alanya asked.

"The attackers took their relative's body home, thinking he was dead. They started preparing the young man for burial, only to discover that he was breathing normally, and that his arm jerked when they pricked it. So they put him to bed. A day later he began to have violent convulsions as the effects of the teméyn wore off. I expect you had those, too?" Alanya nodded.

"Then, like you, he was completely limp from the mindlock. A devoted sister cared for him for about two weeks. After that he slowly began to recover. But that youngster needed a lot of help to deny the lies the Mindbender had implanted in his brain. It was over a month before he could walk without help. Which puts your achievement in perspective, I think."

There was more drumming of hands on knees.

"Shambor's the one who needs to be killed," Fira declared grimly. "Then every Mindbender in the land would freeze, and their slaves could be set free."

Perrely sighed. It sounded terrible to talk of killing people. But the Mindbenders were utterly evil. Removing them was part of banishing the darkness and cleansing the Way—which was what the Restorers had come to do.

* * *

Bishop Shambor was prowling up and down the corridors of Darthane Cathedral like an enraged *garzin*. Also like the famed mountain bear he was growling under his breath. *Five days* had passed since Alanya and Shiván disappeared, and they still hadn't been caught.

Twice they had slipped through his fingers. They almost fell into his trap at Ganneret's house; then at the last minute they simply vanished! His idiot of a subordinate had only thought to mention a day later that the Land Elder's daughter had disappeared as well. If he, Shambor, had known that *before*, he would have had them scouring the area for *her*! It was obvious from Alanya's memories that the girl was a sympathiser. She must have been the one who'd warned them. *But what had she done with them?*

He wiped a hand over his mouth. The whole area had been thoroughly searched, everyone entering and leaving had been checked, but they hadn't shown up anywhere. It wasn't as if they were inconspicuous, either, with two foreigners whose auras reeked to high heaven, and one of them being carried as an invalid! It was inconceivable that Alanya could have broken free of the mindlock this soon.

Only one certainty remained—Carreck Manor. Well, he'd ordered every available Guardsman and regular army unit into that area, and there were informers patrolling all the roads. He would wipe out that nest of rebels and scoop Danîsha in. Maybe she would know where Gelmion was—which would speed up the last part of his search. But first he'd prepare a pleasant little reception for the two delinquents when they reached the Manor.

He'd make them regret ever imagining they could defy the Mindruler of Dûrion.

* * *

Next morning there were sad farewells as Frengor and his priests set off south-west towards Finien. Any further into the forest and they would have been too far off their normal route. This was where, as Frengor put it, the Restorers of the Way must come into their own. Shiván and his friends had returned the priestly garments and were their normal scruffy selves again. They all stood with their hands raised until the last purple robe had vanished among the trees.

"Well, guys, better get moving," Shiván said. The Blade of Dar-thane felt awkward against his right leg, and he hated having to wear it. On the other hand, if fighting became unavoidable he'd rather make do with an unknown weapon than use his martial arts. Everything within him shuddered at the thought of using his hands or feet to inflict deliberate injury. That one event long ago was enough. Never again.

He wanted to reach Carreck Manor before the Bishop's forces, if humanly possible. But Fira had told him they had more than forty *aldoret* to travel through the forest. He'd worked out that the Dûrian *aldor* was about three quarters of a mile. That meant over thirty miles through dense woodland. No way they could do it in a day. But they'd get there as early as possible tomorrow and warn their friends.

They set off, Fira leading along paths she knew. Shîr, Câr and Lannie brought up the rear, indulging in mock arguments as usual. Lannie had slept well; her voice—and walk—were more fluent to-day.

So he'd ended up in the middle with Perrely, which pleased him. They'd chatted on the journey yesterday, and he'd found out what happened to her on that day of the massacres in Berûvis. She'd apologised for joining them against her father's wishes.

He was surprised how much he enjoyed talking to her. She was a young kid barely out of school—yet he sensed a kindred spirit. She, like him, longed for reality with God and didn't care about conventions.

He glanced at her with genuine admiration. Here the little rich girl was, calm and self-possessed after suddenly being ripped away from her family and thrust into the harsh, outdoor lifestyle of a band of fugitives. He'd been afraid it would be too much for her. Not in the least! Last night she'd mucked in willingly with everyone else, doing more than her fair share in building the lean-to, preparing the meal, and cleaning up afterwards.

Now, despite a chilly night on the hard ground, her dark, bluey-purple eyes were sparkling, her simple green robe was neat and her golden hair carefully done up. Slung over her shoulder was a brown cloth bag which she'd told him contained her copy of the Book — the only possession she'd had with her when the Guardsmen invaded her home.

"Have you done this before, Perrely?" he asked. "Camping out, I mean, and living rough."

She looked at him, and a mischievous dimple appeared in her cheeks. "You mean, you didn't expect the pampered rich girl to do so well?"

It was so exactly what he'd thought that he was at a loss for words.

Perrely threw back her head and laughed. It was pure, infectious merriment, and Shiván found himself chuckling too.

"Shiván, I need to explain something," she said, a grin still lurking round the corners of her mouth. "I've been the despair of my parents. They've always wanted me to be the proper lady: to dress in pretty clothes, attend hearth and society functions with them, meet just the right eligible bachelor, get married, and become a pillar of society with my husband — just like themselves. But I was hopeless! Always going off to the Travellers' waymeets, getting mud on my clothes, and being seen in the worst areas of town with the worst kind of people."

Her face suddenly sobered. "My parents are in the Prince's care now. But one thing's for sure: if they knew I was here, they'd say I was in my element at last."

Shiván nodded slowly. "I can see that," he said. "I'm glad you're with us."

To his surprise she flushed and dropped her eyes. "Thank you," she murmured. Then she was looking at him again with that direct gaze of hers. "Even though you find it hard to be the *Aténnelor* — the Overguardian?"

He shrugged, a little awkwardly. "Ever since arriving here I've believed that we were the Restorers of the Way. But you're right—I do find it hard to see myself as the leader, when I'm the youngest."

She nodded. "I think that will come gradually. You'll learn the truth of who you really are, and then you'll need to believe in yourself."

He looked at her quizzically. Quite a knowing head on such a young girl. "Maybe."

She flushed again and changed the subject.

* * *

Another cold and damp night under the trees had passed. Today, though, the sun was shining. Shiván revelled in the splendour of the red-gold forest and the warm brightness when they passed through an open glade.

He was relieved that they'd covered about twenty-six aldoret — almost twenty miles—yesterday. Only ten left for today. Lannie had walked well, steadily regaining control; and Perrely was still not having any trouble adapting.

Carreck Manor must be quite close now. They were approaching cautiously from the north-east along a narrow path through dense undergrowth. Fira shared the lead beside him. There was tension in every line of her body, her glance darting to and fro, her hand on her sword hilt. Shiván had his eyes peeled for the first sign of open country through the trees ahead. They had to avoid accidentally stepping out of the forest and being seen by hostile eyes—if any. He fervently hoped not, but they couldn't count on it. He felt a heavy responsibility for Perrely, walking behind him. She was unarmed, not a fighter in any way. Mind you, so was Lannie. But that was— different.

There was a large glade ahead of them. They paused for a careful look—but not careful enough. As they stepped into the open, eight Bishop's Guards walked out of the trees opposite.

For a moment both groups froze. Then the Guard leader smiled and reached up for the hilt of his longsword, protruding over his left shoulder. There was a clang of rasping steel as they all drew their swords.

"Back, Shiván!" Fira hissed, and turned to run.

But conflicting emotions held Shiván rooted to the spot. Here was the physical combat he'd been dreading. His common sense screamed at him to listen to Fira. Yet if he ran now, he would always run. He had to face his fear and overcome it. What had Perrely said? "You'll learn the truth of who you really are, and then you'll need to believe in yourself."

He was the *Aténnelor* now, the Overguardian, sent to restore the Way of the One in Dûrion. Those workers of evil facing him had no place in this country. It belonged to the One Creator God. His job was to cleanse it of just such filth as this. And what might they already have done to Danîsha and their friends at the Manor?

Fira could say what she liked, but he was not going to retreat. A righteous rage filled him. "*Attack!*" he yelled.

He drew the Blade of Darthane and ran full tilt at the approaching Guardsmen.

Chapter 36: *Of Bellaril and Dorbian*

WHAT HAPPENED NEXT was the very last thing Shiván expected. As he charged the Guardsmen, their eyes darted to the left and right of him, shock spreading over their faces. Then they turned tail and fled! He heard them crashing through the undergrowth, shouting frantic warnings.

He skidded to a halt, thunderstruck, still holding the Blade of Darthane over his head. There were cries of amazement behind him.

He lowered the sword and stared at its gleaming blade. What had Frengor said? A time would come when it would again strike terror into the forces of darkness. Good Lord. Well, it certainly had.

Perrely came running up and caught his arm. Her eyes were shining. "Shiván, that was wonderful!"

He felt embarrassed. "I did nothing! It was the Blade..."

"But *you* charged — we were all running away — "

"Shiván!" Fira was there, her narrow face lit up with excitement. "The One be thanked! We must give chase — we may be in time to save our friends at the Manor..."

"Let's go!" he shouted, darting off along the trail of crushed greenery the Guards had left behind. He glanced over his shoulder. They were all running after him, the rebel soldiers with swords drawn, Perrely smiling, her golden hair streaming behind her. Even Lannie was running! Joy surged through him. This was so crazy, yet so right! He knew he was doing what God had sent him to do.

They burst out of the trees, and Shiván's headlong charge faltered. There, across a wide swathe of grass, stood the familiar blackened ruins of Carreck Manor. Cantering towards them, summoned by their comrades' cries, were twelve mounted Guardsmen. The eight Guards they'd put to flight ran through the horsemen's protective line and turned to face them.

Shiván felt a sudden cold shaft of fear. Was this going to be the real, hand-to-hand stuff? But God was with them! He raised the Blade of Darthane. *"In the name of the Prince!"* he yelled and charged straight for the centre of the line. He heard the others' voices echoing his cry.

All around them a rustle of clothing and a thudding of feet arose. There were shouts of alarm from the approaching riders. The line parted in the middle as they desperately wheeled their mounts aside. The Guardsmen on foot turned and fled any way they could.

Flushed with victory Shiván led his companions on towards the Manor. Then to the south a squadron of mounted Guards appeared — and there was a thunder of hooves from the north-west. More grey-cloaked riders were bearing down on them.

"Not the Manor, Shiván!" Fira called out. "West! To the forest!"

He saw what she meant. They would be trapped in the Manor. And with all these troops it was looking unlikely that the basement had escaped discovery. He felt a sudden stab of anxiety. Looking behind, he saw that the Guards they had just passed had regrouped and were coming after them. There seemed to be grey flowing cloaks everywhere, carried by the thunder of hooves.

"To the forest!" he shouted. They ran west past the Manor. He was panting, but he saw to his relief that both Perrely and Lannie were keeping up. The horsemen to the south and north changed direction, angling to cut them off. Those behind were gaining. The rising tide of grey was sweeping in to swamp them.

"We won't make it," he gasped. "Form a circle!"

They stumbled to a halt and quickly arranged themselves with Perrely and Lannie at the centre of a tight circle. Perrely's arms and eyes were lifted heavenward in prayer. Shiván raised the Blade of Darthane and shouted, "In the name of the Prince!" — but his voice lacked conviction. The horsemen were closing in on every side, their longswords drawn, their faces grim.

Shiván's earlier confidence ebbed away. It would be a hand-to-hand fight after all, one that they could never win. But even in the face of death he couldn't bring himself to use his martial arts. He'd rather fight with the sword, a weapon he'd never used. He glanced at Cârin and tried to imitate his stance, with the Blade poised and ready. He'd defend himself and the others as well as he could. But he could not deliberately kill.

* * *

Bishop Shambor rubbed his hands as he sat at ease in the private reclining room of the Bishop's Palace on the hills near Sûrilane. He and his entourage had moved here a couple of days ago. Secretary

Estaron was building up a fire in the hearth to ease the chill of rain-gold—though in fact it was one of the season's rare sunny days. Flames glinted in the rich brown gloss of the furniture. He took a sip of his drink and sighed contentedly. He wasn't a man who relaxed for long, but it was good to be out of Darthane for a while.

And despite the initial setback, his welcoming committee was doing well up at Carreck Manor. Young Shiván had again taken him by surprise, he had to admit, by suddenly producing the Blade of Darthane. *That* hadn't been in Alanya's memories. But however he'd come by it, he was now discovering it wasn't all it was cracked up to be. Yes, it could strike fear at a distance with the illusion of a huge army; but press in close, as he'd forced his men to do, and it lost its magic.

He settled back to watch the final round-up of the fugitives through the eyes of his subordinate at Carreck Manor.

* * *

Lannie stood in the centre of the circle, panting. So this was it, then. She felt terrified and useless. While her heart thudded wildly in her chest, her mind observed all that was happening with a numb detachment.

For a while it had seemed as if Shivvie's trick with the Blade would carry them through. That was truly amazing. She'd never have thought he had it in him. All Frengor's stuff about him being 'Overguardian' she'd taken with a pinch of salt. Yet today there was no doubt about it—he'd led, decisively.

Now, though, he seemed to be running out of steam. His latest flourish with the sword had achieved nothing; the riders were closing in on all sides. And she didn't even have a knife to fight with. She and Perrely were the helpless females needing protection. She glanced at the girl beside her. Perrely was praying, her hands raised. How could she *do* that when she might die any minute? On the other hand, prayer was about all the two of them were good for. She tried to focus her mind on God, but heard only the thunder of hooves and the thudding of her own heart.

The approaching horsemen eased to a trot. They were closing in slowly, swords pointing inwards; taking no chances. Shivvie was holding the Blade ready, but he didn't look comfortable with it. She hoped he wouldn't hit one of *them* when he started swinging the thing around. What would it feel like to have a sword bite into your flesh? She shuddered and gripped her shoulders with her arms. She might know all too soon. One of the approaching riders was looking at her: a baleful, uncompromising look. His sword pointed straight at her heart. She'd always been fearless when facing new challenges—some would say foolhardy. But now she was more terrified than she'd been in her life.

One of the riders struck at Cârin. He blocked the blow with his shield. The sudden dull clang was like a signal, and fighting broke out all around. Lannie huddled in the middle with Perrely, fists clenched, her head swivelling one way and another in the chaos to try and see what was going on. A longsword whistled past her ear and she jumped aside, knocking Perrely to the ground. Fira leapt in front of her, a knife in one hand, sword in the other, parrying and thrusting at two riders simultaneously. Câr had ducked under his opponent's guard and was jabbing upward with his dagger. Shiván was—

"*Shiván!*" she screamed at him.

He turned just in time to avoid a vicious downward swipe. Another Guard was coming at him, and he tried to parry the blow, but the Blade was knocked out of his hand. Shîrin came charging in, engaging the second rider. Horses reared and neighed. The uproar was deafening.

Lannie saw Shiván whip round and grab his first assailant's free arm, yanking him off his horse. The man crashed to the ground. Shiván drew back his foot to kick—but suddenly seemed to hesitate. The rider rolled away as another Guard urged his horse at Shiván. Shivvie was reaching for the Blade, but the Guard's longsword was already raised...

Then a new sound made itself heard. Music wafted out of the forest to the west. *Music?* Everyone turned towards it, and a sudden stillness fell. Her jaw dropped as she realised that all the riders and their horses had frozen. They stood, sat or lay with perspiration bedewing their foreheads, each face a mask of agony.

This was unreal. Lannie couldn't believe her eyes—or ears. The music was that old church hymn, "Amazing Grace"! Had she just been killed and fallen into her grandparents' heaven?

Then her astonishment was swept aside as chaos erupted. Something that looked like a great, grey-white wolf leapt snarling in front of her, and she screamed. The horses were also screaming, rearing and plunging. Riders were being thrown and trampled as their animals bolted. The wolf leapt on many of the fallen Guards. None of them stirred, while the music filled the air with light.

Lannie and the others stared about them, dazed. They were standing untouched at the centre of an earthquake. "Holy Flame!" Cârin breathed. The hoof-beats of riderless horses dwindled in the distance.

Someone was approaching from the forest, playing— a bellaril. *Danîsha!*

"Shiván! Lannie!" she called. "We knew it was you."

Lannie's reply was wiped from her lips when the wolf spoke.

* * *

Bishop Shambor had never felt anything like it before. The Light that he'd barred from his mind since childhood was streaming in through the senses of his subordinate at Carreck Manor. He screamed at the man to close his eyes, turn away, block his ears— but nothing got through. The fellow was blinded and in agony, deaf to his master.

The Bishop rolled on the floor in his black velvet reclining robe, arms and legs thrashing as he tried to ward off that terrible Light. His cup crashed against the wall. He felt hands plucking at him, anxious voices calling his name. He struck them aside. Appalling visions filled his mind, fire engulfed him. *Flames!* His life and all he cared for were going up in searing white flame. He himself had started the blaze! Now it was consuming him. Him and... *No! How could I have done that? How could I have burnt her?*

"*Amma!*" he screamed as the world darkened.

* * *

Much later he awoke. He was on his bed. The drapes were closed and lamps were lit. Was it night already? Keepers were leaning over him, fear on their faces. Estaron stood at the end of the bed, impassive as always. A cold compress was strapped to his forehead. With an oath he ripped it off. He sat up suddenly, then fell back, giddy.

"Get out!" The room cleared rapidly, Estaron bringing up the rear with measured steps.

He had to think. Something terrible had happened. What was it?

Carreck Manor! All his troops disabled — the Restorers gone. Fury filled him. *Again! How did they do that?* He had a dim recollection of a blinding white light and a terrible, soul-jarring music. Try as he might he could remember nothing else. They'd used supernatural means. The Restorers of the Way. The almighty power of the One Creator God was with them — he had no chance. He was finished.

Stop that!

He would deal with this as he'd dealt with every crisis. Logic and determination. These so-called Restorers and their hangers-on were very few. The rebels in the Manor basement had already been executed — he didn't know by whom, but it was just as well. After the recent failed Rebellion the Restorers weren't likely to attract new followers in a hurry. Their little band might pull off the occasional stunt like this, but in the end they'd be overwhelmed by sheer numbers.

Every soldier in western Dûrion would be mobilised. He reached out with a shaky, hurting mind and gathered under his control the sorry remnant of his Guards at Carreck Manor. He tried to mind-speak his subordinate, but found only a silent void. The Mindbenders of Berûvis and Stillárre, then; and the army Legate in Finien. No point in revealing his temporary weakness more widely. But those three would empty their garrisons and find the fugitives. Their lives depended on it.

* * *

"Lady, I greet you!"

Danîsha saw Gwargif squat down respectfully before Lannie, who cowered back against Fira. "It's all right!" Danîsha called in English. It felt strange to her tongue. "He's a friend." She hurried towards them, but had to keep playing the bellaril, which was difficult.

Gwargif moved to Shiván, who stared at him with wide eyes.

"Warrior of Light, I welcome you!"

He sat patiently until Shiván found speech. "Er, yes, we welcome you too. Thank you for — saving our lives just now."

Gwargif loped back to Danîsha, who was picking her way among the fallen riders. His eyes were bright with excitement. "Mylendel, it is true! Is Warriors of Light!" Without waiting for a reply he ran back to the newcomers. Danîsha smiled. Sometimes he was just a great, friendly dog.

"All of you, follow me!" Danîsha called. "I have to keep playing, or the ones still alive will start waking up."

She led them through the forest like the Pied Piper to the cave on an open hillside where she and Gwargif were staying. There, finally, she stopped playing. She embraced her friends warmly, the tears flowing, and they all settled themselves on the sandy floor. It was so good to be with people again. Shiván introduced her to Perrely. The girl seemed sweet enough, but very young. It was hard to believe the string of daring deeds Shiván credited her with. He had a slightly proprietary air towards her. Well, well.

Then Fira and the twins began telling her how magnificent Shiván had been. He looked embarrassed, but Perrely's eyes were bright. Well, well, *well*.

"But where are the other two soldiers who left the Manor with you?" Danîsha asked. "Tornoret and Fiminor?"

"They got separated from us in Berûvis," Shiván told her. "We'll tell you more about that later."

In all the talking she sensed a subtle shift in authority from Lannie to Shiván. People looked to him as the leader — though when they'd left the Manor it had been Lannie's group. Interesting. Lannie had little to say. She looked strained, and thinner. Something had happened to her that people weren't talking about.

She herself, of course, introduced them all to Gwargif. "A warrior leader of the Lightened Dorbians," she called him. He did a snort-and-bob to them all. They jumped, and she chuckled. She described briefly how he'd suddenly turned up one day. She could see the Dûrians struggling with their deep-seated antipathy to the dark Dorbians who had long plagued their northern borders. And she could see Shiván and Lannie struggling with a more fundamental problem — the one that had confronted her when she first met Gwargif. She would have to speak to them about that.

"But 'Neesh, tell us what's been going on here," said Lannie, casting an anxious eye in Gwargif's direction. He was lying at the mouth of the cave keeping watch, as always. "What happened at the Manor? Was there an attack? Did the others escape, too?"

This was the moment she'd been dreading. She couldn't help it, the tears began flowing. As she saw the shock dawning on their faces she broke down completely. Gwargif came and sat beside her and licked her hand. She put an arm around him and buried her head against his shoulder. She couldn't speak. To her relief, he took over.

"Dark men come. Is know, is find way inside Manor. Mylendel — Da-nee-sha — is near forest. Dark men is attack, is try catch Mylendel. She make song — like today. Dark men fall off horse. She go with Gwargif, she go in forest."

"And — the others?" There was a catch in Shiván's voice that was like a knife to Danîsha's heart.

"Is dead."

"*All* of them?" There was horror in Fira's hushed question.

Gwargif gave a small whine.

"The children?" Lannie whispered.

Another whine.

"Oh, dear Prince," Shîr muttered.

The deathly hush that followed was broken as others were unable to restrain their grief. They crowded down next to Danîsha, held one another and wept together. It was such a relief to grieve with others who shared her pain. She felt a heavy burden lifting.

They hadn't seen the basement, though, God be thanked. Her fingers gently caressed Teynel's comb in her tunic pocket.

She glanced round and saw the girl Perrely quietly making chass. God bless her.

"Gil was there," she said when she could trust herself to speak.

"Gil!" Shiván and Lannie exclaimed together.

She described the strange conversation she'd had with him, pinned down by Gwargif. He was wearing the same uniform as the other riders, so he had to be one of them. Yes, a grey cloak. "Bishop's Guards," Shivvie muttered, loathing on his face. She told them of the tear that had squeezed from Gil's eye, and her conviction that he was somehow being forced to do this against his will. Shock registered on their faces.

"Mindbent!" Six voices spoke in unison.

"Oh! Is that what it's called? I remember we talked about that at the Manor..."

"We've learnt a lot about mindbending, 'Neesh," Shiván said quietly. "Lannie was mindbent, too."

So that was it! She looked at Lannie, who met her gaze steadily. There was a shadow of pain in her eyes.

"What happened to Gil?" Lannie asked.

"As far as I know, he left with the other grey-coats... Bishop's Guards."

"Where did they go?"

Danîsha looked at Gwargif. "Child-killers go to left of sunset," he said.

"South," she interpreted.

"That would be Mesten or Stillárre," Fira said.

Gwargif sucked his breath in sharply—the opposite of snort-and-bob. "Not Mes-ten. Dark men go far. Gwargif smell."

"Stillárre, then. So he's one of Dhelgor's mob." There was loathing in Fira's voice.

"Is he the Mindbender of Stillárre?" Lannie asked.

"Yes. One of the worst."

Perrely began handing round the chass. When Danîsha had received her cup, she turned to Lannie. "Tell me about this—mindbending," she said. "But start from the beginning, so I can get the story straight."

They all helped out. Danîsha wept afresh when they described the executions in Berûvis, though she'd known there was little hope for Frem, Margay, and their group. But her amazement grew as they continued their dramatic story. Each of the isolated exploits they'd mentioned earlier now found its place in the overall whole.

She felt a new admiration for every one of them. What a grim trial Lannie had been through, mindbent by Shambor himself! How bravely she'd fought her battle, alone in the prison of her mind. What a bold plan Shiván had come up with to rescue Lannie—and it had succeeded! How skilfully Fira had kept them out of the hands of their pursuers. And Perrely—after that amazing vision!—adrift in the world, but without tears or self-pity.

When they described what Frengor had said, and how they'd formally accepted their rôles as Restorers of the Way, she and Gwargif looked at each other and a bolt of excitement passed between them. The Dorbian barked for joy.

"That's just what Gwargif keeps telling me!" she exclaimed. "He calls us 'Warriors of Light'—that must be the Dorbian for *Atenámbaret*. And Shiván, he called you 'Father of Warriors'—and that's the leader of the Warriors of Light, isn't he, Gwargif?"

"Is *Hrarkhez*—Leader of all Warriors."

"That's the same as what the priest called you, isn't it? — the 'Overguardian', leader of the Restorers of the Way."

Shiván shrugged, looking bemused. "Must be."

Fira was drawn in despite the doubtful glances she'd been giving Gwargif. "And what is this name the Dorbian calls *you*, Danîsha? *My*— something."

"*Mylendel*. It means 'Lady of Song'."

"And Frengor called you the 'Restorer of Song'!" Lannie exclaimed.

"I do not understand," Fira said, frowning. "Can these Dorbians *read*? Do they have the Book? How do they know these things?"

"Dorbi have *Varlezagh* — holy men," Gwargif answered. "*Varlezagh* read and draw words. But not have your Book. Shining One speak to them."

"And tells them exactly the same things about the Restorers…? Is he the same as the One Creator God? Do you believe in his son, Prince Orrénne?"

"Dorbi of Light believe Shining One is only true God. Long ago he send son Hren, come speak to us."

"*Hren* — you mean, Orrénne?"

Snort-and-bob.

"Orrénne came and *spoke* to you?"

Danîsha stared, fascinated. All five Dûrians looked thunderstruck.

"Yes." Gwargif was faintly surprised by their reaction. "You not know? Hren come Dûrion, then over mountain. Is Dorbi is live that time *Khalmiskar* — Bel-lar-nyar. Hren come, show true Light."

"The Prince visited *Bellarniar?*" Cârin exclaimed. "I've never heard of that."

"Yes, he did!" Perrely told him. "Elanesh says so, in his Account of the Prince's life. Only he calls it by the old name, 'Calamar'. And it doesn't say what he did there…" She was paging eagerly through a thick tome she'd pulled from her bag. A Bible scholar! Danîsha warmed even more to the girl.

"Dorbi smell Light," Gwargif was explaining. "Dorbi know if person follow light or dark. Always smell light and dark in people. Then Hren come. Hren is… *all* Light. Great Light. Is…" He struggled for words. "Is like sun shine for first time. Dorbi never smell such Light! Is every Dorbi is fall down, is blind from Light of Shining One." His voice shook. Danîsha had never seen him so moved.

"Hren say— He say, 'Open eyes and see. Be children of Light'. Dorbi open eyes. See him. Smell Light. Never want darkness again. Want to stay always with Hren. But Hren must go—" He paused, overcome. There was an electric silence in the cave. "He must go, die. He must die to bring people to Light. He leave us, say, 'Take my Light, kill darkness, children of Shining One'."

He drew a deep breath; then smiled. "Dorbi of Light do that. Smell Light, kill darkness. Is why Gwargif come, find Warriors of Light."

For a long moment no one moved. Then Fira said in a small voice, "So— who are the Dorbians who steal our crops?"

"Not Dorbi of Light!" Gwargif declared angrily. "Is dark Dorbi, Dorbi refuse Light, run away, do bad things. Dark Dorbi not part of people. Not smell Light."

Fira nodded, a new respect in her eyes. "And the One—the Shining One—he told your holy men about the Restorers?"

He did his snort-and-bob.

"That's amazing," Shiván said, shaking his head.

"It's more amazing than you realise," Danîsha said, looking at her shaggy friend with pride. "Gwargif has come all the way here from the far north—a three-week journey!—just to find us. And when he returns and tells his people that the holy men's prophecy was true, they'll *all* come to support us in the fight against darkness. Five thousand fighters like Gwargif! To root out those monsters, those... child-killers—" She choked up.

"We fight for Shining One," Gwargif said gently. "We smell Light; we kill darkness. You are leaders, Warriors of Light. You say fight here, we fight. You say fight there, we fight. Till darkness gone, is Light only."

Chapter 37: *The story of Prince Orrénne*

THE DAYMEAL WAS OVER. Shiván sat on the rocky ledge outside the cave, giving Gwargif a break from guard duty. They'd all gone foraging in the afternoon, with the Dorbian constantly sniffing the air for any whiff of 'darkness' nearby. They'd found enough late roots and pulses for a decent meal. En route they'd looked out from the shelter of the trees at this morning's battlefield. Many bodies lay still, both of men and horses. Gwargif told them he smelt only death around the Manor—though in the distance some men of darkness were "walking home". None were approaching. They'd given Shambor a bloody nose.

Shiván felt a shock of disbelief every time he heard Gwargif speak. An intelligent, non-human species! Something from the pages of a science fiction novel. Until now Dûrion had seemed so similar to Earth. Gwargif was a sharp reminder that they were on an alien planet.

He heaved a sigh. The day had started so well, with the Blade of Darthane showing its power in that glorious charge. Then somehow… everything had gone pear-shaped. He'd raised the Blade when they were surrounded, but nothing had happened. He'd tried to fight with it, but it was a miracle he hadn't been killed. He'd switched to his martial arts: but when a single kick would have killed that Guard on the ground… he'd frozen again. He just couldn't do it. How could he claim to be Overguardian if he couldn't even fight alongside those he was supposed to be leading? Another heavy sigh escaped him.

"Can I join you?"

He looked up and saw Perrely. His spirits lifted. "Take a chair." He shifted over to make room on the rocky ledge.

She was looking at him intently. He stared back. Perrely wasn't hard to look at. He liked the smile crinkles around her friendly, purple-blue eyes. She flushed, but held his gaze. "Why are you sighing?"

A light-hearted disclaimer sprang to his lips; then he saw her genuine sympathy. He looked away.

"Because of this morning, mainly."

"How can you say that?" she exclaimed. "You were wonderful this morning! You followed where the Light led you. You revealed the power of the Blade of Darthane."

"Yes. But when it really mattered, when we were surrounded, somehow I lost it. I raised the Blade, and nothing happened. If it hadn't been for the Dorbian — and Danîsha with her bellaril — we'd all be dead or captured now."

She shook her head. "That sounds as though you were trusting the Blade, rather than the One. Maybe he didn't intend you to use it in the final battle. Have you thought of that? Maybe he *chose* to use Danîsha and Gwargif. First, you and the Blade; then, Gwargif, Danîsha and the bellaril. *He* is the one who saved us."

Shiván nodded, staring away into the forest. "You're right. Maybe 'Neesh and Gwargif were the One's instruments. But I still failed. In a different way..." His voice tailed off. Should he be telling Perrely this? She was so easy to talk to.

"How did you fail?"

He saw the concern in her purple eyes and knew the whole story would come out.

He told Perrely about his skill at unarmed combat, and cut short her appreciative comments. "But I can't use it. That's what I should have done in the battle this morning when I lost the Blade. I simply couldn't."

"Why not?"

He swallowed. He'd hardly told anyone about the episode that had blighted his life. "About eight years ago when I was at school, I got into a fight with one of the older boys..."

He described how Dave Garner had mocked him to the point where he could no longer restrain himself. How he'd let loose with the most damaging kick he knew. How he *had* damaged Garner — seriously; how the school had ostracised him afterwards.

"It was the worst thing that ever happened to me. I swore I would never do that to anyone again. Afterwards I became so... sad and cut off from everyone, that I even thought of killing myself."

Perrely's eyes were deep wells of sympathy.

He drew in a long breath. "Yes. But in one way it was a good thing: it brought me to God. My parents had told me about him, but I thought I could manage on my own. Now I knew I couldn't. So I told God my life was worth nothing, but if he wanted it, he could have it."

Perrely was nodding, her face alight with understanding. She'd been there, too.

"But he told me I was wrong. He said my life was worth the highest price in the universe: the life of his own Son. And he said —" He struggled to control his voice. "He said the price had already been paid. The Son of God had given his life — for me. I only had to accept it."

A silence fell between them; but there was no strain in it. When Shiván could trust himself to speak he continued, "So God took me over. He was the one who lifted me out of my depression and got me relating to people again. But since that time I've never been able to use my martial arts in a real fight."

"Do you need to?"

He gave her a crooked smile. "Well, I'm no good with the sword. Twice now someone else had to rescue me: Fira, down near the Larwood; and Shîrin this morning. Do you think that's right, for the Overguardian?"

She smiled back. "No, I suppose not. But don't be discouraged. It's only happened twice. The third time, God will enable you to fight the way you need to."

"Thank you. I'd better believe that." He stared at her apprecia-tively for so long that she put out her tongue at him. He did the same, with interest, and they both laughed. A restful silence fell again. He'd never met a girl who was so easy to be with.

"How did you meet the Prince?" he asked.

She shrugged and looked down, suddenly embarrassed. "Oh, it isn't a dramatic story like yours. I went to a Lightist school, so I knew all about the Prince; but one Anderil in my last year I was — um — outside the school, and —"

"Aha! Without permission?"

"Yes, without permission. Stop grinning. Did *you* never do any-thing without permission?"

"Oh, all the time."

She gave him a look. "Anyway, I saw a big crowd of ordinary people standing in a muddy field, listening to a travelling priest who was preaching from the back of a cart. He was getting all car-ried away and throwing his hands about. I thought it would be fun to join them. So I did. And I've never been the same since. It was Frengor, and he was telling the story of Prince Orrénne."

"Frengor himself! That must have been something."

"It was. I'd never heard it told like that before. He made it so real, so personal. The rightful King, surrendering his throne and his life, so that ordinary people could have their darkness burnt away. Then Frengor pointed his finger right at me and said, 'That means *you!*'" She smiled. "And I discovered it did."

Shiván smiled back. They sat quietly for a few moments staring out over the forest. Then Shiván said, "You know, I've never really heard the full story of Prince Orrénne. I know that he was burnt to death and came back to life again, and I've heard a lot of stories about him. But who *was* he? How did his death and resurrection come about?"

"You've never heard the story? Oh, Shiván. I would *love* to tell you."

"Go on, then."

She composed herself, hands folded in the lap of her green robe, a faraway look on her face. "I won't try to explain everything about the Prince's background—it would take too long. You'll have to take my word for it that he was a genuine prince, in direct line to the throne of Selmion—that's the country to the east of us."

"Got that. A real prince."

"But at that time the royal family were in exile, living in a little fishing village called Andelar. So in everyday life he was the son of a fisherman."

Shiván grinned. "Interesting."

"Selmion was a country completely dominated by the Lightless cults—except for the community in Andelar. They believed in the One Creator God. Orrénne was sent out by the One from Andelar into the rest of the country and the surrounding nations. He was sent to show people the darkness of cultism, and to open a Way back to the Light.

"He began travelling around Selmion with a group of followers, preaching and healing the sick. Some of the cults offered healing spells—for a price—but they seldom really worked. Orrénne truly cared about sick people. He healed them completely, for free. Blind people could see again, the deaf could hear, the lame could walk."

"Wow," Shiván murmured. This was sounding so familiar.

"The people of Selmion flocked to him. They loved Orrénne. He opposed all those who oppressed them—especially the powerful cults. In one of the towns he drove all the priests of Minórre out with a whip, before teaching the people about the Way, and healing the sick. In another place the votaries of Sharn tried to place a death curse on him, but it rebounded on themselves and *they* died! All the time more and more people were coming to him, being healed in body and mind, and following him.

"The rulers of the country began to take notice. They tried to stop him—but indirectly, so as not to inflame the people. Eventually they found his family in Andelar, and… slaughtered them." Tears glinted in her eyes. They were silent for a moment.

"Orrénne was now the only surviving heir to the throne, and he decided to leave the country. For five years he and his followers preached the Way of the One and healed people in all the surrounding lands—Dûrion, Thrinar, Marûvin, Pandiar—and Bellarniar, as we now know. Then he returned to Selmion, and found that in his absence he'd become a national hero. Thousands welcomed him as their king! He headed straight for the capital city, Orselm, with more joining him every day. Everyone thought he would overthrow the evil rulers and take the throne—and he could easily have done it.

"But he didn't. Orrénne refused to lead the crowd in an attack on the city. He said that was not why he had come. He had come to offer himself as a sacrifice for the people so that they too could enter his Father's Light. They didn't understand. They pleaded with him. When he continued to refuse, they became disillusioned and abandoned him.

"The authorities immediately arrested him and put him on trial for treason. For treason, when he was the rightful king! But when they accused him, he didn't say a word in his own defence."

Wow. *As a sheep before her shearers is dumb, so he opened not his mouth.*

"They found him guilty, of course. And they sentenced him to a traitor's death…"

She named the penalty, but Shiván had to quiz her to find out what the Dûrian word meant. He became increasingly horrified as she explained. There was a word for it in English: *dismemberment*.

Each limb was cut off while the victim was still alive: starting at the extremities, fingers and toes, and working inwards. His stomach churned. Perrely's face was a mask of pain at having to spell it out. When he'd finally understood she dropped her eyes and murmured, "That's what he went through to rescue *us* from darkness."

"And the burning?" Shiván heard himself asking in a hoarse voice. "Where did that come in?"

To his surprise she smiled. "That was their big mistake. His parts were thrown into the fire on the altar, as a sacrifice to the One Creator God, who he claimed was his Father. *They* made his death a sacrificial offering! They had no idea what they were doing. And in the midst of it all, he prayed for his executioners."

Father, forgive them; for they know not what they do.

"Finally, in great agony, the Prince died. His head and torso were also thrown into the fire. His followers drifted away, thinking it was all over."

"But it wasn't, was it?"

"No! It was only the beginning. The fire on the altar was left to burn out—only it didn't. Witnesses found it still smouldering three days later. Then it grew brighter and brighter, and in the midst of it they could see Orrénne's body re-forming! It was shining as though made of pure light. His arms were lifted to heaven. He shouted, 'Father, let Your Light break through!' There was a loud roaring noise, and the altar and the roof of the temple started collapsing. The witnesses fled for their lives. Later it was found that every altar in every cult temple had been reduced to rubble."

She was silent for a moment, looking out into the forest as the shadows deepened. Then she turned back to Shiván. "After the Prince returned to life, he was often seen by his followers. He told them to spread the truth he had taught them, until his Father's Light reached every land—and then he would return. He filled them with that Light themselves, so they became channels of his truth and healing. Then one day he stood with his arms raised in blessing, and as they watched, his body became brighter and brighter, till they couldn't bear to look. When they opened their eyes again, he was gone. He has never been seen since, but his presence is with everyone who has entered the Light."

Shiván found that there were tears in his eyes. "It's as if I've heard the story of our own Lord Jesus for the first time."

Her eyes were also full. They were silent for a while. Then Perrely said, "You told me yesterday that the Son came to your country as a different person. Was that his name? Jîzis?"

"Yes."

"It still seems… strange to me. How was he killed?"

He told her the story simply, as she had told him. She was distressed at his description of the crucifixion. "Hanging by nails on a wooden post…! What a terrible way to die."

"It's amazing how your mind can accept things. Dismemberment sounds far worse to me, because it's the first time I've heard it."

He finished the story.

For a while they stared out into the forest. It was fully dark now. The folk inside were laughing at some joke of Shîr's.

Eventually Perrely said softly, "The stories are the same. They really are the same. Only the details are different. But why would the Creator send his Son as a different person to *you*, and not to the Khrell, or the Dorbians, or the Gnarthrog? They are also strangers, though their countries are not as far away as yours."

As Shiván considered how to respond, Perrely sat quietly waiting, hands in her lap. The firelight from the cave entrance turned her hair into a golden halo.

"Um… I don't know if this makes sense, but Danîsha, Alanya and I have worked out that we must be from a completely different place. I don't mean a different country—I mean a *completely* different place. *Much* further away than those people you mentioned. Further than… anything you or I can imagine."

He paused. Not very clear. He was starting again, when she took his breath away.

"Of course."

"A place— *What?* What do you mean, 'of course'?"

He caught a glimmer of that cheeky smile on her face. "I mean 'of course'. You are from a different sky. Like the Founders. We know that."

"I— You— …" So many questions collided in his mind that he latched on to the simplest. "Who are the Founders?"

"People sent by God three hundred and sixty-three years ago, who set up our nation to follow his Way. They, too, arrived here suddenly and didn't know how they'd made the journey. You have their leader's sword—Garion don Lûcas. They were from a different sky."

To his whirling brain it was clear at least that 'sky' had to mean 'world'.

"But how —? So you know about different skies?"

"We know that when the One sends his messengers here, they come from a different sky. The Founders did. It makes sense that the Restorers would, too. You arrived in the same way, wearing strange clothes."

"The Founders had strange clothes?" He clutched his head with his hands. "Wait! Tell me — did they live at Carreck Manor?"

It was her turn to be taken aback. "I don't know... Yes, I do! I remember reading it. One of them spent the last years of his life there."

He looked at her intently. "Was his name James Turner?"

"No — he was Jemmet dos Simion."

"Jemmet... James. It was him. I'll bet his father was Simeon Turner."

"Shiván, what are you talking about?"

He told her about the English objects they'd found in the storeroom under Carreck Manor: the two coins; the lorgnette; the snuffbox; the timepiece inscribed on the back with the name 'James Turner'. And of course his precious King James Bible. It was amazing to realise that both the Bible and the sword he carried had belonged to Founders of the Dûrian nation — who had also been sent here by God over three hundred years ago... from Earth.

"So the Founders were Inglish," Perrely murmured wonderingly. "They were from your sky. Would they also have believed in Lord Jîzis?"

"Must have done. People on my... under my sky have been believing in him for almost two thousand years. I think the Son of the One came as a different person to each different sky."

Perrely nodded. "Maybe that explains it." She grinned at him. "Then it's all right. You believe the same as the Founders. I can approve of you."

"Hah!" He reached out to cuff her, but she ducked. They went back into the cave laughing.

_____

Chapter 38: *Interrogation*

"YOU HEARD ME, DHELGOR. A search of both northern routes — at once!"

Mindbender Dhelgor struggled through the mists of sleep to bring his master's words into focus. It must be the early hours of the morning. Shambor's voice kept fading, as though he were a novice just learning the art of distance-speaking. Strange.

Dhelgor rolled on to his back and tried to clear his head. It had been a late night of pleasure.

"Yes, Mindruler." Crisp and alert. The efficient subordinate.

"A nest of rebels has been found at Carreck Manor. All dead. Do you know anything about that?"

Dhelgor's eyes shot open. Suddenly he was wide awake and sweating. Denial was impossible: Shambor was in his mind, and no amount of mental autonomy as a trusted subordinate would prevent his master detecting a direct lie. *"Er, yes, Mindruler. I found them and … dealt with them."*

"Why was I not informed?"

"Forgive me, Mindruler. I was intending to, but …" His mind leapt desperately over the options. He couldn't tell Shambor about Gelmion. That information coming on top of the other would be disastrous. A half-truth, then. *"Word had reached me that there were rebels up there, so I went and disposed of them. But a few escaped, including some foreigners. I have been trying to find them in the hope of making a favourable report to you."*

It went better than he'd hoped. The sharpness in the Bishop's tone eased. *"Very well. But don't act alone in future. Keep me informed, and involve the Mindbender responsible. Hollet of Berûvis was not happy that he'd been bypassed."*

Dhelgor suppressed a grin. *I'll bet he wasn't.* "Yes, Mindruler."

"Keep looking for the foreigners. They are your top priority now. One is called Shiván" —he sent a rather fuzzy mental picture, doubtless second-hand— *"and another is Alanya."* A much clearer image. Shambor had met this one. *"With them are three rebel soldiers"* —more names and blurry images— *"and a young noblewoman, Lady Perrely en Nelláy a GarMadin. If they fall into your hands, they are to be sent to me at once. Do you understand?"*

"*Yes, your Dominance.*"

"*They must be found at all costs. At all costs, do you hear me, Dhelgor? The foreigners'* shiláy *is unmistakable. A third foreigner, Danîsha, may be with them.*" Another fuzzy picture. "*There could also be a fourth — Gelmion …*"

Dhelgor's blood froze. Shambor knew about Gelmion? "*Yes, Mindruler,*" he responded crisply, before Shambor could read his reaction. Thank the dark god he was an autonomous subordinate. A slave would have been found out instantly.

"*Another thing. I want you to interrogate a Selmian merchant and his family who live in Stillárre. Name of Taboru Lanida — known in Dûrion as Taboru dol Lanion. He belongs to the Cult of Minórre, but his daughter Jomel is a member of your temple. They left Selmion under a cloud ten years ago.*

"*Find out all they know about his wife's sister and her husband Ganneret. He is the Land Elder of Sesten. He is also a rebel sympathiser. We've ignored this until now because of the importance of his armoury. But recently we discovered that he's been offering open support to these foreigners. His daughter Perrely is the young girl who has joined them. Their Stillárre relatives are cultists, but I want independent confirmation from you whether they might still have rebel leanings. Find out all you can from Taboru's daughter Jomel about her cousin Perrely. We've learnt from Ganneret's sons that the two girls were close friends at school.*"

"*Yes, Mindruler. May I ask … are these foreigners planning another rebellion?*"

There was a pause. "*I will say this, Dhelgor. These foreigners pose the most serious threat to the Dûrian state since I became Bishop.*"

Dhelgor swallowed something jagged. "*I will spare no effort to find them, your Dominance.*"

"*You'd better not. Lives depend on this — including yours.*" The overbearing presence faded from his mind.

Dhelgor drew a deep breath and expelled it. That had been close. He climbed carefully out of bed to avoid waking Chery, the little rosebud he'd plucked from the temple. He threw on his turquoise indoor robe and padded softly into the reclining room. A subtle testing of the mindwaves showed that Shambor was otherwise occupied. He began pacing up and down, thinking.

He'd managed to wriggle off the immediate hook, but he was still in a tight spot. At most only three foreigners would be found —

because he had the fourth. If *that* came out, it would be the end of him. Not only had he failed to consult Shambor before mindbending Gelmion in the first place, but he hadn't reported the matter even now, when Shambor had specifically named him. He tasted bile in his throat. What the Mindruler would do to him didn't bear thinking about.

His desperate thoughts threw up only one possible solution. He *had* to find the other three—before the Bishop himself, and above all, before Hollet of Berûvis. That long, thin snake would be darting through the undergrowth looking for a coup to put him one up. But if he could snare the foreigners first and present all four to Shambor, the Mindruler might eventually forgive the fact that Gelmion had already been mindbent—though Dhelgor could count on suffering for it in the short term.

But... what if he could present Shambor with a new and improved version of Gelmion? Now there was a thought. When the smoke cleared, he might even have enhanced his standing.

He added a few logs to the smouldering embers of the fire and stretched out on a recliner facing it. He needed to think this through. At the moment Gelmion was trying a typical ploy of the soft-hearted. He was playing tough in order to win promotion. After which he fondly imagined he'd be in a position to curb excesses. Dhelgor knew how to deal with that tactic. Give him enough chances to play tough and he'd start losing the ability to distinguish between 'playing' and reality. Either that or he'd crack completely; but he didn't think Gelmion was the cracking kind. He'd start to find he liked it.

So... how about giving that process a boost, while at the same time solving the other little problem Shambor had dropped in his lap? The problem of Jomel.

He hadn't been entirely open with his master there, either. If the Mindruler had known Jomel was the victim for the equinox sacrifice—and therefore unlikely to co-operate in her interrogation—he might have insisted Dhelgor mindbend her. And there was no way Dhelgor wanted to do that. He wasn't alone among Mindbenders in his extreme distaste for being mentally tied to a condemned prisoner. Their constant inner wailings and moanings had a way of pulling you down that was dismal, to say the least. Then you had to go through their death throes. His mouth puckered in distaste.

Besides, mindbending Jomel was out of the question right now. That was another thing he couldn't have explained to Shambor. With Gelmion he'd reached his limit. He knew Shambor himself was an exception—he had twelve immediate subordinates, including Dhelgor—but most Mindbenders couldn't manage more than about eight. Gelmion was Dhelgor's eighth.

He went to the tall, glass-fronted cupboard in the corner and took out a pear-shaped bottle that glinted with amber fluid. He poured a few fingers of shandil into a crystal goblet and returned to the recliner. The fire was beginning to crackle as the logs caught. He lay on one elbow sipping as he soaked up the warmth.

But... how about if Gelmion were to interrogate Jomel? He already had a grudge against her for landing him in his present predicament. That in itself was a strong inducement to brutality. Besides, she was an attractive woman. He could give Gelmion leave to do whatever he liked with her. And she, in self-defence, would try to seduce him again—which, from what he'd observed of Gelmion, would only annoy him and make him rougher with her. That might force out the information Shambor wanted—as well as pushing along Gelmion's brutalisation. Yes! He liked it.

He would keep Gelmion here for the meantime, then, to interrogate Jomel and be the bait in a trap for his foreign friends. When one of the northern search parties found the foreigners, Gelmion would be sent to join them before all four went to the Mindruler.

Dhelgor sat up, full of grim determination. He took pleasure in jerking two of his lieutenants from their slumbers to organise the detachments to go north. He himself would keep a sizeable force on constant patrol locally. He *had* to be the first to find those foreigners.

* * *

The next morning Gil found himself struggling with conflicting emotions. His body—Gelmion—was striding with two fellow Guardsmen across the market square towards the imposing façade of the Temple of Gadesh. Dhelgor had ordered Gelmion to interrogate Jomel. His exact words had been, *Do whatever you like with her, just don't break any flesh or bones.* They needed an undamaged victim for the ritual sacrifice in two days' time.

It was his first assignment with some responsibility: maybe a step towards promotion if he performed well. A perfect opportunity to 'play along' with the brutality. Too perfect, maybe. Gil felt dangerous undercurrents within himself. He still had a serious grudge against that slut Jomel for seducing and betraying him into this present mess. Could his inner mind remain objective while Gelmion beat her up—or would he be cheering Gelmion on?

On the other hand he felt a guilty gratitude toward Jomel for taking his place as a human sacrifice—even though she hadn't done so of her own free will. What's more, she was physically attractive. Against his better self—and his love for Lannie—he found himself sexually aroused at the prospect of "doing whatever he liked". He tried to suppress those thoughts; but he hadn't had much practice in that area. He arrived at the temple confused and on edge.

A couple of acolytes met them in the temple portico. One took his companions to where a group of adherents were giggling together. *They'd* have a good time. The other led him through the imposing, high-roofed sanctuary to one of the cubicles along the side. If his memory served him right, it was the same one Jomel had taken him to before. The acolyte pulled out a bunch of keys and opened the door.

Gelmion walked in, closing the door behind him. Jomel was sitting with her feet up on the bed. She was thinner than he remembered—but still beautiful, with the dark hair framing her oval face and blue-green almond eyes. Fear flashed briefly in those eyes when she saw his grey cloak. He came and stood over her.

"Remember me, Jomel?"

Shock registered on her face.

"Gelmion," she murmured.

"That's right. Gelmion. The man you seduced and betrayed." Gil tried to suppress a surge of anger. "How does it feel, Jomel, sitting locked in a room waiting to be cut up like a joint of meat? That's where *I'd* be now, if you'd had your way." At least since being mindbent he could express himself properly in Dûrian.

She looked up at him with tears in her eyes. "I'm sorry."

"*Sorry!*" He couldn't believe the woman. "Oh, of *course* you are! So dreadfully sorry, when it's *you* waiting on death row. You've ruined my life, you know that? And what for? *Nothing!* You were condemned to death before, you're condemned to death now. In the meantime all you've managed to do is get *me* condemned to a lifetime of slavery."

Jomel stared at him with wide, sorrowful eyes. He found he was breathing heavily. Who had just said that? Gil or Gelmion? Would Gelmion slander the Bishop's Guard? But he had no time to think about it now.

He sat on the chair and stared grimly at the slut. That's all she was: a sly, manipulating slut who was getting a lethal dose of her own medicine.

"Answer my questions!" he barked. She jumped. Good. He softened his voice in the interrogation technique he'd learnt only too well. "If you answer fully and truthfully, your death sentence will be lifted. This is your last chance. Do you understand?"

She looked at him for a long moment. No relief dawned in her eyes. "I understand," she said. Was that irony in her voice?

He launched into the questions Dhelgor had for her. "Your father is Taboru Lanida, your mother Berenel es Silmia. Do they respect the Bishop of Dûrion?"

She considered the question. "Yes."

"Yet they are cultists."

"They respect him as head of state."

"But *not* as head of the Dûrian Hearth?"

"Yes, in that capacity too."

"How can they, when they believe differently?"

"They have no trouble respecting others with different beliefs. My mother's family are Lightists. We respect their beliefs, they respect ours."

" 'We'? But you are a devotee of the Cult of Gadesh. How can you respect the Lightists?"

"I can respect them without sharing their beliefs."

Her eyes taunted him. She was neatly side-stepping every answer that might suggest rebel sympathies. There was a sharp crack as his hand shot out and connected with her cheek. She cried out, and he felt a stab of pleasure.

"Tell me about your uncle, Lord Ganneret. Does *he* respect the Bishop of Dûrion?"

She stared at him defiantly, her cheek reddening. In her reaction to the sudden blow she'd jerked back, and her shift had slipped off one shoulder. She hitched it back on again. Gelmion remembered that bare shoulder. She'd left it uncovered at their first encounter. Now, when he had power over her, she was covering it. For some reason that annoyed him.

"Answer my question! Are Lord Ganneret and his family rebel sympathisers?"

"You know the answer already," she said contemptuously.

His anger flared. He grabbed her arm and began twisting it. She groaned, struggling to break free, her body twisting in sympathy.

"Tell — me — the answer — to my question," he ground out.

"They probably are!" she gasped. He let go. "What's the point?" she panted, her eyes smouldering as she nursed her arm. "I'm only telling you what you already know."

"Then tell me something I don't know. Tell me about your cousin Perrely. You were at school with her. What were her likes and dislikes? What places did she frequent? What outside friends did she have?"

"We were at school. We didn't go anywhere or see anyone outside school."

"You're not being very helpful! If you want your death sentence lifted, I suggest you tell me *everything you remember about Perrely!*"

Jomel leaned forward, her eyes hard. "Dhelgor! I'm talking to *you*, not this puppet. I know you'll never cancel my death sentence. I have nothing to lose, and I'll tell you nothing about Perrely."

Something snapped in Gelmion. He grabbed her roughly and began manhandling her. She screamed, her clothing ripped, and a powerful desire erupted within him.

* * *

Later, as he and his comrades left the temple, the other two were roaring with laughter about their exploits among the adherents. Gelmion was silent — and Gil within him. He hated himself for what he'd done to Jomel. He hadn't been a puppet at all. He'd been actively involved — in fact, most of the time it had felt as though *he* was deciding what to do, not Dhelgor. Yet hadn't this been necessary in order to 'play along'? Did it matter what he'd done to Jomel, who was a condemned victim anyway, if it helped him achieve his goal of greater freedom of action?

He chose to ignore a small voice within, which whispered that he was achieving freedom only to do the very things he hated.

* * *

Jomel slowly picked herself up from the floor where Gelmion had left her. She was aching all over. A careful examination revealed no blood or broken bones. Dhelgor had seen to that, she thought bitterly. She painfully poured water into a basin to clean herself up. Oh, yes. A sacrificial victim must be undamaged — physically. What happened to her emotions didn't matter.

Looking back over the interview, she realised she'd been led astray by remorse. Seeing Gelmion playing the part of Dhelgor's puppet — and not realising what was happening to him — had filled her with regret for what she'd done to the innocent foreigner. He was right. In the end all she'd achieved was to ruin his life as well as her own.

Well, at least she hadn't pulled Perrely down with her. What had her cousin done to attract Dhelgor's attention? She felt a pang of sorrow for dear, innocent Perrely. It sounded as if some wild prank of hers had put them all in serious danger. Being convicted as a rebel sympathiser carried the death penalty. Yet Perrely believed so earnestly in the One Creator God. She, Jomel, also believed in him now. Did that make her a Lightist? There was so much she needed to learn. "Creator God, please rescue Perrely," she murmured. "Please don't let her die."

She eased the remains of her shift off her bruised body and groaned as she bent to pick up a wash cloth.

As for those clumsy attempts to incriminate her own family... well, there was no way *they* would stick. Her people were cultists — it was ludicrous to imagine Father throwing in his lot with a bunch of Lightist rebels! He was also a pillar (financially and otherwise) of the local Temple of Minórre. Dhelgor would never wantonly antagonise another cult. No, that had all been a rather pathetic attempt to frighten her, followed by the phoney offer of freedom. Dhelgor would never set her free. By abusing the favour he'd bestowed on her, she'd so antagonised him that even if she presented him with twenty sacrificial victims, he'd still find an excuse to send her to the altar.

But it was the despicable tactic of using Gelmion's grudge against *her* in order to brutalise *him* that had aroused her sympathy. She knew that this incident would have been one of many designed to change Gelmion from the fallible but basically decent man whom she'd seduced last time, into a typical thug of the Bishop's Guard, ruthlessly trampling all who stood in his way. The male equivalent of what she herself had been, not long ago.

She wiped herself thoroughly, using as little water as possible. Who knew when Chand and Guriet would get round to refilling the jug? She dried herself off with the heavy outdoor robe that never got used these days, and wearily pulled on a fresh shift. Then she slumped back on the bed and stared up at the pink ceiling with its delicate pattern of whorls and curlicues.

So, she'd refused to co-operate. What would Dhelgor do? She knew he wouldn't mindbend a victim on the verge of dismemberment. Would he try mesmerising and mind*reading* her? Surely not. Those two powers were weak at best, useless at worst. If her mind were strongly opposed and on guard against them, they'd fail. She herself had only succeeded in mindreading Dhelgor because he'd allowed her to. On the other hand... he was a Mindbender. She'd underestimated him once. She mustn't do so again. A shiver of fear ran down her spine. "Oh, God, please keep me from revealing anything that would harm Perrely."

A deep depression settled over her. She was due to be sacrificed the day after tomorrow. Could she even last out till then? Every day was worse than the one before. Her impending fate seemed to inflame the patrons to greater heights of violence against the body that was soon to be butchered. She gave them drinks laced with her soothing potion as a matter of course these days. Priest Sarmion and his acolytes had several times had to drag a rampaging patron off her. It was sick. There was a waiting list of worshippers wanting a go at her before the festival. She hadn't needed a daytime mauling by Gelmion on top of that.

Her thoughts went back to that vivid encounter almost a week ago with the One Creator God. She treasured the memory in a secret place deep inside. It was the only thing that kept her going. She had begged the Creator to rescue her. And he'd answered. He'd stood before her in this very cubicle—more real than anything she'd known—and told her gently that her request had been heard.

As she'd done then and many times since, she whispered, "Thank you".

But a week had gone by and nothing had happened. Her heart knew that *this* God did not break promises. He was too great, too awesome. If he said it, it would be done. Yet her mind struggled to understand. "Why, Creator God?" she murmured as she lay on the bed, her hands clasping and unclasping. "Why do I have to keep on going through this? When will you rescue me? Why do you allow it to hurt so much?" Her face crumpled and she began sobbing, her breath coming in deep gasps of pain.

There was no dramatic presence this time, no words echoing in her heart. She just knew she could trust him. The sobbing eased, her face cleared, and peace enfolded her. Like a small child held safely in her father's arms she drifted off to sleep.

Chapter 39: *Escaping the net*

SHIVÁN AND PERRELY HAD JUST REJOINED THE OTHERS in the cave when a low growl began deep in Gwargif's chest, swelling to a continuous rumble. He rose and walked stiff-legged to the entrance, where he stood staring out towards the east. Perrely instinctively backed away from the large creature, whose hackles were up. She'd never met a Dorbian before, and found Gwargif an awe-inspiring mixture of gentleness and sheer physical power.

"Gwargif, what is it?" Danîsha said.

The growl vibrated through the Dorbian's words as he replied. "Is darkness is come! Is come towards Manor."

He had everyone's attention.

"How many?" Fira asked, her narrow face taut in the firelight from the cave entrance.

"Gwargif not know. Is above eight dozen. With horse." The ominous growl continued.

"A hundred cavalry," Shiván muttered.

"The Bishop's Guard. Shiván, we must leave."

Gwargif had gone out on the ledge. The others joined him. His growl intensified as he sniffed the air, staring south. "More darkness come," he said. "Great blackness. Ten dozen."

"That makes over two hundred." Shiván shook his head. "We must get away now, before they start searching for us."

"Where will we go?" Perrely asked.

"Good question. Any ideas? Think fast!"

An urgent discussion broke out. All agreed that they somehow had to get to Stillárre. That was where Gwargif had detected Gelmion's contingent of Guards heading after the massacre at the Manor. And Stillárre was also where the headquarters, or Domicile, of the Travelling Order was. Frengor and his priests had been heading there when they parted two days ago. He could advise them about freeing Gelmion, and perhaps provide temporary sanctuary in the Domicile.

"We need to ask the One about it," Perrely said.

Gwargif's tail thumped. "Lady of Prayer is right." Perrely jumped. *Lady of Prayer!* Was that what she was? The title neatly summarised what the One had shown her in her vision. It also tied in with what Frengor had said. The Dorbian's insight was uncannily accurate.

Shiván nodded, smiling at Perrely. "Of course. Let's also ask the One to show us how to get there."

They all prayed, Gwargif included. Unlike his exuberant manner of talking, his prayers were quietly-spoken and full of reverence. While the Dûrians sat with their palms upward on their knees, he stretched himself out with his head between his forelegs. Occasionally he lapsed into a strange language of snuffles and throaty sounds that could only be Dorbian. Each in their own way asked the One to save them from the net being thrown around them, and bring them safely to the destination he had prepared for them.

Afterwards when they looked at one another there was no doubt in their eyes. Stillárre was where they needed to go.

"How do we get there?" Shiván asked, looking round the group.

"I have an idea," Fira said.

* * *

"Darkness coming!"

Gwargif's urgent warning and the rumble of his growl woke Fira instantly. She'd been afraid of this! She began shaking the others. They'd walked half the night; then against her better judgment Shiván had allowed them this rest.

Soon they were stumbling out of the small cave, still heavy with sleep. "Gwargif, how near are they?"

"Is dark men from Manor is close. Is others from left of sunset is far."

"Shiván, we must hurry!"

Fira led the way through the dark forest. The path was narrow, and there were stumbles and bitten-off exclamations from behind. She needed to find the old road.

Gwargif came loping up from his position as rearguard. "Is behind. Hide!"

They plunged into a clump of undergrowth and hunkered down. Soon the distant sound of trotting horses made itself heard. There was some muttered conversation, and the horses separated. One group branched off to the south. The other came on along the path. Four riders trotted past their hiding place. The figures were indistinct, but the short capes told her they were mounted infantrymen. A little further on another two branched off.

Flame! They were taking up positions throughout the forest. The group would have to work their way past them without being seen. Harsh thoughts jumped to mind about Shiván's decision to take a rest. But he was the One's appointed leader.

When the hoof beats had faded she murmured to Gwargif, "Lead us south between the watchers." The great grey Dorbian growled acknowledgement and rose to his feet. "Follow Gwargif," she told the others. "Don't make a sound!"

She took the rear position as Gwargif led them at a careful pace. He paused frequently and sniffed the air. Sometimes he would abruptly alter direction. She thanked the Prince he was with them.

Eventually Gwargif stopped. "Is past watchers now. End of forest close."

She heaved a sigh — partly relief, partly anxiety that she had no idea where they were. When they left the forest, would they walk straight into the new troops Gwargif had sensed coming from the south — "from left of sunset"? He reassured her they were still far away.

They came out of the trees into the grey pre-dawn light. The landscape before them was a formless jumble of hills falling away from the high forest. There were no soldiers in sight. But to the southwest was a glint of water. The One be thanked! The River Mest.

Fira led them across ridges and dales to the river valley. Gwargif kept sniffing the air, but it seemed the Bishop's forces were either in the forest or just approaching Carreck Manor. Dawn came, with heavy clouds. It looked like rain — which would be both good and bad. Good, because it would help to hide them from their enemies; bad, because it might hinder their journey.

At last they stumbled down a steep hillside to the bend in the river where the old lodge stood with its attached boathouse. There were exclamations of recognition from Danîsha, Shiván and Alanya. They well remembered the occasion, weeks ago, when they'd come here to gather fireclay. Inside the boathouse, to Fira's great relief, were the three rowing boats, raised out of the water and covered in patched oilcloth, just as the fireclay party had left them. They were simple *garrilet* — long and narrow, with pointed prows and sterns. Each had three seats.

"Remember how much work we had fixing those boats?" Alanya said.

Shiván nodded. "Yeah! We couldn't reach the sandbars in the river till we'd made those wrecks seaworthy. I hope they still are."

They pulled off the tarps and found paddles and painters inside. Shîrin and Cârin tested the boats in the water. One had a slow leak, and would need bailing. They were discussing who would travel in which boat, when Gwargif began growling. "Darkness coming!"

There was a scramble for the boats. Shiván, Perrely and Shîrin ended up in one, Fira in another, and Cârin and Alanya in the one with the leak.

"Danîsha, here! Hurry!" Fira called.

Shiván's boat was already surging out into the river, with Shîrin paddling on one side and Shiván on the other. Cârin and Alanya were wavering to and fro in the boathouse as they tried to match each other's strokes.

Danîsha was saying farewell to Gwargif. He'd told them he would see them to the river; then he had to return home and tell his Great Leader that he had found the Warriors of Light.

"*Mylendel*. Shining One will guard you now."

Tears were trickling down Danîsha's cheeks. "Goodbye, Gwargif. Thank you. May the Shining One go with you."

The Dorbian leaned forward and licked her cheek. "Be happy. We meet soon." With a sharp little bark he turned and was off through a hole in the boathouse wall. Danîsha stood staring at the spot where he'd vanished.

"Danîsha! Into the boat! We must leave before they see us!"

Slowly she turned and stumbled towards them. Fira grabbed the bellaril and Danîsha's shoulder pouch and stowed them under the seats. The older woman climbed unsteadily aboard. Almost before she was seated Fira began paddling furiously.

They approached the river bend, gaining on Cârin and Alanya. Câr had taken over the paddles now, and was digging into the water on both sides.

As they rounded the sharp curve in the river, she glanced back. There were no cloaked figures pointing at them from the shore. She heaved a sigh of relief. The River Mest passed through sparsely populated country far from the major highways for most of its journey to Lake Stillárre. This would be the last route their pursuers would expect them to take.

* * *

After more than an hour sitting in cramped positions, they pulled the boats up on a sloping pebbled beach on the west bank of the Mest. The party climbed out. Danîsha was glad to be able to stretch her legs. Cârin and Lannie turned their boat over to tip the water out.

Danîsha stood staring at the grey river as it lapped against the pebbles. Her thoughts were still with Gwargif, as they had been since the sudden parting at the boathouse. No one could have asked for a better friend. Throughout that terrible time after the massacre he had sat with her, listened to her, made food for her, prayed with her. God had given him to her in her time of need. It was through Gwargif that she had at last truly accepted her rôle as a Warrior of Light—a Restorer of the Way. Now he was gone. It would be many weeks before she saw him again.

Her heart mourned for her own loss, but rejoiced at the thought of seeing him return with thousands of fellow-warriors. It was wonderful how the One was weaving them all together into *his* plan for this world.

She looked across the river. On the opposite bank a short way downstream was the town of Mesten. It was the first major popu-lated area they had to pass. A ferry boat and a number of pleasure craft were moored there. Several more were on the water.

Fira was staring intently at the waterfront. "I can't see properly from here," she muttered. "We need to be sure there aren't troops watching the river when we pass." She was silent for a moment, then her face lightened. "Alanya! You used your bess a couple of days ago, and you heard Danîsha talking to Gwargif. Could you use it now to hear what's being said on the jetties over there?"

Danîsha blinked. "You heard us talking? Before you even reached the Manor?"

"Yes, but…" Lannie frowned doubtfully. She glanced at Danîsha. "I thought of *you* while I was holding the bess to my ear—then I heard you speaking."

"She heard you talking about many soldiers," Fira added. "That was what warned us to be careful as we approached."

"That's amazing!" Danîsha exclaimed.

Lannie was still frowning. "I don't think it would work here, though. There's no one I know on those jetties."

"Just try it," Fira urged.

Lannie shrugged. "I suppose I could concentrate on a place instead of a person. I don't know that town, but I can see it."

Lannie moved a little apart from the others. She held the shell to her ear with both hands, staring intently at the Mesten waterfront. After a moment her eyes lit up, and she gave Fira a quick nod. Thank the Prince! Danîsha thought. The 'instruments' the One had given them were proving their value. Lannie continued to listen, her face tight with concentration.

Danîsha lowered herself awkwardly on to the pebbled beach. Fira had squatted down near Lannie. Not far away Shiván was regaling Perrely with some story about his life in England. Shîrin and Cârin were laughing together. Ten minutes passed in welcome relaxation.

Then Lannie uttered an exclamation. "There's someone asking questions. Sounds official."

"What's he saying?" Fira demanded.

" 'If you see the... something... three disobey...' Oh darn, I can't make out the words properly!"

"Keep listening! Tell us whatever you do understand."

Finally Lannie lowered the shell. "There were at least four of them. They were asking people if they'd seen a group of rebels—I think. They told everyone to keep looking. They sounded like— Mindbenders. The same kind of evil voice I heard when I was mindbent."

"Not Mindbenders," Fira said. "Subordinates. Bishop's Guards." She bit the words off grimly. Danîsha felt the old anger and grief rise in her at the thought of those callous killers.

"So the Guards are warning everyone to watch out for us," Shiván muttered.

"But not on the river! Am I right, Alanya?" Lannie nodded. "What happened at the end? Did they leave the waterfront?"

"Yes. I was able to follow them a short way. They went back into the town." She sounded weary. Concentrating on the bess seemed to be tiring work.

Fira turned to Shiván. "We have to take the chance. At least they haven't left anyone watching on the jetties."

He nodded. "Right, let's do it. Look happy, everyone. We're a rich family out enjoying the river!"

Shîr and Câr immediately put on an exaggerated swagger and began talking loudly in lordly tones as they strutted to relaunch the boats. Danîsha had to smile at the shocked expression on Perrely's face. Her ladyship had clearly never seen anyone openly mocking the nobility.

Danîsha offered to take Lannie's place in the leaky boat. It needed constant bailing, and Lannie was ready for a rest.

In a few minutes they reached the waterfront, and began paddling quickly past the craft moored at the jetties. The flat-bottomed ferry was just being poled out toward the western landing, loaded with passengers, several deer, and a grûn calf. Fira's boat and Shiván's slipped through ahead of it, but Cârin had to back-paddle their craft and veer aside for the ferry to pass.

As it did so a voice shouted, "Hey! That's them!"

_____

Map 11:
Voyage to Stillárre

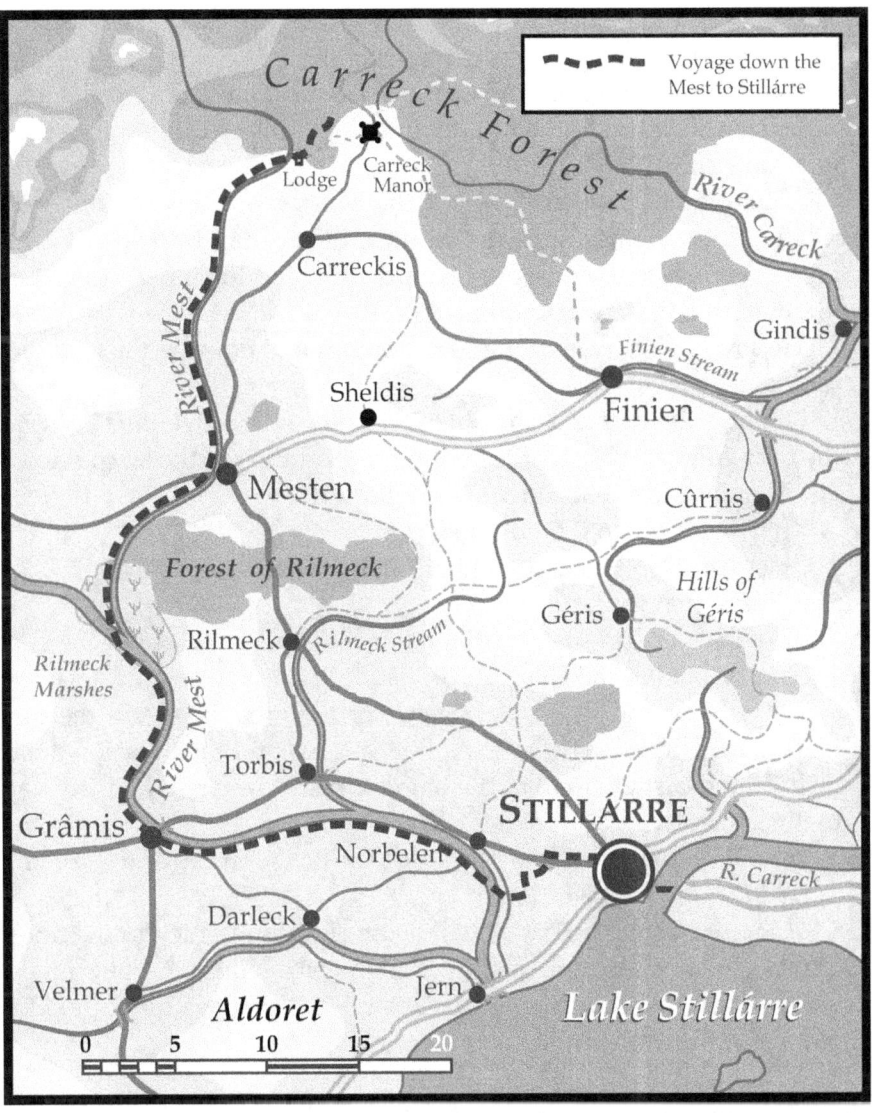

Chapter 40: *Downstream*

THEY ALL PADDLED FRANTICALLY downriver. There were no other shouts or sounds of pursuit. Still Shiván wouldn't let them ease up. Each boat swapped rowers and carried on.

Eventually, after half an hour had passed, Shiván heaved a sigh of relief. He raised a hand to indicate a slow-down. But they wouldn't stop. Not yet.

"That ferry was crossing to the west bank, away from the town," Perrely said. She was sitting in the small bow seat facing him. "Whoever recognised us would have had to go back to report it. They probably didn't bother."

He smiled. She was trying to reassure him. "I'm sure that's it," he said.

"Or else the whole of the Stillárre Guard will be waiting for us at the next village," Shîrin offered. He was paddling in the stern seat.

"Thanks, Shîr, that so relieves my mind."

"I like to look on the bright side."

"Heaven help us when you're looking on the dark side."

"I leave that to Cârin."

They paddled in silence for a while. Shiván stared out at the barren, rocky land to the west. Shîrin had told him it was grûn-farming country. They had seen a few herds of the great beasts in the distance. There were some isolated homesteads and the occasional village. To the east the many little hamlets near Mesten had given way to thick forest.

"We'll be coming to the Rilmeck Marshes soon," Shîr told them.

"Still trying to cheer us up?"

"Oh, they're not so bad. We'll be all right if we stick to the main channel. The marshes stretch for about six aldoret." Four miles, Shiván thought. "Even after that it's reeds and bogs on both sides of the river most of the way to Grâmis."

"Charming."

"I'm giving you good news! That whole area gets swamped in spring when the Mest comes down in flood. That's why there are no towns or villages along the river. Between the foothills of the Kennissôr Mountains and the marshes on the plains, Mesten is the only inhabited area the river passes through. That's why it's such a safe route for us."

Shiván nodded. "Well, that might just qualify as good news."

As the land became flatter, the banks on either side of the river gave way to broad-leafed reeds. The eastern forest receded, and the world closed in on them. Soon they were gliding between high green walls surrounded by an eerie stillness. The river lost its impetus, and they had to paddle continuously. He glanced back at the other boats. Fira and Lannie seemed to be doing okay, but Danîsha was bailing furiously as Cârin paddled. Oh Lord, keep them afloat! If Shîrin was right, it might be some time before they reached dry land.

"We're sailing into a massive storm," Shîr said.

"Still looking on the bright side?"

"No. At the sky ahead."

Shiván looked up. Perrely twisted round for a glance, and gasped. The clouds were a deep, purple-black. Lightning flickered, and there was a distant rumble of thunder.

"We've got to get out of the marsh before *that* breaks!" He called out to the others, pointing to the sky. Danîsha grabbed a paddle from Câr and they redoubled their efforts. Fira and Lannie did likewise. Shiván turned back and dug deeply into the water. The narrow boats began speeding down the sluggish river.

Shiván was relieved when the western bank reappeared. They landed and emptied out the leaky boat. He and Danîsha swapped places. She rescued her precious bellaril, wrapped it in an extra cloth, and tucked it under her tent-like robe. Shiván climbed in with Cârin. They started off down the river again—and the storm broke. There was a crack of lightning, an enormous blast of thunder, and the rain started pelting down. It was all he could do to keep bailing out the water that flowed in from above as well as below.

When they reached Grâmis an hour later the rain was lashing down in sheets. They enjoyed a moment's respite as they glided under the ancient stone road bridge. Beyond was the dock area, but not a soul was to be seen as they paddled by. If the moored barges belonged to anyone, they were safely indoors. Shiván envied the comfortable citizens sitting in the rosy glow that spilled from many windows.

They battled down the wide, slow-moving stream for what seemed like forever. The rain was so thick and hard, it was like rowing through a waterfall. He and Cârin pulled in to the spit of land between the Mest and another river that joined it. They called out to the others, but they didn't hear. After pouring out the lake in the bottom of the boat, they set off again, Shiván sharing the paddling. They found the other two craft on the southern bank, waiting for them. There they emptied out the water yet again and held a hurried conference.

"There are patrols on the Stillárre road," Fira told him, her voice raised above the roar of the storm. The anxiety on her narrow face was stark in the dim light. "We were close to the other bank, and we saw an infantry patrol stop a group of travellers. They examined their faces by lamplight and asked questions. Then they moved on west."

"There are travellers out in this?" Shiván asked in disbelief as the rain pounded on his hunched shoulders. 'Neesh sat huddled under a bush hugging her bellaril. Lannie had squatted down next to her.

"Oh, yes," Cârin said. "Many will be trying to reach the city before nightfall. The roads are normally crowded at this time of day."

"What do you suggest we do?" he asked Fira. She hesitated, looking uncertainly eastward. He knew the original plan had been to disembark where the Grâmis–Stillárre road ran close to the river, near a village called Norbelen. But that was just where they'd seen the patrols.

"Why don't we go beyond Norbelen, where the river turns south?" Perrely asked. "That's further from the road, and people are unlikely to see us."

"There'll be troops stationed in the village," Fira said.

"They won't notice us in this downpour, if we hug the southern bank. In any case, they'll be watching the road, not the river."

"Yes, that's true..." Fira shot Perrely a surprised glance.

They glided past the dim lights of Norbelen unseen. It was not yet night, but in the seething rain everything was indistinct. Once the village had vanished behind them, they crossed the river to the northern shore. Finding a place to disembark was not easy. Eventually Câr in the leading boat gave a muted cry and led them into a small inlet sheltered from the river by an embankment. Several sizeable river craft were moored to a jetty, and dimly beyond them houses loomed. They tied their little boats to the supports of the jetty, where they would hardly be noticed.

The twins scrambled on to the jetty and helped the others up. Shiván gave his boat a farewell pat before climbing out. It had served them well. He briefly wondered what the well-to-do folk in the nearby houses would make of the three battered rowing boats. Then they all hurried off the jetty, and he gave silent thanks to the One for the teeming rain that hid them as they trotted past the houses into the countryside beyond.

They made their way towards the lights on the Stillárre road along rural paths that were more like young rivers. But constant detours around farmland and hamlets made Shiván despair of ever reaching the highway.

At last, however, the road came into view through the sheets of rain. Next to it was a patch of woodland on a small rise. They made a beeline for it. Shiván joined in the general sigh of relief when the relentless battering of the rain suddenly eased under the trees. Danîsha spread her robe like a tent and anxiously examined the bellaril. He and Perrely moved to the far side of the copse and peered out at the road.

Groups of travellers were hurrying along, hunched over against the storm. In the distance to the east Shiván could dimly make out a massive stone structure: the wall of Stillárre. Blurred lights shone here and there on the battlements. Where the road met the wall there was a faint glow. The gate was open and the gate tunnel lit. But what caused Perrely to clutch his arm was the slow-moving huddle of people stretching back along the road.

* * *

Lannie was tired, cold, and soaking wet. Stumbling along slippery paths through lashing rain had been the last straw after a day of constant rowing and bailing. She'd forced herself to keep up. She was proud of that—though it had taken it out of her. She'd get back to normal soon. She had to.

They were resting under the dripping trees when Shiván and Perrely rejoined them. Something was brewing between those two. It made her miss Gil. But right now they had the look of people bursting with news.

"There are patrols going up and down the road," Shivvie said, "and others checking the country lanes and villages. We also saw the city gate." He paused for effect. "There's a queue back down the road. They're checking everyone entering the city."

"Oh, holy flame," Fira groaned. "That's all we need." She buried her head in her hands. Lannie's heart sank.

"Why, Lieutenant, don't tell me you forgot our invitations?" Cârin asked, frowning. His brother looked at him pityingly.

"You think *we* need invitations? We'll get in on our faces. They'll welcome us with open arms."

Lannie shot the twins a dark look. Sometimes their banter got on her nerves. "So what are we going to do? Does anyone have any *useful* ideas?"

"Useful ideas...?" Shîrin said musingly. "Don't think I've had one of those. What about you, Cârin?"

"Not really, no. Plenty of the other kind, though."

Lannie glared at them while Shiván and Perrely chuckled.

"Well, if it comes to a fight, I can't play the bellaril," Danîsha said. "Not in this downpour. It would be ruined."

Shiván and Perrely had squatted down on the ground with the others. Their clothes were sodden anyway. "Let's see," Shiván said. "We can't enter normally through the gates, because they'll recognise us."

"If we don't get caught by a patrol on the road first," Fira muttered.

"Right. Is there any other way we could get into the city?"

"No."

"No underground tunnels, or windows in the wall, or..."

"Of course not!"

"Just exploring possibilities. So we either enter through a gate, or not at all?"

"Yes. And if this gate is guarded, all the others will be, too."

"What are the chances of fighting our way in?"

"Not good. They seem to have every available soldier out looking for us—ordinary troops as well as Bishop's Guards. We'd soon be overpowered."

"So. We don't have Gwargif, and Danîsha can't play the bellaril. That leaves the Blade. If they thought we were a large force charging the gate, they'd close it. If we waited till we were being questioned, it would be close quarters. The Blade didn't work when we were surrounded at Carreck Manor. And if we escaped into the city — "

"We'd be caught like fish in a trap," Cârin offered.

"Right. Our only hope would be if we could reach Frengor's 'Domicile'. Lannie, do you think you could raise Frengor on the bess?"

"I can try," she sighed.

"We know where the Domicile is, Shiván."

"I realise that, Fira. I'd just like to know if he's there."

The others were silent while Lannie lifted the shell to her ear and wearily concentrated on her mental image of Frengor's cheerful, wrinkled face.

"*...stopping people everywhere in the city.*" It was the priest's voice! He was... over *there*. Not far away, in Stillárre. Sudden joy reinvigorated her. She smiled at the others, and there was a pleased murmur. She turned her attention again to Frengor's words. "*Yes. Tell all the brothers —*" He broke off suddenly. There was a silence, and another voice spoke. "*What is it?*" After a pause Frengor said, "*Nothing. Thought I heard something, that's all. Where was I? We must be ready to take them in if they arrive in a hurry...*" The discussion went into detailed arrangements to have watchers in position, bedding and dry clothing laid on, food prepared...

She lowered the shell and told the others what she'd heard. There were murmurs of relief as they realised that Frengor was not only in the city, but actively preparing to welcome them.

"Right," Shiván said, taking charge. "So Frengor will be waiting for us at the Domicile. The problem is how to get there. We can only enter through a gate. We need to avoid fighting if possible. So what I say is — if you can't beat them, join them!"

The expression sounded strange in Dûrian. Fourteen puzzled eyes met his. He proceeded to explain. Lannie thought it was a crazy idea. What else could you expect from an undergraduate student? Yet, as they thrashed it back and forth, it began to gain credibility. It might work. In any case, it seemed the only hope they had.

They all went over to the edge of wood overlooking the road. From there Lannie could see the gate — between squalls. She summoned up her fading energies to use the bess again. It all depended on this. By a painful effort of concentration, staring at the distant gate, she managed to overhear snatches of conversation. She had to keep lowering the shell to rest. They sat there for a long time, the others silently supporting her. Perrely was praying. Finally she heard what they needed. She gasped out a word, and Shiván said "*Yes!*"

Fira repeated the magic word and jumped up, barking out commands. Soon she had everyone hard at work preparing makeshift ropes from the vines on the trees in the little wood. Lannie was surprised at how tough and pliable they were when stripped of their leaves and fruit. The others had a cold supper off the fruit. Lannie was too tired to feel hungry.

Shîrin and Cârin went to the edge of the wood to watch for an infantry patrol on the road. It wasn't long before Câr trotted back to tell them an eight-man patrol was approaching on its way to the city. The group took up prearranged positions inside the wood. Then Lannie and Perrely began screaming.

They had no trouble catching the patrol's attention. Seven infantrymen and a sergeant came plunging into the wood to investigate. The two women ran deeper under the trees. The patrol crashed after them.

The ambush took place in a small glade. Shîr and Câr jerked a vine rope taut as the soldiers charged across. The result was entirely satisfactory. When those on top of the pile tried to get up, they froze with the cold steel of four swords on their necks.

"Get up slowly one at a time when we tell you," Shiván said. They did so, and Shiván held the Blade of Darthane at their throats while Lannie, Perrely and Danîsha disarmed them. They had the infantrymen remove their military capes, their breastplates, helmets, outer tunics and boots, and gave them their own robes in exchange. Two were wounded trying to break away. The others learned from their comrades' mistakes.

Soon they were sitting in a sorry circle while Fira, Perrely and Danîsha tied them firmly with the vine ropes after binding the two flesh wounds with cloths. There were six men and two women. Shîr, Câr and Shiván stood by with drawn swords. Lannie looked on from the sidelines, breathing heavily from her recent exertions.

The soldiers stared at their captors. Their eyes were drawn to Lannie, 'Neesh and Shiván, and several looked puzzled. Couldn't make out the foreign shiláy, Lannie thought.

"You're *them!*" one of the infantrymen suddenly exclaimed, his face lighting up.

"If you mean the Restorers of the Way, yes, we're them," Shiván said. "We're sorry to put you to this inconvenience. We won't harm you as long as you co-operate."

"But we're on your side!" one of the women exclaimed. She had a broad, squarish face, with laughter lines around her mouth and eyes. "We're also Lightists. Test our shiláyet. We serve under Captain Garset. He's a dedicated believer." There was a chorus of agreement from the others.

"If we'd found you on the road, we'd have taken you to him," a solemn young man added. "If he thought you were genuine, he'd never hand you over to the Bishop's Guard."

"Oh, I'm sure he wouldn't," Fira said. "I've also seen deer that can fly." She tested the knot on the woman's wrists. "You'll have an uncomfortable night, but we can't help that. Your excellent Lightist Captain will no doubt send a party out to look for you in the morning." It was obvious that Fira had no time for Lightists who hadn't joined the Rebellion. As for 'dedicated believers' in Shambor's army... Lannie felt that had to be a tall story. Yet the woman and the po-faced young man seemed completely sincere.

"What is your unit?" Shîrin asked. Fira gave him an approving nod.

"Sixth patrol, third foot cohort, second company, fourth legion," Po-face recited dully.

"Good. That's *us* now. You? A suspicious bunch of strangers."

"You'll never get away with this! Captain Garset is—"

"Shut it." Shîr muffled the man with a strip of cloth Perrely had been tearing. He obviously shared his Lieutenant's contempt for Lightists in the regular forces.

When the soldiers were thoroughly bound and gagged, they dressed themselves in their gear—all except Lannie. Fira put on the sergeant's cape with its light green edging. They made a fine bunch of regular army soldiers.

When Cârin gave the all clear that there were no other patrols on the road, they marched out of the wood with Fira leading and Lannie in the centre, carried on Câr's back. She was a sick woman they'd found collapsed by the side of the road (which Lannie felt was not far from the truth). If this errand of mercy got them through the gate, they would head straight for the Domicile of the Travelling Order.

As they left the copse the rain hit them, and in her restricted field of vision Lannie saw Danîsha hug the bellaril closer. She'd kept her robe and used it to wrap the instrument. Lannie was glad the bess was sitting snugly in her shoulder pouch. If questioned, they'd describe the bellaril as a confiscated item for the Captain's eyes only.

When they reached the road, Fira led them at a brisk pace to the gate, where they marched through the tailback of people waiting to enter. Citizens scrambled to get out of the way. Lannie grinned to herself. Jumping queues was a useful perk of being in the military. She quickly sobered, though. What lay ahead was no laughing matter. What if their bluff failed? 'You'll never get away with this,' Poface had said. As they approached the desk that had been set up just inside the gate tunnel, she found herself wondering anxiously whether he might be right.

The first line of defence was a group of military types at the lamplit desk, led by a stern-faced officer wearing a dark green cape trimmed in gold. In the shadows behind them Lannie could see three more infantrymen—and four grey cloaks. Bishop's Guards! *Lord help us.* Fortunately their attention was on the travellers who had just passed through.

Fira came to a halt before the gold-trimmed officer. Cârin lowered Lannie to the ground, and she stood leaning against him, with Shîrin flanking her on the other side. There were long vertical lines on the officer's face. His light green eyes were weary, but not arrogant or hostile. Fira—demoted to Sergeant now—snapped off a smart hand-to-chest salute.

"Password?"

Fira repeated the word Lannie had picked up with the bess earlier on.

The officer subjected them all to a long, leisurely stare.

"What company are you with?"

"Sir. Second company, fourth legion."

The green eyes suddenly became very sharp and interested. There was a rustle of movement around him, and one of the other officers started to speak. He held up a hand.

"Second company, eh? Why are you returning, Sergeant?"

Lannie's heart was in her mouth now, but Fira took it in her stride. "Sir. Bringing in this woman we found at the roadside."

"What's wrong with her?"

"Sir. She'd collapsed. Unable to walk."

The captain nodded. "Where are you taking her?"

"Sir. She asked to be taken to the Travellers' Domicile. But we'll report first to our company commander." There was a stirring of unrest among the other officers. Green-eyes held up his hand again.

"And who would that be?"

There was a tense silence. Fira had forgotten! Garset! *Captain Garset!*

"Sir. Captain Garset." Lannie let out her pent-up breath slowly.

The green-eyed officer leaned back in his chair. "Then you need go no further. I am Captain Garset."

Chapter 41: *At the Domicile*

"WHAT'S THE HOLD-UP, CAPTAIN? Your men are blocking the tunnel."

Danîsha wrenched her mind away from one disaster to the next. A grey-cloaked Bishop's Guard was staring impatiently at the tableau before Captain Garset's desk. Fira stood bereft of speech, while the captain allowed his gaze to travel slowly over each of them.

He looked up when the Guardsman spoke.

"No problem. They'll be on their way at once." He spoke to the aides with him. "Tarlion, Fen. Escort this patrol to the barracks, will you?"

The two younger men gave their captain a strange look, but moved out from behind the table. Fira saluted again, and turned to follow the officers. She looked dazed—they all must. What would happen now? Danîsha hoped the soldiers they'd tied up were right about the sterling qualities of this Captain Garset.

They started moving along the short tunnel, which was lit by lamps on both sides. It was full of people shuffling into the city. Then, suddenly, it happened.

"Hey!" the Guardsman shouted. "Stop! That patrol. Halt!"

The two officers leading them paused and looked back. All four Guardsmen came striding over. Danîsha's heart was in her mouth.

"There are foreign shiláyet here. Why was this not reported?"

Captain Garset came up. "Is there a problem?"

"Yes, Captain, you've failed in your duty. You were ordered to hand over any foreigners to us. We'll take these people."

With a ring of metal Fira, Shîrin and Cârin drew their swords. Danîsha jumped aside, shielding the bellaril with her body. There were screams as the travellers in the tunnel scrambled out of the way. The Guards shouted to Garset and drew their longswords. Garset called out something Danîsha couldn't understand. His men began manoeuvring towards the Guardsmen. Shiván raised the Blade yelling, "In the Name of the Prince!" The rebel soldiers and Perrely echoed him, surging towards the Guards. Lannie huddled next to Danîsha.

Then suddenly the Guards were down. Garset and three of his officers were standing where they'd fallen, looking grim. Four grey-cloaked figures lay still on the tunnel floor.

Shiván stared at Garset. They all did. The other travellers had
vanished; they stood alone in the lamplit tunnel. To Danîsha's
amazement, a slow smile spread over the captain's face as he
sheathed his sword. He clapped a hand to his chest in salute. His
officers did likewise. He jerked his head toward the city end of the
tunnel. "I'd leave right away, if I were you."

"We will. Thank you." Shiván returned the salute. Then he
turned and led them out into the streets of Stillárre.

* * *

Shîrin and Cârin guided them at a rapid pace through a maze of
small alleyways towards the Domicile of the Travelling Order. It
was a wonder the twins could find their way in the unlit caverns
between the tall buildings. All of them were shaken. Lannie's face
was a ghostly white in the gloom. Shiván's own mind was reeling
from the sudden turn of events—and that incredible moment
when the captain had saluted him.

The rain was still sheeting down, and it was getting dark. He was
glad of his military helmet and cape. Their uniforms made ordinary
citizens avert their eyes and other troops ignore them. Not that there
were many folk about.

They sheltered for a moment under an overhanging roof. Fira
was the first to speak. "That was unbelievable!" Her voice cut
through the hiss of the rain.

Shiván grinned at her. "You didn't think much of Lightists who
refused to join the Rebellion, did you? But you've been proved
wrong twice—first Lord Ganneret, and now Captain Garset."

She shook her head. "I owe that patrol in the wood an apology.
They *were* on our side. But who would have thought a captain in the
regular army would deliberately disobey orders?"

"He liked the Bishop's Guard as little as we do," 'Neesh commented. "He shouted a special command to his men—did anyone
hear what it was?"

"I did," Perrely replied. "He called out, 'Snake time'!"

"Iiah! A signal to kill those Guardsmen," Shiván said.

Fira pulled her cape tighter. "He planned this! He decided to let
us through—even if it meant killing Bishop's Guards. That was not
only dangerous, it was treason! He took an enormous risk."

"Will he be found out?" Perrely asked anxiously.

"If he has any sense, he will have taken his men and disappeared by now."

"You mean—we've just destroyed their army careers?" Lannie asked.

Fira smiled. "Strange things happen. Maybe they'll rejoin their legion when it's posted elsewhere, and everyone will say they've been on leave." She shook her head. "I'd like to meet him again, and give him an extra high handshake."

"Here!" Cârin was gesturing them urgently into a side alley. They all crowded into the narrow space between two buildings. Shîr had his hand up for them to be still. "Guard patrol," he mouthed.

After a while they heard the tramping of boots above the drumming rain. Six Guardsmen passed the entrance to the side alley. They shrank back into the shadows. One of the Guards glanced into the alley, but didn't see anything. They breathed a collective sigh of relief when the boots faded away.

They continued their journey in silence, turning aside whenever they saw military capes, grey or green. Now, though, they'd reached the more upmarket part of town. The alleyways had given way to broad streets.

"We're nearly there," Shîr murmured.

At the same moment Câr, acting as rearguard, hissed an urgent warning. "Horses behind!"

Shiván looked back through the veils of rain, his heart beating rapidly. There was nothing to be seen, but now he could hear the clop of approaching hooves: a patrol coming along a cross street. He glanced around. Nowhere to hide—the avenue they were on was lined with the smart frontages of merchants' townhouses.

"Quick! We turn at the next intersection," Shîr told him. "The Domicile is right there."

They rounded the corner at a half run. Câr stopped and peered cautiously back the way they'd come. He rapidly caught them up again. "Guard patrol. Coming this way."

A priest appeared from an alleyway, peering at them through the rain. It was Brother Lannet. "Lannet, it's us!" Shiván called. "This way!" the priest replied. He ran down the street, leapt up some steps and beat a distinctive tattoo on a large wooden door. At any other time Shiván would have paused to admire the marble pillars, domed roof and stone ambon of the impressive portico. As it was, he followed on Lannet's heels without a second glance.

The door was thrown open almost immediately. The familiar, solemn face of Brother Ongaret greeted them.

"*Mel anéy nalestas!*" he exclaimed. "Welcome! We've been expecting you." He didn't show the least surprise at their military uniforms. "Come in!" He quickly closed the door behind them, and Shiván felt a burden roll off him. They all exchanged tired, relieved looks as they removed their helmets. Their sodden clothes began to steam in the warmth of the elegant entrance hall with its roaring log fire, light trees and recliners clustered in groups across the marble floor. The sound of singing floated through from elsewhere in the building.

They were soon surrounded by purple-robed priests clapping them on the shoulder and welcoming them.

They had made it to the Domicile.

* * *

"Come quickly," Ongaret urged them. "There have been patrols at the door all day." Shiván was only too glad to follow. They all needed somewhere to rest.

Ongaret led them out of the hall through a series of tiled passages that became progressively less grand, until they reached what seemed to be a walk-in clothes cupboard. Tunics, robes, breeches, sandals, hoods, belts, boots and underwear of all kinds were stacked on shelves and hanging from hooks. There was a clean smell of freshly laundered fabric.

"Clothing donated by novices' families," Ongaret muttered. "We give them to the poor. Stay there, please."

He went to the end wall and fumbled under a shelf. There was a squeak and a groan, and a whole section of the black-and-white tiled floor between themselves and him slid downwards to reveal a dark hole. Perrely gasped. Shiván grabbed her arm as she stepped hastily back.

The priest took a lamp and led them down a steep ladder. When they reached the bottom, they found themselves in a sizeable chamber stretching away in all directions, supported by sturdy masonry columns. Ongaret was walking round lighting lamps in sconces on the walls. There were plaques with inscriptions on the floor and walls, and several areas enclosed by wooden partitions, ornately carved.

"This is the crypt," Ongaret told them. He led them to one of the partitioned areas and lit lamps inside. It must originally have been a small chapel. A wooden ambon hung from the roof and a Book stood on a lectern at the far end. Chairs had been moved aside. A table against one of the wooden partitions carried a jug and a loaf of dark bread, with mugs, plates and a knife. But what caught their immediate attention was the four beds, neatly made up, with a lampstand, basin and towel beside each. On the end of each bed was a pile of clean, folded clothes.

"We thought the ladies might sleep here," Ongaret said.

For a moment they were all speechless. Then Lannie flopped on to the nearest bed with a groan of relief and closed her eyes, her expression blissful. Ongaret took the men out and led them to another partitioned area that was similarly appointed. He showed Shiván and Danîsha various other facilities for an extended stay, including pipes that delivered hot and cold water and a cord hanging down beside one of the columns.

"Please, make yourselves at home," he said. "Warm food will be brought to you. The Visionary will be coming soon. When he leaves, he'll close the trapdoor. It can't be opened from the underside. But if you need anything, pull this cord. It rings a bell in the Visionary's office."

"The Visionary?" 'Neesh asked.

"Oh yes." A rare smile appeared on Ongaret's narrow face. "The head of our Order will see you personally."

Shiván and Danîsha thanked him warmly, and the young priest tramped up the ladder. They returned to the others. Shiván was deeply grateful to have everyone safe at last.

He wondered where Frengor was. He also wondered what this 'Visionary' would have to say. Frengor had orchestrated their warm reception, according to what Lannie had heard in the bess. But had the Visionary sanctioned it? Would he be as wholehearted as Frengor in his support? They would soon find out.

They filled the basins beside the beds from the hot and cold taps that stood over a trough on one wall. Drawing the curtains across the chapel entrances, the men and women washed in their separate 'dormitories' and changed into the dry clothes provided. The woodland fragrance of fern-oil soap mingled with the homely smell of beeswax polish from the wooden partitions. They all gathered afterwards around a large charcoal boiler in the centre of the crypt, rubbing their hands and laughing together from sheer relief at being warm, dry, clean and safe.

There was a tramp of feet on the ladder. Frengor arrived, his wrinkled, bearded face wreathed in smiles. He greeted them all warmly with the high handshake. Shiván was relieved. It would be good to chat with Frengor before facing the Visionary.

"Singer of Truth!" Frengor cried when Shiván introduced Danîsha. He seized both her hands in his. "Welcome to Dûrion!"

"Er, yes. Hello."

Shiván smiled to see 'Neesh at a disadvantage. The priest's ebullient manner took a little getting used to.

Then Frengor had them sit around the table in the men's chapel with drink and bread, and tell him all that had happened. He listened intently, exclaiming in delight as he heard how God had enabled them to slip through the Bishop's net. Part way through four priests arrived carrying bowls of a fragrant nut-and-bean stew seasoned with *dimas* and *emil*. The guests all dug in eagerly, dipping the dark bread into their stew.

Between mouthfuls they continued the story. Frengor shook his head in wonder when he heard how they'd entered Stillárre. "The One be thanked for that captain!" he exclaimed. "We saw the patrols and the check-points at the gates, and we thought if it wasn't a foreign army, it must be you! How you would get into the city with all those troops about, we couldn't imagine. But you are the Restorers of the Way! We trusted God to do the impossible—and he has. If you were surprised at finding the beds ready, it was because we've been preparing for your arrival since mid-afternoon."

"We know," said Lannie, with a twinkle in her eye. "We heard you."

For a moment Frengor was nonplussed. Then the penny dropped. "You listened with the bess!"

She nodded. "I heard you telling someone that everyone must be ready to take us in if we arrived in a hurry."

"That's right! I was talking to Brother Ongaret—" Suddenly Frengor went still. "Do you know," he said slowly, "I *felt* something while I was talking to Ongaret. He even asked me what the trouble was…"

"I remember that. You said you'd heard something."

"But it wasn't exactly hearing. It was more... a sudden, very strong impression that you were nearby, and in urgent need of shelter. That's why I told him to be ready to open the doors, and had brothers watching in the streets."

"Well, we can't thank you enough," Shiván said. After a pause he continued, "Tell me, Frengor, you organised all this — the people looking out for us, the beds, the food — and we're tremendously grateful. But what about your leader? The — er — "

"*Bissan* — the Visionary," Perrely supplied.

"Yes. I guess he must approve, but does he also accept that we're the Restorers of the Way?"

Frengor turned a fathomless gaze on him. "Who's been talking about the Visionary?"

"Brother Ongaret. He said the Visionary would be coming to see us soon. I just wanted an idea of what to expect."

The priest sighed. "Ongaret may look serious, but he does like his little joke." He paused. "I am the Visionary."

Seven pairs of eyes widened. Shiván stared at Frengor in amazement. This ordinary, friendly priest was head of the whole organisation?

Perrely broke the silence. Her eyes were huge. "But— how can you be? You travel the roads with the other brothers. You— I've known you all my life!"

Frengor grinned. "That doesn't stop me from being the head of our order! In fact I believe it makes me a better one. In any case, it's not something I regard as important. A leader is needed, to give direction and to make difficult decisions; but that doesn't give him the right to lord it over his brothers. The Prince said if anyone wants to be first, he should be last; if anyone wants to lead, he should serve. That's the rule I follow."

Perrely was still gaping at him. "So it was *you* who spoke to Father and persuaded him to let me join the Restorers! You said the Visionary was in Berûvis... but it was you all the time!"

Frengor smiled and nodded.

Shiván was stunned. If he'd understood aright, the Travelling Order had hundreds of priests in Dûrion, and more in the surrounding nations. It was an international organisation. Yet here was its leader, a humble man who tramped the highways with his brothers, sharing the One's Light with all he met. Wow.

The effect of Frengor's words on the Dûrians was even more dramatic. Perrely slipped to her knees, followed awkwardly by the twins and Fira.

"Forgive me, your Wisdom!" There were tears in her eyes. "I never knew —"

Frengor made an impatient gesture. "Oh come, please!" He took her hand and raised her to her feet, signalling to the others to do likewise. "None of that nonsense here. We're old friends!" His mouth quirked in a grin. "If you were an embassy from Thrinar seeking our help with drought relief, I'd surely let you kneel. But not sons and daughters of the King!" He let his gaze wander over them all. "And certainly not the One's Restorers! It's our privilege to serve *you*. We're delighted to give you refuge here. And in the days to come we'll be spreading the news of your arrival throughout Dûrion and the surrounding nations."

He turned to Shiván. "But now I must leave you to sleep. You've had a heavy day, and I believe Alanya has dropped off already." Sure enough, Lannie was propped up against the partition, snoring softly.

"Sleep in peace," he said. "You'll be surrounded by prayer all night."

But Shiván found it hard to sleep. He snuggled down under the many blankets the brothers had piled on his bed. He had some serious thinking to do. And praying. Tomorrow he had to come up with a plan. A plan to rescue his linguistics lecturer, who by an amazing string of events had become both a fellow-worker for God, and a pawn of the dark power that ruled Dûrion. Reality had a way of being stranger than one could ever imagine.

* * *

Lannie felt much better the next morning. It was amazing what one night in a warm, comfortable bed could do. She could move almost normally, too. The enforced exercise yesterday must have helped.

Ongaret had brought them a hot breakfast—a large kettle of chass and a pot of porridge with honey. Lannie scandalised the Dûrians by adding honey to her chass as well as the porridge. They'd just finished, and were sitting round the table in the women's room to discuss the burning question on everyone's mind: what to do next. They needed Frengor's input, though. Shiván rose to go and pull the cord that would ring a bell in the Visionary's office; but Lannie stopped him with a raised hand. She wanted to check where he was first. She was enjoying her new-found power of 'hearing'.

She lifted the bess to her ear and pictured Frengor's smiling face. There he was! She instinctively glanced upwards. He was above them—not the next floor, but higher; probably in his office. She listened idly for a moment as Frengor discussed everyday matters with one of the priests. It occurred to her that she was eavesdropping. She was about to put the bess down, when she heard the door of Frengor's office burst open. The Visionary broke off in mid-sentence. "A patrol!" the newcomer exclaimed.

Lannie jerked upright. "A patrol!" Everyone in the crypt froze and stared at her. At the same time there was a startled query from Frengor through the bess. "Who said that?"

"Visionary, Brother Hendor—"

Without thinking Lannie fell into telephone mode.

"Hello, Frengor, this is Alanya. Is there a patrol?"

The Dûrians in the crypt were staring at her wide-eyed. Danîsha and Shiván were merely surprised.

In the bess there was the sound of someone sitting suddenly in a chair. "Alanya, I can hear you!" She clicked her tongue. "Has a patrol arrived?" she asked urgently.

"Yes, I— How are you doing this?"

"Never mind that now," she snapped. "We need to know what's happening!"

"They're searching the Domicile. Just wait and pray!"

At that moment Brother Lannet came running down the ladder to give them the same news. He charged back up again, and they heard him adjusting the trapdoor to make it completely flush.

"Alanya, were you talking to Frengor? With that *shell*?" Fira demanded.

"Yes."

"Light protect us!" Shîr murmured. Eight Dûrian eyes were as large as chass mugs. Lannie felt herself grinning.

They sat on the beds in the women's room. If the trapdoor opened, they could see who came down through a small hole in the carved partition. They discussed in hushed voices what to do if they were discovered. Their best hope was the bellaril. But could they be sure the intruders would carry no memory away with them of the crypt? That would be disastrous for Frengor and his priests. For themselves, too.

Lannie lifted the shell again and tried to 'find' the patrol. With neither a person nor an exact location to focus on, she failed. She thought of Gil. *There!* Not in the Domicile, but to the south-west, moving east, about half a mile away. She heard the tramp of several pairs of feet against a dim medley of street noises. Joy flooded her and she opened her mouth to speak to him. Just in time it hit her how disastrous that would be. Just one word and he'd know she was here — and so would his Mindbender. She quickly lowered the bess. Oh, Gil. So near, but so far.

They sat for an hour, waiting and praying. Their hearts were in their mouths when boots clumped across the clothing cupboard floor. But the black and white tiles hid their secret well. After some scuffling the footsteps disappeared. Finally the trapdoor opened and Ongaret announced that the patrol had gone. They let out a ragged cheer.

They made more chass from the kettle on the charcoal boiler. It must be mid-morning by now — teatime back home. Home seemed so far away; a different world, a different life.

As they were refreshing themselves, Frengor came down and joined them. After the normal greetings, he turned to Lannie.

"That was an amazing thing that happened with the bess just now. Did you know it made distance-speech possible?"

She frowned. "No, I didn't. Is that what you'd call it? Distance-speaking — like the Mindbenders?"

"Freng— I mean, Visionary, I don't like this!" Fira exclaimed. "Are we sure this shell is the One's instrument, and not a device of Gadesh?"

"Just call me Frengor," the priest said. "And remember the prophecy: The 'Shell of Hearing' is given to destroy the lies that pervert the One's Way. It is not a device of Gadesh. Why should the Mindbenders alone have the benefit of distance-speaking? In *itself* it's not evil. We can all 'hear' the thoughts of others in a small way. That's what the shiláy is all about — had you realised that? We take it for granted, but in fact we're sensing the thoughts of the other person, though very dimly. The Mindbenders have learned, with the help of teméyn, to magnify that sense many times over. If the holy bess does the same for the One's Restorers, we should welcome it! It'll be a tremendous gift in the battles that lie ahead."

Fira shook her head doubtfully while the twins joked about using the bess to scare the wits out of an enemy commander. Lannie herself was rather pleased: the only person on the planet with a mobile phone. Not bad!

"We need to discuss what to do next." Shiván called the meeting to order.

Strange. Lannie found herself beginning to accept this callow undergrad as leader. That would have been unthinkable a fortnight ago. But he'd rescued her from the Bishop. He'd led their charge at Carreck Manor. He'd got them into Stillárre against all the odds.

"We have to try and rescue Gelmion," he was saying. "That's the main reason we came to Stillárre."

Frengor nodded. "I agree. And your main problem is that he's in the Bishop's Guard. How do you plan to rescue him from Dûrion's elite fighting force?"

Shivvie was silent for a moment, staring into the middle distance. Then he said, "On our way to Carreck Manor, you told us a story."

"Which one was that? I tell so many."

"The one about the Mindbender who was killed. All his slaves 'froze'. One of them was rescued by his family and later recovered."

"Oh. *That* one." Frengor's smile faded.

"Shiván, you can't be serious!" Fira exclaimed.

An icy fist gripped Lannie's heart. The Guards were the Dûrian police force. All chaos would break loose if they 'froze'! Scenes from TV flashed across her mind: rioting and looting; mob violence; Gil being seized by many hands, unable to help himself—

"What other option do we have?" Shiván asked quietly.

Over their protests he outlined his plan. He had an answer to every objection. It was a crazy scheme, on a par with dressing up as soldiers to enter Stillárre. But that had worked. This might, too. They'd better pray it did.

Chapter 42: *Mission unaccomplished*

"*SO YOU STILL HAVEN'T FOUND THEM.*"

Dhelgor's knees went weak at the sound of his master's voice. It needed all his self-control to preserve a calm front. The expensive fittings in his 'throne room' — the grey floor-covering, the black leather chair he sat on, the sturdy money chest — suddenly failed to impart their usual sense of power.

"*No, your Dominance, we have not found them yet. But every Guardsman at my disposal, as well as the entire Stillárre garrison, is out searching the streets. It's only a matter of time —* "

"*TIME!*" The word exploded in his brain. "*You had time yesterday, Dhelgor! And what did you do with it? You let them slip through your fingers down the river. You let them overpower a patrol. You let them walk right in through one of your gates! Now they've hidden themselves in the city like salt in the sand, and you're pleading for* time!"

Dhelgor couldn't keep the tremor from his voice. "*Your Dominance, I assure you —* "

"*No, Dhelgor, I assure you. You'll have time. I'll give you until noon tomorrow to present me with all four foreigners and their hangers-on. Fail me — and I think you know the consequences.*"

A tidal wave of fear engulfed the Mindbender. Yes. He knew the consequences. He would become a slave at his master's pleasure. Several of his former colleagues had suffered that fate. Shambor delighted in displaying them to his subordinates as an object lesson. None of them had ten fingers. All were cruelly disfigured. All were in constant pain — both physical and mental. But never enough to kill them.

A stench arose in his plush office. He'd soiled himself.

There was a cruel humour in his master's voice. *I'm glad you appreciate the gravity of the situation. Now, do you have anything to say for yourself?*

He tried to gather his wits. There was only one thing that could redeem him in his master's eyes — and that was the capture of these foreigners. But he already had one of them ... "*Your Dominance, forgive me,*" he stammered. "*I didn't tell you before, but I have one of these foreigners in my service.*"

"WHAT? Which one?"

"Gelmion, Mindruler."

"You've mindbent him? He's in the Guard?"

"Yes, Mindruler."

"When did this happen?"

"Ah... Ten days ago, your Dominance."

"Ten — days — ago."

Dhelgor wondered desperately if confession had been such a good idea. *"I had hoped,"* he rushed on, *"to be able to present you with all four together. I was keeping Gelmion here to lure the others. He knew they would come searching for him —"*

"No, Dhelgor, that won't wash. You mindbent Gelmion before the present emergency. What were you up to, I wonder? It was around that time you wiped out those rebels at Carreck Manor, wasn't it? I see. The foreigners with them escaped, and you said you were seeking them for me. But you weren't, were you? You had Gelmion, and you wanted the other three for yourself! Do I detect a little empire-building, Dhelgor? Enhancing the prestige of the Stillárre temple — not to mention your own — by sacrificing four deliciously-innocent foreigners?"

Dhelgor was silent. Nothing would help him now.

"Not quite, Dhelgor. The only thing that will help you now, is to present me with the four foreigners and their sidekicks by tomorrow noon. If you do that, we'll consider this incident closed."

Dhelgor felt a sickish sense of relief. He'd go to any lengths to avoid becoming a plaything for Shambor's sadism. He screamed and arched in his seat as a bolt of pain transfixed him. The Bishop was reading his mind, invading his autonomy!

"Yes, Dhelgor," the voice ground out grimly. *"You've lost the right to autonomy. And if you fail you'll learn all about my sadism, believe me. I have no mercy on subordinates who try to exalt themselves.*

"Now." He was suddenly brisk. *"The searches continue redoubled, do you hear? If the military give you any trouble, refer them to me. Send men out to the villages. The surrounding towns will be checking all new arrivals."*

"And as for Gelmion... You'd better make sure you don't lose him, *as well. I'll be watching you, Dhelgor. I'll be watching you very closely. Now go and clean yourself, you filthy slime-bag."*

* * *

Danîsha hid her misgivings as Shiván outlined his plan. She couldn't think of any other way of rescuing Gil; but this was very risky. For once she was feeling her age. This was a young person's plan. Bold, daring—brilliant, if it worked. But too many things could go wrong. And she had to admit she was tired. Yesterday's constant physical exertion, and the tensions of each successive crisis, had taken it out of her. She could have done with a week of rest. But somehow God would keep her going.

She sighed. She felt lonely, too. Her family on another planet; Teynel dead; Carreck Manor a tomb; Gwargif gone. She was the odd one out among these youngsters—all of them still in their twenties.

Frengor came over to her while the others were telling Brother Ongaret what clothes he should find as disguises for their planned expedition. The Visionary lifted Danîsha's hands from her lap and looked into her eyes. "Mâra, there is much that lies ahead. You will play a crucial part in it." He gave an encouraging squeeze. She felt tears start in her eyes, and smiled gratefully as he sat down next to her. *Mâra*—her nickname at the Manor: respected mother, grand-mother, aunt. Maybe these young folk did still need someone like that.

"Now, my friends," Frengor said, "we must look beyond the immediate situation. Time is short, and you need to prepare for the expedition you've planned. But allow me to share with you quickly the thoughts on my mind.

"The first is that for a short time you should put both Gelmion and yourselves beyond the Bishop's reach. There are various out-of-the-way corners of Dûrion where you could hide. You might consider the Tallissôr Mountains; or Khoreyn in the south-west; or the Sestiar Wilderness; or any of the great forests on our borders."

Danîsha's heart lifted. She could do with a period of rest in a safe place. But Lannie didn't like the idea. "That sounds like running away."

"Only for a time." Frengor's eyes sparkled. "You Restorers are planning to stir up a nest of killer wasps here in Stillárre. It's a wise person who runs from killer wasps. You need a temporary refuge where Gelmion can recover. Perhaps there he will also enter the Light and discover the One's path for him as a Restorer of the Way."

That held Lannie. Danîsha smiled to herself. The younger woman sat with unfocused eyes, no doubt picturing long scenic walks with Gil while she nursed him back to health.

Ongaret came clambering down the steps, a bundle of green clothing in his hands. "Fira, Perrely! I've found two sets of servants' livery for you. Would that do?"

"Perfect!" Perrely exclaimed. To her this was still an exciting adventure. Danîsha hoped the awakening, when it came, wouldn't be too painful.

"To find a good hiding place," Frengor continued, "I suggest you go to the town of Dhembis and ask discreetly for a woman called Nist." A smile tugged at the corners of his mouth. "You'll like Nist: an extremely efficient lady who has helped many refugees from Shambor's wrath to disappear for a while."

He became brisk. "Time is running out. That's my first thought. I wanted to tell all of you these things so you can help one another remember."

Ongaret reappeared. He had a ghastly wide-brimmed hat on his head. He held up a tunic with attached tights in two shades of brown. It was quite large. "Danîsha, this will turn you into a minstrel!" Everyone laughed. Danîsha shuddered, but managed to nod her head gamely.

"Secondly," Frengor said, "there's the long-lost Ambon of Sûrilane."

Fira frowned. "Don't tell me you want us to go hunting for the Ambon! Hundreds have tried that and failed."

Frengor continued undeterred. "The Ambon of Sûrilane will be essential if—*when*—you challenge Shambor's full military might. As you know, this ambon was made by the Founders of Dûrion. It summons children of the One to the defence of his cause. You will need it to raise an army quickly."

"Just one little problem," Shîr objected. "It's vanished."

"So we've often been told," Shiván said. "How did that happen?"

"It was placed on the wall of the Sûrilane Hearth three hundred years ago, at the end of the Founders' campaigns," Perrely told him. "Fourteen years later, it disappeared. People hunted everywhere for it. Huge rewards were posted for its recovery. But it was never found."

Quite the scholar, young Perrely, Danîsha thought. It struck her that in Dûrion God seemed to delight in showing his power through physical objects: her bellaril; Lannie's shell; Shiván's sword—and now this special ambon. It seemed uncomfortably like magic at first, but there were biblical parallels: the hem of Jesus' garment—and Samson's hair; the Ark of the Covenant; Moses' staff...

"The Ambon will be another day's challenge," Frengor said. "Today you have your expedition to prepare for; and I have an Order to run. I'll see you again before you leave. The One lighten and strengthen you."

* * *

Midmeal at the Domicile was over; all the preparations had been completed, and now their planned 'first expedition' had begun. Perrely was walking through the city, enjoying the open air and the crowds of leisurely strollers.

It was Anderil—the One's day—and that morning she'd had a severe bout of homesickness. The ache of the sudden parting from her family was always there, but now she'd found herself missing the house, the relaxed Anderil activities, the fellowship with others at the Hearth or Travellers' Chapel. It was Anderil a week ago that she'd watched from the hill as the Bishop's Guards invaded her home. Now here she was, a fugitive in disguise, walking openly down Stillárre's wealthy Bishop's Avenue with Fira! How her life had changed.

The storm had blown itself out during the night. The sky remained overcast, giving way to occasional showers; but these had eased off as the day went by. The same couldn't be said of the patrols. Several times already soldiers had marched purposefully past to some destination, probably in search of *them!* It was crazy. Even more crazy was the presence of Shiván, Danîsha, Alanya and the twins not far behind. Craziest of all, it had been her own idea!

Their goal was to discover the Mindbender's movements. That the foreigners themselves had come was a great risk, but Shiván wanted the bellaril there to protect them, and the bess to keep Frengor informed. Alanya had said nothing would stop her anyway, because this was to do with rescuing Gelmion. Perrely gathered that Alanya and Gelmion were all but betrothed—though Fira had looked rather sour when Alanya put it that way. That left only

Shiván with no specific reason to come; and he'd said, looking at Perrely, that he couldn't stay behind while they all went out and faced danger.

Another patrol of Guards coming towards them! These were on foot, scanning the faces of pedestrians. She and Fira kept their eyes on the paving stones as they scurried along. That wasn't unusual. Most people averted their faces from the hated Bishop's Guard. Besides, they all had their disguises.

It was quite exciting, really. Danîsha had mixed charcoal with oil and painted shadows under their eyes and hollows in their cheeks to make them look older. She and Fira had put on those smart green-and-gold servants' outfits Brother Ongaret had found in the clothing cupboard. Alanya, Shiván and the twins were dressed in priests' purple robes with hoods over their heads. Danîsha had put on the brown two-tone tunic and leggings with the broad-brimmed hat Ongaret had given her. She did look rather like a minstrel — which accounted neatly for the bellaril. The five of them had sand-wiched themselves between two large family groups out for an Anderil stroll.

The patrol passed them by with only a cursory glance, and they came out into the market square. More troops were moving about at random among the crowds. She was shocked to see several stalls doing business — on the One's day! There was even a pen of grûn calves for sale — plus the usual troupes of jugglers, clowns, minstrels and acrobats earning their living when others were at leisure.

Fira glanced behind them. "The others are waiting by the animal pen," she said in an undertone. Perrely nodded. From here on they were alone.

They marched up wide steps into the imposing portico, not of the Hearth, but of the Temple of Gadesh. She felt a shiver of fear run down her spine. It was like walking unarmed into an enemy citadel. No, not unarmed. Words from the *Songs of Travail* came to her mind. *Even if I walk through the valley of death, I will fear no darkness: for you are with me. Your sword and your staff protect me.*

"Yes, what can I do for you?" The abrupt challenge startled her. A pasty-faced young man in a grey, official-looking robe was sur-veying the two of them dubiously. He looked as though he couldn't decide how to respond to their servants' livery — whether to be brusque, to those of lesser rank; or deferential, to the representatives of a potential donor. Perrely put on her best aristocratic manner.

"Our master desires information from one of your members. A young lady called Jomel em Berenel. Can you tell us where to find her, please?" She fixed him with a haughty stare.

It had the desired effect. The young man blinked and swallowed. "Ah, yes, certainly. Ummm... She's here, but ..."

"Here? In the temple?"

"Yes. But, you see, she's... under discipline at the moment. I'm not sure if... Please wait while I speak to the priest."

Not a good idea. She took a bold gamble.

"No, we certainly will *not* wait! Our master's business is urgent. If this Jomel is here, take us to her! We are not to be kept waiting like tradespeople."

For an agonising moment he dithered, looking this way and that; then he caught her indignant glare full in the face. He dropped his eyes. "Very well, come this way," he muttered.

Perrely's heart was hammering as he led them from the portico into the actual sanctuary itself. Her knees felt weak at the black pall of evil that hung over the place. This was where those demonic rituals were performed! She glanced fearfully at the rising tiers of seats, the tree-like columns, the dark ceiling way above — and the high altar that brooded over all. There animals were sacrificed to appease a god of darkness who knew no mercy. It was rumoured that at times that grey slab of marble ran red with *human* blood! How had Dûrion, the Land of Light, ever come to this?

The grey-robed official was leading them towards a row of small doors that lined the left side of the sanctuary. She wondered what Jomel was doing here outside of worship hours. And what had the young man meant about her being 'under discipline'?

It had been Perrely's idea to seek Jomel out. As a member of the Cult of Gadesh, she was their best prospect for information about the Mindbender's movements. She might know when he was due to attend an important ceremony at the temple, or what regular trips he made.

Not that she would tell Jomel the *real* reason they needed that information! Perrely would make out that this whole thing — she and her friend Fira dressing up as servants — was one of her wild pranks. Her family was en route to Stillárre, she would say, and she and Fira had come on ahead. They were wearing Fira's family livery as a lark. Their next lark was to get really close to the Mindbender himself. It was the sort of thing she and Jomel had often done during their school holidays, and accounted for half of Father's grey hairs. (Grim Fira, of course, made an unlikely prankster. But Shiván had insisted on the most experienced member of the group escorting her.)

They reached one of the small doors, and to her surprise the official pulled out a bunch of keys. They kept Jomel locked up? Suddenly she remembered how the One had moved her to pray for Jomel, that day up on the hill above her house. Later events had driven it from her mind. She'd felt a deep anguish for Jomel, convinced that she was facing some terrible disaster.

The door lock clicked. The pasty young man turned to them. "I'm sorry, but I'll have to lock you in. I'll be nearby. Call when you need to leave." He allowed them through and turned the key behind them.

And there was her dear Jomel, sitting up on a large bed that filled half the cubicle. She looked thinner, and so drawn! "Jomel!" she exclaimed, and rushed to hug her.

Her cousin jerked back, alarmed. The disguise! "Jomel, it's me, Perrely!" She joined her on the bed.

Amazement spread over Jomel's face. "Perrely?"

Then Perrely was hugging her, and Jomel was weeping. She clung to her, crying her heart out. Perrely heard Fira settling in the chair. It must be awkward for her, but Jomel wouldn't let go. She wept and wept.

At last Jomel relaxed her grip, and the two sat together on the bed. Perrely introduced Fira as 'a friend', and Jomel merely nodded. Her eyes were all for Perrely. *What a difference!* Perrely thought, as she looked at her. The face was thinner, but it was real. That dead mask had fallen away. The sophisticated young society woman was gone. This was the true Jomel she'd always loved — though older, and worn by suffering.

"Have you come to rescue me?" Jomel whispered.

Perrely stared at her. Fira was frowning.

"What do you need rescuing from?" she whispered back.

Jomel's shoulders sagged and she buried her face in her hands. Then she looked up, her face haggard. "I'm sorry," she said, tears trickling down her cheeks. "For a moment I hoped... But of course, you don't even know."

"Know *what*, Jomie?"

Her cousin looked at her sadly. "That I'm due to be sacrificed tomorrow."

There was a grunt of shock from Fira. As the appalling words crashed into Perrely's consciousness she felt the blood drain from her face. She stared at Jomel, not believing, not comprehending what she'd heard. Jomel? Dragged on to that evil altar? Carved up, chopped apart, as they did with meat? *Jomel's* blood running down the marble steps? Dizziness threatened to engulf her.

She jerked as someone slapped her cheeks. "Don't pass out on us," Fira muttered. "That won't help anyone."

Jomel took her hands, looking earnestly into her face. "Perrely, I've met the One! The Creator God that you Lightists believe in. *He* promised to rescue me. It's just that... I thought he was using you, today. But I know he *will*—"

There was a rattling in the lock, and the door burst open. A large man in a white robe surged in. His florid face was suffused with anger.

"This is an unauthorised interview!" he exclaimed. "You will please leave at once." Behind him the pasty-faced one was cowering.

Fira took charge, to Perrely's relief. "We're just going, priest," she said contemptuously. "If the interview was unauthorised, you should have instructed your subordinate accordingly." She swaggered past the fuming dignitary, letting her elbow dig into his protruding belly. Perrely was desperate to stay, to comfort Jomel, to find some way of freeing her—but Fira's hand was clasped firmly around her wrist. Tearing her eyes away with difficulty from Jomel's tear-stained face, Perrely followed.

She stumbled out of the temple in a daze, barely able to keep from tripping on the marble stairs. Music was playing somewhere, and Fira was pulling her faster. The music stopped, and so did Fira.

They stood for a few moments staring out over the crowds. But neither of them saw the patrol. Fira gasped "Gelmion!" as a heavy hand descended on Perrely's shoulder.

Chapter 43: *Captured!*

GELMION FELT A THRILL OF PRIDE as he surveyed his patrol. They were walking slowly along Bankers' Row towards the market square, scanning the faces of those they passed. Five Guardsmen who were his to command. It was amazing how that ability had come to him as soon as the authority was given. He was exercising telepathic control—unbelievable a couple of months ago, but as natural as breathing now. His slaves did what he told them, went where he said, came when he called. They were like extensions of himself.

He was Ensign Gelmion now. He'd achieved his goal of autonomy sooner than expected—because of his high mental potential, the Mindbender had told him. It wasn't full autonomy, by any means. He was still at his master's beck and call. But gone was the constant presence in his mind, the sense of always being watched. Gone, too, was the inability to make even the simplest decision himself. How precious that became once you'd lost it! He didn't intend to lose it again. No undue squeamishness would prevent him carrying out his master's commands.

His present orders were difficult, he acknowledged. They were searching for three foreigners and their four Dûrian companions. He knew who those foreigners were. He also knew three of the four companions. But that wouldn't stop him ordering their arrest. Since the episode with Jomel he'd done a lot of rethinking. What it came down to, was that he could no longer afford his former scruples. They belonged to a different life. In Dûrion it was the law of the jungle. Kill, or be killed.

One of his Guardsmen was scrutinising a thickset young man who might have been Shiván. He had a look through the trooper's eyes. It wasn't. He cursed the fellow and sent him on to the next group of pedestrians. The trooper had less reason for error than his comrades in other patrols. They had their images via their lieutenants and ensigns, who in turn had them from Gelmion. Much was lost in transmission. *His* slaves had theirs directly.

And if that *had* been Shiván? Well, his heart would have been torn, but he'd have ordered his arrest. Likewise Danîsha. But Lannie…? That was what he really dreaded. If he came across Lannie, would he be able to give the order in cold blood, knowing he might be condemning her to death – or worse?

But then, he might be condemning himself as well. He wasn't blind to the fact that his master urgently wanted all four foreigners. Would he, Gelmion, have served his usefulness when the others were caught? He could only hope not. If he had high mental potential, and was serving his master's interests, he would surely be allowed to continue in the Bishop's Guard. He was counting on it. And who knows? He might even be given Lannie as a reward.

They entered the market square. He led his patrol slowly towards the imposing Temple of Gadesh, scanning the faces they passed. He glanced at the marble stairs leading to the portico of the temple. There were a couple of servants in green-and-gold livery coming down. One of them was walking oddly, stumbling as though she were drugged. The other – He looked more closely. There was something familiar about her. She seemed older than he remembered, but wasn't that… Fira?

Yes, it was! He'd know that thin, hawk-like face anywhere. And the fair-haired girl with her bore a definite likeness to the fuzzy image of Lady Perrely en Nelláy a GarMadin that he'd been given. This would be a feather in his cap – an Ensign for less than a day, and the first to capture some of the fugitives! He had no qualms about arresting those two. Perrely meant nothing to him; and Fira was the one who had driven him out of the Manor in the first place, with all the misery that followed. He'd enjoy being rough with her.

He glanced around the area at the foot of the stairs. There was a band of minstrels producing a raucous treble, and beyond them a pen of grûn calves providing the bass. A tall woman with a wide hat was standing beside the minstrels. She was carrying a bellaril. As she shifted the instrument in her hands, it tipped the hat back. He saw with a shock that it was Danîsha.

This changed everything. He had strict orders not to arrest the foreigners himself. Apparently they were extremely dangerous – though he couldn't imagine what harm old 'Neesh could do with a fancy guitar. He pushed through the crowd to the nearest infantry patrol.

"That woman over there with the bellaril – arrest her at once," he told the pudgy sergeant.

"What woman?"

He cursed the man, and pointed to Danîsha. She saw him, and their eyes met. He felt an irrational flush of shame.

"Hurry!" he snapped to the sergeant. He looked at Fira and Perely. They'd paused near the bottom of the stairs. He ran with his slaves towards them, glancing at Danîsha as he went. She raised the bellaril to play —

— and an explosion of Light burst into Gelmion's mind. He was blinded, paralysed, overwhelmed. He felt himself falling, knocking someone over, tumbling to the ground. He clasped his hands over his head in a feeble attempt to hide from the most mind-numbing purity he'd ever encountered.

As suddenly as it had started, it stopped. He slowly unclasped his hands. There was a throbbing blank in his memory. He looked up. What was he doing lying on the paving stones? His last conscious thought emerged shakily from the debris of his mind. The two women! He scrambled to his feet. He felt weak at the knees. What had come over him?

The women were still standing at the foot of the temple stairs. Fira was staring at something over to his left. He glanced that way. A tall minstrel with a bellaril was being arrested. It was a timely distraction.

He gathered up his shaken troopers and hurried to the stairs. The women didn't see them till the last moment. Fira suddenly met his eyes and gasped his name. Then his men had both of them pinned by the arms.

"Well, well. It seems you remember me, Fira."

"No, I don't remember you, Gelmion. Not as you are now."

Her head snapped sideways as his hand cracked against her cheek.

"That's just for starters," he murmured. "You got me into all this, Fira. There's a lot coming to you. If you want some more, you only have to speak."

"Oh, there's no point talking to *you*, Gelmion. It's your master I'll be dealing with."

He punched her in the stomach and she doubled over. He was about to strike the back of her neck when he felt a restraining influence.

Not too much. I want her in one piece.

Odd. The Boss also sounded a bit shook up.

Yes, Master.

Take the two of them to the Guardhouse. You'll escort them to Darthane tomorrow.

Yes, Master.

Fira had straightened up slowly and was staring at him with burning eyes. The other girl looked dazed and not quite with it. Pretty, though. He saw now that they'd smudged their faces to make themselves look older. A lot of good it had done them.

When his troopers had bound their hands, he led them off across the square. He hadn't gone far when an infantry patrol intercepted him. They had the minstrel in their midst, her hands tied, the broad hat shading her face. One of the infantrymen was carrying her bellaril.

The pudgy sergeant addressed him. "Here she is, Ensign."

He stared at the man coldly. "Yes?"

The man frowned. "You told me to arrest her. Don't you want her?"

"Are you too lazy to—" The woman lifted her head to look at him, and shock wiped the words from his lips. It was Danîsha!

"What are you waiting for? Hand her over," he snapped. The infantry sergeant gave an expressive shrug.

"Are you sure you want to do this, Gil?"

The sorrow in her face and the gentle concern in her voice nearly unmanned him. A tide of suppressed emotion arose. This was 'Neesh! How could he betray her like this?

"Well done, Gelmion! An Ensign for less than a day, and you're the first to have captured one of the foreigners! You'll be well rewarded. By the way, look after that bellaril. It must also come to Darthane."

He turned away from Danîsha. The ranks parted, and she was shoved alongside Perrely and Fira. One of his troopers had a firm grip on the rope that bound her hands.

They marched off towards the Guardhouse.

* * *

Lannie watched in horror as 'Neesh, Fira and Perrely were led off between their grey-cloaked captors. She, Shiván and the twins stood helpless beside the bellowing grûn calves. Shivvie's face was a mask of anguish.

Part of Lannie's pain was for her three friends; part was for the leader of the Guard patrol. She'd recognised Gil, of course. When she first saw him standing tall above the crowd, she'd had to stop herself from running to him. Then she'd seen his cold, set face. Later she'd watched him slapping and punching Fira. She had to keep telling herself it wasn't really Gil doing that, it was some monster of a Mindbender.

But now the three of them were being taken to that Mindbender! This was a disaster.

"We must see where they go," Shiván muttered, plunging into the crowd. Lannie and the twins followed. It was good Gil was so tall. They kept his head in sight as he moved steadily across the market square.

They emerged into a wide, prosperous street. With fewer people around, they had to hang back so as not to attract Gil's attention. He turned right. A couple of minutes later he stopped at a black door. It was in a blank stone wall with only a few shuttered windows way up on the third storey. Two grey-cloaked Guardsmen flanked the entrance. Others were patrolling the street. Shiván dodged into a side alley.

"Use the bess," he hissed. "Get the password!"

By the time she'd extracted it from her robe and thought of Gil, he was already inside the building. "Congratulations, Ensign," a voice was saying. "Thank you, sir," Gil replied. There were footsteps, and the door closed. It occurred to her that for the first time in many weeks she'd heard Gil's voice. But there'd been no warmth in it. It was the voice of a stranger.

She relayed the conversation to the others.

"Oho! *Ensign* now, is it?" Shîrin said.

"Our boy's rising through the ranks." Cârin nodded grimly.

"Does that mean he has more authority?" Shivvie asked.

"Oh yes. Leads his own patrol. Can make decisions for himself."

Lannie's heart sank and tears started in her eyes. So his brutality to Fira *hadn't* been forced on him. Oh, Gil. What's happened to you? Will I even know you if we meet again?

Dodging in and out of side alleys, they made a circular tour of the Guardhouse. It occupied its own irregularly-shaped block between four streets. Sheer walls rose on all sides. The slate roof had a wide overhang. Watch turrets stood at each corner. At the back, on a narrow street parallel to the main thoroughfare, a row of dilapidated houses ran along the foot of the wall. At the far corner, the third floor windows were bigger and more elaborate. Below them a new addition was being built. The end house in the row had been demolished, and new walls extended at right angles from the building to enclose the area it had occupied. So far they were about twenty feet high, surrounded by scaffolding.

"Looks like the captain's new quarters," Shîr muttered. "Dhelgor does himself proud."

The light was starting to fade. "Why don't you two do something useful?" Lannie said to the twins. "Climb the scaffolding and have a look inside those new walls."

"Honoured lady, your expectations are too *high*," Cârin told her, looking up at the rickety wooden framework. But Shiván gave them the nod, and they did it. Lannie and Shiván waited in the dark entrance of a tenement block opposite.

The twins came back looking full of themselves. "Inside the building works, an opening has been made in the wall," Shîrin announced. "A temporary entrance into the main building," Cârin expanded. "And — get this —" He looked expectantly at his brother.

"*It was not guarded!*" Shîr hissed, his eyes wide.

"You think we can get in there?" Shivvie asked, hope dawning.

"A much better chance than at the front," Shîr said. "Even better late at night."

"If we can slip across without the men in the turrets noticing," Câr added.

"Sounds good. Okay, it's getting dark. Let's go home."

* * *

Inside the Guardhouse, Perrely sat on a narrow bed in a tiny cell. The bed itself, with its thin padding and single filthy blanket, could barely accommodate her lying on her side. But she couldn't have fallen off, because there wasn't enough space between the bed and the opposite wall. Sitting as she was, her knees were touching cold stone. A dim flickery lamplight filtered through the grille above the door from the corridor outside. There was no window.

She was struggling to adjust to the rapid pace of events. First that devastating news about Jomel; then she and Fira arrested — by none other than Gelmion, the fourth Restorer! Who was now revealed as a traitor. He hadn't been a mere mindbent slave. She'd seen that. He'd been in charge of that patrol. He'd deliberately assaulted Fira.

And now she was in the Guardhouse, locked in this one-person cell. Solitary confinement: the cruellest Dûrian punishment short of death. It was reserved for violent criminals and traitors. Presumably she fell in the latter category. Or maybe Mindbender Dhelgor was trying to weaken her resistance, before... She didn't want to think about that. But at least her loner tendencies made her better able to cope with the situation than others.

Nevertheless, she had to face facts. She, Fira and Danîsha would be mindbent. That meant they'd reveal where the others were — which would be the end of the Restorers of the Way. Had this all been a delusion, like the Rebellion? Had she been deceived twice? Yet her vision had proved true in every detail. No, she wouldn't listen to Gadesh's lies, tempting her to despair.

Time went by. She spoke to the One, and knew he heard her. He was there, though she missed human companionship.

Pictures of her family floated into her mind: Father and Mums; her brothers, Larion and Barlet. Happy, relaxed Anderil afternoons together. She sighed. Where were they now? Were they dead? Were they slaves of the Bishop in Darthane? What had they been through first? She had to admit she was afraid of being mindbent. With that fear came memories of stories she'd heard of the unspeakable torments inflicted on prisoners by the Bishop's Guard. She pleaded with the One to fill her with his Light, to drive out the darkness of fear.

Suddenly there was a voice in her mind.

"Perrely!"

She sat up, startled. Again —

"Perrely!"

No, this wasn't the One. "Alanya, is that you?"

"Hush! Don't speak out loud. Just think what you want to say."

"It's wonderful to hear you!"

Alanya talked quietly in her head, reassuring and comforting her. She'd spoken to Fira and Danîsha, who were also in solitary confinement. She and Shiván and the twins were coming to rescue them. Tonight. She must wait and pray. They would get her and Fira out — *and* Gelmion. They'd found an unexpected way into the Guardhouse.

"Now Shiván wants to talk to you..."

And there was Shiván's voice. He asked anxiously how she was, and she assured him she was unharmed mentally and physically. She asked after the rest of them, and Shiván said they were fine. There was an awkward pause. She found it unsettling being able to hear Shiván, but unable to see his face and gauge his reactions.

"We're coming to get you. Everything will be all right."

Her heart warmed at the sincerity in his voice. She didn't know if they would succeed in rescuing her—but it would be all right. Her Prince was there beside her, strengthening her. He had said *I will never leave you on your own or abandon you.*

"Thank you, Father."

"What?"

"Thank you, Shiván. I know I'll be all right. I'll be waiting for you."

* * *

"Any sign of Gil yet?"

Lannie shook her head. She'd been sitting on her bed in the crypt of the Domicile for the past hour, following Gil's movements in the bess. He was out on patrol—and they needed him back in the Guardhouse so they could rescue him along with the other three.

Shiván's nerves had been on edge ever since the arrest. The thought of Perrely being tortured and ... *mindbent* was too horrible to contemplate. At least they were able to keep in touch with her and 'Neesh and Fira. Thank the One for the bess! They knew their friends were so far unharmed—and they could track Gelmion's movements.

They were all sitting in the women's enclosure in the crypt, packed and ready to go, dressed in their 'borrowed' infantry uniforms. Cârin had an extra sword, and so did Lannie—they were for Fira and Danîsha. The priests had filled their pouches with water bottles, dry food, and changes of clothing. They were ready for a long journey when this was over—to the Tallissôr Mountains or further. Unless of course they paid an involuntary visit to Bishop Shambor instead...

Time went by. It must be well after midnight now. Lannie was the only one with anything to do. He envied her. She was constantly busy with the bess, but doing it silently now. He'd offered to help, but she wanted to keep tabs on Gelmion. Periodically she looked up at them and shook her head—Gelmion was still out on patrol. The rest of the time she was chatting in turn to the three prisoners. She allowed Shiván an occasional word with Perrely, but there was little to say. Fira, she'd told him privately, was finding the solitary confinement hard.

Frengor came down to join them. His cheery presence lightened the atmosphere at once. They prayed together. Their emergency plan needed all the prayer it could get. No bellaril; the Blade just an ordinary sword at close quarters. Attempting a break-in at the Guardhouse under those conditions was madness, humanly speaking. *But with God all things are possible.* They were banking on that.

"What?" Lannie was clutching the bess. Their heads all snapped round to look at her.

"Where?" There was a pause. She looked at the others, her eyes round with anxiety. "Two Guards have just hauled Perrely out of her cell. She doesn't know where they're taking her..." Shiván's heart did a somersault.

"Plan B!" he exclaimed. "We must get the three out, and try to find Gelmion later."

"Fira ...? Danîsha? ... Oh, thank God ..."

After a moment she turned to the others. "Danîsha and Fira are still in their cells. Gil is out on patrol, but I think he's heading back to the Guardhouse now."

"Right. We're off."

They hurried to the foot of the ladder, where Frengor held up a hand to stop them. "Let me commit you all to the One Creator God." They linked arms in a circle like the Ring of Orrénne, that amazing constellation. The Visionary lifted their rescue mission up to the One in his simple, practical way. Then they stood silent, committing themselves to God. It was a solemn moment.

"It may be a long time before we meet again," Frengor said, holding each of their eyes in turn. *"Ney len silmend*—Light stay with you."

"Illi ristend—And keep you," they all responded softly.

"Thank you, Frengor," Shiván's heart was overflowing with all he'd like to say to this humble, wrinkled priest who'd done so much for them. But there wasn't time.

Frengor smiled. "Lead in the One's strength, Overguardian."

Then they were up the ladder and out into the night, marching as fast as they dared to the Guardhouse.

* * *

Dhelgor decided to risk it. Gelmion was away on patrol. Shambor was not watching him at the moment. The three women were in his power. The Mindruler had said they were not to be harmed — but this was life or death. He wouldn't harm them — not seriously — but he had to find out where the other two foreigners were. The patrols had still not found them, so the women were his only hope. He could *not* allow himself to become a plaything of Shambor's sick fantasies.

He couldn't mindbend the women. The Mindruler would never forgive that — he wanted them for himself. A little physical pain, though, only to extort the whereabouts of their friends — that might be overlooked.

He'd start with the youngest one. The old woman looked a tough nut — and he'd been warned about the foreigners. He'd stay clear of her. But the young girl... He knew how she could be broken — without any physical harm, which was perfect. If for some reason that failed, then the rebel lieutenant could have a foretaste of the kind of pain she'd be living with daily before long. Something sudden and extreme might make her crack. He'd seen it happen in the Rebellion. Those rebel officers thought they were tough, until they visited the Guards' torture chambers.

He sent Guardsmen to fetch Perrely. He roused the torturer and his assistants, and outlined the treatment Fira should receive — when he gave the signal.

It wasn't long before two Guards delivered Perrely to his third floor apartment. She looked rather fetching in the green and gold livery. A charming young serving girl one would like to know better — if it weren't for that nauseating Lightist shiláy. Her gaze was direct and unafraid. Perhaps she didn't realise who he was. He would enlighten her.

"My dear, do come in. Have a seat," he said, taking her gallantly by the arm and ushering her to a recliner in front of the fire. She sat upright, watching him calmly. Dhelgor lay on the recliner opposite, propped up on one elbow to observe her responses. He took a sip from a glass goblet on the recliner's built-in receptacle.

"I am Dhelgor, Mindbender of Stillárre," he told her casually. "I need your help with a few things." Her expression didn't change;

her hands lay relaxed in her lap. Was she stupid? That announcement usually had people swallowing and fidgeting nervously. Shock tactics were indicated.

Leaping up and towering over her, cape swirling, he snapped out, "*Where is the rest of your group?*"

She looked up at him with the same calm gaze. "What will you do if I tell you?"

"*I* am asking the questions! Will you co-operate, or not?"

"I can only co-operate if I know you're going to help my friends. Not harm them."

His hand lashed out. She gave a gasp as it struck her cheek. He felt a thrill of satisfaction. "You will co-operate, you stupid bitch, because if you don't I'll harm *you*."

"You'll mindbend me, you mean? If you're going to do that, you'll find out everything you want to know anyway. Why should I co-operate? Just go ahead and do it."

For a tantalising moment, in his fury, he looked inside her mind. The shining barrier was very bright. But he could get round it— He caught himself. That was not an option.

He smiled at the red hand-print blooming on her cheek, and sat down. He leaned back. "No. I won't mindbend you." Her face showed a flicker of surprise. "I could rape you, though." The purple eyes widened. Of course that wasn't true—Shambor would find out—but as a shock tactic it was working just fine. "Would you like me to do that? No one will hear your screams. I can be quite rough, you know." He went on to describe in detail how rough he could be, watching her narrowly. His annoyance flared as he saw her face settle into an expression of calm resignation.

He'd have to take it to the next level.

* * *

Lannie tried to keep the bess to her ear as they hurried through the darkened streets. It wasn't easy. Fortunately there weren't many patrols; it must be about five in the morning. Gil's patrol was definitely headed for the Guardhouse—from a different direction, fortunately. She told Danîsha they were coming; and let Shiván know that Mindbender Dhelgor had just introduced himself to Perrely. He increased the pace.

A few minutes later she heard two things that made her almost drop the bess. "Shiván!" she gasped. "We're out of time! The Mindbender's about to rape Perrely!"

"Oh, my God!"

Shiván shot off like an arrow from a bow, and they were all running flat out to keep up with him. Lannie was trailing behind. She *had* to keep up! There was no way she was going to miss wreaking the One's vengeance on that Mindbender.

* * *

The girl was staring calmly at Dhelgor, her lips moving silently. He leapt up and grabbed her. She gasped and began to struggle. Bearing her down under him on the recliner, he gripped the top of her tunic with both hands and wrenched outwards. With a staccato rattle a volley of gold buttons shot around the room, and her shift was exposed. He stared in surprise at the delicately embroidered satin. He'd forgotten for the moment that Lady Perrely en Nelláy a GarMadin was no serving girl.

To remind him, she punched him in the nose. He jerked back, eyes watering. She almost got away, but he grabbed her from behind, locking both arms around her in an iron grip.

He could of course have summoned his slaves to subdue her, but that would have spoiled the fun. He issued a mental command that he was not to be disturbed.

Chapter 44: *Frozen*

THEY REACHED THE SCAFFOLDING at the back of the Guardhouse. There they stopped, breathing deeply and quietly to catch their breaths. Shiván stared up at the unfinished walls of Mindbender Dhelgor's new living quarters, standing like the ruins of a haunted monastery. Beyond loomed the bulk of the Guard fortress. There was no sound from the watch turrets at either corner of the main wall.

This was it. Here he would finally face his fears and overcome them. Perrely's life was at stake. He would fight for her in the most lethal way he knew how—whether with the Blade, or with his martial arts. She herself had encouraged him, that evening they'd sat together outside the cave in Carreck Forest: "The third time, God will enable you to fight the way you need to."

Dear Prince, break the barrier that's held me back for eight years. Let me fight the way I need to.

"Let's go," he muttered.

They climbed the scaffolding. Shiván stopped at a window gap in the unfinished wall. Above their heads was the next level of planking. The tang of mortar was heavy in the air. Through the gap they could see the enclosed area, filled with all the rubble and clutter of a building site. Beyond rose the main wall of the Guardhouse—and as the twins had said, there was a newly-made opening facing them. It was partly covered by a wide board. There was no guard outside. Was there one standing just within? They'd find out.

Shiván gestured to the others to move away from the gap, so they were out of sight from the Guardhouse.

"Okay, we're here. Can we get in without being seen?" he asked.

"If we keep to the shadows under the left wall," Cârin murmured. "And move slowly."

"Once we reach the wall of the Guardhouse, we won't easily be seen from the watch turrets," Shîrin added, speaking in a rapid undertone. "But if there's a Guard at the entrance—beyond that board—we'll have to hope his controller is asleep."

"His controller? Why?" Lannie wanted to know.

"Because, dear lady, he's a mindbent slave. The instant a Guardsman dies his controller knows about it—*if* he's awake.

There's a good chance that this one's controller, being an officer, will be asleep. But we'll have to kill him unseen, and fast—so he has very little reaction to disturb his controller. Even so, the death blow might do it."

"I think that has to be your job," Shiván said, looking at the twins.

Câr scowled at his brother. "Thanks!"

Shîr bowed. "Any time."

Shiván was restraining himself with difficulty. "Let's go!"

They climbed through the window gap and lowered themselves to the ground. Then Shîr and Câr led them step by careful step along the new walls, crouching behind piles of stones, water barrels and stacks of timbers, until they reached the safety of the main Guardhouse wall. They stood pressed against it.

The twins eased their shoes off, then drew their swords with a faint metallic rustle: still no response from the watch turrets. Shîr raised a hand to halt the others, and he and Câr moved silently past the temporary board until they reached the opening. Shîr peered slowly round the end of the board. He withdrew his head, mouthed a few words to his brother, and the two of them slipped smoothly inside like a pair of sinuous black panthers.

Shiván waited with Lannie, his thoughts chaotic. By delegating this to the twins, had he been putting off the moment when he'd have to fight himself? No, this required stealth, and the twins were professional army scouts.

There were a couple of distant thuds. Shiván and Lannie froze, expecting shouts from the watch turrets. None came. Half a minute passed, then Cârin appeared. He beckoned to them. They sidled past the wooden board to the entrance, carrying the twins' shoes.

They found themselves in a bare utility area lined with tools, wheelbarrows and work tunics. A brazier with glowing coals stood in the centre. Its dim glow revealed a closed door opposite the entrance, a flight of stairs to the right—and a body lying on the floor. There was something odd about it. "Don't look too closely," Shîr whispered. "Had to, er, separate the head."

"Oh!" Lannie gasped.

"Only way to silence him instantly," Câr murmured. "He was warming his hands at the brazier with his back to the door. We crept up behind, and Shîr swung his sword like a scythe at harvest." The twins took their shoes and began putting them on.

After a moment of shocked silence, Shiván turned to Lannie. "What's happening to Perrely?"

Lannie lifted the bess to her ear and winced. "She's struggling with him! We must get to her quickly. I'll just check on 'Neesh and Fira... Yes, we're here, 'Neesh. We'll be with you as soon as possible... You too. Bye. ... Fira?" Her eyes widened. "Oh no! They're taking Fira somewhere... downstairs... A huge man and two others? *Torture?* Oh, Lord..." She took the bess from her ear and stared at the others.

Shiván ran a hand over his eyes. Everything in him was bursting to find Perrely, but Fira also urgently needed help... "At least one trained swordsman must stay with us. Câr, could you go...?"

The Dûrian nodded. "I'll see what I can do for the Lieutenant. Which direction, Alanya?"

She listened in the bess then pointed to the inner door facing the entrance. "Somewhere through there. Down below!"

Cârin saluted, hand on heart. "*Ney mel sharras*—Go with the Light."

"*Ney mel shar*," they replied. He opened the inner door and left.

"The Mindbender's apartment is on the top floor," Shiván muttered. "Let's go."

He leapt up the stairway. The Blade glinted in the dim lamplight. Lannie and Shîr followed. The first floor landing was empty. But halfway up the next flight Shiván suddenly stopped. They heard distant shouts, followed by doors slamming and a growing uproar.

"Uh-oh. The controller woke up," Shîr muttered.

"Hurry!" Shiván gasped.

The second landing was still empty, but there was a shout from down the long passage that led to it. In a brief glance Lannie saw Guardsman, many of them half-dressed, running towards them.

"Up there!" Shîr shouted, pointing to a narrower stairway that ran up the opposite wall to the third floor. At the top was a small landing with a single ornate door.

They sprinted up the stairs. Guards came pouring on to the landing below. The first arrivals began climbing the stairs in single file, longswords drawn. There wasn't space for two to fight abreast.

A muffled scream filtered through the ornate door from the room beyond.

"Go to her!" Shîr told Shiván. "Alanya and I will hold off the Guards." He whipped out his sword. Lannie fumbled to free hers from the sheath.

Shiván sheathed the Blade and tried to open the door. It was locked. He drew a deep breath and raised his foot.

*　*　*

Fira sat gasping in the chair. The two hulks on either side of her relaxed their grip on her shoulders. Opposite her the chief torturer sat, surveying her dispassionately. He was huge, impressively muscled, with a black sleeveless tunic and leggings: short dark hair, small unblinking eyes in a craggy face like a hard grey tuber. He exuded implacable determination.

All around the dimly-lit room were the grisly tools of his trade. What she'd first taken for machinery turned out to be a rack, a wheel, a chair of nails, a garrotte, a flaying table, thumbscrews, and other abominations whose use she didn't want to guess.

They'd started her off gently, she supposed. She'd been strapped on to this chair with her hands stretched out in front of her on the table. Her elbows and wrists had been strapped down. Her fingers were splayed out, each digit fixed to the table by a u-shaped, double-ended nail. The nails were made for small fingers, and her tormentor hadn't been gentle. She was sure a couple of hers were broken. Then the real agony had begun —

"Where are your foreign friends?" His voice was a cold *basso profundo*. Prince have mercy, she didn't know how much more of this she could take. *Give me your strength*, she cried silently to the One, *mine is finished*. She stared defiantly at the torturer.

He took a blood-stained splinter of wood with a sharp point and held it up for her to see. She closed her eyes. The two heavies were pushing down on her shoulders. Fingers gripped the tip of her left middle finger and her whole body tensed, knowing what was coming next. She kept her eyes squeezed shut, feeling tears trickling out of the corners. Then agony exploded in her hand and through her whole body. She screamed. Pain soared off the scale as the splinter was driven further in. Blackness swept over her. One thought lingered in her brain as she passed out:

There were nine more fingers to go.

* * *

Shiván smashed the door open.

The first thing he saw was Dhelgor sitting on top of Perrely, pinning her to the floor. Perrely's clothing was torn. She was screaming and writhing under him.

The Mindbender looked up, startled. Shiván let loose a vicious kick, sending Dhelgor crashing backward off his victim. He leapt at Dhelgor, but in a single agile movement the Mindbender rolled aside and up on to his feet. Perrely scrambled away. Dhelgor lunged towards her. She screamed as his clutching hand just missed her. Shiván leapt between them, but before he could do anything Dhelgor ran the opposite way. He grabbed a longsword from its hook on the wall.

"Not so clever, hey, boy?" The Mindbender advanced slowly towards him, weapon poised. Shiván hastily drew the Blade. It wavered slightly in his grasp. "I don't think you're much good with that, are you?" the Mindbender taunted. "Better off without it." Quicker than Shiván could have imagined the longsword flashed out. Instead of countering with his own weapon, Shiván instinctively leapt aside—but not far enough. A sharp pain stung his sword hand, and he dropped the Blade. In a moment Dhelgor had kicked it out of reach. There was a cry from Perrely.

The Mindbender moved forward with a twisted grin. Shiván slipped into martial arts mode, body sideways-on to his enemy. He could feel a trickle of blood on his left hand, but the wound wasn't serious. He *had* to get that longsword out of Dhelgor's hand. It had been a mistake to try the Blade. He knew he could demolish the Mindbender with his martial arts, if he could just bring himself to…

He consciously forced himself into combat mode. His eyes devoured Dhelgor's every movement, watching for the tell-tale signs of an impending strike—a tensing of the muscles, tightening of the face, flick of the eyes.

The Mindbender's sword moved fractionally, and Shiván lashed out in a circular kick with his left leg, hitting the flat of the blade with the heel of his shoe and sweeping Dhelgor's sword arm aside. Using his own momentum, he planted his left leg on the floor and launched his right foot at Dhelgor's unguarded body. The light kick sent Dhelgor staggering back, giving Shiván the moment he needed to leap forward and grab the arm holding the longsword. He twisted it, forcing his enemy to drop the weapon with a yell of pain.

Dhelgor recovered quickly, wrenching his arm free and punching Shiván in the side. But even as Dhelgor lunged for the longsword, Shiván's foot sent it spinning under a recliner.

"I agree. Better off without them."

The Mindbender's mouth set in a hard line.

With half an eye Shiván saw Perrely sidling towards the corner of the room where the Blade had landed. She would have to pass behind Dhelgor. He wished he could tell her he meant what he'd said, that he was better off unarmed. But his heart swelled with admiration for her courage.

He and the Mindbender faced each other. Dhelgor was half-crouched, his fists clenched in a boxing position. He shot a rapid glance at the door. A flash of irritation crossed his face. The reinforcements hadn't arrived. Then he subjected Shiván to a long, intense stare. Shiván felt a prickling at the back of his head and a stab of fear. Was he being mindbent? But again, that flash of irritation. No go, my friend.

Perrely was creeping past Dhelgor. Shiván was trying to work out how he could signal that he didn't need the Blade, hesitating to attack the Mindbender with Perrely so close. Dhelgor must have seen something, because suddenly he whipped round and grabbed Perrely. Shiván leapt forward, but Dhelgor spun Perrely between them, one arm locked on her throat, the other gripping her waist. Perrely screamed, her purple eyes wide with shock. Shiván stood rooted to the spot.

A sardonic smile appeared below Dhelgor's cold eyes. "Perhaps it's time to talk."

* * *

On the landing Shîrin stood poised with his weapon at the ready as the first Guardsman came to a halt below him—a large brute with a bulbous nose and closely-spaced eyes. Shîr had the advantage of a higher position; the Guard had the advantage of a longer sword. With narrowed eyes they measured each another up. Lannie hovered behind Shîr with her sword raised, trying to imitate his stance.

There was a clash of metal as the first Guardsman's longsword lunged forward and Shîr parried. While the longer weapon was rising for a second blow, Shîr slashed the Guard's shoulder on the back stroke. He staggered, and Shîr jumped down a step, inside the man's guard, sword flashing in every direction. The Guardsman achieved a glancing blow on Shîr's arm before the former rebel soldier drove his sword into his enemy's side. The Guard collapsed, and Shîr leapt back to the landing as the second Guardsman's longsword flashed out. Lannie watched from behind with wide eyes, clammy hands clutching her own sword uselessly.

The fighting became both fiercer and more skilful as Dhelgor's minions realised what they were up against. Shîr's sword seemed to be everywhere at once, thrusting, parrying, scything through the air — somehow holding off one Guard after another.

But as each enemy fell or moved back wounded, another leapt forward to take his place. The fallen were passed down the stairs, while others joined the queue. Shîr's breath was coming rapidly now, the sweat standing out on his brow. Lannie's heart was in her mouth. How much longer could he last? Through the broken door she caught glimpses of Shivàn and Dhelgor fighting, but she daren't leave Shîr.

There was a buzzing noise in her ear, and a *thunk* of something biting into wood. It took her a moment to realise that the thing quivering in the doorpost was an arrow. She whirled round and ducked as two more arrows whizzed by and shattered against the wall. None had hit Shîr — but he was moving too fast to be an easy target. She saw the archers below swiftly fitting new shafts to their bows.

Desperately she looked around, and her eye fell on a small table beside Dhelgor's door. A tray with dirty plates and bowls stood on it. She dropped her sword, grabbed the tray and threw it over the railing, hoping it hit the Guards below. She quickly turned the lightweight table over and broke off two of the legs. Holding it by the other two legs, she raised it over her head and shoulders and ran to stand behind Shîr.

Just in time. With a splintering sound an arrow burst through the table top — but its force was broken, and it fell harmlessly to the floor.

Feeling at last that she was doing something useful, Lannie kept herself and her table between Shîr and the archers. They could only shoot from one direction to avoid hitting their own people. Several more arrows crashed into the table top, some sticking there, others breaking through. One grazed her cheek, another hit her arm. No serious damage.

Then Shîr cried out and staggered into her. He recovered immediately, sword flashing back at his opponent, but his other arm hung useless. In a quick glance Lannie saw blood oozing out through a wide slash in his tunic. He couldn't carry on much longer! Protecting him wasn't enough. She had to be ready to continue the fight— somehow. Stretching out a leg till it touched her sword where it lay on the floor, she scuffled it towards her with her foot. If the worst came to the worst—

It did. Shîr uttered another cry, and crashed to the floor. She threw the table down, snatched up her sword and whirled round to face the Guards, the weapon swinging wildly in her hand. There was a soft thud—it had embedded itself in the oncoming Guard's neck! He was toppling towards her. With a scream she leapt away, tripped over Shîr and fell on her back, banging her head against the table. The Guard slumped on top of her, pinning down the lower half of her body—and her sword.

The Guardsman behind him leapt up to the landing, saw the jumble of bodies, and met Lannie's horrified gaze. He smiled and poised his sword like an endlessly long dagger at her throat.

* * *

Rage flared up in Shiván as the Mindbender's arm tightened around Perrely's neck. Blood suffused her face and her eyes bulged. She struggled, but Dhelgor's grip was too strong. Shiván's mind raced through various options, rejecting one after another. Dhelgor watched him over Perrely's head with cynical amusement. He relaxed the arm around her throat and she sagged, gasping and coughing.

"You have no chance of winning, boy. It was a good attempt, but not good enough. Your loyal friends outside can't hold my Guardsmen off much longer. They'll break through any moment." The clash of weapons on the landing bore him out.

"Go and sit on that recliner, and I'll let your ladylove go. Then we can decide what to do with you all. Maybe this has simply been a misunderstanding, and we can help you return to your own country."

Shiván's fury rose a notch or two. This guy must take him for a complete sucker. But what could he do? He looked at Perrely, and saw her eyes fixed intently on him. Deliberately she looked down and to the right of Shiván, then back up. He followed her glance: on the built-in receptacle of a nearby recliner stood a large goblet half-filled with amber fluid. Dhelgor's night-cap, which had somehow escaped the violence. When Shiván looked back at Perrely, she lifted her foot and mouthed the word *shaddon* — 'kick'. He gave her a slight nod.

Dhelgor took the nod as agreement. "Good. Just sit down slowly, and — "

Perrely's foot rose and jabbed backwards. The heel of her shoe struck Dhelgor hard on the shin. He yelped. Shiván snatched up the goblet and hurled the contents at the Mindbender, just as Perrely ducked her head.

The liquid struck Dhelgor full in the face, and a reek of alcohol filled the room. He cried out, and snatched his arm away from Perrely's neck to wipe his eyes. She jerked forward and almost broke free, but his other hand clutched a fistful of clothing and dragged her back.

However Perrely's movement left Dhelgor open, and like an enraged bull Shiván charged the Mindbender, all fears and inhibitions forgotten. Grabbing Dhelgor's tunic at the neck he ran him backwards toward the wall.

Perrely was jerked out of Dhelgor's grasp. Legs flailing to find a purchase, Dhelgor could only throw wild punches at Shiván — some of which connected. Shiván hardly noticed.

There was a loud *crunch* as Dhelgor's back hit one of the green and gold wall hangings — and with a shock Shiván realised there was a window behind it. He'd forgotten the Dûrians used hangings rather than curtains. The glass hadn't shattered — yet.

Pinned against the window, Dhelgor struggled violently. Shiván yanked him forward and head-butted him between the eyes. Taken by surprise, the Mindbender stood dazed — giving Shiván the extra seconds he needed.

He didn't hesitate. He'd done it once before, and it had been a terrible mistake. Not now.

He leapt back and launched himself into the air in a three-hundred-and-sixty degree spin. Letting out a roar, he poured every ounce of effort into the most powerful kick he knew. His leg shot out, the heel punching into Dhelgor's chest.

With a resounding crash of breaking glass, the Mindbender catapulted through the window. His wheezing cry as he fell three storeys ended abruptly.

Shiván staggered after coming down from the kick, and grabbed for the nearest support—which turned out to be Perrely. Suddenly he discovered he was holding her tightly against his chest. She looked up at him with shining eyes.

* * *

The Guardsman had his sword poised to drive it through Lannie's neck. But the fatal thrust never came. Lannie watched in amazement as his eyes glazed and the longsword fell from his hand. He stood frozen. All sound died in the hallway, except for the rustles and thuds of bodies falling.

Dazed, Lannie heaved the other Guardsman off her and scrambled to her feet. There was a litter of fallen bodies on the stairs and below. Many remained standing—but they were still, arms hanging at their sides.

Suddenly it dawned on her, and she let out a yell of pure joy. *Shiván had killed the Mindbender!*

* * *

Movement ceased in the Guardhouse, except in the prisoners' cells. Like a deadly ripple the effect spread slowly outward across the city, until the Mindbender's hundreds of slaves and informers were still.

Chapter 45: *Escape and rescue*

SHÎRIN HAD TWISTED HIS ANKLE, which was what had brought him to the ground. He had also taken a deep gash in his right arm. "Good thing I can also use my left," he muttered as Shiván tore strips off the extra tunic he'd brought from the Domicile. He bound the injured arm as best he could. Inside Dhelgor's apartment, Lannie was helping Perrely put on fresh clothes, using her own spare Domicile garments. Shiván had been immensely relieved that her only injuries were cuts and bruises.

The two women came out. Perrely was wearing a simple blue tunic. He'd never seen anything so beautiful. He stepped forward and held out his hand. Perrely flushed, but took it. Her small hand in his was the most natural and glorious feeling.

Shîr chuckled. He was leaning against the railing, looking pale. "Careful, Shiván. Next thing her father will be asking for half the wedding costs."

"What?"

"Don't pay any attention." Perrely smiled up at him. "Only rustic Dûrians still follow those old traditions. And I'll bet *you've* held plenty of girls' hands without getting betrothed, haven't you Shîrin?"

The accused cleared his throat.

Shiván looked down at Perrely. Her eyes said it all. His heart felt like bursting.

Lannie ruined the moment. "Stop gawping at each other, you two. Danîsha's still locked in her cell, and we need to find the others."

"Yes, ma'am! Let's wade through these Guards. Keep a lookout for Gelmion."

They struggled through the bodies on the stairs. He and Perrely helped Shîr over the obstacles. Lannie spoke to 'Neesh in the bess. They stared wonderingly at the Guards still standing, eyes glazed, arms hanging at their sides, longswords sagging to the floor. Shiván pushed one towards his fallen comrades, and he toppled over in slow motion.

"Don't *do* that, Shiván!" Lannie snapped. "It could have been Gil."

He made no reply. This was the most wonderful night of his life, and nothing could spoil it. Perrely's hand still nestled in his.

Lannie led the way down to the unfinished room on the ground floor. Shîr limped on his twisted ankle, but managed to keep up. Lannie opened the inner door Cârin had used. They found themselves hurrying down a long, straight corridor lit by intermittent lamps. The walls were of undressed stone, the floor well-laid paving blocks. They passed a group of Guards, some standing, some fallen. All were still, their eyes unseeing. It was an eerie scene in the empty passage. Perrely's hand tightened in Shiván's.

Lannie swerved into a side corridor, obviously following the direction the bess had given her. This passage was lined with narrow doors. She stopped in front of one of them.

"'Neesh, are you there?"

"Lannie! Oh, thank God!"

She tried the door, but it was locked. "Just wait, we'll find the key!" She turned to the others. "Those Guards we passed—they must have been on duty here. We'll have to search them."

They hurried back and began feeling in the tunic pockets, on the belts, and round the necks of the frozen Guardsmen. If merely seeing them was eerie, this was ten times worse. Shiván kept expecting a roar of outrage and a hand seizing the scruff of his neck. But the Guards stood immobile like waxworks. Finally Lannie exclaimed "Bingo!" and produced a bunch of the thin metal slivers from one of the Guards' pockets. They quickly returned to Danîsha's cell.

Lannie handed the keys to Perrely, who slipped them into the lock with quick efficiency until she found the one that fitted. She opened the door, and Danîsha came tumbling out of the tiny space. She was overjoyed to see them. After a round of motherly hugs and some tut-tutting over Shîr's arm, she exclaimed, "What happened? Why is everything so quiet?"

"Shiván killed the Mindbender," Perrely told her.

"You did it!" Danîsha exclaimed. "You know, I thought this was a wild, impossible plan, but you've proved me wrong!" Her smile broadened as she took in the clasped hands. "Well, I can see that *you* both came through it all right!"

"What happened to your bellaril, 'Neesh?" Shiván asked.

"They took it away from me. I do hope it hasn't been damaged."

"We'll look for it. But first we need to find Fira and Cârin."

As it happened it was Câr who found them. They heard a shout from a side passage as they walked by, and he and Fira came out and joined them. Fira was walking slowly, holding her left arm away from her body. They gasped when they saw the swollen, bloodstained tip of the index finger. The nail was missing. "I fainted," she told them. "When I came to, the torturer and his assistants had frozen. Then Cârin arrived and released my fingers. That was the worst part..." Shiván's knees felt weak. Fira's survival of that ordeal seemed a greater triumph than his own.

Danîsha examined Fira's finger from every angle, clicking her tongue in dismay. "This needs hospital treatment, with antibiotics!" she muttered angrily in English. "How could they do such a thing?"

In a storeroom they found basic first aid supplies. They took bandages, a jar of salve, and several packets of dried herbs the Dûrians said were good against infection. With infinite care Danîsha applied some of the salve to Fira's fingers and wound a bandage around the hand.

They continued to search the ground floor for Gelmion. The corridor ran around all four sides of the Guardhouse. From time to time they passed groups of 'frozen' Guardsmen. In some rooms Guards were sitting, standing or sprawled on the floor. One or two were bleeding from injuries when they'd keeled over. No time to help them now.

On the first floor they found the prisoners. Voices were calling out, wanting to know what had happened. Here there were many more Guards standing frozen in the corridor. They began unlocking doors, using the keys Lannie had found. Prisoners were crammed into each stinking cell like sardines. They were pathetically grateful to be released, and scurried out of the Guardhouse — those who could. Many had to be carried.

There was a shout from Cârin. "Shiván, look who's here!"

He looked — and gave a shout of joy. "Captain Garset!"

He hurried over and gave the dishevelled captain a high handshake. He'd lost his cape, and his tunic was crumpled. One eye had been blackened, and there were cuts and bruises on his forearms. Behind him were the officers who had been with him in the gate tunnel. They also looked the worse for wear.

"Captain, that was a wonderful thing you did! If it weren't for you, we might be slaves now. Instead, you've had to suffer. I truly am sorry."

"Our service is to the One Creator God—and the Restorers of his Way. Who have already established their credentials, it seems." A smile of understanding passed between them.

"Fira! You wanted to see Captain Garset again, to give him an extra-high handshake. Here he is!"

Fira came forward and held out her right hand. "Captain, you did us a great service."

He gently gripped her arm and raised it high. "It was my privilege." Then he turned to Shiván and saluted, hand on heart.

"If I and my men can be of further service, you only have to give the command."

Shiván shook his head. "Captain, there will be chaos in Stillárre before long. We've got you into enough trouble already. I suggest you and your officers rejoin your legion. There will be no one now to remember your... 'error'."

Garset bowed his head. His green eyes glinted as he looked up. "You are right, young man. It's true that every soldier will be needed to restore order in the city. May the One lead you and your companions on to great things. I believe we will meet again one day."

"I hope so! *Ney len silmend*—Light stay with you."

"*Illen destend*—And keep you."

With a final salute Garset turned and led his men out of the Guardhouse.

Shiván led the way up to the second floor, which housed the Guards' personal quarters. There were dormitories, common rooms and wash areas. Besides the crowd still clustered motionless on the Mindbender's landing, the passages were clogged with others who had been on the way to assist their master when disaster struck. Towards the end Dhelgor must have called out every man he had. Each Guard had to be checked, though. One might be Gil.

They turned a corner, and Lannie gave a cry of delight. There he was—standing a head taller than the other Guards. They hurried through the frozen crowd. It was uncanny to see his familiar face staring unseeing towards the next turn in the passage.

Shiván and the twins carried Gil to the nearest empty dormitory. The Doc was no lightweight, and Shiván's heart sank. How would they get him out of Stillárre like this? He was an unbending statue. It took all three of them to manoeuvre him through the doorway.

While the women stayed outside the men removed Gil's night-wear and the Guard's tunic he'd thrown on top. Then they dressed him in clothes they'd brought from the Domicile. Everything was a little short—there was nothing for a six-footer. With difficulty they wrestled him into a dark green tunic, leggings, and a brown robe. Shiván searched through his old tunic and found the blaise—his two-handled glass—in an inner pocket. He tucked it into the pocket of the brown robe.

The women came in, and Lannie ran and embraced the still form on the bed. "We must ask the One to heal him," she declared. "How long did Frengor say the slaves stayed frozen after the Mindbender was killed?"

"A day, till the teméyn wore off, I think," Perrely said. Fira nodded.

"It has to happen sooner for Gelmion! Somehow he must be able to walk and run by himself, *now*—tonight!"

Shiván looked round at the others. "Right. Let's talk this over with God."

They sat on the floor between the beds and asked the One to break the hold the drug had over Gil. They asked him by whatever means to enable Gil to walk, even to run. Now. Today.

After about half an hour Lannie got up and took hold of both Gil's hands. She pulled—and his torso came upright, bending at the waist. Shiván and several others exclaimed in delight. Lannie was thrilled. She let go. His arms dropped to the bed, but he remained upright.

"It's coming!" she cried. "Now we must ask God to let him stand up."

They came and clustered beside the bed. Once again they asked the One to enable their friend to walk.

Lannie leapt up and took Gil's hands again. "Time to stand up, Gil." She gently swung his arms round towards the edge of the bed.

His torso twisted slowly with his arms. Then they gasped as he moved first one, then the other leg to the floor, so that he was sitting on the side of the bed.

Still holding his hands, Lannie moved away from the bed, pulling him towards her. He stood up. She let go of his hands and moved further away. "You need to walk, Gil. Walk to me."

Gil walked slowly to Lannie and stopped in front of her. His eyes dropped to hers.

"Lannie," he said.

"*Yes!*" She threw her arms around him. He lifted his arms and held her. Shiván and Danîsha cheered. The Dûrians looked askance at the display of affection, but murmured their thanks to God. A weight lifted from Shiván's mind. This would make things a lot easier.

Gil didn't say anything beyond that one word. But he could walk, stiffly. Lannie led him out of the dormitory.

"We have all four Restorers!" Shiván declared. "Now to find the bellaril."

They eventually discovered it in Dhelgor's office on the ground floor. It was leaning against the wall behind his blackwood desk. Danîsha ran and scooped it up with a cry of joy.

Meanwhile at Fira's request Cârin forced open a small chest sitting in the corner. Fira pulled out a leather bag with her good hand, and shook it. It jingled. She gave a grunt of satisfaction. "This may ease our way when the instruments fail." She glanced round at the others. "Just a pity you foreigners can't ride, or we'd help ourselves to their horses, too."

Sounds of increasing uproar were filtering in from outside the Guardhouse. They went to the main door and opened it.

* * *

The day had started, and there was a confused rumble of many voices in the distance, punctuated by individual shouts and screams. People were running along the street. A little further down a group seemed to be fighting among themselves. Danîsha saw grey cloaks in the centre, and realised what was happening. She felt sick. Thank God they'd put Gil into different clothes.

"Quick! We need to get away," Shiván said. They slipped out and closed the door behind them. Just in time. A crowd was surging up the street led by a tall fellow with wild purple hair brandishing an improvised club. "*To the Guardhouse!*" he was screaming. "*Destroy the vipers' nest!*" The Restorers pressed themselves against the wall on the opposite side of the street to let the mob pass. With a roar they crashed the door open and poured in. Danîsha shuddered to think what the crazed mob would do to all those frozen Guardsmen inside.

They began walking quickly down the street towards the city centre, Fira holding the wrist of her injured arm with the other hand. She looked pale. Danîsha kept herself between Fira and the crowd to prevent her being jostled.

Behind them Lannie was leading Gil by the hand. He was taking long, awkward strides, but was able to keep up, thank God.

They reached the group they'd seen earlier. There were fewer now, most having followed the larger crowd to the Guardhouse. But several self-appointed wreakers of vengeance were still attacking the frozen Guardsmen. "Take *that*, you slime!" a working man with a hunched shoulder cried, crashing his fist into the only Guard who remained standing. A trickle of blood came from the Guardsman's mouth. His eyes stared calmly ahead. The body jerked with the blow and toppled to join three others on the ground, where the workman and his cronies proceeded to kick, spit, and stamp on it.

They hurried past, trying not to look. Danîsha felt faint. It was one thing to watch riot scenes on TV in the comfort of your living room; it was quite another to see it in real life, with no 'Off' button.

"Shiván, we must leave the city!" she exclaimed when they were out of earshot. He was walking with Perrely, just ahead of her. "Next thing they'll be turning on foreigners or anyone else they've taken a dislike to!"

He turned and nodded. "Cârin is taking us to the Eastgate. From there we'll find our way to the Forest of Janulane and on to Dhembis."

"But, Shiván—" Perrely looked up at him with pleading eyes. "We can't leave Jomel to be killed!" She'd told them the awful story of how her cousin had been condemned as a human sacrifice.

Shiván stared at her. "That won't happen now, surely? With Dhelgor dead?"

"The Bishop's Guard don't control the Temple of Gadesh," Fira told him.

"Oh. And where's the Temple of Gadesh?"

"In the market square."

Shivvie fell silent, frowning. Perrely kept glancing at him anxiously. Danîsha's heart clenched. She felt for Perrely, but how could they risk everything to rescue her cousin?

"Alright. Cârin said we'd have to pass through the market square. We'll see how things are at the Temple. If we can do something, we will." His face was sad as he looked at Perrely. She nodded and bit her lip.

* * *

Gil walked stiffly beside Lannie. He couldn't speak, but she was saying enough for them both. He savoured the feel of her hand in his. It was amazing that she still cared for him.

His mind was dazed by the speed of recent events. A mere two hours ago he'd been a Mindbender's slave, searching for Shiván and Lannie to apprehend and imprison them. Instead they had apprehended him, after killing Dhelgor! Everything had been turned on its head.

He knew he ought to be grateful for being rescued — especially after seeing how the mob were dealing with his former comrades... But it was too big a transition to make so suddenly.

Could he ever be 'normal' again? He doubted it. Too much had changed inside him since that bitch Jomel had betrayed him into the Bishop's Guard. And she was the one they wanted to rescue next! He'd love to sabotage *that* little act of kindness, if only he could move more freely...

He caught himself. Thinking like a Bishop's Guard wasn't healthy in this company. Lannie, Shiván and 'Neesh were obviously glad to have him back, but he'd seen the dark looks Fira and the twins were giving him. He'd have to work on keeping his shiláy grateful and repentant...

Yes. Readjusting to life with these former friends would not be easy.

* * *

Jomel lay on the bed in her cubicle, her eyes closed. Unless the One Creator God did something soon, this was the last day of her life.

At dawn she had been ceremonially washed and arrayed in the scarlet robe of the sacrificial victims. Her ankles and wrists were tied. She was available to be 'used' by any of the temple staff — since that night she'd be meat on the altar fire. Already several —

including acolytes Chand and Guriet—had availed themselves of the opportunity, gloating over her. She was aching.

Her thoughts drifted off to her family. They were out of the city visiting relatives at the moment. They wouldn't even know she'd died until they came back later this week. A tear tickled her cheek; she shook her head, unable to brush it away. She'd spent so little time at home recently. Her parents had irritated her with their constant anxious questions about her life in the Cult of Gadesh. How right they'd been! Now their worst nightmare was about to be realised… unless the Creator God stepped in.

She remembered that awesome moment just over a week ago when he had met her in this very cubicle. The utter humility she'd felt in the presence of such absolute truth and purity. What he said, would be done. Anything else was unthinkable. She had asked him to rescue her. Her request had been heard. *Somehow, today, he would rescue her.*

Outside her door, in the sanctuary, preparations were being made for the autumn festival. Adherents and devotees were chattering and laughing, stringing up garlands of autumn leaves, bringing in supplies of wine and sweetmeats, scrubbing the floors. Acolyte Chand's voice rose above the others.

"Derisay, why haven't you done the altar? … No, *first!* Otherwise the dirty water runs down and the *floor* has to be washed again."

So… the altar would be clean to receive her blood. All her fears rose up afresh to choke her. *Creator God, help me!*

The happy babble continued outside. Someone started up a favourite autumn song, and everyone joined in. They'd be singing that tonight.

Then Jomel frowned through her tears. For a moment she thought she'd heard a jarring noise amidst the frivolity. There it was again—a scream, faint but clear! The voices outside her door suddenly fell silent. There was a distant clatter of many feet on the marble portico. A double crash—the sanctuary doors thrown open. A volley of screams and shouts from the temple workers! What was happening?

A harsh, workman's voice rose above the others. "Get 'em! They're cultists and evildoers! Murderers and whores! Drag 'em outside, let 'em face justice!" Beyond the immediate sounds was the full-throated roar of a large crowd in the square.

The cries of her former colleagues rose in volume. Then a plummy voice made itself heard. Priest Sarmion.

"What is the meaning of this outrage? This is sacred property! Leave at once, or —"

"Or *what*, slobberchops?" the harsh voice interrupted. "The Bishop's Guard are done for! *We're* the law around here now. *Grab him!*"

There was an outraged yell from Sarmion; then he started blubbering and pleading.

"Keep him for later," the voice commanded. "Smaller fry first. *You!*"

Jomel heard a woman's terrified screaming. It was Chery, one of the young adherents. Her voice faded as she was dragged out of the sanctuary. The distant roar swelled to a bloodthirsty howl. She shuddered. But behind the horror, hope began to dawn. Was this the Creator's rescue?

That thought was abruptly shattered. There was a crash not far away; then another, nearer. Her heart leapt into her mouth. They were breaking open the cubicle doors —

Her own door smashed open. A heavyset woman with lank, greasy hair and a large wart on her nose burst in. She gave a cry of triumph when she saw Jomel. "*Here's one!*"

"Please, I'm not —"

"Shut it!" A large hand crashed against her face. "We know what you are, you filthy pile of *drikh!*"

Two other women crowded in. A thin, black-haired hag screamed and pointed at her robe, which the last 'user' had left lying open. "*Harlot! Whore!* Exposing y'self in broad daylight, 'ticing our men from us! *Have you no shame?*"

She leapt forward and began slapping and punching Jomel. The heavy woman pulled her away.

"Today she'll pay for everything, Jalla. Untie her and bring her outside!"

Struggling was pointless. Jomel sobbed as the three women freed her from the bed, yanked her upright, tied her robe, and dragged her from the sanctuary.

True God, keep your promise!

* * *

419

It was not yet the first hour of the day, but Bishop Shambor was already hard at work. Secretary Estaron sat opposite him at the wide blackwood desk in his reception chamber, taking notes.

"Then after the opening of the new Temple of Sharn, Estaron, I want you to make time for me to speak to the Marûvian trade delegation. I know they were only scheduled for noon tomorrow, but bringing them forward will show how highly I value their business. The Marûvians have been buying cheap metalware from Khrellárre, and we must persuade them that ours is better in the long term."

Estaron glanced up from the wax tablet and nodded as the intent eyes bored into his. For some reason Shambor always needed him to understand. "So cancel whatever was arranged. I need a clear half—"

The Bishop broke off with a strangled yelp, jerking as though someone had stabbed him. Estaron leapt to his feet. But no hidden assassin appeared.

"*Dhelgor*—" Shambor gasped. He sat frozen, white knuckles clasping the edge of the desk. The blood drained from his heavy features. He stared ahead sightlessly. Estaron's eyebrows rose. "What is it, your Radiance? Are you not feeling well?"

"Dead! He's dead, Estaron. Dhelgor has just been killed." He turned wide, disbelieving eyes on the secretary.

"The Mindbender of Stillárre? But how—?" Estaron had learnt to be impervious to most things in Shambor's service, but this was new.

Shambor's gaze lost focus again. "I caught his final thought the instant before he died." He spoke in a low voice, half to himself. "It was, 'Shiván'. Shiván killed Dhelgor, Estaron. The leader of the four foreigners we've been hunting. The Restorers of the Way. They killed a *Mindbender*. An entire network, gone. In Stillárre— the second city of Dûrion! The whole area will fall into chaos..."

His eyes widened further, and his voice sank to a shuddering whisper. "They come in the power of the One Creator God, and none can stop them. They will rebuild the broken path and restore the Way and cleanse his rescued people. All who stand against them will be swept aside..." His voice tailed off.

Suddenly his grey eyes grew sharp and his face darkened. "No! I will *not* let that happen, Estaron!" He slammed a hand on the table.

"Dhelgor was a fool. I told him the Restorers were dangerous, I threatened him, but he never took it seriously. He let them slip into Stillárre — and he's paid the penalty. But now — Now they face *me*, and I will not make the same mistake. There are only a few of them; soon I'll have them in my power. I have one asset they know nothing about…"

He looked into the middle distance and the muscles of his face twitched. Estaron recognised the symptoms of mindspeech.

When he'd finished he buried his head in his hands. He looked up, his expression tormented. "Only *one*, Estaron! Out of all the hundreds of Guards and informers in Stillárre. Only *one*, and I can't use him! Or should I…?" He stared into space again, wiping a hand over his mouth. Estaron had seldom seen him so agitated. "No! Too risky. I must stick to the original plan. Even if it means chaos in Stillárre, and allowing those so-called Restorers to escape. The earliest any outside Guardsmen could reach the city would be…" He glanced at the water clock in the corner. "…After midday. The foreigners will be long gone by then."

Light suddenly dawned on Shambor's face. "*Wait!* Dhelgor had requested help with the search from Mindbender Jastor in Dhembis. Jastor's Guardsmen were due to reach Stillárre this morning…" His jaw set in a hard line. "I'll contact Jastor, as well as Hollet in Berûvis and Meldior in Janulane. They'll alert all the garrisons around Stillárre. I'll throw out a net to catch those upstarts…

"Cancel all appointments, Estaron. I'll be directing this myself."

* * *

The Stillárre market square was a seething mass of people. Many were looting the wealthy buildings that faced on the square. Perrely exclaimed angrily when she saw a couple trotting out of the ancient Hearth, holding a silver ambon, a gold-bound copy of the Book, and several silver platters and goblets. They brandished them aloft, shouting to friends below.

But the mob's attention was focused on the Temple of Gadesh. A cold fear settled in Perrely's stomach when she saw people being dragged out on to the raised portico. Today had obviously been a Gadeshite festival. Broken streamers of autumn leaves dangled from the opulent frontage. Strands of coloured ribbon lay all round the square, with the fallen white poles that had recently held them.

An impromptu tribunal had been set up on the portico. As each white or grey-robed figure was dragged out a thickset, red-faced fellow in a carpenter's apron bellowed their position in the temple. He had a stentorian voice. "*Ad-herent! Whaddaya say?*" "*Guilty!*" the crowd roared back. Then the screaming individual was thrown down the broad, marble steps and seized by the crowd. They weren't seen again.

"Dear Prince, they've gone mad!" Fira exclaimed.

Perrely swallowed down the bile that rose in her throat. Everyone knew that the Mindbenders and the Bishop's Guard were closely linked to the Cult of Gadesh. In the popular mind they were one and the same.

"Jomel!" she cried despairingly. Oh, what had happened to her? Were they too late?

"We're going in closer!" Shiván shouted to the rest. He started barging through the crowd, pulling her behind him. She felt a rush of gratitude. He was going to attempt a rescue.

Perrely looked round. Danîsha was ploughing after them with the bellaril raised above her head. The others were following. Dear Prince, please bring us out of this safely—otherwise it'll be my fault...

They reached the front of the crowd, at the foot of the temple portico. She'd checked every mangled body en route. To her unspeakable relief, none was Jomel.

More hapless adherents and devotees came tumbling down the steps, to be trampled by the crowd. Her heart went out to them. They were in bondage to the god of darkness, but they deserved a chance to choose the Light—as Jomel had done. That thickset carpenter and his cronies would have to answer one day to the God of Truth.

"Shiván, can we get up there?" she shouted against the noise of the crowd.

He shook his head. "Too dangerous. This is their show. If Jomel appears, we'll take her." He shouted something to the twins and Fira.

"*A-co-lyte! He helps the priest!*" the carpenter roared. "*Guilty!*" the mob thundered. Next moment the pasty-faced fellow who had taken them to Jomel came tumbling down the steps towards them, squealing. The crowd surged up, and they were carried along.

Shiván pulled her back as those in front began kicking and stamping. She suppressed a wave of nausea.

Suddenly the crowd's shouts rose to a thunderous roar. A fat, grey-robed man had been thrust on to the portico. Every chin was trembling. "Don't hurt me, I've done nothing!" he was screeching in a high, penetrating tenor. "I'm only a simple priest—"

"*The priest of Gadesh!*" the stentorian one bellowed.

"*Guilty!*" the crowd roared with one voice.

Four sets of arms sent the fat man toppling down. He crashed on to the hard marble, howled, rolled over a couple of times, then was swallowed by a great swell of the mob. His screams soon died away.

Then a scarlet-robed figure was dragged on to the portico by three women. They spoke to the carpenter. He turned to the crowd, his face redder than before. "*Temple whore! Whaddaya say?*"

"*Jomel!*" Perrely screamed.

"*Guilty!*" the crowd roared.

"*Now!*" Shiván yelled.

As Jomel was sent staggering down the steps, Shiván and the twins ran up them. Moving at lightning speed Cârin intercepted Jomel and scooped her into his arms. Shiván and Shîrin leapt between her and the crowd. There was a howl of fury, and the mob surged forward. With a clear metallic ring Shiván drew the Blade of Darthane. Shîr's sword was in his left hand. The crowd froze. Perrely and the others ran up to join their friends, Alanya towing Gelmion.

"We are on the Prince's business," Shiván declared in the sudden silence. "This woman is a *victim*. She was going to be killed tonight—a human sacrifice! We are taking her to safety. Let us pass! Show the way, Câr."

Cârin led them at a trot obliquely down the temple steps to the south-east. There were doubtful rumbles from the mob. Some again pressed towards them. Shiván raised the Blade. "Back! In the name of the Prince!" Once more they paused, uncertain.

Then a new sound made itself heard: the rhythmic clop of horses' hooves. A large contingent of grey-cloaked Bishop's Guards swept into the far side of the square.

"Oh, dear Prince. Guards of a different Mindbender!" Fira exclaimed. The mood of the crowd swung abruptly from vengeance to panic. With cries of alarm people scrambled out of the way of their dreaded oppressors. The carpenter and his tribunal suddenly vanished. Cârin put Jomel down, shouting *"Follow me!"* The others leapt after him, sprinting towards the Eastgate Road next to the temple. Perrely grabbed Jomel's hand and dragged her along. Jomel was sobbing. "Come, Jomie, you must run!" A smile suddenly appeared amidst her cousin's tears. Thanks to the One! They raced after the others.

Perrely glanced back. The Guards were heading directly towards them! People scrambled frantically out of the way, but there was chaos in the square. Her heart was trying to escape her chest. Could they outrun them?

* * *

Pedestrians in the Eastgate Road scattered as they charged down it. Gil was running alongside Lannie—thank God that he could! Behind them the Guards were forcing their way rapidly through the crowd. Danîsha was panting. Dûrion had toughened her, but how long could she keep this up? The bellaril was an awkward burden.

As if in answer, Perrely swerved alongside and took the instrument from her. They rounded a bend and the gate appeared up ahead. Huddled grey mounds were all that remained of the gate guards. The drumming of hooves grew louder. She glanced over her shoulder to see the first of their pursuers turning the corner behind them. They wouldn't make it in time!

They sprinted through the gate tunnel on to the dock area. Crates were stacked beside warehouses near the city wall. Empty and half-laden wagons were dotted about. Wooden cranes stood among bollards and coils of rope on the riverside wharf, where five ships were moored. Danîsha's eyes briefly took in a forest of tall masts and rigging. There were two larger vessels, with cranes hovering over their holds; a medium-sized ship; and a couple of fishing boats, their decks strewn with nets, barrels on the wharf being filled with their morning catch. A thick aroma of fish, spices, tar and sacking filled the air.

The road from the gate ran down a long, sloping ramp recessed in the raised wharf to where a flat-bottomed ferry lay idle. Long-haired sailors in brightly-coloured tunics and breeches, and dockers in more sombre garb, turned to stare at them.

Shiván suddenly whipped round and stood with the Blade raised. Danîsha stopped beside him. Perrely thrust the bellaril into her hands. The horses charged out of the gate tunnel, their grey-cloaked riders looming up like an express train about to roar over them.

Danîsha started to play. The horses skidded to a halt. Two riders went sailing over their mounts' heads. She and Shiván leapt aside as others crashed into those in front. Soon there was a mound of frozen Guardsmen lying on the wharf, and a group of horses — some with riders — standing motionless behind. The riders' brows were beaded with sweat, their knuckles white on the reins. The girl Jomel — and the sailors and dockers — were staring open-mouthed.

Shiván winked at Danîsha. "Good on yer, 'Neesh!" She continued playing.

He turned to the others. "Let's get us a ship!"

"Someone help me with Gil!" Lannie exclaimed.

He was standing stock still, sweat on his forehead.

Shiván frowned. "He can't walk?"

"He must still be affected by the bellaril," Lannie said. "He's not off the drug yet. He may have to be carried till you stop playing, 'Neesh."

Shîrin and Cârin hoisted Gil up between them like a fallen statue. They followed Shiván, who marched up to the medium-sized vessel with Fira murmuring in his ear and pointing. Danîsha brought up the rear, still playing. The ship was a two-master, rather like a small Chinese junk. The crew stared at them wide-eyed, sail lines in their hands, arrested halfway through raising the ribbed foresail.

Shiván led his motley party up the gangplank, Danîsha struggling to keep her balance on the springy board while still playing the bellaril. A commanding figure with weather-beaten face, hooked nose and a wide-brimmed hat — clearly the ship's master — stood at the stern, staring, his hand on the tiller.

Shiván planted himself immediately in front of the man, arms akimbo. "Can you take us across the lake?" he asked, raising his voice over the bellaril. "To Palderen. We need to leave at once. We'll pay you."

Amazement faded from the master's face at the mention of money. "Let's see the colour of your coin," he said huskily. Fira held out her hand and opened it. In it were four gold *demeret* from the

Mindbender's chest. The captain blinked, and nodded. "For that you get service as well. Those Guards—you killed 'em?" He pointed to the motionless grey-cloaked figures on the wharf.

"No," Shiván told him. "When our friend here stops playing, they'll wake up."

"And when they do, you don't want 'em finding out where you went?"

Shiván nodded in agreement.

The captain turned and hailed the other ships. "*HALAA!*" he roared in a voice that echoed round the entire dock area. "*Those Bishop's vermin ain't dead. When they come to, they'll be after us. Up sail and out of here!*"

Sailors and dockers alike were galvanised into action. Cranes were hastily swung aside, gangplanks removed, cables unhitched, sails raised. The dockers melted away, slipping past the frozen Guards into the gate tunnel. The ferrymen rowed across the river to the other side. The sailors on their own vessel rapidly pulled in the gangplank, hauled up the sails, and cast off.

As they swept out of the River Carreck into the wide expanse of Lake Stillárre, Danîsha finally stopped playing.

Chapter 46: *Last thoughts*

THE SUN CAME OUT, and all nature seemed to be rejoicing with them. Shiván and Perrely stood at the rail on the ship's prow with a following breeze ruffling their hair. The ribbed brown sails were taut above them, the mast creaking, the lake water hissing as they cut through it. Perrely's hand lay in Shiván's, and joy filled his heart.

Nearby Danîsha was getting to know Jomel, now dressed in a sober green tunic and brown robe brought from the Domicile. Behind them on the main deck Lannie was talking softly to Gil, who was leaning against the mast looking shaken; Fira had her elbows on the rail, holding the wrist of her injured hand as she stared out across the lake; and Shîrin and Cârin were exaggerating their exploits to a couple of bemused sailors.

But by the One's gift, they *had* achieved something, hadn't they? The Mindbender of Stillárre was dead. They'd rescued Gelmion — all four Restorers were together at last. Perrely, Fira and Danîsha had been freed — and Jomel was an added bonus. He himself had begun to learn something about servant leadership, as Father Martin had predicted all those weeks ago. He thanked the One Creator God; and asked his healing for the wounded city of Stillárre, now dwindling behind them.

Their immediate destination was the town of Palderen on the eastern shore of the lake. From there they would head across country to the Forest of Janulane. Fira had been relieved that in this way they could avoid the Janulane road — which the Bishop would already have used to send reinforcements to Stillárre. The only point of danger was Palderen itself, through which the highway passed. Once they reached the safety of the deep woods they could make their way south by forest paths towards Dhembis. There they would look for the lady Frengor had mentioned, who they hoped would find them a short-term refuge where they could recover, take stock, and find out what God had in mind next.

He looked at Perrely. She smiled up at him. Life was good.

* * *

Gil was getting over that harrowing experience earlier on. Lannie had told him it was caused by the bellaril, of all things! Who would have believed that a simple musical instrument could have such a devastating effect? He'd felt as though he was unravelling like a badly knitted jersey. He had no memory of how it started.

Anyway, it was good to have Lannie chatting beside him, his past mistakes obviously forgiven. He was still prevented from replying, but that didn't matter. Soon she would be his.

As Lannie continued to describe her adventures, he heard his master's voice. *You will be given a supply of* teméyn *as soon as possible. Keep it well hidden. And make your thoughts sympathetic to confuse the shiláy.*

Yes, my lord Bishop.

Continued in Book 2, *The Restorers*
(coming soon)

Dear reader,

In the new world of publishing, word of mouth is often the most important factor in a story finding its readers. If you enjoyed this book, it would be fantastic if you would consider rating it and leaving a review on **amazon.co.uk** *or* **amazon.com**.

Thank you — and enjoy the sequel!

— Steve Pillinger

Appendices

Of Dûrians, the Dûrai, and a sky called Malane

Dûrion is just one nation under the sky. The sky—known as Malane—covers many nations and peoples (who live *under* Malane: no one lives *on* or *in* the sky). Dûrians are of a people-kindred called the Dûrai.

(Please note: the country is Dûri*on*; someone from there, and the language they speak, is Dûri*an*.)

Space forbids a complete history of the Dûrai people and the origins of the Dûrian nation; suffice it to say that at the time of the events described in this book they had risen to prominence under a small patch of Malane. There for several centuries Dûrion and its sister Dûrai nations—Selmion to the east, Thrinar, Marûvin, Pandiar and the city-state of Calardane to the south—had prospered in relative freedom after the overthrow of their Gnarthrog oppressors by the Dûrian Founders. Until, that is, an evil cancer developed that threatened to destroy them from within: a cancer called *mindbending*.

The beginnings of the eradication of that cancer are described in this book. These Appendices provide further information, especially about Dûrion and the Dûrians, that I hope will enhance readers' understanding and enjoyment.

How to Pronounce Dûrian Words & Names

Generally I have tried to spell Dûrian in an 'English' way, which has done violence to my principles as a linguist: but I have sacrificed these to the greater good of helping English readers pronounce the language more correctly.

The name **Fira**, for instance, is spelt that way so that English speakers will pronounce it as 'Fire-ah', which is a lot closer to the Dûrian pronunciation than what an English person would say if faced with the linguistically more accurate **Faira / Fayra**.

In most cases, therefore, you can just go ahead and pronounce Dûrian words and names the way they look. But there are a few things to bear in mind:

The letter-combination **dh** stands for a sound that exists in English, but is misleadingly spelt 'th' in words like 'this', 'that' and 'bathe', as opposed to 'thin', 'thank' and 'bath'. So the first syllable of the Dûrian town name **Dhembis** is pronounced like English 'them'; and Mind-bender **Dhelgor**'s name begins with the same sound.

The combination **th** is pronounced as in English 'thin', 'thank' and 'bath'.

The combination **kh** represents a sound that English only encounters in loanwords from other languages, which it writes with a 'ch', as in Scottish 'loch', German 'Bach'. Likewise **zh** represents the French 'g' in 'rouge', 'gêne', etc.

Ch is pronounced as in English 'chase', 'chill', 'each'.

J is pronounced as in English 'jump', 'joy', 'ajar'.

G is always hard as in 'get', never soft as in 'gem'. Thus the first syllable of **Gilmane** is pronounced like 'gilded', not 'Gillian'.

C and **k** are both used for the hard 'k' sound at the beginning of a word. C is never pronounced like an 's', as in English 'ceiling', 'city', 'receive'. Following English usage, Dûrian words beginning with **ke-** or **ki-** are spelt with a k: **keldon**, **kim**, **kion** (cf. English 'keep', 'kind', 'king'), thus avoiding any temptation to pronounce an initial **c-** with an 's'. However **c** has been retained elsewhere for its 'softer' look, as in **Cârin**, **cay**, **colárre**.

R is always rolled, as in Scottish English.

The syllable **ey** always rhymes with 'say', never 'see'. Thus **teméyn** (which is a loanword in Dûrian) is pronounced 'temane';

and the name of Danîsha's protégéé **Teynel** is pronounced 'Taynel'.

Accents: The optional **acute accent**, as in the final syllable of **Shiván**, shows where the stress falls. Steve Harston's Dûrian name is pronounced 'Shiv-VAN', not 'SHIV-ven' (or, heaven forbid, 'SHY-ven'!).

Dûrian has quite a few words that are not accented on the first syllable (as English tends to be). To make this clearer, I have adopted a quasi-French spelling in a number of cases: for example, **Stillárre**. A straightforward transcription of the Dûrian spelling of this name would have been **Stilár**: which most English readers would have pronounced as either 'stiller' or 'styler'. But by doubling the final consonant and adding a silent **-e**, I hope I have encouraged English speakers to read this correctly as 'stil-LAR'. Similar examples are **Durónne** ('du-RON'), **calénne** ('cal-LEN') and **sinélle** ('sin-EL').

By contrast the name **Jomel** has no final accent, and is not spelt 'Jomelle': the pronunciation is 'JOE-mel', not 'joe-MEL'.

(Note that I could not bring myself to apply the French spelling to the name **Shiván**: '**Shivánne**' would have looked altogether too feminine. Here the accent alone indicates the stessed syllable. In any case, these are merely helpful representations of the Dûrian script, which contains no accents or French-style spellings.)

I have not indicated stress where it seems obvious, as in **Alanya** ('a-LAN-ya'). The chances of this being wrongly pronounced as 'Alan-ya' seem fairly slim.

The other accent used is the **circumflex**, as in the second syllable of **Danîsha**. Circumflexes indicate long vowels (which in the Dûrian writing system have separate letters). They also tend to carry the stress, and are pronounced as follows:

â: 'ah' as in 'calm', e.g. **Cârin** ('CAH-rin').
ê: 'air' as in 'cairn'* (no example in this book).
î: 'ee' as in 'see', e.g. **Danîsha** ('dan-EE-sha').
ô: 'or' as in 'thorn',* e.g. **Dôrion** ('DOR-ee-yon').
û: 'oo' as in 'boot', e.g. **Dûrion** ('DOO-ree-yon').

(*British English. Americans and others who pronounce the 'r' in such words will have to try and imagine how they would sound without an 'r'...)

As an example of the difference between short and long vowels, compare **Dûrion** and **Guriet**: **Dûrion** has a long 'u' as in 'suit'; **Guriet** has a short 'u' as in 'soot'.

Pronunciation of some of the names and words in the book:

Alanya:	a-LAN-ya
ambon:	AM-bon
bellaril:	BELL-a-ril
Bellarniar:	bell-AR-nee-yar
Berenel:	BEH-ren-el (first syllable rhymes with 'Ben'; not 'burn')
Berûvis:	beh-ROO-vis
blaise:	BLAZE (or more properly, 'BLACE')
Câr:	CAHR (final **r** pronounced)
Carreck:	CA-reck (first syllable rhymes with 'cat')
Cârin(or):	CAH-rin, CAH-rin-ore (not 'CARE-in-')
colárre:	col-LAHR
Darthane:	DAR-thane
Damion:	DAY-mee-yon
Danîsha:	da-NEE-sha
Demárre:	dem-MAR
Denny:	DEN-nee
Dhelgor:	THEL-gor ('th' as in 'them')
Dhembis:	THEM-bis
Dôrion:	DOR-ee-yon
Dûrion:	DOO-ree-yon (not 'DYOO-ree-yon' or 'JOO-ree-yon')
Durónne:	du-RON (short **u**, as in 'put')
Finien:	FIN-ee-yen
Fira:	FIRE-ah
Frengor:	FRENG-gore
Ganneret:	GAN-ner-et
Gelmion:	GEL-mee-yon (hard 'g' like 'get')
Géris:	GEH-ris (hard 'g' like 'get'; first syllable rhymes with 'get')
Gil:	GIL (hard 'g' like 'get'; not like 'Jill')
Gilmane:	GIL-mane (hard 'g' like 'get'; not like 'Jill')
Gnarthrog:	NAR-throg (for English and Dûrian speakers: the Gnarthrog themselves pronounce the initial letter as a hard 'g')
Guriet:	GUR-ree-yet (short 'u' as in 'put')

Gwargif:	GWAR-gif (**ar** as in 'are', not 'war'; second 'g' hard as in 'gift')
Janulane:	JAN-u-lane (short 'u' as in 'put'; not 'JAN-you-lane')
Jomel:	JOE-mel
Kennissôr:	KEN-nis-sore
Khoreyn:	khor-ANE (**kh** pronounced like 'ch' in Scottish 'loch')
Khrellárre:	khrel-LAHR (**kh** pronounced like 'ch' in Scottish 'loch')
Lômack:	LOW-mack (more properly 'LAW-mack', but English speakers can be allowed some licence here)
Mâra:	MAH-ra
Margay:	MAR-gay
Marûvin:	ma-ROO-vin
Mesten:	MESS-ten
Nelláy:	nel-LAY
Nerick:	NEH-rick (first syllable rhymes with 'net')
Ongaret:	ONG-ga-ret (hard 'g' like 'get')
Orrénne:	o-REN (first syllable rhymes with 'on')
Pandiar:	PAN-dee-yar
Perrely:	PEH-reh-lee (first 2 syllables rhymes with 'pet'; not like 'pearly')
Sarmion:	SAR-mee-yon
Selmion:	SEL-mee-yon
Sesten:	SES-ten
Shambor:	SHAM-bore
shandil:	SHAN-dill
shiláy:	shil-LAY
shiláyet:	shil-LAY-et
Shîr:	SHEE-r (not 'shee-yer': the 'r' immediately follows 'SHEE-')
Shîrin(or):	SHEE-rin, SHEE-rin-ore
Shiván:	shiv-VAN
Sûrilane:	SOO-ree-lane (not 'SURE-ree-lane')
Taboru:	tah-BOR-oo (not 'TAY-bor-oo')
Tallissôr:	TAL-lis-sore (first syllable rhymes with 'pal', not 'tall')
teméyn:	tem-ANE
Teynel:	TAY-nel
Thrinar:	THRY-nar (first syllable rhymes with 'try')
Thrinari:	thry-NAR-ee
Veynel:	VAY-nel.

Telling the Time in Dûrian
Years, Months, Weeks, Days, Hours

During their weeks at Carreck Manor, the Restorers learnt a little about how time is reckoned in Dûrion and the Dûrai nations. Gelmion eventually made a record of what they had worked out, which may be summarised as follows:

There are 358 days in a **Malanian year**, and each day is about 6 minutes shorter than a terrestrial day. The Dûrai divide their year into 12 months, and their day into 20 hours. (The Dûrians also have a seven-day week: see below.)

Dûrians **number their years** from the Foundation of their nation. The year in which the events described in this book took place was 363 NF: 363 years *ne Fistanar*, 'after the Founders'. (Years prior to the Foundation are tagged 'LF' — *lô Fistanar*, 'before the Founders'.)

The main **daily unit of time** is the *kion* ('KEE-yon'), which is translated 'hour'. The Restorers did not find it easy at first to match the Dûrian 20-hour system with their terrestrial 24-hour one, especially as the Dûrians begin numbering the hours at dawn, not at midnight. Thus 'the first hour of the day' refers not to one o'clock in the morning, but to the hour from approximately 6 to 7 a.m.

However they soon realised that their primary reference point had to be midday: this was 'the fifth hour of the day', while midnight was 'the fifth hour of the night'. Once that was established, 'the first hour of the day' was seen as a year-round theoretical 'dawn'-time — though of course the actual moment when the sun rose varied with the seasons. The same applied to sunset, the tenth hour of the day, which corresponded roughly to the terrestrial hour from 5 to 6 p.m.

(There are informal smaller units of time than the *kion*, but these will not be considered here.)

Since its Foundation, the nation of Dûrion has followed a **seven-day week** like that of Earth:

      Sunday: *Anderil*
      Monday: *Marneril*
      Tuesday: *Dûrneril*

Wednesday: *Vanderil*
Thursday: *Tharderil*
Friday: *Freyneril*
Saturday: *Stenderil.*

These names are believed by some to have originated with the Founders, being adaptations of the weekday names in their language, Inglish. Whether or not this is true, each name ends with the Dûrian word **deril** (*'day'*); *but only the first day,* **Anderil,** *has an overall meaning, i.e. 'the One's day'* (**Am-deril**). *These weekday names are only used in Dûrion.*

The names of the **twelve months of the year**, however, are used with minor variations in all the Dûrai nations, and their origin can be traced to an ancient lunar calendar based on the phases of the larger moon:

1. *Tûland* (January) .... 29 days
2. *Gammerand* (February) .... 30 days
3. *Emmerand* (March) .... 30 days
4. *Bardiand* (April).......................... 30 days
5. *Sîmand* (May) .... 30 days
6. *Hammorand* (June) .... 30 days
7. *Mallerand* (July)........................... 30 days
8. *Rônand* (August)........................... 30 days
9. *Jerenand* (September) .... 30 days
10. *Nargand* (October) .... 30 days
11. *Dormeland* (November).............. 30 days
12. *Larmand* (December)................... 29 days

Year:. *358 days*

(The month names all end with *-and*, a reduced form of the Dûrai root word *yand*, meaning 'month'.)

The identification of the Dûrai months with their terrestrial counterparts is based simply on seasonal similarity to Earth's northern hemisphere.

The six Dûrian **seasons** are: *Sunblaze* — roughly 6 weeks spanning late *Hammorand* (June), all of *Mallerand* (July) and early *Rônand* (August); *Raingold* — *Rônand* (August) to late *Jerenand* (September); *Goldshine* — late *Jerenand* to late *Larmand* (December); *Winter* (late *Larmand* to late *Emmerand* (March); *Flowering* — late *Emmerand* to late *Sîmand* (May); and *Flowerchill* (late *Sîmand* to late *Hammorand*). Sunblaze and Raingold together correspond to the notion of 'Summer', while Flowering and Flowerchill correspond to 'Spring'. Goldshine is the Dûrian equivalent of 'Autumn', without the rain and mists (which occur in the preceding season): it's a season of bright, cold weather when the deciduous leaves enter their full glory of colour.

Note that the **solstices** and **equinoxes** occur about two weeks into each season: Thus Sunblaze is considered to start before the end of Hammorand (June); but the summer solstice occurs on 4th Mallerand (July). Likewise the autumn equinox occurs on 4th Nargand, though the season of Goldshine generally begins before the end of the preceding month, Jerenand.

Distances and Currency

Distances: The main Dûrian unit of distance is the **aldor** (plural: *aldoret*). It is equivalent to about 1.25 kilometers or 0.776 of a mile.

A smaller unit of distance is the *gani* ('stride' or 'pace', plural: *ganiet*), equivalent to approximately 78 cm or 30 inches. There are 1,600 ganiet to the aldor.

Currency: Each Dûrai nation has its own currency, deriving from a common origin in ancient times. In Dûrion the primary unit is called the **demeril** (plural: *demeret*), and most of the other Dûrai nations use a similar term. Its value is approximately one tenth of a labourer's daily wage.

However because of the enormous influence of the Gnarthrog Empire, Gnarthrog *zhôrek* are also widely used, especially in international trade. At the time of the events described here (the last quarter of the year 363 NF) one zhôrek was worth approximately 5.75 Dûrian demeret.

The standard demeril is a debased silver alloy coin. Bronze coins of smaller denominations (half-demeril, quarter-demeril and the *cumil*, or twelfth-demeril coin) are also in wide circulation. However, almost as a separate currency, the **gold demeril** is the medium of exchange used by the seriously wealthy. Made of solid gold, these coins are worth over 300 standard demeret each. It was gold demeret that Jomel offered the Gadeshite adherents to betray Gelmion; and that Fira gave the ship's captain from Mindbender Dhelgor's chest.

Some Basic Dûrian Words and Phrases

*Note: **Month** and **weekday** names are listed in the Appendix* Telling the Time in Dûrian, *p. 434.*

aay .... alright (*reluctant concession*)

aldor (*plur.* **aldoret**) .... Dûrian unit of distance (±1.25 km or 0.776 miles)

am .... one

Am .... the One, God

ambon .... Lightist emblem (*circle intersected by a vertical rod*)

amma .... mama, mummy (*child's name for mother*)

anéy .... we, us

bânor .... father

bar .... path, road, way through

bas .... then, in that case

bel .... sing

bess .... shell

bis .... see

bist .... can, be able

blaise (bleys) .... magnifying glass

bond .... fight

callénne .... honour, privilege

câr .... four

car .... live, be alive

cay .... potato-like tuber

chass .... beverage similar to tea or coffee

col .... stand

collin .... come, approach

dâr .... why

dem .... (*introduces a polite request*)

dembar .... how

demeril (*plur.* **demeret**) .... coin; primary unit of Dûrian currency

denôro .... where to

deril .... day

deylan .... sky

dîm (1) .... fill
dîm (2) .... meal
dimin .... lead, escort, guard
dissil .... forget
don .... son
dôr .... three
elor .... thank, affirm, support
em .... daughter
eréy .... our, ours
eshan .... never
essin .... no, no way
estôr .... nothing
estûr .... stranger
farn .... wheat-like grain
fellen .... leave
fend .... want
fil .... run
flisht! .... (*strong expletive*)
fonâr .... help
ganal .... call, name, address as
ged .... engage in combat
Gesh! .... By Gadesh!
gid .... kill
grûn (*plur.* grûnet) .... ox; bovine beast-of-burden
haa .... yes, right, okay
halaa! .... (*rallying cry*)
hallár .... blessed, glorious
hây! *or* hâya! .... hey! look! (*exclamation of surprise*)
heyn .... manor, nobleman's country house
heyss! .... oh no! (*exclamation of annoyance or dismay*)
hinnay .... more
Illi/Illen dîmend .... And fill you (*midday greeting response, singular & plural*)
Illi/Illen ristend .... And keep you (*evening greeting response*)
Illi/Illen steylend .... And guide you (*morning greeting response*)
is .... me
isset (*plur.* istar) .... friend(s)

jed .... stop, cease, desist
jil .... hear
kel .... king
kim .... ask
kinnéy .... different
las .... be
li eloris, len eloris .... thank you (*singular and plural*)
lim .... thought
lîs .... six
mal .... kindle, set alight
Mâra .... auntie, granny (*respected older female relative*)
mel .... with, among
min .... now
nal .... rest
nar .... fire
neldin .... enjoy
Ney li/len omalend .... Light enfold you (*midday greeting, singular & plural*)
Ney li/len silmend .... Light stay with you (*evening greeting, sing. & plur.*)
Ney li/len tarrend .... Light find you (*morning greeting, sing. & plur.*)
Ney mel shar(ras) .... Go with the Light (*farewell to one leaving, sing. & plur.*)
ney .... light
Neylas .... Light be here (*first-time greeting and response*)
or .... die
ost .... worship
ris .... protection, defence
rist .... keep, guard, protect
sen .... two
shar .... go
sheck .... quickly
shiláy .... aura, mental 'signature'
shild .... resist, oppose
sid .... have, possess
steyil .... guide, direct, oversee

sûlack .... already
tar .... find, find out
târ .... these
tem .... bring
teméyn............................... mindbending drug
ten .... make, build, create
thal...................................... catch
thet...................................... five
thond .... be sick
toldor................................. young man (*polite term of address*)
vey.. learn
vildor .... old man, elder (*polite term of address*)

---

www.ingramcontent.com/pod-product-compliance
Lightning Source LLC
Chambersburg PA
CBHW070858260626
47162CB00007B/2495